YELLOW BIRD'S SONG

*Based on the lives of John Rollin Ridge
and his parents, John and Sarah Ridge*

Heather Miller

*Edited by Alex Hammond
Line Edited by Norma Gambini and Lydia Popiolek
Cover Design by White Rabbit Arts*

Copyright © 2024 by Heather Miller

All rights reserved. No part of this book may be reproduced or transmitted in any form or by any means, electronic or mechanical, including photocopying, recording, or by any information storage and retrieval system, without written permission from the publisher.

This is a work of fiction. Although many of the characters, organizations, and events portrayed in the novel are based on actual historical counterparts, the dialogue and thoughts of these characters are products of the author's imagination.

First Edition published by Historium Press

Images by Shutterstock, Imagine, & Public Domain
Cover designed by White Rabbit Arts

Visit Heather Miller's website at
www.heathermillerauthor.com

Library of Congress Cataloging-in-Publication Data on file
Library of Congress Control Number: 2024901687

Hardcover ISBN: 978-1-962465-23-6
Paperback ISBN: 978-1-962465-22-9
E-Book ISBN: 978-1-962465-24-3

Historium Press, an imprint of
The Historical Fiction Company
Macon, GA / New York, NY
2024

For my Jon

TABLE OF CONTENTS

Prologue	7
Chapter 1: Iron and Salt	9
Chapter 2: The Wild Half-breed May Ride	18
Chapter 3: Civilized	27
Chapter 4: Chess	41
Chapter 5: Black Drink	53
Chapter 6: Such Rest to Him Who Faints upon the Journey	67
Chapter 7: Queen Bee	73
Chapter 8: "My Life Upon Her Faith"	82
Chapter 9: Balm in Gilead	94
Chapter 10: It Matters	105
Chapter 11: White Man's Flies	109
Chapter 12: A Garden of Three Sisters	120
Chapter 13: Broken Strings	131
Chapter 14: Mercy	144
Chapter 15: Lily of the Valley	152
Chapter 16: Too Impatient to Wait for God	158
Chapter 17: Not Seeing, I Have Seen	170
Chapter 18: A Newspaperman's Shoes	177
Chapter 19: Worlds Collide	188
Chapter 20: Feather, Gobble, Strut, and Spur	200
Chapter 21: "Our Liberty – Most Dear"	211
Chapter 22: Cursed	220
Chapter 23: Chasing the Sun	227
Chapter 24: Riding Blind	234
Chapter 25: Bronze Eagles	245
Chapter 26: The Shepherd	257
Chapter 27: Lion's Roar	268
Chapter 28: Betrayal	276
Chapter 29: Unsanctioned Integrity	288
Chapter 30: Golden Gate	298
Chapter 31: Know Nothing	306
Chapter 32: Hollow	317
Chapter 33: The Gambit	325
Chapter 34: With Clearer Soul and Fine-tuned Ear	334
Special Thanks	345
About the Author	346
Notes	347
Bibliography	355

PROLOGUE

To the Cherokee Tribe of Indians East of the Mississippi River,

You are now placed in the midst of a white population. Your peculiar customs, which regulated your intercourse with one another, have been abrogated by the great political community among which you live; and you are now subject to the same laws which govern the other citizens of Georgia and Alabama. You are liable to prosecution for offences, and to civil actions for a breach of any of your contracts. Most of your people are uneducated and are liable to be brought into collision at all times with their white neighbors. Your young men are acquiring habits of intoxication. With strong passions, and without those habits of restraint, which our laws inculcate and render necessary, they are frequently driven to excesses which must eventually terminate in their ruin. The game has disappeared among you, and you must depend upon agriculture and the mechanical arts for support. And yet, a large portion of your people have acquired little or no property in the soil itself, or in any article of personal property which can be useful to them. How, under these circumstances, can you live in the country you now occupy? Your condition must become worse & worse, and you will ultimately disappear, as so many tribes have done before you.

Of all this I warned your people when I met them in council eighteen years ago. I then advised them to sell out their possessions East of the Mississippi and to remove to the country west of that river. This advice I have continued to give you at various times from that period down to the present day, and can you now look back and doubt the wisdom of this council? Had you then removed, you would have gone with all the means necessary to establish yourselves in a fertile country, sufficiently extensive for your subsistence, and beyond the reach of the moral evils which are hastening your destruction. Instead of being a divided people as you now are, arrayed into parties bitterly opposed to each other, you would have been a prosperous and a united community. Your farms would have been open and cultivated; comfortable houses would have been erected, the means of subsistence abundant, and you would have been governed by your own customs and laws and removed from the effects of a white population. Where you now are, you are encompassed by evils, moral and physical, & these are fearfully increasing.

Look even at the experience of the last few years. What have you

Yellow Bird's Song

gained by adhering to the pernicious counsels which have led you to reject the liberal offers made for your removal? They promised you an improvement in your condition. But instead of that, every year has brought increasing difficulties. How, then, can you place confidence in the advice of men who are misleading you for their own purposes, and whose assurances have proved, from the experience of every year, to be utterly unfounded?

I have no motive, my friends, to deceive you. I am sincerely desirous to promote your welfare. Listen to me, therefore, while I tell you that you cannot remain where you now are. Circumstances that cannot be controlled, and which are beyond the reach of human laws, render it impossible that you can flourish in the midst of a civilized community. You have but one remedy within your reach. And that is, to remove to the west and join your countrymen, who are already established there. And the sooner you do this, the sooner you can commence your career of improvement and prosperity...

The choice now is before you. May the Great Spirit teach you how to choose. The fate of your women and children, the fate of your people to the remotest generation, depend upon the issue. Deceive yourselves no longer. Do not cherish the belief that you can ever resume your former political situation while you continue in your present residence. As certain as the sun shines to guide you in your path, so certain is it that you cannot drive back the laws of Georgia from among you. Every year will increase your difficulties. Look at the condition of the Creeks. See the collisions which are taking place with them. See how their young men are committing depredations upon the property of our citizens and are shedding their blood. This cannot and will not be allowed. Punishment will follow, and all who are engaged in these offences must suffer. Your young men will commit the same acts, and the same consequences must ensue.

Think then of all these things. Shut your ears to bad counsel. Look at your condition as it now is, and then consider what it will be if you follow the advice I give to you.

Your friend,
ANDREW JACKSON.
Washington, March 16, 1835.[1]

CHAPTER I: IRON AND SALT
Rollin Ridge
Near Springfield, Missouri
May 1849

Once lightning strikes a mighty oak, it often burns the tree to cinders, and its remnants fall to the ground as useless char. With a single touch of God's fingertip, flames consume the pulp, erasing its record of earthly time. Split and frayed limbs sag toward erupting roots, teeming with groundwater steam, hoping to escape the grave and ascend to the Nightland.

If, by happenstance, the tree survives, the cursed oak never grows straight again. During the storm, rainfall baptizes the flames while roots hold fast to deep water. For years after, those spine-like trunks reach beyond their scars, never rising straight, and never as weak as they once were. New sprouts leaf, like a young man's dreams, and reach the straightest path toward Heaven.

Year after year, that cursed oak perseveres, but trembles, insecure at each incoming storm. Through each lover's shower or volleyed deluge, the tree strengthens to the cadence of rain. If a rancher were to sling an ax, attempting to down the oak for a cabin or fence, the knotted grain would make it impossible to fell. Truth be told, God's lightning was necessary; it hardened the wood.

What hopes have we not all buried; what dreams have we not all mourned that come to us again with the music of the rhythmic rain? Have we trusted and been deceived? Have we lost what we loved? Have we seen joy after joy fade in the sky of our fate? All come to us again in sad and mournful memory as we listen to the patter of the rain.[1]

A lone crow cawed above my head, the prophetic harbinger of storm. The onslaught would end soon if heavy drops fell, but if the first drops were small, the barrage might last the day. Grandfather often said so. I had no complaints; our crops needed rain. Missouri's earthy musk told me no time remained before the clouds set their rainwater free.

Tiny drops speckled and smeared my last sentence. With the edge of my shirt, I patted the words dry, corked the inkwell, wrapped it together with pen and journal in their waxy cloth, tucking them under my vest. Crossing the wheat field for the barn, behind me, the wind lurched, pushed, taunted me with flash and rumble. So, I thought, God packed his pipe and lit His tobacco with lightning.

Yellow Bird's Song

Wacooli and I took advantage of the morning thunderstorm and lit the forge to shoe horses. Rain from the barn's open doorway cooled the heat radiating from the forge. He pumped the bellows, swirling gales of blurred woodsmoke hovering through smells of stale horse manure and damp hay. Our backs were warm, while our shirtfronts speckled dark, wet with blowing rainwater. We were caught, in between.

I wedged a hoof between my thighs and opened and closed my hand, implying Wacooli should hand me his knife. But my brother paid me no heed. I followed his gaze and dropped the hoof. Two riders raced through the graying downpour. Wet red hair flew in time with the incoming horse's mane. It was my sister, Clarinda, and her husband, Skili, riding bareback on her medicine hat mare. The storm must have caught them, and my farm was the closest shelter. I unhooked the halter and returned the horse to his stall, clearing the doorway before they arrived.

Both were drenched. Twigs stuck in Clarinda's hair. Her torn shirt sleeves were belted around a rust-colored skirt that stuck to her legs, exposing her moccasins. Tree limbs had scratched Skili's bare chest and gartered biceps, leaving red nettles on his copper skin.

Wacooli called out, "Mighty storm this morning." He tilted his hat down to keep the rain from pelting his eyes and escorted their mare under the cover of the barn.

The mare snorted water from her nostrils when my sister threw her leg over her mount and slid to the ground. Then, with plant-stained fingers, she grabbed my face, eyes urgent and straightforward. Something was wrong.

I signed to her, "Is Mama all right?"

Clarinda dismissed my question with a wave and held her fingers apart, pointing from her eyes to my own. She spelled my horse's name with her right hand, then pointed with two fingers, parallel to her forearms, and slid her arms apart.

I shouted above a rumble of thunder. "Someone stole my horse. How do you know?"

She watched my mouth speak, even though I asked the question with my hands. She gestured to Skili and herself as witnesses and spelled the thief's name, "K. e. l. l."

"He took your Appaloosa from the grazing prairie," Skili confirmed in Cherokee, flicking away slick black hair clinging to his face.

I knew Kell's theft for what it was: an answered prayer, an inevitable challenge to duel. Fate finally answered my appeal for justice, what I'd hoped would find me every day since Papa, Grandfather, and Cousin Elias' murders ten years ago. On that single day, weary with grief, my family descended from royalty to peasant, banished and fragmented—June 22, 1839.

My feet charged into the tempest before I thought through the consequences. Rain pelted my face, and I turned my chin away from the stinging wind.

Clarinda followed and grabbed my arm. She signed, "Brave brother, you can't go."

I made the insistent sign for "must"—a crook of my pointer finger, a flick of the same wrist. My wide strides left her behind. Although she couldn't hear me, I said, "You know why."

I burst through the door and passed Lizzie rocking our infant daughter near the stone fireplace. All I could think was to retrieve my pistol inside the cedar box under the bed. I heard, rather than saw, Lizzie's boots hit the floor with a solitary thud.

The quiet told me Clarinda spoke, telling Lizzie of Kell's crime. When I returned, pulling the belt tight to trap the colt to my side, Clarinda added how she and Skili witnessed Kell tie sinew to geld my Appaloosa.

I signed and spoke, startling Lizzie by standing behind her. "Kell's goading me. He knows Dickie is mine. No one near here grazes Appaloosas." There was only one reason Kell stole that horse. "Chief Ross commanded Kell to take me down. Force me to come to him." Ours wasn't a new story, one of betrayal and revenge.

Lizzie turned around with Alice in her arms and blocked the cabin door, blown open at her back. She shouted panic over Alice crying and the roar of blowing rain. "Why now? After a decade's passed since your father died?"

"I'm finally old enough to kill."

Lizzie squeezed her closed eyes tight. She dropped her head to my chest, resigned, and gripped my shirt. "Would that I had words to stop you."

None existed, so she attempted no further. Regardless, I wouldn't have heard her over the hum and crackle in my ears, like the sound the ground makes before lightning strikes. I reached for my coat. A still, small voice spoke through my thoughts as each arm passed through each wool sleeve, a voice heard every day since Papa died.

"A raven-thought is darkly set
Upon my brow—where shades are met
Of grief, pain, toil, and care—
The raven-thought of stern despair!"[2]

I shrugged the black coat over my shoulders and put on my hat. Yes, despair was the right word.

Yellow Bird's Song

No matter how I turned, Lizzie blocked my escape from our cabin's narrow walls. I put my hands on her arms to still her and shook her, so she'd open her eyes. "I can't let this bide." I spoke and signed the words over rhythmic slaps of one palm against the other. I said, "What would Mama be like if Papa were alive? If he were chief instead of Ross? If Grandfather could still ride his beloved Priest across the prairie, advocating for Cherokee statehood? If Cousin Elias still printed news of our cause? Listen to me, Lizzie. There's no one else alive to do it. Cousin Stand took down Foreman. It is my turn. God knows what I want."

I touched baby Alice's plump face with the back of my knuckles. I grabbed Lizzie's waist and kissed her hard for what might be the last time. After, she stood speechless; no time remained to argue.

Still, Lizzie wouldn't let go. Clarinda took her hands away. My sister and I locked our eyes. Instead, she touched a whistle, her talisman our grandfather gave her. She pulled the leather strap to release it from her damp shirt. I removed my hat and bowed. When I rose, Clarinda signed, "It will keep you safe. While you're gone, I'll call Kell's Raven Mockers."

Saturated and waiting just outside the door's frame, Wacooli handed me the horse's reins. I mounted and rode hard to the west, toward the storm over Cherokee Nation. Under diagonal sheets of rain, falling beneath a canopy of God's smoke, I rode one life back into another.

The evening's red sky horizon stretched its wide arms behind Judge Kell's dogtrot, extending into the dust. A dead tree stood as an ineffectual sentry between his corn crib and smokehouse, visible through the open-framed breezeway. I salivated, smelling pork fat lingering in the air. No longer able to afford to slaughter hogs, my family could only recall bacon's salty taste.

Inside the paddock, my appy lay on his side. Castration's fresh blood tainted his coat of bronze and cream. Blood gathered under his hind quarters. If Kell had cut his femoral, he'd die from blood loss. That horse was Dick's grandson, the pony I begged Papa to bring west from Running Waters.

The porch door squeaked, then slammed behind him. Kell expected me. He rolled tobacco in paper, sealing it closed with his tongue. His eyes squinted from the western prairie's sunlight sliding low behind me.

He struck a phosphorus match against the porch post, lit the end of the rolled tobacco, held it in his lips, tilted his head to the side, and inhaled. Through smoke, he said, *"Look at you, Rollin, standing on my land like some Mexican bandit. I believe your post is south of here.*" Kell's sarcasm snarled like poisoned saliva foaming from the jaw of a rabid dog.

"*I'm in the right place,*" I said, more confidently than I felt, flying on vindication's wind alone.

"*That is where you and I agree. Not much else, but that singular point.*"

He sauntered, with spotless leather boots, to the edge of the steps extending into the western dirt, just dust over the granite under Indian land.

I nodded left toward his painted paddock fence. "*Kell, you take my Appaloosa stallion? His markings are unmistakable.*"

Kell gestured with his smoking hand, pointing the two fingers toward my injured animal. "*You mean that gelding?*"

"*Who made him so?*"[3]

"*I did and am willing to stand by my deeds with my life.*[4] *Found him in pastureland. Horse bucked and rammed me. Without balls, he'll settle right down.*"

"*As a judge, you should know Cherokee don't own open tribal land. No reason he should be here.*"

Judge Kell gripped his porch rail but remained atop its planks on the high ground. Then, his unoccupied, dominant hand recognized his bowie knife's handle, sheathed, and slung low on his hip. He said, "*Can testify to nothing.*"

His lies didn't dampen my resolve. I saw through him. We both knew the real reason I was there. I shouted, "*My sister can.*"

He leaned against his porch post with carefree nonchalance. "*The deaf and dumb sister? I don't know what that feeble-minded woman could mean.*"

I touched the leather strap of Clarinda's whistle around my neck. "*She doesn't need to speak to witness. She is a medicine woman.*" Then I separated my boots, furthering my stance against the inevitable explosion of powder and ball from the iron under my palm.

Kell scoffed. "*Then remind me to stay well. That woman's a witch.*"

Wouldn't be illness that killed him. I couldn't allow Kell's wit to move me to fire first, no matter what insults he hurled at my sister. To make justice legal, Kell must first try to take my life, although that didn't mean I couldn't provoke the inevitable.

I matched his sarcasm. "*Now isn't the time to insult my family. Come down off that porch. Clarinda and Skili followed you, saw what you did. You've cost me far more than future foals. That blade in your grip took my father's life.*"

Yellow Bird's Song

I spoke the Cherokee words fast, having memorized their phrases from a thousand daydreams. Still, this time, the words echoed in the abandoned cave of my chest with heavier resonance—measuring the phrase's increased weight by speech.

He spoke his smug reply through smoke. *"Your father's signature on that treaty stole nearly four thousand Cherokee souls. So, I believe, son, both that horse and your father,"* he smiled before finishing his thought, *"got what they deserved."*

"According to whom? Your justice? Chief Ross'? It's his bloody hands you're hiding."

Kell pulled a rogue piece of tobacco off his tongue with his thumb and pointer finger. *"See now, truth rests in each man's perception. Your father knew that, at least."*

"Papa understood Cherokee sovereignty could not exist in the East. My family stood in the way of Chief Ross' greed; Ross sent you to kill him for it."

Kell's searing sarcasm furthered his attempt at intimidation. He shook his head, clicking his tongue. *"By accusing Chief Ross of such crimes, you make a steep accusation for a raven so young."* But then, his snide tone became more cynical. *"Your family received lawful Cherokee blood vengeance. So's I heard."*

It wasn't only his voice; every crack of bare earth mocked me. But what he didn't know, what the ground couldn't predict, was that this time, his blood would run. Cherokee Nation's rocky soil would soak in it, dilute him in its groundwater, and spit his remnants through every winding river and well.

Kell offered an aside, turning his face from me. *"You're still breathing."* He looked back, continuing his threat with closed-tooth menace. *"When this knife reaches you, that'll end. How ironic—"* He stopped short, mid-thought, and exhaled a chuckle before inhaling again from his lit tobacco. His eyes looked at me from my worn boots to my mother's pale eyes.

I finished the sentiment on his behalf, *"That the same knife would assassinate a father and murder his son? Admit your part. You were there in '39; the same knife hangs at your side."*

Kell unsheathed and admired the blade in his hand as if he hadn't seen his distorted reflection in it for years. *"She's a beautiful weapon, don't you think? Buckhorn handle. Metal inside the bone. Streamlined and strong. Son, this weapon ended many a man's life with its peaceful vengeance."*

I barked, *"Vengeance is a fickle whore. She strains her rulings through a sieve she calls morality, leaving behind rocks and politics. Justice's bullet is fair and fast. Even blindfolded, her shooter doesn't have to stand close to hit where he's aiming."*

Years ago, the image of Kell's bowie knife forged in my mind. Its craftsman burned the bone handle with the image of an arrowhead—no shaft, no flight feathers—only a killing point. Kell's knife required wind and aim, powered by his quick reach, and forged will. My twelve-year-old eyes remembered his blade. At twenty-two, my memory dripped in images of Papa's blood.

Impatient and blinded by the reddening dusk, Kell spoke with vigorous staccato, hefting his significant weight down the stairs. *"Take your thumb off that trigger, boy, before you start a war."* Then, with sight restored, he dirtied his spotless boots, kicking a wandering rat snake slithering between us, seaming a dividing line in prairie dust.

I shook my head in disgust. *"War began ten years ago. Your whiskey breath is as rancid as your soul. I can smell it stronger now."* I studied his smirk, offering my own in exchange. *"Stinks so bad, I thought someone died."*

Kell and I stood in paradox: I, in the shadow of a tree, him in the dying sunlight. His age to my youth, wealth to my poverty, appointment to my banishment, and vengeful intent opposing my righteous confidence.

He cocked his head and smirked, glanced over to my horse, and crushed the remnants of his smoke into the dust. *"You think this will end with you? Cousin Stand leading your teenage brothers and Boudinot's boy against my grown sons and Chief Ross' men in some unsanctioned feud? The few against the many?"*

"No, justice ends with me. If you approach, you will lose your life."[5] I wouldn't retreat from his taunts, knowing them for what they were. If Cousin Stand and I took down Chief Ross, it wouldn't be a feud; it would escalate an already brewing Cherokee civil war.

His face flushed red as he studied my eyes for any movement of my hand, raising his commanding voice. *"You're trespassing on my land. I am judge here; my rulings stand in place of vengeance."*

"How would you rule in my case? You stole and castrated my horse. Reason enough for me to be here."

Kell spoke through gritted teeth. *"Give me that pistol, boy."*

I didn't move. We faced one another, distanced only by the unspoken rules of a gentleman's duel with the western wind gathering speed between our stationary bodies.

"I'm in no mood for giving," I said.

He inhaled once before the blade left his hand with a flick of his wrist. Instinctively, I twisted and leaned away, not moving my feet. The flying

Yellow Bird's Song

blade grazed my chin, missing my skull, its intended target. Instead, it embedded itself in the ground behind me with a solitary thud.

From there, its point could do no further harm, and Kell stood before me, unarmed. I touched the blood dripping from my chin to my tongue and savored the taste of iron.

Hammer cocked.

Focus tuned.

Wrist snapped.

Colt Walker drawn.

Breath inhaled.

Trigger squeezed.

My horse was startled with the pistol's report and neighed his incarnate war cry. My breath didn't shift the cloud of gunpowder smoke. Only the vast prairie and the snake in the grass witnessed what I had done.

A stream of crimson escaped the black cave between Judge Kell's eyes and poured like molten lead boiled soft over white-hot coals. He fell straight back and hit the ground, with no mind left to command his knees to bend.

I walked to the paddock and gathered my appy's reins. I checked his nethers. After assuring myself the bleeding was under control, I led him past Kell's body and tied his guide rope to my horse. On impulse, I walked back to the tree and plucked the bowie knife from the ground. With his blade in my hand, I stood over Kell's body, sat on my heels, and cut out his heart. Blood dripped over his unfocused eyes, afraid of what the living couldn't see. His face held a surprised expression and faced God's judgment, forced to accept the consequences of living with a hypocritical heart.

I usurped Ross' faction with a .44, took Kell's heart with his own blade, satisfying only part of my blood revenge. I told his corpse, "*My sister summoned the Raven Mockers you see. I am no raven. My father named me Cheesquatalawny, Yellow Bird.*"

After wiping blood on my pant leg, I untied the knife's sheath from Kell's belt and thigh and strapped it against my own. Like a condemned man's chains, this weapon would be my weighty reminder of where I'd come from, no matter how far Chief Ross might force me to flee this sin.

At that moment, that second, I knew freedom. I'd made my choice, and in it, there was no guilt, no anger, no restless remorse. But with each tick of the pocket watch Papa bequeathed to me, my deep-seated principle of revenge returned, a will never satisfied until it reached Ross. I must do all I could to bring about that moment.[6]

Covered in dirt stuck to blood, the horses and I went to water, standing together in the dusky shallows of the Neosho. I removed my clothes and left them on the sand. The horses followed me deeper, rinsing dirt and blood from our bodies downstream.

It was a wrathful God who constructed man's body with strength and hate enough to kill, but his conscience, his memory, to preserve such a sin. Such contradiction explained why man rose and fell in God's once wild Eden. If man confessed, sought baptism among Earth's winged and gilled creatures, God's forgiveness was as assured as the hum of summer bees. But the wind rose and trapped unearthed anger beneath my skin, muting any such confession. The mockingbird's screech interrupted the glissade of water.

Upon the summit of yon tree
How gaily thou dost sing! How free from pain.
Oh, would that my sad heart could bound
With half the Eden rapture of thy strain!
I then would mock at every tear
That falls where sorrow's shaded fountains flow,
And smile at every sigh that heaves
In dark regret o'er some bewildering woe.[7]

Falling from the treetops, a camouflaged whippoorwill rebuked the mockingbird's sympathies. It said, "Too late! Too late! The doom is set. The die is cast!"[8]

CHAPTER 2: THE WILD HALF-BREED MAY RIDE[1]
Rollin Ridge
Fayetteville, Arkansas
April 1850

No questions remained unasked. Each possibility led to contrasting alternatives: run or hang. I grew weary of the word "danger," hearing it spoken in every uttered phrase from Mama, my cousin Stand, my brothers and sisters—Flora, Herman, AJ, Susan, her husband, Josiah, and my beloved, Lizzie.[2] Clarinda never signed the word. So, I stayed beside her to avoid hearing its repetition. Wacooli and Aeneas planned to go West with me, their banished brother, to renew our family fortune in California gold.

In my absence, Mama insisted my wife and daughter abandon the Missouri cabin for the time being and stay with her, saying they'd keep one another from worry. But Lizzie refused, insisting that wherever I was to go, she was to follow. At last Sunday's dinner, Mama said, "Sometimes a good wife can't follow her husband, even though she loves him most." Her words silenced all who shared our table and ended any further debate.

I held Lizzie against my chest on our last night together, memorizing the smell of her hair. We'd temporarily escaped our upcoming separation by traveling back to the days when our lives were free to love one another. Days before our wedding, we'd ridden in a canoe downriver to a small island near her family's home and made love under its sheltering trees. We'd returned to the same place tonight and done the same.

I squeezed her tighter, dedicating the moment, 'To Lizzie'. "She that called me to her arms, was first, was all, that stirred my soul.[3] The night we met, you've understood me like no other."

She propped her chin on her hand, resting the weight of both on my chest. "I know you, Rollin. Better than the professor's daughter."

I stretched to kiss her, saying, "There's no comparison."

She replaced her cheek against my smattering of chest hair. "I don't know what you saw in her. She's a frumpy girl, meant to marry a minister and remain covered from neck to ankle her entire life." After saying so, Lizzie raised her bare thigh and wound her ankle around my knee.

My hand found the bend of her hip. "A beauty among mortals, with eyes that make peacocks envy." My hand traveled across the curve of her bones, up her resting arm, and settled beneath her hair, gripping the back of her thin neck. Lizzie's closed eyes and audible hum assured me I'd renewed a pleasing memory. "I sat alone in Reverend Washbourne's school house, in near darkness, feeling sorry for myself. There is little in life more melancholy than a poet forced to study the law. I knew better than to write without a muse. Crumpled paper covered my desk."

She continued in my stead, "Until I burst in and let in wind enough to blow out your light."

"The moonlight silhouetted you, until you slammed the door and the latch fell." I took a deep breath. "I spoke to you in darkness. 'Ma'am, are you in need of assistance?' You asked me not to tell anyone you'd been there, but I could hardly say, since I didn't have the pleasure of knowing your name."

"I walked toward your voice, out of breath. There was a cattywampus. He was right behind me."

"I reached into my pocket but dropped the matches. I touched along the floor for one, stood, and relit the candle. When I saw you, an arrow pierced my poet's heart. You handed me one of the crumpled papers from the floor."

"My dress was smattered with mud."

"I don't remember the mud, only your brown curls gathering at your nape, and blue eyes deeper than a cloudless sky reflected in a lake diluted with limestone dust. My stolen white girl."[4]

Lizzie kissed me and said, "You're innocent of theft. I followed you willingly."

"I remember. I handed you the light and grabbed the shotgun off the mantle."

She recalled, "You said, 'I know these woods. I would be happy to escort you home, armed against the roaming eyes of wampus cats.' I didn't know whether I should have gone with you. There are many dangers to a woman from a man."

I said, "The same exists in paradox, darlin'. When I took you home, there were no paw prints of mountain lions. Just horse tracks, probably from Stand's band of Cherokee riding west to take down Ross' men. Had he let me, I would have painted my eyes and joined him."

She whispered, "God did not mean for you to ride that night."

"That mystical cattywampus became my good fortune." I rolled her to her back on the quilt under us, sliding my arms under hers. She intertwined thin ankles behind me.

"My people have legends of such a cat, the Ew'ah," I said, stretching the vowels with my breath. "Cunning Ew'ah feasted on the thoughts of village children and terrorized their dreams."

Lizzie's eyes grew wide under the blue moonlight peeking through the spring green awning above us.

Yellow Bird's Song

I said, "They chose Standing Bear, the village's strongest brave, to kill the demon cat." I reached her ear, interspersing kisses with whispers of the remaining tale. "Shamans and war chiefs gave Standing Bear their best weapons when he left the village on his quest to kill the cattywampus. His woman, Running Deer, followed him to the edge of their village until she couldn't see him any longer."[5]

She held me to her with one arm while the fingers of the other brushed the line of my spine. I continued speaking in her ear, mimicking the dawdling rhythm of her hand. "Weeks went by with no word from Standing Bear. Then he returned, screaming, with claw marks beneath his eyes. Running Deer knew her husband was lost, never again to be the man she loved."[6]

"Don't tell me anymore. Not tonight, not any night."

I kissed her neck and slid down her body to rest my head between her breasts. "Running Deer wanted to avenge her husband, so as a weapon, the village elders gave her a booger mask carved like the face of the mountain lion. On her journey, breaking sticks woke Running Deer in the middle of the night. Afraid to meet the cattywampus' gaze and suffer the same fate as her husband, she put on the mask and followed the sound. She sprang from the thick brush beside the stream and scared the mountain lion."[7]

Lizzie's hands found my hair. She scratched my scalp with her nails and pulled her fingers through its thick, black strands. I said, "The Ew'ah fell on its side in the water. It clawed and tore at itself. The booger mask turned the Ew'ah's powerful magic back on itself. Running Deer ran the night through, back to the village, back to her husband, never once looking behind her toward the stream or the bleeding cattywampus."[8]

Lizzie asked, "Did Standing Bear return to his former self?"

"No, he was never the same man. But Running Deer was called a Spirit-Talker by her village. She still protects her people from demons lurking in lost places."[9]

She reached for my face, brought me to her, rubbing her thumbs against my cheekbones. She kissed me tenderly at first, with desperate passion trailing close behind.

She only released my lips long enough to say, "There will never come a time I will not hear you."

I climbed the squeaking steps and knocked on Mother's bedroom door to say goodbye. I didn't speak, unsure which words would keep her from grieving three sons, even though our hearts beat. Waiting for her answer, I looked at the pale spot on the wooden floor, recognizing the grain on the planks which had been my bed for the long year after Papa's death. Mama refused to talk for so long. She wouldn't sign, only nod in acceptance or refusal. After so much silence, I think I slept there so I could be the first to hear when her voice returned.

"Come," I heard through the door. Her voice barely made sound enough to listen.

I turned the knob and inhaled her smell—morning earth covered in dew, yeast and flour, milk and lye soap. After Kell's death, since my crime, her hair, once a vibrant auburn, dimmed to rust, streaked white from wisdom's cause and worry's effect, yet she remained only a woman of forty-seven years. Her sunken cheeks were lit by a candle, despite the incoming dawn. She stared out the window, seated at her writing desk, with a cup of tea next to her folded hands, and her Bible opened down the middle, assumedly to Psalms.

Her focus was outside the window, and she said in Cherokee, "*There's a mockingbird.*" From her expression, I saw her as a young bride with vibrancy as vivid as her sunlit hair. Mother found her way among her husband's people, finding a family so distinct from her own. She found the language challenging to speak yet understood its nuances. She recognized Papa's sarcasm or his worry. All the while, fearing the return of his cough, afraid the same disease that brought them together would return and tear them apart.

Not long after she and Papa settled in Cherokee Nation, her mother, Grandmother Northrup, sent teacups and saucers, blue-and-white pearl-ware, as a wedding gift. When I could barely walk, Mama moved those cups to our home, Running Waters. Then, when I was ten, when our family prepared for removal, with trembling hands, she'd crated them again, placing each porcelain piece among straw and wood shavings in a pine box.

Our family traveled across the country with many such wooden crates, first carried north by wagon and then south by riverboat. At Honey Creek, she helped my father build a new home, a school, and a store stocked with supplies for the Cherokee who would arrive later. After the war party assassinated Papa, she packed her precious porcelain and fled, holding one hand with widowed Grandmother Susannah and each of us with the other.

The same cup and saucer sat on her desk, chipped and full, with the same purpose. How many cups of mourning had she sipped from their rims? Aunt Harriet, Quatie, Honey, Elias, Grandpa, Papa, and only recently, Grandmother Susannah. More than her birthday, each chip marked her years—a move, a passing.

Yellow Bird's Song

Overcome but holding back tears, she sipped from the cup and returned it to its saucer. She filled her lungs. I'd memorized her gasps and silences, recalled from midnight sobs after Papa died in her arms. The same air hovered around her now.

"I will write to you and Lizzie and Cousin Stand." I spoke the assurance, despite my genuine doubts about our survival. "We will stay alive, Mama. You won't have to cry anymore."

"You said the same to me when you were a boy." Then, after composing herself, she stood slowly, expecting a renewed spasm in her chest. Her hands brought me closer to her, smiling through tear-swollen eyes. I took her hands and studied her curved, knotted knuckles gripping my calloused hands. I memorized each frail bone inside her thin skin, weathered from needle and thread, seed and weed, flour and egg, water and lye.

She said, "I have papers for you before your journey." She put her hands on my shoulders and slid them down, holding me at arm's length, memorizing me in return. Mama touched Clarinda's whistle around my neck and smiled. She touched the fob chain of Papa's watch and forced her chin higher. Then, her eyes stopped on Kell's blade, hanging on my hip.

Watching her expression shift, I said, "It will never again be in the hands of anyone who intends to hurt our family."

She nodded in affirmation and let go of my arms to walk to her dresser. She pulled a stack of letters and a bound journal from the top drawer. After she handed them to me, the sight of the top letter's script shocked me, and in a heated flush, I sat in the chair she had just vacated.

"He wrote this to you just days before they came. You were playing in the room when he penned it. I don't think he knew I watched him study you. I thought he was trying to imagine your face older. At the time, he was so ill. Your father thought the cough would take him then. But…" She stood above me and brushed the bushy hair from my eyes. "Time on your journey to read the others. Read the letter he wrote before you go. I know what it says. I'll give you some privacy and wait for you at the bottom of the stairs."

I couldn't speak. My hand shook when she closed the door, and I slid my finger under the sticky wax seal. He dated it June 20th, 1839. Ross' war party, led by Kell, assassinated Papa two days later.

Cheesquatalawny, Yellow Bird,
　　To soothe your cries as a baby, I held you in my arms and promised you Cherokee's eastern land as your legacy. I promised you an education worthy of leading our people, giving you the

wisdom to guide them from ignorance to knowledge, from superstition to faith. But, with a broken spirit and fractured heart, I must tell you, son, I failed you, despite my every effort to the contrary.

From the days of my youth, President Jefferson promised that native blood would mix with the new country's immigrants and create Americans, together becoming a civilized people. However, during my generation, Jefferson's prophecy never came to fruition. Rollin, you were born when I believed Jefferson's hope a genuine possibility.

As you may remember, I was in Washington the December of '35 when your grandfather and Cousin Elias signed the Treaty of New Echota. I led our cause, left with no alternative to Georgia's violence and oppression. Even after the Supreme Court recognized Cherokee Nation as a foreign country, President Jackson refused to send federal troops to protect our people from Georgia's thievery and abuse. He said it wasn't his place to violate the states' autonomy. Politically, Jackson wouldn't infuriate the southerners who'd voted him into office—not once, but twice.

Most Cherokee hated General Jackson, but after our meeting in '32, I found him a man loyal to his friends, a scarcity indeed. Jackson offered me honesty where my people, led by Chief John Ross, tendered lies and betrayals. My journal and these letters corroborate Ross' character and unceasing avarice.

Ross already counts my demise as certain. Yet, for even this, I am prepared. To release our people from their degraded bondage, who would not freely lay down his life? Our character may now be slandered, our motives impugned, and we may perish in the cause of our blind nation. Retribution and justice will arise over our ashes. I hope you will point with pride and say, 'My father was an honest man. He died in pursuit of his people's preservation. In my veins is the patriotic blood of a noble parent. I will finish his intentions.'[10]

Son, no matter what you may hear, I never took a bribe and never committed treason. I am an honest man. But because of my choices, the Ridges continually blocked Ross' passage. Their family hates ours for knowing the secret seditious control they hold over the lives of our people, both in the east, and now, the west. When a government is afraid of the people, there is freedom; when the people are threatened by their government, there can be only tyranny.[11]

Yellow Bird's Song

For the lives lost during emigration, by my signature and seventy others, I confess and accept their blame. I'm haunted by it. I have often thought about which needed more courage: facing a premature death or keeping Ross' treachery hidden. But here, while he forces his hand, I must keep silent. Once an ally and friend, I refused to disavow Ross' strengths entirely because of his flaws. The Cherokee needed Ross' leadership to move our nation westward. Despite his grand opinion of himself, he is not a God. Ross is only a man, steepled by stubborn pride, yet eager to placate the same enemies lying in wait to attack him.

If I die, Rollin, take care of your mother. Carry my watch and my ace, an As Nas playing card won in a hand dealt by a devil, a Black Crow, the first to tell me of Ross' greed. Study the card's portrait carefully. The horse and the lion are not natural enemies. Horses don't approach lions. The lion never begins an attack it does not plan to finish. In a wild encounter, the lion might spring onto the horse's back and sever its spine with a single bite. From that perspective, the lion would kill the horse. But, if that lion were to pounce and miss, falling below the horse, a single kick or stomp from the thousand-pound animal would kill the lion. Nature never lies; the mightiest animal overcomes. Yet, from the portrait on the playing card, no one can tell which animal wins. The result of their entanglement lives in an unknown future.

My son, you were born during a fight for two worlds, one with the lion's prowess and the other, a horse's brave agility. Your mother and I raised you and your siblings to live in freedom, uniting each animal's strengths in your blood. Don't spend your future blinded by emotions, but balance them with truth, passed down from philosophers and shamans alike. Be loyal to your soul's unbound spirit. I've watched it fly on our journeys to the sun. You won't be content only holding it in your palm.

Papa

With so many years spent longing to hear his voice, I thought I had forgotten how he sounded, how he breathed when he spoke, how he inhaled to think through his thoughts before voicing them aloud. But I hadn't misplaced him. In my mind, it was his tone, his inflection, speaking his letter's words.

When I came down the stairs, I couldn't look at Mama. I didn't take her hand when she and I passed our sanctuary's threshold. Abandoned by its loss, she left my side to embrace my brothers. She told each to protect the other, declaring before God in Heaven that each was her favorite. Wacooli's father, Peter, put his arm around her after she put her handkerchief over her mouth and said how quiet the house would be without all our noise.

I kissed Lizzie and promised again to send for her and Alice when I had the proper means to ensure their safe travels. I knew, on this journey, Lizzie constructed my consciousness with her tears, my fortitude from her love, my endurance purchased at the cost of her bravery. After mounting, I held her beautiful face one more time. Then, I touched the crumpled parchment in my pocket, reassured the poem I began the night we met remained close. Still unfinished, the lingering words interrupted our last goodbye.

The prairies are broad, and the woodlands are wide
And proud on his steed, the wild half-breed may ride.[11]

Mother's credit supplied us a month's provisions and three pack mules. God only knew how she afforded to do so. Aeneas and Wacooli mounted their horses. I touched each of my talismans again: Clarinda's whistle, Papa's pocket watch, Kell's bowie knife, Papa's letters and journal, and pen and ink wrapped in their waxy cloth.

Mounted high on my horse, I watched Mother's retreat. Anger welled in me. I didn't want to feel it, but it surfaced regardless. In these last moments between us, I blamed her for Papa's death and all that followed. I called her to account with a singular question. "Mama." She turned. "Why did you wait so long to give me his letter?"

She wilted from my blast of bitterness. I turned my eyes from the sight of her and stared toward the horizon. I said, "If I'd had this evidence before, I could have brought Ross to account." Papa's letter made me question whether I needed to leave Lizzie, Alice, Arkansas. Gripping the reins, I fisted glove and leather reins around the saddlebow. "I wouldn't have killed Kell if this evidence brought Papa justice. Do you expect me to forgive you for keeping quiet?" My emotions ran higher than flood waters, too treacherous to cross, too heavy to carry across the deep, rushing waters.

From the open doorway, her grief rose and crumpled her stature, unable to find my eyes for shame. Mama said, "My sin was in my silence. Forgive me, Rollin. If I'd given you the knowledge before now, I'd have lost you too. For as long as I could, my heart clung to every word your father ever said." And she returned to the house's ghosts, stepping into the shadowed doorway.

With words spent, sensing Lizzie trailing behind my horse, I heeled for speed, passing beyond the mules and my brothers, hoping they wouldn't

Yellow Bird's Song

see my unmanly tears. I flew past them before the drops hit the ground, hoping, for a moment longer, to delay wet wings, grounding us, drowning us in swaths of inevitable rain.

CHAPTER 3: CIVILIZED
Sarah Ridge
New Echota, Cherokee Territory
July 1827

I held a crying Rollin, shushing and swaying him in the morning sunlight. Honey bustled into the room carrying a white box, wider than her demure frame. She peeked around it, trying to see her feet, and set it on the bed. "Brother John already dressed and waitin' for you outside. It's getting late this mornin'. This feedin' will do. Rollin eat all day long, if'n you let him. And before you ask, we be fine while you two is gone."

I laid Rollin in his cradle. His legs kicked free of his light blanket, and his fists stretched and contracted, trying to hold the morning sun warming his face. Above him, perched on her knees atop a chair, Clarinda's eyes watched through the glass window, keeping faithful sentinel duty.

"Trouble follows Clarinda. Rollin's cries bring more. They need so much attention, Honey. Are you sure you can manage? John must go; I'll stay."

"We won't be lookin' for trouble from crows," Honey reassured.

She flipped the box open. "Oh, Sarah, you'll be the finest dressed white woman at da Vann's." Inside the box was an emerald-green satin gown with flouncing sleeves and ribbons running across the bodice, interlacing to allow the dress to fit as snugly as the wearer wished. A parasol and hat draped across new elbow-length white gloves.

"He shouldn't have bought me such a fine gown. I'll leak through my shift. I shouldn't go."

"Nos, you won't. I brought dem cabbage leaves. Go on, now. Mister John gets lost talkin' to all da Cherokee. You 'minds him of his English."

"I won't ask," I said, tempted into vanity by the green sheen running through my fingers. "I'll just assume Mother Susannah gave the cabbage leaves to you and put them wherever you tell me." According to Honey, cabbage leaves could remedy nursing mothers away from their hungry sons.

"That's the way of it." Honey put her hands on her hips and stood taller, proud she knew more than me—albeit a common occurrence. Honey was my linkster with my husband's people. I would trade my life to save hers, had once before. Born into servitude, after her father's death, her body and soul were free. By choice, she became a Ridge. I loved her as a sister.

Honey helped me dress while John waited on the porch of Mother

Yellow Bird's Song

Susannah's cabin near New Echota. When I closed the door behind me, John checked the time and returned his pocket watch to his waistcoat.

He must have heard me walking behind him and offered me his matching sleeve. "You're stunning," he said, "like you flew here and landed on my arm, *walela*." John's compliment, the Cherokee word for hummingbird, reminded me of our courtship.

I whispered, "I'm going to melt inside these stays." My pragmatism was no match for his poetry. His linguistic prowess was not limited to English but began in his native Cherokee tongue.

"The moon is still out. We can go back inside if you'd like. Take the stays off. I'll do as you please." He smirked.

"How would that help?" I asked, even though I knew he would best me again.

"You and I could populate Cherokee Nation with beautiful and intelligent people instead of attending horse races and talking politics." He held on to the lapels of his coat and raised his head. "Both are for future generations, after all."

I smiled at him and him at me, although he kept his eyes closed, soaking in the heat from the morning sunlight on his face. I thought for a minute, hoping to remember the proper phrase. I spoke with the intonation of a question, raising my voice. "It is the very error of the moon. She comes more nearer Earth than she was wont. And makes men mad."[1] John chuckled and smiled and kissed my hand with the memory. We read *Othello* two winters ago and memorized lines that fit our moods. I accredited Rollin's conception to the tragic love story.

He turned, holding my cheeks in his hands, and barely touched my lips with his. "Perhaps there will be an eclipse today, where the heavenly orbs will meet." Then, leading me toward the awaiting carriage, he said, "An eclipse, *nvdo walosi ugisgo*—the frog eats the sun, more or less." My Cherokee culture and vocabulary lessons continued.

I said what he already knew. "Even during the day, you find moonlit words to say."

He ignored my sentiment and continued his lesson. "When Cherokee people see an eclipse, they beat pots or pound drums. They shout and stare wildly at the sky to scare the frog away from the sun, thinking themselves victorious when the moon drifts, returning order to the heavens.[2] Ridiculous."

John tried to rid his people of superstition and bring them to education, such as he learned from missionaries. Unfortunately, most of his people had not had the educated advantages his family's wealth brought him. He hoped to transfer his love of learning to all those he met.

John picked up a familiar case, a telescope given to the Major by Doctor Gold in Connecticut. I don't think the Major examined it out of the case more than a few times, but John used it constantly.

"Harriet and I looked through that telescope when we were children. It was a special treat, although I never understood what I was looking at. Why are you bringing it?"

"To loan it to a friend. What was Harriet like as a child?" he asked.

"Precocious, outspoken, stubborn. For a long time, I thought Harriet insincere, although I witnessed the contrary."

"What made you change your mind?" John stopped to ask.

"Before you returned, after my parents sent you home, I was unwell, so heartsick, I didn't eat. Everyone tiptoed around me, avoiding any room where I occupied myself. Harriet came to distract me, and we walked to Kellogg's Mercantile. Mister Kellogg and Mister Copeland spoke cruelly of the native students, past and present. She stood up to them, told them their words were unchristian."

"Did she now?" John continued the walk to the carriage, pleased by my recollection.

"Boldly. Harriet always wanted to be a missionary."

Major Ridge guarded the open carriage door. John escorted me inside to join his already seated mother. After freeing his hand from mine, he and his father stood upright, framing light entering the darker carriage, mirroring one another's pride and fortitude. War shadowed the elder; English words and law enlightened the student. Like bookends, they embodied the transition taking place in the Cherokee Nation.

We rode the Federal Road to Vann's mansion in the Coosa district. Today, "Rich" Joe held horse races and served a picnic for the Cherokee Council and white guests during the Constitutional Convention. Chosen intentionally, July 3rd aligned Cherokee independence with America's independence from Britain. So, while Georgia celebrated freedom, Cherokee Nation did the same. After living here for three years, this would be my first opportunity to meet with so many people John and his family held in such high esteem. Yet, my accustomed fear of their judgment slipped through my thoughts, while reassuring myself that this land was my home.

Orchards greeted us in neatly planted rows, dense with peaches and apples, creating a fragrance in the air like home. Servants' quarters bordered the tree line of flat valley land surrounding Diamond Hill. Joe Vann's large manor, a two-story brick home with expensive glass windows and large white columns, held verandas on the front and the rear of the house. There were corncribs, smokehouses, and outbuildings for weaving

Yellow Bird's Song

and cooking. Given the abundant number of horses and carriages, many attended. A surge rushed through me, nerves on fire, reminding me of the importance of the event, framed by the fear I'd make a mistake.

Our carriage rolled through Vann land between a row of walnut trees bordering endless green pastures. Black and white cows, silent sentinels, gnawed grass and watched as we passed, undisturbed. As the horses pulled us the last distance, I saw an open door at the side of the house. From it, trails of servants carried trays and crockery from the exterior kitchen to the main house near white linen tablecloths and white-washed ladderback chairs in neat rows. Their movement reminded me of fire ants seeking sweets, and, in a line, returning to their self-constructed dirt abodes. Other servants turned a pig on an open fire, slaughtered for the occasion. The smell of salt and fat from the roasted meat mingled with the aromatic sweet apples hanging on the trees. The bees hummed louder amidst such plenty.

Most whites were surprised to know slavery existed among the Cherokee. John and I argued over the institution. The Ridges treated their servants like family. However, their will to choose their lives was the identical desire of John's people, fighting for God-given liberty to govern themselves. While we still lived with his family, I could do little but speak to my husband and pursue change. But I knew a time would come when America and the Cherokee Nation must make the moral choice, no matter the economic difficulty such a choice might bring.

Once I stepped from the carriage, John held my gloved hand and said, "I'm instituting the wink law." John's top hat shaded half of his face, so I couldn't see his eyes in the bright sunlight. I predicted his expression from his carefree tone. "Are you familiar, Mistress Ridge?" he asked.

"I am not, Mister Ridge. However, I would hate to violate without intention."

"Ignorance of the law is no excuse. It is in the Constitution."

"I'm aware." I grinned.

"One wink means I have ten minutes to end my conversation and take you home."

"What does a whole blink mean?" I asked.

I surprised him with my question. "I don't know. You have something in your eye?"

"A whole blink means I'm proud of you and content to remain by your side, but thank you for saying so. You know I am worried about leaving Rollin and Clarinda with Honey. She can manage one, but if Rollin wails…"

"Amendment duly noted, Mistress Ridge." He rechecked his watch.

"I'll have you back to our children in hours." His promise was sincere, just under the surface of his sarcasm.

I pulled him close so I could whisper. "Promise me you won't leave me alone too often." For a man so aware of time, he lost hours debating politics.

"Agreed. I hope we get to mingle with the many guests in the time we have. Some have traveled great distances and are new here."

Major and Mother followed us into the sunlight. A row of white women adorned in a rainbow of pastels held fast to their matching parasols with white-gloved hands and whispered about the heat while their white-breeched, black-booted husbands stood in small circles gesturing about important matters. White pipe smoke hazed around their heads.

Shirtless Cherokee separated themselves by sitting on their heels on the ground. Cherokee women walked through the guests with red and purple baskets in their arms and yellowed gourds slung from leather straps around their necks. Like John's family, wealthy Cherokee slipped easily between these two groups. As for me, I did not know where I'd fit in this mix of classes and attitudes.

A close family friend, John Ross, stood atop a stump near a stand of hickories which offered him an arc of shade. His English words spoke to the purpose of the Cherokee's new Constitution to an array of men, Cherokee and white alike, separated by class but listening, Cherokee men stood closest to Ross, outlined by Rich Joe Vann's curious white guests, standing at a distance but still quite able to hear Ross' prepared speech.

Ross bellowed the words written on the page in his hand. "There is every reason to flatter us in the hope that under wise and wholesome laws, the preponderating influence of civilization, morality, and religion will secure us and our posterity an ample share of prosperity and happiness."[3]

Turbaned warriors clapped at Ross' eloquence, followed by a delayed reaction from some white men who discovered a sudden motivation to stray.

Behind Ross, near the trunk of a neighboring tree, I noticed a small woman dressed in pale pink. She was Cherokee but wearing European styles. Her black hair parted down the middle, swept from her face, and was bound by a simple wrap next to a pink rose. She held gloved hands in front of her and waited with penetrating eyes, studying the men's faces in the crowd. She angled herself to survey those who'd turned away from Ross, who'd denied him applause or remark.

Still, many clapped and extended their hands as Ross stepped down. I couldn't take my eyes from the noble woman behind him. Noticing the direction of my stare, Mother Susannah said in slow English, "Quatie

Yellow Bird's Song

Ross," and gestured toward the woman. I pulled my arm from John's, who was already leaning toward the ambient sounds of English spoken around his father. Mother Susannah took me to meet the woman of my attention.

Quatie Ross' face carried lines between her eyes and around her mouth, denoting her age. She seemed older than me, but the indentations were perhaps from sun and work instead of years. I curtsied with Mother Susannah's Cherokee introduction, hearing my name mid-sentence. Quatie, in return, studied me and reached out to touch a tendril of my hair. It was not intimidating, only a reaction I'd come to expect. There were few white missionaries in the territory with red hair.

In English, she asked, "Do you speak our tongue?"

"I understand more than I speak correctly." Better to be honest about my understanding of Cherokee verbs rather than make a fool of myself.

"Then, I will speak English for you, *and Cherokee for Mother Susannah.*"

I opened my parasol when we stepped away from the grand shade supplied by the house and followed Quatie Ross. She led us to a group of older women seated near a separate glade of oaks. I did not belong. Their attire was more muted and homespun than our trio's elegant gowns.

I overheard an unfamiliar white woman speak with a familiar New England accent. "It is a shame Reverend Gambold couldn't come. His presence might deter some of the gambling, drinking, and ball games, sure to follow all this political talk. He is unwell. May never regain his strength. He never stopped mourning Anna's passing years ago."

Following her comment, she closed her eyes and shook her capped head. My mother would have said something similar, dressed in the same fashion as this stranger.

I knew of the man she spoke. Minister Butrick and his apprentice, Arch, introduced me to the aged and infirm Reverend Gambold at Oothnaloga Mission's services.

Quatie responded first in Cherokee and repeated her sentiment in English. "Their passings gave us all pause. It was God's will that Peggy and Anna died so close to one another, buried together beneath 'God's Acre.' Do you remember? It was the same night a fireball crossed the sky. A star fell."

"Who were Peggy and Anna?" I mumbled.

Quatie whispered, gesturing toward the mansion. "This house once belonged to Peggy, Rich Joe's mother. Anna was Reverend Gambold's wife. They were close friends."

Quatie angled her body gracefully, as if she moved through water, asking Susannah, *"Peggy was your niece, was she not?"*

"She was. My heart still grieves the loss." Susannah's hand behind my back put me on display, as these women examined me themselves. *"But, with death comes new life. My daughter Sarah, John's wife, has two children. Rollin is only three months old."*

Quatie's eyes widened. "I remember nights of little sleep and the long days that followed when my children were infants. Ross was rarely home to help." She returned her gaze to her husband but spoke to me. "My youngest, Jane, is six years old."

I said, "It is difficult for us to be away from our children, even for a short time."

A woman approached us, wearing a European-fashioned gown of crisp yellow with firm pleats. The toes of her white shoes peeked from under the hem. She trod to our flock, looking behind her, escaping some annoyance. Ironed curls lay in ringlets around her gaunt cheeks, making her eyes appear larger than they should have been.

"I cannot stand to hear one more minute of that man's boastings," the stranger said.

Quatie asked, "Which man?"

"That Ross fellow. His skin is not red, yet he talks as if it is dark as yours. Excuse my mention of the obvious. You speak English, I see? Far better than those slaves of Vann's. His Pleasant is anything but." She scoffed when looking back at the men attending Ross' continued recitations. John stood near him, with his forearms crossed over his knee, and the foot of his weaker leg perched on the stump where Ross had delivered his speech only moments ago.

Quatie listened but turned her back to the woman in yellow, looping arms with Mother Susannah. After the unsavory comment about her husband, Quatie left me behind to speak to the arrogant woman by myself.

"I'm Julianna Connor, here with my husband on a visiting tour."

"I'm Sarah Ridge. My husband is John Ridge." At the mention of his name, I looked back at him, hoping to catch his attention and blink.

"Oh, I heard him speak once in Philadelphia. I was only a girl. Such rhetoric and prose. He's nothing like the Indians gathered here. These natives seem made of dirt and confusion, far from ideal. Until this party, this visit has been neither orderly nor comfortable." She hid her whispered words behind a gloved hand. "So many of these women dress like unchristian witches, exposing so much skin to the light. It's indecent." She changed the subject and her tone so quickly, I shuddered. "It must be love, for you to choose to live so far away from—" She expelled a forced cough while searching for a careful word, "—civilization." She assumed since we were white, she could reveal her true thoughts, and the Cherokee women

Yellow Bird's Song

around us would be none the wiser. She couldn't have been more wrong.

She cackled mocking glee. "Your gown is lovely. Although, if I may say so, the bodice's binding is last year's fashion. No matter here." She exuded insincerity with every pleat of her gaudy, yellow dress.

I said, "My husband bought it for me. I disagree entirely with your conclusions."

"About the gown? I know the day's fashions. Trust me," she said.

"No. I'm honored to wear what John selected. You are wrong about the Cherokee."

"Surely, you recognize their heathen nature, their savage ways. So many in poverty, yet the wealthy own slaves? God forbid." Her language was such that I had not heard in three years, but cruel words rarely change. Mistress Connor was not what I expected today.

"You didn't mind the slaves when they obeyed you. I find these people, my husband's people, to be honest, kind, spiritual, and clever, masters of their world. They carry the souls of the smallest and oldest on their shoulders. Warriors bear the weight and do so with joy. They are generous people with spirits of fire, matching the irrelevant color of their skin."

Mistress Connor scoffed when Quatie returned with Mother Susannah, distracting me from the ridiculous woman.

Mother Susannah addressed me in Cherokee. All I understood was "Sollee" and "horse," so I curtsied to excuse myself and reopened my parasol, hoping its shade might hide my exasperation. I bowed to excuse myself, leaving Mistress Connor alone, to scan the crowd for company she deemed appropriate.

Many gathered near the fences to watch the horse race on Joe Vann's illustrious track. Some believed he wasted valuable cropland when he ordered servants to construct it. However, cultivating so much land, I imagined he did not feel the monetary loss.

From my view, a tall gentleman in a black vest stood with his arms across a fence post bordering the racetrack. He watched as fourteen-year-old Sollee Ridge mounted her horse. John met us when we inched closer to the rail near the starting gate. The gentleman turned and at once recognized John.

"How's the leg?" the man inquired.

"Better in the summer. How were your travels, Sam?" John greeted him with an animated handshake. "Or should I address you as Governor Houston?"

"Not yet, and if the newspapermen get their way, perhaps never." He chuckled a belly laugh. "I'm here as Joe Vann's guest and your father's friend. Couldn't miss Sollee's race. Glad the weather held. Hot and muggy. No rain until later this afternoon, I imagine." He nodded toward Diamond Hill, remarking, "Up there, your father was speaking Cherokee so fast, I couldn't keep up. My knowledge of your language was meager to start with and has not aged well."

"You're modest. You speak the language better than most. Better than Ross." Then, catching sight of me, Mister Houston acknowledged my presence with a gracious nod.

"Who is this lovely young woman?" he asked with the deep bow of a tall man.

"May I present my wife, Sarah. Sarah, this is Sam Houston. He marched with Father, and Ross during the Red Sticks' War."

Houston again bowed his head, after I held out my hand.

"Welcome, Mister Houston," I said, noticing his shadowed, kind blue eyes. His receding hairline spoke of too many hours on horseback wearing hats.

"That accent is from nowhere near here, Mistress Ridge. Where are you from?"

"Connecticut, sir."

"Oh, don't call me sir. Call me Sam."

As we spoke, I noticed Quatie Ross standing apart from the men led down the slope by Joseph Vann.

"Excuse me. I'll be right back." Squeezing John's arm, I left him to talk with Sam Houston and intercepted Quatie's approach.

Once she was under the shade of my parasol, I whispered, "I owe you a debt for taking me from Mistress Connor's conversation."

"I was pleased to hear your observations about my people, Mistress Ridge. I'll soon be preparing for winter. Join me? So many candles to make and blankets to weave. Come to my home. Bring your children. I'll send the particulars."

With the simple reminder of Rollin and Clarinda, my body renewed its insistence that my attendance at this function needed to be short. I put my hand on my heart to measure whether Honey's cabbage leaves had done their job. They had. Nonetheless, I felt an impending milk surge in my chest. Her eyes followed my hand and smiled, understanding the gesture.

"I'm honored," I said. "Thank you for your kindness. Unfortunately, there are few to talk with here I can understand."

Quatie looked into my eyes and said, "It is a shame this is our first meeting. Ross and the Ridges are quite close, as you know." Then she nodded and moved away to stand taciturnly near her husband's magnetic voice. She did not take his arm. Instead, she stood behind a gathering of

Yellow Bird's Song

other Cherokee men collecting nearby, listening. It seemed a curious place for her to remain alone. A hot breeze followed her departure and blew wisps of hair into my face.

From the hill above, Mistress Connor followed the remaining guests, trailing behind her much older husband. He carried a brandy in one hand with a smoking cigar wedged between his fingers and the glass. Major, one of the tallest in the crowd, walked down the hill and joined John and Sam Houston, each resting a foot on the fence rail. Without words, their relaxed bodies assured confidence in Sollee's victory.

Parallel to the starting gate, Rich Joseph Vann's feet reached the top of a freshly painted white box to announce, "With the Federal Road, you all could attend today's monumental occasion."

After returning to my husband's side, he whispered, "What Rich Joe meant to say was that now more whites will make the journey. Easier to drive their wagons down the Federal Road." Few listened to Vann. Instead, his guests discussed odds, tallied bets, and clasped hands to seal wagers.

Sollee mounted her horse sidesaddle at the end of the track, the only female among five male competitors. With a crop in her hand, Sollee's riding boots peeked under her orange gown, draped over layers of crisp white petticoats. Next to her, a bare-chested rider glanced over his shoulder, gawking, and mocking her elegant attire. Undeterred by his taunts, her focus remained on the finish line while whispering in her mare's ear. Then she laughed at the Cherokee rider, never turning her head to address him.

Mister Sam said, "Look at that girl, John. She is afraid of no one. It wouldn't surprise me if Sollee marries a rancher and works harder than he does. She's riding sidesaddle. I don't see how our women do so."

"Father would like nothing better—the marriage, I mean, not her riding style," John clarified, and assured that the assumption was precisely the Major's plan for his daughter.

Vann's pistol shot stirred the dust under the horses' hooves. Whoops rang from outside the fenced gate bordering the track. Sollee's dark hair unwound from its strict curls and tangled in the ribbons of her bonnet while speeding across the track. She rode clear of any competition, victorious in the bout. After crossing the finish line, she cantered her mare past the unfortunate losers in total control. She offered no second glance to the weaker competition and approached the fence and Sam Houston. Once seeing him, she adjusted her hair with her free hand. Then, she petted her horse's neck and whispered in its ear. What did she tell the animal, I wondered?

Mister Sam took the reins from her as John held his hand to help his little sister dismount. Already an accomplished lady at fourteen, she sighed from her accustomed exertions and smiled at Sam Houston. Once her feet met the ground, she acknowledged him, asking, "When are we going to Washington City again, Mister Sam?"

"Say the word, and we will ride there together." He escorted her up the hill toward the house, stopping intermittently to greet those wanting to thank her for their bountiful winnings. Major offered Susannah his arm and followed them toward lunch, anticipating that John and I would follow.

Servants propped open the doors to the house so guests could travel through. The dining room's walls were in hues of aged copper, olive, and maroon, with a large portrait of the home's first owner hanging over an intricately lathed mantle. Silver candlesticks lit the sideboard, full of adorned, green-rimmed, white candy dishes full of ribboned sugar and a large platter holding a fresh tea block beside a steaming silver teapot. John and I walked through the dining room to the foyer, lofting high and steep with a split staircase dividing the middle of the house. Streams of children barreled from the top floor to the bottom in hungry anticipation. We followed them to the rear entrance shaded from the afternoon sunlight by the mansion's second story. Servants bordered the long tables, covered with roasted pork, watermelon, corn, and pies cradled in elegant white ceramic dishes trimmed with painted violet wildflowers like those growing through Vann's vast pastureland.

John escorted me to a table occupied by Reverend Sam Worcester's family, New Hampshire missionaries building a home in New Echota. Next to them sat the homespun, northern woman I spoke with earlier. When she saw me, she stood and extended her bare hand to my gloved.

"I knew your accent was familiar. I'm Sophie Sawyer from near Boston, a small town called Grassy Pond. You?"

"Cornwall, Connecticut. My father is the steward at the Foreign Mission School there."

Sophie Sawyer was a plain woman, young, not yet a spinster, with a loud voice drawing the attention of those nearby. "I work with the Worcester family, teaching and training the Cherokee to be proper Christians. I hope you will send your children to Brainerd School when they become of age."

"We live too far away, I'm afraid. It will be years before Rollin is old enough. Our daughter will learn at home from her father and grandmother."

She tilted her head, curious why Clarinda would not attend school. But she asked no further questions, nodded, and took her seat beside the

Yellow Bird's Song

awkward Ann Worcester. I didn't want Ann to feel excluded, so I said, "Ann, your new home looks beautiful. Two stories in the shade of hardwoods, with a well dug so close to the house. You must be eager to move."

She hunched her shoulders like an elderly woman. Mousy brown hair escaped her cap, with fuzzy wisps surrounding her plain bonnet. "The well will be of the utmost convenience." Her remark did not invite further conversation.

Finally, Reverend Sam stood and silenced the crowd to pray a Christian blessing over the feast, and after, leaned into the table and scooped servings onto his plate. It amazed me how much thin men could eat.

He said, "John, what do you expect from Georgia's Governor Forsyth regarding the Constitution?"

"I imagine it will not please him. Won't help our cause now that Governor Troupe warms a Senate seat." After speaking, John leaned back in his chair and stretched his free arm behind me.

"Ross spoke of your revisions to his Constitution, asking for an oath from the Principal Chief to the Divine Being. I appreciate the Lord's inclusion. Ross' mention of the geographic boundaries may be, shall we say, necessary in the future."

John replied, "It was right to amend them both. The Principal Chief answers to God, the Great Spirit, in his thoughts and deeds. The chief must function as His hand, protecting the flock. As you know, reasons to include the boundaries are ever-present." He gestured to a table filled with white Americans. "For the benefit of all, Elias will print the Constitution in his *Phoenix*."

Reverend Sam spoke across his wife, who speared tiny bits of food, chewing with little change to her dismissive expression. "Have you heard from Elias, John?" Reverend Sam asked, reaching for the bread plate.

"He has matters to attend to in the North. He's soliciting subscriptions to support his press."

Worcester tore into a loaf of bread and handed my husband a piece. "Yes. 'De Ave Phoenice'—where the sun shines eternal brightness to the place where the soul ascends, nourished with food reminiscent of the sacraments."[4] He squinted, raising his head to the unforgiving sunlight. "Especially on a day like today, with so much evidence surrounding us— the Cherokee people rising from the ashes—engaging in civilization, education, spiritual renewal."

"We were right to call you *Atsensuti*, the messenger.[5] As you know, the more Georgia pushes against us, the more our people need education."

Near the Capitol, I knew this to be true, but I wondered if such advancements stretched beyond the Coosa district, to the mountains of North Carolina and Tennessee. What might the Cherokee lose by the exchange?

John continued, "Elias is campaigning now. Relationships he's establishing will prove fruitful in the future."

Worcester gestured with bread in hand. "I pray daily for my friend's safe travels."

Latecomer, Stand Watie, Elias' brother, interrupted Mister Worcester's response. "My brother needs to return home from that pale woman he loves. No offense, Mistress Ridge. Nothing like having a world traveler for an older brother. I haven't had a belly laugh since he left. Won't till he returns."

"Stand, glad you could join us." John stood and shook his cousin's hand. Stand was a bold man, funnier than Elias if such a thing were possible. His constant expression was that of a smile, with long black hair brushed away from his face, so thick the wind barely disturbed its deep waves. John told me his name meant, "two persons standing together, so closely united in sympathy as to form one body."[6] I'm glad his parents shortened it for daily use.

"There are two good reasons for my tardiness, cousin." Stand grabbed a chair, spun it in his palm, and sat in it backward, leaning mighty forearms on its back.

"No doubt. All is well?" John asked him.

"It is. I have no excuse for my tardiness other than family obligations, ladies. I hope that ensures your forgiveness." Stand examined his fork for cleanliness and once satisfied, filled his plate with fruits and vegetables. He speared individual green beans, eating one after the other.

Once the meal was done, the intruding clouds escaped. After their departure, the shade turned to fiery sunlight. A late approaching coach stopped at Vann's intersection with the Federal Road. A bushy-headed gentleman exited the carriage and extended his hand for another inside. Then, the two clasped hands and began their ascent up Diamond Hill.

I held my hand above my eyes to shade them from the afternoon's sun. With a sharp inhale, I gasped, knowing those two anywhere, although never having seen them together. With her hair in braids twisted around her ears, in a black-and-white striped gown, Harriet Gold Boudinot caught sight of me. She left Elias behind to follow with his leisurely gait. I handed John my parasol, lifted my gown to free my feet, and sprinted to meet her. Neither of us slowed our pace, not even when we wrapped our arms around one another. She smelled the same—like sugary tea parties from

Yellow Bird's Song

my childhood.

"Oh, Sarah, Elias is all I wished him to be. So completely wrong my mother was. No number of wrinkles on her forehead from fretting and worry could stop me from swearing my life and love to him." Harriet didn't let me go nor did I her until she finished speaking. Meeting us, John shook Elias' hand and embraced him.

John bowed to Harriet. "Mistress Boudinot, in our carriage, I thought I'd return a gift, one to help you and Elias see a long and happy marriage."

I said, "The telescope? You knew."

John grinned and nodded, then asked, "Is Cornwall as we left it?"

Elias shook his head. "No. Worse. Now they're burning effigies in the front yards. On a brighter note, I earned enough in donations to finish paying for the press. You know how it is. Every speaking engagement is the same. Half of the congregations think I plan to scalp them, and the other half thinks I'm some piteous, exotic savage in need of saving."

Harriet spoke with confidence. "So much of the lack of civilization people imagine—"

Her remark was interrupted by grunts from a ball game on Rich Joe's racetrack. Shirtless, wearing only buckskin breechcloths, players hurled a ball violently from baskets at the end of wooden sticks. Blood smeared around their noses and over their cheeks. Sunlight glared across the players' bare chests, shimmering with bear grease, ensuring no opponent could hold them down.

Harriet finished with newfound hesitation. "—is untrue."

John and Elias' expressive smiles lifted even more while they removed their coats, handing them to us.

John winked to ask, "Another ten minutes?"

Harriet stared at the game and passed Elias' coat to me without looking at her hands.

Elias said, "I hoped we wouldn't be too late to watch the game."

Unapologetic to his new wife's shock, he took my husband by the shoulder to study the game's strategy from the fence.

I, too, was shaken, but certainly less than Harriet, who withdrew her handkerchief from its hiding place in her sleeve. I escorted her to shade, hoping to revive her of the appalled expression fixed across her already sunburned face.

CHAPTER 4: CHESS
John Ridge
The Road to Tuckabatchee, Creek Nation Territory
November 1827

I turned my eyes away from the searing cuts of wind. Our buckskins and furs warded off the November cold far better than white man's clothes. The sky challenged us but had yet to follow through with its threat of rain, making this journey to Tuckabatchee, at Opothle Yoholo's request, far more miserable. We rode into the gray clouds blurring the peaks of the southern Appalachians.

Vann tore a piece of salted jerky in his teeth and talked while he chewed. "This mist makes my bones cold. The Great Spirit needs to decide, either rain or clear."

"That is the truest story you've told on this trip."

"Me? Exaggerate?" Vann grinned, showing his teeth.

"There's no way you caught a fish that big with a hook you whittled from bone. An utter lie."

"I swear. The trout fed four men." He lifted his chin and smirked. "Call them embellishments." He used the jerky in his hand to point. "You're one of the few men I'd allow to speak to me with such disregard for my fishing skills."

"Father taught both of us. We have the same skills." I countered, mimicking his smile, recalling a memory with my oldest friend. I saw his face as it was then, under the bright summer sun, grinning with absent front teeth, standing waist-deep in the Oostanaula.

Vann said, "My skills are more attuned—from natural ability."

I laughed. "Whatever helps you sleep at night. Should we change your name to *atsadi*?"

"Yes. We'll need another night on soggy twigs with rocks in our backs to finish this survey."

"Even after we get to Yoholo's house, we might not sleep well. Yoholo's invitation said he'd written to Secretary McKenney. Told him he'd invited us as legal counsel and linksters. I can't imagine McKenney wants us here."

"Yoholo can ask whomever he wants to his councils. He doesn't suffer fools. Well, unless forced." He hit my chest with the back of his hand. "We don't either."

I pretended to be proud. "Listen to you, two truths in a row." Feigning

Yellow Bird's Song

concern, I touched his forehead. "You ill?"

He swatted away my gesture and laughed, tossing the remaining jerky from his hand into his hungry mouth.

We couldn't see more than a few feet in front of us. From the slope above, horses rushed down the embankment. Startled, we pulled our reins away. Our horses responded with steaming whinnies and bucked at the near miss.

"Good to see you, friends," Chief Talladega called.

Vann sighed in relief, dismounted, and drank from his canteen. He passed it to the chiefs now in our company.

I swung my leg around my horse, regained balance on the ground, and extended my hand to shake each of theirs.

Chief Cheaha said, *"I'm glad you both came. Cherokee will keep Washington honest while considering the annuity from last year's treaty."*

Vann said, *"We will try. You startled us. I thought you two might be Governor Forsyth's surveying agents."*

Talladega replied, *"I'm insulted. And here I thought we were friends."*

Georgia's Governor Forsyth sought an end to the violence—Creeks slaughtering settlers who believed Creek land was already theirs to inhabit. So, Forsyth insisted on a survey. But because of it, all parties discovered the treaty omitted borderlands between Georgia and Alabama, 192,000 acres. Savannah's newspaper reported that Fort Mitchell's Colonel John Crowwell, the Creek's Indian Agent, led the charge to convince Chiefs Little Prince and Opothle Yoholo to sell the treaty's missing tract. It wasn't long before McKenney added the American government's power to Crowwell's negotiations. Yoholo's letter requested our presence for council and our opinion about the acreage.

I asked, *"Have you seen any rogue white men who don't know where they are going?"*

Talladega replied first. *"Only one. He rode in circles. Crossed the river twice. Saw no reason to straighten him out."* The man's candor hid little, like the valley land of his people.

Cheaha was as wise as his ancient, rolling mountains. He said, *"For those who claim intelligence, white men can't see right in front of them."*

We let our horses rest and walked with our friends further into the woodland cover. The four of us leaned our backs against the same wide trunk of a leafless oak. Stretching my aching hip, I said, *"From what I can tell, these acres would be difficult to clear and cultivate."*

"Still, Colonel Crowwell wants the land," Cheaha remarked. He pulled his pipe from a leather satchel and packed it with tobacco. *"John, have you met Colonel Crowwell?"* I smelled the tang when he ignited the dried herb.

Then, after puffing, he passed his pipe to me.

I inhaled and passed the pipe to Vann. *"No. Only by reputation, but I'm sure Father has met him. I'll ask when we return."*

Vann's disjointed voice came from his feet. *"My cousin, Rich Joe, told me the Crowwell brothers are fond of racehorses and owe gambling debts because of it."*

Vann passed the pipe to Talladega, who said, *"All trust Major Ridge's word."* Then, he pounded drying mud from the bottoms of his moccasins, remarking, *"Crowwell's brother, Thomas, was once Chief McIntosh's business partner. That alone should give you a notion of the family's character."*

With the pipe again reaching its owner, tobacco burned through, we dusted our clothes free of pine needles and leaves. When we returned to our wandering horses, I said, *"Yoholo granted us permission to survey the acres. You two ride ahead and get free of this mist. We must spend another night and day with compass and Gunter's chain."*

Our two trusted friends mounted their horses. Cheaha nodded and heeled for speed. He shouted over his shoulder. *"We will tell Yoholo of your arrival late tomorrow."*

We mounted but didn't follow them down the path toward Tuckabatchee. Instead, we turned deeper into the pines. Spending the day marking the territory, Vann and I rode in single file, stopping only to take notes and directions. With the day's meager light dissipating, night fell on us with a single blink.

Downed branches from earlier storms supplied popping pine for a cook fire, but with wet wood, we earned more smoke than warmth for our efforts. Eventually, Vann sizzled salt pork over the fire, dipping cold cornbread in the grease. I walked over to his mare, asleep on her hooves. She did not stir when I patted her side and took the chessboard from her saddlebags.

Vann's mare, patched in sorrel, was an exquisite specimen, athletic and independent, with a painted white face surrounding unique blue eyes. She was gentle yet firm at fourteen hands high. Her name was Equoni, "the river," for her broad back and predictable bends. Painted hat mares were for spiritual women, not warriors like Vann, skilled only with sarcasm, pistol, and ink.

With a look over my shoulder, Vann was transfixed on the fire. I opened the brass latch on the wooden chess set and put the black knight in one pocket and the white knight in the other. Chance could decide the match's aggressor.

Without asking him to choose, Vann said, *"Left,"* never turning his

Yellow Bird's Song

head from the mesmerizing flame. Our game was afoot.

"Stars say you go first, brother." I passed the white knight over his shoulder.

I pulled the foxtail fur around my ears, trying to burrow from the wind cutting between us, stealing the fire's warmth. Vann brushed nearby needles and rocks away to place the board flat and arrange the chess pieces. We laid on our sides, feet to the fire, straddling a gentleman's checkerboard battlefield.

I asked, *"Sell me Equoni? I'll give you a fair price. She's too beautiful for you to ride."* I placed the black pawns on white squares to begin my volley.

"That depends. Are you going to ride her?" He aligned his white soldiers against my opposition.

"I was thinking of her for Clarinda."

"Your toddling daughter?" Vann knew of our daughter's deafness, watched her learn to share her thoughts through the movements of her hands. Clarinda's sign for a horse was as darling as she was, two fingers up by her ears, like the animal she described. Since she rode atop my shoulders, she could ride a horse in the paddock. *"Yes. Time for her to learn to sit a horse."*

"Time for you to learn to sit a horse."

I placed the black rooks to guard my flanks. It reminded me. *"Don't move your rooks. Exchange them to protect the king."*

Vann stopped his hand and scoffed at me with an accustomed smirk. *"I do not need your reminders on how to play chess."*

When we were children, we'd learned to play at Brainerd Mission with Reverend Gambold, learning English along with strategy. Since then, I reminded Vann of the rook rule with every match. Desperate to avoid checkmate, he usually forgot.

Per his habit, he blew the cross atop his white king for luck and centered the piece on the row closest to him in the middle of the black pattern, like a temporary throne. I placed my opposing king. Our game began, although horse bartering remained unconcluded. Clarinda would convince him to sell Equoni if I could not.

Each move started in quick succession but slowed as we captured successive pieces, taking more time to expect the opponent's entrapment.

Vann voiced his thoughts. *"There's little here but scrub pines. The only benefit to the land is the Tallapoosa riverfront and that unmanned ferry. How many acres did you say it was?"* Vann thought about the Creek's battleground, not the chess match.

"192,000." Vann was right. It held little value, yet Colonel John

Crowwell's negotiations persisted. *"It is simple ground. There's little pastureland, few hardwoods, and fewer settlements. Little sign of game."*

Vann studied the board with puckered lips. He moved a pawn, a wasted move. I'd already seen my path to check.

I said, *"It isn't only the property Georgia desires. They want to print 'Victory' in headlines written across the narrow columns of her newspapers. Governor Forsyth needs to guarantee the safety of his constituents away from Creek's 'merciless savages'."*

We both shared that nightmare, spawned from reading too many articles depicting the oncoming assault from the white king.

Our game advanced to capture. I took Vann's knight after he earned two of my pawns. Behind us, twigs snapped. Leaves shuffled. Vann looked over his shoulder and whispered, *"Perhaps the surveyor found his way after all."*

We continued our game with slower hands and more attuned ears. Vann watched over my shoulder while I scanned over his for horizontal movement through the vertical woods.

I remarked, *"Maybe it's fortunate the Governor's survey didn't include this patch of land. Gives the Creek an advantage."*

"Not as—" Vann forced a cough before continuing, *"—lucky as you are by gaining both of my knights. Are you sure they did not list this parcel in the treaty?"*

I said, *"Based upon the map in McKenney's office compared to what I've seen of Alabama's survey, this ground was not included. Crowwell wouldn't be after it so bad if the government already held the deed."*

"Then, the U.S. must buy it—if Yoholo will sell. How will you advise him?" Vann asked.

"There's little worth keeping. The land here couldn't sustain crops of any kind, not without seasons of labor. The money might serve their people better."

Vann slid his queen to save his bishop. I sheltered mine. The queen's moves were limitless.

Distant bawling hounds interrupted his move. Vann stood while I stretched along the ground, focused on the distant trees, and searched the dark for shifting shadows. Vann gathered his pistol from Equoni's saddlebag and lay down again. He placed the retrieved weapon beside the board, discreetly loading the gun with his back to the approaching dogs.

Vann whispered, *"What do you think they're following? It's too late for rabbits. Opossum, maybe?"*

Before he completed his question, I greeted an approaching shadow. A young, black man, shivering, panting, barefoot, stopped some distance

Yellow Bird's Song

from our horses. He looked behind him at the approaching dogs and, again, at us. Fear beamed from the whites of his wide eyes, attracting the moonlight. He wore rags, a dirty shirt falling from one dark shoulder, more noticeable by contrast to the other. The youth's cheekbones were deep, recording their lack of nourishment. Still, he found energy enough to run circles around our campsite.

I stopped his movement, asking in Cherokee, *"What's your name?"* People thought the worst when others spoke in an unknown tongue. Still, he must have decided we were the lesser of two evils. Near our horses, he squatted, rolling himself in earth and pine needles. He brushed them along his face and chest, wincing after pulling sweet gum briars and broken hickory nutshells that spurred his exposed feet.

"What's your name, strange friend?" I asked again, in English.

The runaway spat pine needles from his mouth and replied, "Peter, sahr."

Vann interjected, crossing his forearms over the pistol. "Seems like you're in a predicament. What are you running from?"

He looked behind him again. "Dem dogs."

I remarked to Vann in Cherokee, *"You've met your match for stating the obvious."*

Barking increased to howls and approached our position. Across such flat land, both master and slave had the same ironic advantage to see and hear across vast distances. The horse-backed rider beckoned his dogs, still tracking Peter's trail.

Vann interrupted the howling. "Young Peter, they have your scent."

Peter approached Equoni and took a handful of her manure, spreading the stench across his arms and neck. He dropped to his hands and feet, scoured on all fours through the surrounding brush, looking to disappear from the hounds' noses. He hid beside a bent sycamore, the land marker of Creek property, and buried himself under leaves and brush. Young Peter wagered his life with the singular hope that nature's cover would keep the tracking hounds at bay.

Vann and I looked behind us toward the Tallapoosa River. Peter could hide in the water, but I doubted there would be time to escape that far. There was only a moment to decide before the predator would approach us and inquire about his prey. So, Peter decided, and we witnessed.

I threw two pieces of jerky into the woods, opposite Peter's man-dug grave. Then, I laid down again to the chess game beside my collection of Vann's pieces.

The hounds' noses shuffled against the ground while their back hips wavered over leaves preceding the man stopping his galloping horse. Their noses wandered apart, losing Peter's scent among the cover. All the dogs quit their baying under moon's blue cold. They found the taste of the jerky distracting, forgetting to use their noses to reveal Peter buried alive.

"*Whose turn?*" Vann whispered.

"*Yours,*" I said, knowing it wasn't.

Vann cocked his pistol before the intruder was close enough to recognize the sound of the metal spring locking into place. Vann rested the gun on the ground near his chest and propped his head on his fist to appear relaxed. The man dismounted and gripped his horse's reins while strolling to our fireside.

"Get over here, you beasts," the white man shouted with a violent gruff.

I spoke to Vann in Cherokee, loud enough for the man to hear. "*To win the game, the initiative belongs to the player who makes threats that cannot be ignored.*"

Vann whispered, "*The last thing I need now is for you to tell me how to play chess.*"

"*Not talking about the game.*" I nodded toward the slave-hunting intruder.

The stranger's reaction revealed that he'd overheard, but he didn't reciprocate in Cherokee. His first words to us were in English. "Now, there's something you don't see every day. Two Indians, sitting by a fire, playing a gentleman's game."

When he stepped into the light, I saw him clearly. Facial scars pitted his pale cheeks. Long salt-and-pepper sideburns touched the corners of his lips. He wore riding attire, clearly imported, which stayed remarkably clean for a man tracking hounds and an escaped slave under cover of night.

He didn't want us to know he'd insulted us, as we didn't want him to know that there was likely no language we wouldn't understand. So, claiming ignorance of English allowed us to avoid lying for Peter's sake while giving us the advantage of talking without this white man's comprehension.

Vann commanded, "*You trespass on Creek land.*" Vann kept one hand on the trigger and, with the other, made friends with the dog. The hound went from sniffing to licking. Its master noticed. Firelight showed his smirk and disappointment at his dog's passive attack. I imagine Vann didn't intend to shoot the dog, but its master didn't know that.

Peter's pursuer held pale palms in front of him and didn't advance further. "Whoa, now. That dog cost me hours to train. Wouldn't be here if it weren't for a runaway slave."

Our uninvited guest carried an unbent hat in one hand and a horsewhip

Yellow Bird's Song

in the other. No doubt he had a pistol buried under his coat, too difficult to retrieve without significant effort. Instead, the whip in his hand was his weapon of choice to abuse beast and slave alike.

The man asked the inevitable question. "Seen anyone come through these woods?" Before Vann had time to second-guess, I responded with a horizontal shake of my head, pretending not to understand his query. Instead, I pointed in the direction the man came from, implying he needed to return. Then, gesturing to myself and Vann, I held up two fingers to insinuate we were the only two here. While the white man scanned the pines behind him, I mumbled, *"Remind me to kiss my daughter twice when we return."*

"It's not Creek you're talking. Guess you've got no English. Seems you two understand well enough."

He didn't leave. Instead, he walked closer, tilted his head to fixate our features in his mind. He studied our game. He looked over Vann's white pieces and said, "Shame you took that queen out. She's the most powerful player on the board. A woman's place is at home, even if she wears a crown." Then, he stepped over the board, purposefully dragging a slowed boot to knock over the pieces. He examined our horses.

It was challenging to know what to do next: allow him to memorize their markings, find the surveyor's chain in my saddlebags or distract him. Either choice would incur further suspicion. He moved closer to Saloli, my horse, and nearer to Peter's newly dug grave. If the man moved another foot forward, he'd stand on top of Peter.

His dogs howled again, informing their master they'd recovered some scent. But Peter wasn't where they hit. His ingenuity in crossing up his scent trail saved his life and perhaps ours.

Still, Vann aimed his pistol and didn't release the dog. The man gathered our intent: we'd protect ourselves by shooting the dog or him. The choice was his. His voice was sarcastic, threatening us with the whip's tail grazing his thighs. With a snide lip and upturned brow, he said, "Sorry I disturbed your game." He backed away from our blaze, mounted, and kicked the horse abruptly to follow his hounds' renewed baying near the riverbank. Vann released the dog, which followed its owner, likely from fear of abuse rather than loyalty.

When the man rode past earshot, Vann asked, *"Did you recognize him?"*

I replied, *"He looked familiar, but I can't place him."*

Vann persisted, *"Is he from the Capitol?"*

"I'll remember when I stop thinking about it."

Vann and I replaced the pieces on the board, made two moves each, and slung more wood on the fire before Peter unearthed himself. Rustling and gasping alerted us, followed by the tang of horse manure.

"I was concerned you smothered under there, Peter." Vann's sarcasm was unintentional and natural. If Vann talked, humor or violence, or both, found their way into his tone.

Once Peter stepped into the firelight, Vann and I gestured for him to warm himself.

Peter said, "That wind that come up was my brother's ghost flyin' by, lettin' me knows I was in safety with yous two. Thank you for sayin' nothin' 'bout me. You don't even know me and still helpin' me. I trust you won't scalp me, if'n you didn't turn me over to the Crow." Peter noticed our chess game. With curiosity, he sat on a downed log to inspect the pieces. He said, "A game of da white man against the black."

Vann asked our grateful friend, stepping away from Peter's fermenting smell, "Who was that man? Neither of us can place his face."

"Dat be Black Crow, Thomas Crowwell. Never forget dat man's voice." Peter picked my black king off the chessboard and held it at eye level. "He like all the other crows, pickin' his dinner from the dead. Black Crow owns a sto' and tavern out Fort Mitchell way." He stretched and replaced my king precisely where it had been.

Vann walked toward our horses, smacked his leg, and breathed through a string of Cherokee terms inappropriate for polite company. I remained seated and asked Peter, "Any relation to Colonel John Crowwell?"

"Yes, sahr, his brother. Da slaves call the Colonel White Crow." He picked the white king off the chessboard, held it in the firelight and continued. "Some crows have white feathers, but most are black. But an all-white crow don't belong with the murder. Plain bad luck for bird and man. Back dat way, Crow brothers movin' da slaves behind whiskey wagons pulled by stolen horses." Peter pointed behind him, toward the west and slid off the log to sit on the ground.

"Dey said to keep the sun behind our backs in da afternoon and the sun in our face in da mornin', which make no sense. We was tied up. We had no choice in which direction we's walkin'."

Vann thought it better not to riddle Peter with questions and clear the air. "Want to wash off in the river? It'll be cold."

"Nah, sahr. Horse manure don't bother me none. Used to it. I'm a blacksmithy, a groomsman. Used to horse Chief's shoes on da land I was born."

"Opothle Yoholo, Little Prince, Big Warrior?" I asked, hoping for a familiar name.

"Nah, sahr. Dem Creeks, east of here, da McIntosh fambly."

Yellow Bird's Song

I circled our camp, thinking. My silence must have made young Peter uncomfortable. So, he rambled, and we listened.

"When Drew, my brother and I, livin' at *Lockchau Talofau*, Acorn Bluff, I tend to da horseshoeing for Chief McIntosh. Big fambly. Dat Chief had two wives. When I worked for dem, they shared their table, fresh fish from the Chattahoochee River and okry and corn in the summer. We's 'lowed to stops da work at sunset and hear da ole folks' stories at night. Gots to go to the Methody church on da Sunday afternoon, after da white men and red women all gone home to eat Sunday dinner. Drew and me went fishin' after services and caught the biggest catfish ever caught in da Chattahoochee. My whole fambly belong to McIntosh, 'fore dem Creeks shoot him up, and burn da house ta cinders.

"After da Creek come, McIntosh's wives, Mistress Peggy and Mistress Susannah, and all der chillun be destitute. Before, dey's rich with gold nuggets hidden in a box in da barn. Every time the whiskey barrels went out, more of dat gold found its way to the box buried under the stable flo'. Wasn't s'pose to know where it was hidden, but I did. Touch none of it, tho'. No man accuse Peter of stealin'.

"After the murder of the Chief, da money stop comin' and dem wives be needin' food for their youngins, so deys sells off my brother and me to Thomas Crowwell. While he there, he look for da gold. Founds it too. Made Drew and I's carry it to his wagon and didn't offer none to them wives and chillern."

I stopped pacing, without realizing, speaking my thoughts aloud. *"Was McIntosh whiskey running? Will that man never die?"*

Vann nodded in agreement while handing Peter his canteen of water. "What happened to your brother?" Peter looked behind him again, drank the full content of the canteen, and continued his tale.

"'Bout two weeks ago, Masser Thomas Crowwell, da Black Crow, gots us up real early. Said new ponies needin' shod for da journey. But he never says we's comin' long. Drew and I sweat buckets from da forge, pounding dem shoes. We sliced off the hoof growth, good and level, so dem horses wear even on both sides. So tired from workin' dawn to dusk, but we's finished dat big job. No big bowl of okry waiting on us, tho'. 'Stead, he tied us up behind four other slave womern. We set off toward the sunset way. 'Fore we go, I give Drew my boots for his feet, and drop farrier pinchers inside. He younger dan I by two years. I turn seventeen when the weather gets warm 'gin."

He shook his head, shaking his brother's clinging spirit from his skin. "We weren't 'lowed no talk and never freed from dem ropes. Had to relieve myself right der by dem womern folk.

"Drew say he don't want dis life no more. He say, 'If God be da fisher of men, dey must have big fish in Heaven. So's if'n I die, least I know I'll eat.' He use dem hoof nippers for whittlin' through dem ropes. Gots de whole line of us free from the whiskey wagon. Dem Crows couldn't see, ridin' in front of the wagon.

"But White Crow, Masser John Crowwell, knew we's gone shortly after we run. Musta heared us breakin' into the woods. Both Crows started shootin'.

"Black Crow shot da womern and my brother in da back. I's hid next to Drew's body, pretendin' I's dead too, for a while. Snuck away when they weren't lookin'. But Black Crow musta found me gone and set dem hound dogs free. Drew's spirit run beside me on da ground. He guide me here."

"We're sorry about your brother," I said.

Peter rubbed his eyes with the back of his hand, and a falling tear smeared with the tan of manure. He shivered once more and stilled. "Drew still close."

Vann called me over toward the horses while Peter warmed his feet, alternating one leg while pulling sweet gum spurs from the heel of the other. Vann whispered, *"You realize what Peter witnessed?"*

I nodded, looking at him. I knew the answer before Vann asked the question. *"Crowwell's running pony clubs and trading slaves and whiskey up these 192,000 acres to profit in the West. Without the Creek here, few would see, and none would stand in his way."* I concluded with the English word, "Greed." With clear recollection, I said, "That is where I've seen the man before, at Joe's horse race, at the Constitution Celebration. Crowwell bet against my sister." My mind ran from gambling debts to chess. Then, summarizing both, I said, "Check."

Peter's cough distracted us, and we returned, handing him more water and jerky.

Vann said, "Peter, we're Cherokee officials on the way to Creek Council. We know why the state wants the land, thanks to you and your brother."

I knelt, with some effort, in front of him. "You led us in a direction we weren't expecting to go tonight."

Leaving him here ensured his capture, whipping, or worse because he ran to escape. But I didn't want to assume he'd choose to come with us. I said, "The choice is yours. We can take you with us now, and you can live with the Creek. Or, after we conclude our affairs, you can return with me or Vann to Cherokee Nation. If you choose to go your own way, you are welcome to stay beside our fire tonight. Either way, we owe you a debt and

Yellow Bird's Song

will not return you to the Crows."

Peter stood tenderly on injured feet and limped to my horse. Then, he raised her front shoes, examined them as well as the firelight would allow, and shook his head.

"Sahr, there's wear here on the left side. I could fix that right for you, so dis horse don't go lame. You and your horse favor the left?"

"We do," I said, while Peter's finger dug mud and manure from my horse's hoof.

Vann remarked under his breath, *"Yoholo expects us tomorrow."*

I said, *"We'll be late."*

The stakes surrounding our game just became infinitely higher.

CHAPTER 5: BLACK DRINK
John Ridge
Tuckabatchee Council Grounds, Creek Territory
November 1827

Elevated on the front porch, silhouetted in careening firelight, Yoholo left his cabin door open to greet us. Feathers perched on the crown of his head like a rook, while his shoulders were laden with a woven blanket. Tall, lean legs stepped off the stairs. Yoholo petted my horse's steaming nose. *"McKenney and Crowwell arrived two days past, even though the council isn't until the day after tomorrow. He wanted to meet with us before you and Vann arrived. I sent them to Reverend Compere's mission house. I didn't want to smell either of them any longer than I had to. White men don't wash as often as our native brothers do."*

Yoholo watched as an unfamiliar Peter slid from my horse after my feet hit the ground.

"This weather makes my bones ache," I said and shook his hand, the other, holding my bad hip. *"Father sends his greetings and tobacco for your pipe."*

Yoholo remarked, *"It is a good night to smoke. Who's this?"*

"Yoholo, this is Peter." I hadn't thought to ask his surname, and he hadn't offered it. However, if he took McIntosh, Peter was wise to keep it to himself, especially in Yoholo's company. *"We met this young man on your acreage running from Crows."*

Yoholo snickered, saying, *"That is what my Creek brothers call Colonel Crowwell and his brother Thomas."*

"Same Crows," I replied without laughter.

Yoholo gestured toward his cabin door. *"Sounds like you have a story."*

Vann said, *"We do."* He entered Yoholo's cabin, leaving us alone to walk the horses to the barn under falling rain.

I unsaddled each with Peter's help and pulled our traveling bags from their sides. Led to their stalls, our horses found well-deserved oats and clean hay.

"Cold bites harder after a moment in the warmth," I said, and passed Yoholo Vann's leather satchel while I slung my own across my chest. In a hurry to rejoin Vann, Yoholo and I were halfway across the yard before we realized Peter hadn't followed.

Peter coughed,and we turned back. He apologized. "If'n it's all the same to you, I'd sleep much better hearin' dem whinnies."

53

Yellow Bird's Song

Yoholo looked at me to translate, and then nodded with understanding.

"My son will bring food and blankets, some clothes, shoes for your feet. You two look about the same size." After my translation, Peter bowed thanks and closed the barn doors behind him.

Yoholo's family's cabin boasted higher ceilings than most, built to accommodate his height and stature. One entire wall encompassed a vast stone hearth, filling the room with orange light from the high flames held at bay by a suspended iron pot. Smells of salted pork and beans filled its walls. A rectangular table covered most of the floor, with a ladder on the periphery extending to a loft where his sons and daughters slept.

Yoholo sat at the head of his table and gestured for us to follow. *"Is there such a thing as good news anymore? John, tell me about your son. He was born after you returned from Washington. What did you name him?"*

"John Rollin—Cheesquatalawny. He's a crier. Had he been our first, he may have been an only child."

"Why? Is your wife not well?"

"She's fine. Rollin was born much faster than Clarinda."

Yoholo's wife entered with hands holding three stacked wooden bowls. Her braided black hair hung down her back and framed her face. Long beaded earrings touched her shoulders. She ladled stew from the hearth pot, filling and setting bowls in front of us. *"Children come faster each time. Our bodies have learned what to do."* Then she interjected, *"Only two children?"* She shook her head. *"You love your wife, no? More love makes more babies."*

Without waiting for my answer, Vann nodded to her with gratitude when she placed the ham hock stew in front of him. Vann spoke to her but gestured at me with his spoon. *"No one could love their wife more than John loves his Sarah."*

Yoholo grabbed his wife's hand over his shoulder and kissed the back of her wrist. In April of '25, Yoholo, painted red and solemn, rode with a feathered spear in tow to McIntosh's home near the Chattahoochee River. It was the first time I'd seen him as a war chief, not a diplomat, ready to die to protect Creek land and his people. A year later, in Washington, the same man held his blade to the thin skin covering his heart. This man, a father, a husband, prime minister, considered taking his own life because of the dishonor he felt from McKenney's coercions. But, by choosing to continue the fight, he put the lives of his beloved people above his shame.

From his dinner table, Yoholo's eyes addressed us, but his words were intended for his wife's ears. *"I could have many wives, but I prefer this one, my woman with the smart mouth and fine backside."* She pulled her hand away and laughed, sauntering into the neighboring kitchen.

Yoholo watched her leave and shook his head. *"Vann? Your daughters? How do they fare?"*

"Lethal. Warriors in skirts. They don't need me, and I'm a worthless father with little left to teach them."

This chief's philosophy surrounding meals, wives, and children seemed simple. *"Teach them to find husbands who take them hunting. Time spent together will keep them fed and bring you many grandchildren."*

Yoholo's wife overheard her husband's sage wisdom, raising her voice to respond. *"Take your own advice, and you will have more mouths to feed."*

Our host leaned on his table, resting his elbows and forearms around the bowl, moving his wooden spoon through the stew to cool it.

He said, *"When I was young, on the banks of the Chattahoochee, there was a beautiful island covered in stately trees, carpeted with thick grass. When my people could find no game elsewhere, a hunter would go to the island and kill a deer. Only one deer, mind you, to share with the village.*

"The banks of this island were sandy. But, when the river flooded, the same banks wore away, and the island shrank. That island is growing even smaller now. Deer have disappeared. If we had only planted grass on that sandy soil, the deer would thrive, and the waters would recede. Now white men come upon us like a flood and wash away the remaining seed."[1]

He stared, recalled footsteps over untrodden paths, memories abandoned and retrieved in pensive hindsight. Silence swallowed the sounds of falling rain on the roof. I knew his regret questioned what he could do now to prevent further loss.

He took his spoon from the stew, and said, *"It defeats my people's purpose to sell the island. There are few deer left elsewhere."*

I said, *"In all ways, we will aid your people to keep the land."* The sentiment was not one I expected to deliver to my friend, not after seeing the 192,000 acres of scrub pines and flood plains. Yoholo's desire, his hope for his people's survival, cleared away the overgrown thickets binding my thoughts. He planned to build a new life and plant grass on that soil, facing whatever repercussions white politicians brought. Vann lowered his eyes without comment, confirming he held the same opinion.

At Yoholo's request, we recounted Peter's tale: horseshoes, hidden whiskey, yellow gold, and perched Crows. Yoholo knew Thomas Crowwell owned a tavern at Fort Mitchell and supplied food and drink for McIntosh's inn near High Falls at the medicinal springs. He added that Crowwell's fort was named for David Mitchell, once its commanding

Yellow Bird's Song

officer, who later was forced to resign amidst accusations of running stolen slaves.

"*Then Crowwell continues the business.*" Vann concluded with a logical assumption.

I shifted in my chair, putting my weight on my good hip, and resting my arm over its woven back. "*Rest assured; Crowwell and his brother steal horses from Cherokee while they are in their cups.*"

Vann crossed his arms over his chest. "*If McIntosh saw gold, he'd swindle his way into collecting more to hide under the floor of his barn. Crowwell negotiated the deals. His brother acted as McIntosh's distributor. McIntosh distilled the whiskey. All three tripled their profits by selling slaves and horses to encroaching whites.*"

Yoholo stood, squeaking the chair's wood along the floor, and gazed into his dwindling fire, throwing an additional log to burn. "*I'm glad you brought Peter. His appearance will provide an interesting interaction when Colonel Crowwell reappears the day after tomorrow and sees the young man very much alive. His reaction will tell us how deeply he is involved.*" Yoholo sounded like my father.

Before I could say so, Vann replied, "*I'll make certain of it.*"

A knock at the door revealed a messenger delivering a note from McKenney and Crowwell requesting a late-night meeting. They didn't ask for Yoholo, only Vann and me.

I said, "*How did he even know we were here? What could they want?*" I was tired, not looking for a confrontation tonight.

"*Isn't it always brandy and coercion?*" Vann asked.

"*Knowing what we know, can we refuse? We must change clothes.*"

Yoholo turned from his fire, face redder from the radiant heat. "*I will stay up and await your return. The ride is not far.*"

Rain stopped, and the night sky cleared, bringing a clinging cold during the hour's ride to Reverend Compere's house. Several men sat on the rectangular home's extended front porch around the structure's perimeter. In silhouette, McKenney's standing stately frame, wrapped in a fur coat, contrasted with Crowwell's seated stature. The lit ends of their cigars flamed while we dismounted. A young Creek boy collected our horses, blowing steam from their nostrils.

McKenney called my name with dripping condensation. "John," he said, "nice to see you again."

Vann mumbled with steaming breath. "*Let the lies begin.*"

I held the railing, marking each stair while McKenney extended his hand to shake mine. Once we reached the porch's top step, he stepped to the side, and gestured toward the man whose reputation preceded introduction.

"May I present Colonel John Crowwell. These are the Cherokee negotiators, John Ridge, and David Vann."

Crowwell did not turn, did not stand. Instead, he bent his arm to bring his cigar to his lips breaking the pattern of moonlight through horizontal porch pickets. The brass buttons on his federal uniform pulled against their holes while thin legs stretched in front of him. His long sideburns compensated for his receding hair. His pronounced cheekbones framed dark eyes, with lips set in an irrecoverable grimace. Smiling wouldn't adjust the resting scowl on his face, not that I imagine he exerted much effort to do so.

Regardless, I extended my hand to shake his. Colonel Crowwell looked at my hand but refused to move from his comfort to reciprocate the gesture. Instead, his dominant hand lifted his brandy glass to his mouth.

I could not account for such a snub. I kept my face stoic, but in my mind, his disrespect reminded me how ignorant some white men could be. They viewed Vann and me as sub-human, for no other reason than the color of our skin. White men in Crowwell's position viewed Peter as a tool, a slave, with their greed overwhelming the young man's humanity. I should be grateful Colonel Crowwell limited his disgust of me only to insult.

Vann saw Crowwell's refusal and distracted McKenney, inquiring about his latest travels, but McKenney noticed. I tilted my head. Then, emblazoned by Crowwell's disregard, I shook the hand of Reverend Compere, sitting beside him in the shadows.

"We've had very productive councils with the Choctaws and Chippewas," McKenney said, touching the pinned gifts given him by their tribal chiefs, worn as proudly as military epaulets. "They were very agreeable to our generous terms." Crowwell cleared his throat with a nod in our direction, implying Vann and I might be the root cause of the Creek's dwindling attention.

McKenney continued his condescending exhortations about the rivers and woods he crossed while delivering the "excellent" speech sent from the Great Father in Washington. He called himself a peacemaker. I didn't think we were at war. I was uncomfortable, still mentally seeking the cause for Crowwell's deliberate dodge from courtesy.

Vann changed the subject, tilting back his brandy before we gathered our horses to leave. He asked McKenney about the five-thousand-dollar debt owed us after negotiating the Creek's last treaty, remuneration for the four hundred and sixty acres offered as compensation for translation services rendered.

McKenney scoffed and remarked, "Let me pass over my mountain first, and then I will attend yours."[2] McKenney's savage metaphors continued, as did my suspicion of his intentions. Why had they insisted on seeing us tonight? What was behind such urgency? To brag, intimidate, overpower? To gauge whether we supported selling the Creek's acreage?

However, this was not the time to reveal our intentions. Regardless of how I felt, it wasn't my story to tell. Yoholo must lead his people in this grave decision. McKenney and Colonel Crowwell schemed to surprise us, attempting to coerce and capture our bishop in a move we didn't foresee. Another move was necessary to uncover his strategy.

The following day, Opothle Yoholo led the purge to prepare for council. He drank first from a gourd full of the black drink, *arsee*. Once consumed, the emetic caused those who consumed the boiled holly berries to vomit the remnants of their stomachs. Younger Creeks arched on their sides and held their stomachs, while elders sat tall, motionless, with smoking pipes resting in painted hands. Little Prince, the eldest and most revered Creek warrior, was noticeably absent, not allowed to consume the black drink because of failing health.

As Creek guests and advisors, Yoholo insisted we take part in the ceremonial ablutions. Yoholo was the first to vomit and return to the council square's firelight with open palms, free of ill will or harsh thoughts against any opposition. The purge freed one's instinct for revenge.

Vann rested his head on the log behind his back. His eyes closed, but no one could sleep with their neck in such an awkward position. His neighbor startled him and passed him the gourd again. He drank while I could consume no more. I waved it off and crawled to the surrounding dirt to lay my face on the wet grass. Retching burned and parched my throat. Too weak to rise, I sank deeper into the ground.

My dreams were vivid. My horse's mane spread wide in a gallop. Grassy patches from the field rose and fell under my stirrups. I followed voluminous war cries and woodsmoke seeping through the thick morning fog.

But in my mind, I understood the past in this present. This attack, led by warrior Menawa and Opothle Yoholo, enacted Creek Blood Law. I recognized the scene from '25: Chief McIntosh's *Lockchau Talofau*, the night of his murder. Instead of watching Creek's retribution from the hill above the house, as I once had, I rode across the pastureland toward the smoking timber of McIntosh's cabin, knowing I shouldn't intervene.

Over rolling, green hills, a dogtrot house stood bordered by sweet gum and walnut trees. Shots reverberated from a battalion of Creek warriors gripping torches in one hand and pointing pistols and red-painted clubs aloft by the other. Threats screamed across the yard in one voice, answered by blasts of pistol shots from behind the smoke escaping from broken upstairs windows. Riderless horses panicked and ran from nearby stables. No one saw me slide my leg over my horse to dismount and slap Saloli's rump to prompt her escape.

Fire blossomed from the porch like orange lilies in full bloom. Windows shattered and fell into smoke so hot that the glass shards curled. I walked through the flames but remained unburned. On the floor to my left, Chilly McIntosh, the Chief's son, dug through a woman's trunk and donned her clothes. A scrolled parchment sat beside him on the smoldering mattress, undoubtedly the original Treaty of Indian Springs. Dressed as a woman, Chilly McIntosh threw a bonnet over his black hair and passed through my ghostly form. Then, he ran to the Chattahoochee River and swam to escape with the treaty in his mouth. Vann and I had witnessed his escape years before.

McIntosh's son-in-law, Samuel Hawkins, kissed his wife, Jane, on the stairs for what I knew would be the last time. He sent her to flee into the trees. But I knew what he couldn't see, the warriors lying in wait. After, Hawkins ran up the interior stairs to assist in McIntosh's last stand.

Hawkins didn't notice when I followed him. McIntosh's back arched over the window frame, firing pistols from each hand. Then he retreated behind log walls, dancing between incoming bullets and broken glass. Behind him, Hawkins reloaded wad and ball.

Heavy feet alerted me to Menawa's approach. Turning around, I met the warrior's eyes, stark white under red paint. He struck my temple with the butt of a flintlock, knocking me to the floor. My initial panic turned into a daze. He pointed the same pistol at my head. Time slowed while he clenched the trigger. The gun misfired.

The angry warrior gritted his teeth and pulled me by my shirt collar close to his red face. *"McIntosh, you will pay for your crime with your life."* He picked me from the floor with violent grabs under my shoulders, pulled me backward down the stairs. Then, joined by a Creek horde, threw me from the house.

"You have the wrong man," I screamed. *"I am not Chief McIntosh."*

Menawa replied, "McIntosh, we have come. We have come. We told you if you sold the land to the government, we would come." Panting between his words, he said, "*You, your children, and their children will die.*"

Warriors circled me, raising glistening knives to stab me. I never lost consciousness, remembering each searing tear of my skin. Smooth-bottomed moccasins buried me deeper with every step.

A woman's screams passed through the sounds of crackling fire and falling treads from the second floor. But it wasn't the voice of one of McIntosh's wives. Sarah's English screams seared my ears, held back by red-painted shoulders surrounded by flaming timber. She coughed, begged them to release me with my true name. "Skahtlelohskee," she yelled, pushing against their shoulders.

I pulled my heavy body from the ground to yell in bloody bubbles at the men. "Kill me. Don't touch her." With my last earthly thought, I knew how much I needed her, how her spirit rooted me. With one last gurgle, the tether between Sarah and I dissipated. Her cries faded, and their loss further caved in my chest.

Blue morning skies faded to dusk's red, merging with the purples of ascending night. My bodiless spirit hovered above my bleeding form. Once thoughts of Sarah left my mind, my soul reshaped into the body of a mockingbird, and I flapped white and gray wings to soar to the Nightland, navigating my way by constellation's compass.

It was the flying that woke me. Realizing where I was, I crawled back to Vann's side but could sleep no more, haunted by my desire for the return of my wings.

Rain dripped on my head from pine needles, one after the other, in predictable drops. At dawn, we dragged our exhausted bodies to the spring and went to water, washing away the night's purging. We drank freely, revived by its cold.

Dressed in a frock coat and tie, I sat near Creek's distinguished chiefs to listen and to translate McKenney's and Crowwell's bloated speeches. Vann hurried in after Yoholo began introductions and sat next to me. I whispered, "Was Peter willing?"

"Yes. Crowwell will do nothing surrounded by witnesses. But just in case, I'll stand beside him with my thumb on my pistol."

McKenney began, and I translated. "I am sent by the Great Father in Washington to visit his red children, those who live where the sun sleeps and those who live in the warm country, his Creek children." Then he spoke in the third person, hoping to gain credibility, as if God Himself had written his speech. "McKenney obeyed and went in stagecoaches and traveled far—then he sat in a great canoe that carries fire in its bottom and sent its smoke to Heaven, and traveled to the Great Lakes, where the winds live and where cold dwells and makes the waters to freeze, so hard, men and cattle can pass over it dry-shod.[2]

"He left his big canoe and entered a bark canoe and went up a river whose rapids were like the falls of the Tallapoosa and found Indians. They were sitting in darkness and had not heard the White Father talk for a while. The Indian's paths were choked with briers, and their feet were bleeding. He gave them their White Father's speech, and with it, light. And the Indians were glad.[3]

"But the Indians said, 'When you go away, the briers will grow again, and our feet will bleed.' He asked them why. Because, they said, 'We have bad birds among us, and they will make the briers grow.' Then, he drove away those bad birds from their country, left a mouth with them, and told them they must listen to that mouth alone; it would talk the voice of wisdom from Washington, and if the birds come back again, to listen to them no more. They promised him they would do as he told them. Then, he shook hands with them, and, in his canoe, traveled down the great father of rivers, the Mississippi."[4]

Vann leaned to my ear discreetly and said, "*McKenney must think we are bad birds.*"

McKenney disguised his courting of his Creek listeners with insulting flattery. Then, finally, he arrived at the only part of the speech that mattered.

"There is a small strip of land," McKenney said, "which the Treaty of Washington did not embrace. Nevertheless, your White Father believes it belongs to him. Last year in Washington City, the delegation promised to sign it to our possession if the original treaty lines did not reach it. So, the Creek must fulfill their promise and resign the acreage, according to the treaty demands."[5]

It was a lie, coercion to avoid paying the Creek for their remaining property. Yoholo stood and held a hand to stop anyone else from talking. Yoholo's crown of feathers did not move when he said the single English word, "No."

Crowwell's surprise brought him to his feet. McKenney rebuked, saying, "It is the Cherokee voices, particularly that of John Ridge, influencing your decision." How was that possible since I'd spoken none of my own thoughts?

Yoholo confronted McKenney. "*When our delegation was in Wash-*

ington, our purpose was to find justice from the United States by the annulment of McIntosh's unsanctioned treaty. Your White Father granted us that, but not without replacing it with an immense sacrifice of Creek land. So fast, we held in difficulty, so unmerciful were those who wanted all we owned. In the Treaty of Washington, the American government outlined the limits of our country—specific, detailed, and guaranteed to us.[6]

"We have little land left, sufficient only to raise our children. After obtaining so much from us, we had hoped for the remission of your earnest attempts for our lands. If such had been the understanding, we would have surrendered the whole chartered limits of Georgia in the treaty, but it is not here so written."[7]

After the translation, McKenney pointed at me. "Ridge promised if the treaty lines came close, his Creek brothers would abscond the remaining acres."

"I said no such thing." In my mind, I heard my father's wisdom. *"Cherokee were wrong, no matter their righteous intentions."*

I watched the wide eyes of the Creek's taciturn elders. They studied our movement with flat faces, waiting, unable to turn their eyes from their expectation of an incoming catastrophe.

In English, I said, "Then, why pay to survey the land?"

Crowwell scoffed before saying, "What do you mean, sir?"

I hated repeating myself. "Why take surveys of the land? If the government already owned the land by the initial treaty, there would be no need for an additional survey at substantial cost to our White Father."

Crowwell, insulted by my question, turned his back to the throng of angry Creek chiefs. Then, to assert his dominance, McKenney stepped in front of Colonel Crowwell. He told Yoholo, "Settling this strip of land is a fulfillment of Ridge's promise."

Yoholo needed no translation and refused any further debate. *"You have heard our talk, and we have no other. If you were to talk as you do now for ten days, this council would not give you another answer."*[8]

For a solitary moment, I pitied McKenney. His pompous chain of successful Indian treaties would end today, a noteworthy humiliation among his colleagues.

McKenney turned his back and opened the door. "I am sorry my Creek sons and brothers have chosen such talk for their White Father. We will gather our belongings and leave for Washington."

"Time to saddle the horses," Vann whispered in my ear.

With McKenney and Crowwell's departure, the attending Creek filed out behind the agents. The two exited their temporary lodgings, bumbling bags in tow, and crossed the crowded yard.

Vann opened the stable door and stepped aside to reveal Peter, leading McKenney's and Crowwell's horses. Then Vann pulled our guarantee claim letter from his lapel pocket and waved it, reminding McKenney of his government's promise to pay.

The faces of the two white men surged with imminent rage at Vann's reminder. One looked at the other in unspoken communication. Then Crowwell bent down and whispered in McKenney's ear.

I stepped in front of Yoholo and asked Colonel Crowwell, "What is the meaning of your whisper? First, McKenney speaks unfounded accusations against David Vann and me, and then you, Colonel Crowwell, whisper to McKenney."[9]

White Crow didn't offer any excuse or explanation. To no one's surprise, McKenney wouldn't do as he promised, remarking how Vann and I did not deserve our wages if we had spoken mistruths about guaranteeing the land.

"Do you feel taller, standing on lies?" Vann said through a smirk and laughed, unsurprised by the unfulfilled promise. He handed Crowwell his horse's reins, taken from Peter's grasp.

Short McKenney remained indignant and disgraced, while Crowwell stood erect and stoic, staring at the young black groomsman with disgust. Peter didn't falter, didn't bow his head or retreat. The two agents mounted their horses and cantered away, looking over their shoulders, rightly expecting a coming advance of red war clubs.

Peter said, "God willin' and the Creek don't rise."

Night crouched, covering our faces in its darkness. With each passing hour, Yoholo and I assumed McKenney rode fast for Washington. Meanwhile, Crowwell would return to his profiteering, protected by Fort Mitchell's palisades.

The next day, the Creek Council convened near the square. Yoholo whooped loudly to quiet his compatriots. Once gaining their eyes, he cried out. *"Instead of pursuing their journeys, McKenney and Crowwell halted on the opposite bank of the Tallapoosa River and spoke to Little Prince, whose mind has left him."*[10] An outcry whirled in the air like a dust storm. Cheaha and Talladega stood beside us with open mouths while the Lower Creeks circled the approaching elder, Little Prince.

Yoholo stepped on top of a rock and continued. *"We are not slaves to the white man's word."* He held out unshackled arms. *"This verbal promise McKenney speaks of is nothing. It is not in the treaty, not binding.*"[11]

Old, arched by a feeble spine, Little Prince parted the crowd with his porcupine roach, moving others aside. He stopped in front of Vann and me and raised his head. A white film glazed his eyes. It took significant effort for him to gather breath enough to speak. Little Prince said, "*The great man says you two made the promise.*"[12]

We could not rebuke his misunderstanding. Without asking us a question, he hadn't granted us permission to speak.

Cheaha, a man of uncompromising courage, talked in our stead to honored Little Prince. "*You sent me to Washington to break McIntosh's bad treaty. We did so and secured ourselves some land, yet scarcely large enough for our people to stand upon. I know nothing of this promise-talk from McKenney. Our friends John Ridge and David Vann know nothing about it. We love the native land under our bare feet and will not sell it. But, if we must concede it, it will be because you did not agree with the rest of us, Little Prince.*"[13]

"*Luckscha. False,*"[14] Little Prince commanded.

Sounds from an incoming rider, a Creek boy delivering a note, distracted the crowd. The missive bore McKenney's writing, addressed to Vann alone. Stiff wind renewed, lifting the tales of frock coats, blowing the red tails of Yoholo's drape. The incoming wind misshaped the porcupine adornments atop Little Prince's hunched head.

Vann read it and wadded it up in his hand, hesitant to reveal its message. Careful with his words, Vann said, "He wants me to use my influence to induce the Creeks to accede. Only then will he see our claim paid."[15]

Drips of rain began their slow assault. Before long, they pummeled and extinguished our fires. Negotiations moved back inside the council house. I sat near the resistance, Yoholo, and the Upper Creeks. No one spoke when we passed a pipe while runners fetched McKenney and Crowwell back.

Near an hour later, McKenney and Crowwell entered, soaked, making them seem more comical and less aggressive.

McKenney began with no greeting, not even offering respect to the attending Little Prince. Instead, he started with his rebuttal. "In Washington, Opothle Yoholo, John Ridge, and David Vann transacted all-important business. These three usually came to the war office and spoke for the Creek delegation. I do not know why my children, the Creek, placed their confidence in these men. I assumed it was because they convinced you they had sense and honesty."[16]

Yoholo stood with unwavering fortitude. *"The delegation is present now and can tell this council whether transactions existed without their knowledge or consent. The treaty recorded the names of the delegation. Call them to testify. Facts do not sustain your claim. You talk much of a verbal promise, not recollected by any others."*[17]

Yoholo continued while I translated. *"We speak truth where your government has a history of lies. Unfortunately, you have not always fulfilled your promises."*

"I do not acknowledge any mistruth, sir." McKenney offered no further refutation. Colonel Crowwell listened but did not speak.

Yoholo gestured to me. *"Our Cherokee friends are honest men. The American negotiators say one thing, and again, do another—"*

McKenney interrupted Yoholo. "My proof of Ridge and Vann's promise remains in Washington City. I will be proven correct, sirs. I will expose Vann and Ridge's dishonesty."

Losing my patience, I spoke in English and Creek. *"I swear on my family's honor, Abraham's God, and my Creator, this man speaks false."*[18]

Laughter fell from the Creek Council, although I didn't think my vow was humorous. McKenney's accusation brought such a reaction, not my response to it.

Yoholo said, *"We know you to be a man of truth, John Ridge. You do not need to swear."*[19]

Then, McKenney made some other disconnected speech, destitute of reason, from anger and embarrassment, disappointed he couldn't produce the document. I didn't need to wonder why; no such document existed.

Before McKenney answered, Yoholo turned his back to the government agents.

McKenney spoke, regardless of Yoholo's refusal. "I will judge the length of my speeches and talk as much as I please. However, I will attend to no further Creek letters if penned by John Ridge."[20] He turned abruptly like the termagant from a morality play and stormed into the rain.

Little Prince would not budge. His mind was thin from fever and age. Yet, as Creek patriarch, he overruled Yoholo. All must follow his lead. Creek doctrine dictated each vote be unanimous. It deluded me how one vote in five hundred could control the will of a nation. But it had, and the Creek's last remaining land in Georgia was given freely to the United States government.

Little Prince's ancient and frail voice spoke to us one last time. *"If you young men come among our people again, I will kill you."*[21]

His last words hung around my head like the cursed albatross in Coleridge's 'Ancient Mariner'. Vann and I walked in silent shame down

Yellow Bird's Song

the empty aisle.

Yoholo met us at the stable as we saddled our horses for home. He held bags containing our fee, given from the Creek Treasury's allotment. The three of us said goodbye, not knowing whether we might see one another again.

Yoholo said, *"If you ever need me..."*

All I could reply was done with the firm grasp of my hand.

I knew then that Vann and I, McKenney's bad birds, never should have accepted the gold.

CHAPTER 6:

SUCH REST TO HIM WHO FAINTS UPON THE JOURNEY[1]

Rollin Ridge
West Desert, Utah
July 1851

Birds rarely sing in the summer desert. The mirrored heat rolling across the glistening sand told them there would be little food to find, nothing but futility on the parched journey. Unlike pleasing birdsong, man complains his lot until he can speak no more—until his throat is so dry under the kerchief, he cannot stand his voice for blame.

Imperfect as I am, I've come this far, surviving on defiant might alone. But this journey to the goldfields, one to escape Chief Ross' vengeance, was not my choice. Leaving Lizzie was not my choice. Papa said a man had no choices when his prospect of gain was nigh. But, regardless of my wants, I'd receive no fair trial on Cherokee land for killing Kell, even though the man's soul was seared long before.

Dawn on the eastern horizon woke me, lit my face, and startled me awake. I sat straight up, panicked with an unconscious desire to return to Cherokee Nation in the East, followed by the waking knowledge I might never hear its waterfalls again. I dreamed of home, but my recollection was only in remembrance of leaving with the sun at our backs. Aeneas and Wacooli slept still, so I took advantage of the quiet dawn with no immediate task to occupy me.

As the sun peeked down the day, with renewed sight to scratch words, I pulled pen and parchment from the roll under my head, uncorked the ink, and began a letter home. My passions rose with my pen, but the words felt like a burning thrust of vomitus bile from my stomach. One loses an appetite for poetry when reason surfaces a truth better left latent.

> Mother,
>
> It is with pleasure that I sit down to write and relieve what I know must be your significant burden to hear from your wandering children torn from you, as they are, cast into the depths, as they so feel. Each morning they rise, then lay down, weary, on this strange and distant land each night. Believe me, it is no ordinary thing to come to California. We three men add insignificantly to the crowd of thousands who travel there, testified by common golden dreams.
>
> This journey for gold costs far more than I reckoned it could.

Yellow Bird's Song

With a quarter due at every bridge over every mud-hole, five dollars lost for each different river we ferried, two hundred and fifty for the purchase of a pack mule or horse. We have less remaining than I would have hoped. Shoeing a horse is four dollars a head. The Mormons charge a steep toll for the road to Salt Lake City. Cured beef costs twelve and a half cents per pound, and the flour is twice as much. I'm shelled, nearly out of money.

As we are crossing the desert, now arrives a tug of war. We expect to reach Sacramento in twenty-five days.

We'll be eating dried beef, which is not very good. Sleeping without shelter is worse—.[2]

Aeneas rose and stretched his back, blocking dawn's light from my periphery, taking me from my complaints. He kicked Wacooli's boot to wake him, poured water from our stores into our coffee pot, and placed it over last night's still-warm coals.

It only took a few moments for them to pack up camp, and they did so in silence. Aeneas' first words came from an unused throat. "Horses and mules loaded, Rollin. Quit scratching to Lizzie and take these." Aeneas handed me a cup of weak coffee first, and leather reins second.

I only accepted the coffee. "This letter is to Mama."

"You done being mad at her?"

I didn't answer. But saying Lizzie's name prompted my hand to reach into my pocket for a crinkled piece of parchment. Aged and weathered these three years, the unfinished poem remained incomplete, paper soft and falling apart, knowing myself to be far more feral now than when I started it.

Aeneas said, "If you told Mama the truth, you better write her another. She doesn't need to wring her hands any more than she's already doing. Make it sound like our saddlebags are as full as our bellies. Don't tell her about the wagon." Aeneas slapped his jenny mule's reins on his thigh. "If you're honest, she'll want us home the minute she reads it. The truth would turn her hair all white."

Aeneas' fortune-telling was correct, but I wouldn't lie. I folded the incomplete letter and put the cork on my ink. Drops and dregs from the bitter chicory coffee in my tin cup fell into cracks in the ground, absorbed and faded like a watermark. I took the reins, wrapped the nib pen, ink well, and unfinished letter inside my saddlebag. I'd complete it when we stopped traveling this evening. Posting it would take longer. If Kit Carson and John Fremont found our bones in the center of the West Desert, crisp, beside arcing, bare mule ribs, and searched my pockets, at least Mama and

Lizzie might read of the events leading to our demise.

Time accompanied our passing through the underworld during the driest month my memory could recall. Our horses were saddled instead of hitched. We abandoned the wagon, as had so many others. Empty from depleted supplies, its rectangular base turned gray and died—damaged beyond repair, with fractured axle, rimless wheels, and broken spokes.

Instead of other travelers along this desert route, we'd found wagon carcasses, adding ours to the lot. Whether human corpses decayed inside, I couldn't say. I didn't stop to find out, ridding myself of guilt for not burying the dead. My body couldn't have done it properly with so little water, not without following directly behind them.

As the afternoon waned, we dismounted and walked beside our thirsty animals. In the desert, a man's horse becomes too weak to carry him. So, he travels on foot, closer to the dust, breathing and clogging his mind with villainous grains. Packs double their weight with worry, heavier with one last blanket of self-preservation. Yet, parched though he may be, his mind sings songs, like uprooted choruses from a withered elder, telling his trials to impatient warriors who already know the legend's end.

Expanses of grass shrunk into patches, peeking through worn spots in the desert, like leg hair peeking through worn and holey farmhand pants. We found the pooled water brackish, the color of tea from iodine, salt mixing with sparse rainwater. It wasn't potable for man or beast. With each disappointment from the lack of soluble water, our progress trickled, nearly stopping entirely.

The sway of horses and pack mules found their rhythm, sluggish though it was. Heat rippled across the sand to just repel back to us from wide mountain berths. Thorny bushes turned pale, a shade lighter than the sand at our feet, desperate for water deep in their roots. Snakes could not reach it and fled, finding no shade.

We pressed forward into the sun, past the mountains near Salt Lake. Each pull at the rim of our hats remained where it was stretched. Bandanas covered our mouths, eyes asquint, leaving each of us absent identity.

Aeneas coughed, attempting to break his silence, rallying saliva enough to articulate some question or another. One which I'd likely have no answer to. He said, "How are we gonna feed the horses, Rollin?"

I was right.

Wacooli answered behind me. "Anee, we'll have to search for grass on foot and bring it to 'em."

From my brother's response to Wacooli's lack of enthusiasm, I knew Aeneas stewed in his thoughts. His concern for our animals was more about him than the beasts.

Yellow Bird's Song

Aeneas said, "You know what I'm hungry for? Grandma's fried bread, Mama's glazed chicken, Honey's pole beans boiled with fatback, and strawberry pie."

"Damn it, Aeneas! Doesn't do us any good thinking about it." I took the fatal risk of putting my thoughts to voice while lingering in Aeneas' conjured savory tastes. I bit my tongue and swallowed twice. "Aeneas, do you remember Papa asking Mama to take all the seeds out of his strawberries?"

"Nope. Too little. You can hold Papa in your thoughts better than me, Rollin. You've got more stock."

When I didn't answer right away, he asked, "What did Papa say?"

"Said they got stuck in his teeth, and she needed to remove them."

"Did she throw something at him?" Aeneas smiled briefly and tried a laugh, but his throat was too dry to form the sound.

"No. She kissed him, as I remember it."

The memory was as sweet as the fruit. Our lives were so predictable then, freedom through synchronicity. Running Waters will always be home, not the cabin in the West at Honey Creek, or Mama's dogtrot in Fayetteville, but our home, Running Waters, in Cherokee Nation East, settled among valley lands in the foothills of the Appalachians.

My parent's extensive farm stretched into the valley on a high hill, crowned with a fine grove of oak and hickory, with a large clear spring at its foot. The orchard was on the left, wheat and cornfields to the right, pastures of cows, goats on one side near the house, and sheep grazing on the other.[3] Behind the house, the running spring gave our home its name. After Grandfather's New Echota Treaty in 1835, we, too, would run over rock, slip on moss, and fall downhill with only brief plains to pool.

The ground whitened under our horse hooves, salted sand gathering in random odd-shaped lines. Only God could articulate their rhyme and reason. Boot tracks marked our path northwest. Each saunter brought another thought: some forward, most backward. Where we'd been, what we'd lost. My thoughts rambled without any respite.

Then my imagination envisioned my hands holding a gold pan. Swirling silt and dirt revealed glimmering rock underneath the water, like treasure from Poseidon's wielding waterspouts. Gold.

This generation's men weren't the first to travel in search of it. Papa's journal was stuffed with clippings from Elias' *Phoenix* and Savannah newspapers, beginning in '28, with headlines reading 'Gold in Dahlonega'. Nothing stopped the white invasion from that first rush, all searching for easy wealth. But those invading hordes found no deserts to overcome. The only things standing in their way were rolling hills sheltering abundant game and laughing rivers sparkling over smooth rocks.

At the time, the Cherokee rejected the white miner's presence, speaking for the land itself. Our people didn't own the ground, not in the same way invading whites read on deeds; instead, we belonged to it. Yet, Cherokee pleas for sovereignty lifted on the western wind, so far away that ignorant white settlers and their Congress couldn't hear, leaving behind my father's people as victims of the intimate crime.

Ridges were the only obstacles plaguing the white man's quest. And when they arrived, clamoring with pan in hand, they filled their empty basins with Cherokee riches. White man's decadent desires overruled his supposed Christianity. I felt hypocritical, knowing I committed the same crime against California natives.

Wacooli broke into my thoughts. "We've got to stop, find shelter from this heat." His eyes were keen, surveying the vastness for any sheltering obtrusion, something to hide underneath. He didn't give us time to protest and let go of his reins. He walked in an expanding circle with bowed legs, stretching his weary back near a patch of disembodied tumbleweeds. Then, shaking his head, he took off his hat and lay down under one, a momentary reprieve from the sun's rays soaking into his dark face.

We followed him and found empathy with back pain released deep in our marrow. The horses stayed close while Aeneas and I repeated Wacooli's stretch over so much waterless ground. In the slight, speckled shade, I lost sight of the past worries and imagined troubles ahead. In the present, my spine spasmed on the baked-hard sand, and I no longer cared.

When we woke, the vindictive sun slid behind the mountaintops, and the temperature turned brisk. Aeneas and Wacooli unpacked our flour, coffee pot, cured beef, and our only frying pan. We each drank our ration of water and ate the cursed dry beef, gristly with salt.

Then, sitting on my horse blanket, I returned to my letter under lantern light and blew into the nib of my pen, hoping grains of sand wouldn't block the ink's stream.

> After traveling over vast sandy plains, traversing here and there, by steep mountains, all day at times to relieve our wearied beasts, having walked many hours, fatigued, worn-out, nearly dead, we've reached our "camping place". We tugged away with our tired hands and legs in fixing the horses, searching high and low for grass, water, and wood, all of which we would frequently be compelled to walk for the distance of a mile or more (owing to the non-proximity of the grass). Then, at last, we sat down, faint and hungry, to strong fat meat that tasted like rust and a piece of

Yellow Bird's Song

bread that made the stomach retch with every swallow. Nothing is comfortable! Yet appetite so strong the stomach, loathed, still called for more.[4]

Oh, sweet such rest to him who faints upon the journey long and weary!

And scenes like this the traveler paints, while dying on the wayside weary.

Sad pilgrims o'er life's desert, we, our tedious journey onward ever.[5]

Across the desert, Man shuffles and breathes in sand, clogging his mind. All the while, with each square boot toe forward, his ears spiral outward in wider circles, mind gyrating upward, hoping to hear birdsong. This desert is too quiet for me.

In all this silence, my mind reeled through memories of you and Papa, back to the spring at Running Waters. Fueled forward, swallowing tasteful memories, we press on to the inevitable surface, hoping to find buried gold in unchartered land where none have staked claim.

Rollin

CHAPTER 7: QUEEN BEE
Sarah Ridge
Ridge Land and Chief Ross' Home, Cherokee Nation Territory
November 1827

S waddled against my chest, Rollin and I turned toward a cawing crow, perched on a pine branch beyond the gold reflections of the Oostanaula. Then, we watched the bird stretch its black wings to glide up to autumn's winds. Clarinda released my hand to wave at the field workers, who returned her gesture. With scythe and sickle handles against their shoulders, they began their work through shorter days. They ushered in the fall, swaying hips and backs, gripping handles of tools with perpendicular blades, cutting hay necessary to feed cattle and horses for approaching winter.

We passed the largest barn, loaded with cotton bales, some seeded, some not. We passed another open outbuilding with hanging tobacco leaves. The corncrib overflowed with the harvest, shielding any hint of sunlight from peeking through the joints. What corn Major Ridge had not already sent to the mill or market hid behind its sheltering silk, ready to be stripped off the cob. Smokehouse fire, its smells carried on salted air, dried meat for winter fare.

After the harvest's larger tasks, women's endless list of chores began, smaller, time-consuming tasks completed from laps seated near kitchen fires. Apples and peaches required drying. We preserved vegetables in crockery and gourd. We soaked white oak nuts while the chestnuts dried. Blankets needed weaving, and socks, knitting. These chores, placed on women's able but weary shoulders, filled the weeks. Beside these, we cleaned shirts, darned socks, prepared meals, and guarded children against the ever-present dangers of hot irons and top-heavy spinning wheels.

No one stood still this time of year. With dawn arriving later and dusk earlier, each sunrise wrapped the harvest in unobstructed blue. These days were noteworthy, a brief reprieve before wind and rain brought down orange and rust-colored maple leaves. This moment of plenty allowed bear and deer, squirrel and crow to prepare for a winter when little could grow. Man's preparations were no different.

Sollee stood in the kitchen doorway. She'd returned home from Salem's Moravian School in North Carolina to help Mother Susannah prepare for winter. This was her home, after all, although she was at school for most of my time here. She and Mother worked without words, interceded only by laughter or gestures. One matriarch stepped to the side

Yellow Bird's Song

of the kitchen fire while the younger passed crockery. Neither needed teaching to work beside the other, gossiping Cherokee banter back and forth. Honey kneaded bread, laughing, too busy to translate conversations that didn't involve me or required too much backstory. I was jealous of their kinship, reminded of how far the distance was between my mother and myself, measured by more than miles.

Out of place, and unneeded, the children and I left the kitchen and returned to our garden. Clarinda and I planted winter vegetables: carrots, onions, cabbage, and beets, rows planted in turnips, broccoli, cauliflower, and mustards. The small contribution seemed minor compared to the work Sollee, Susannah, and Honey accomplished, and I felt useless on top of ignorant. No matter how much I learned, none of their tasks came quickly, as though everyone needed to teach me on top of their other endless labors. Not that I did not want to try. I just needed to be trusted with a charge without constant correction from another woman who knew more. I wanted to be involved in their hum, instead of being a bother because I didn't know the song. No one spoke so aloud, but I remembered the feeling, the same one my mother's sighs never let me forget.

While the sun traveled across the sky, a post rider found me enacting my frustration against runaway vines through the onion plants. Against my back, Rollin wiggled and cried, while dusty Clarinda crushed red dirt clods in her hands.

"Little Spider? Is that you?" After shouting up the hill, Arch kicked his horse into a gallop and rode toward us with a full satchel strapped across his chest. Then, swinging his leg over his horse, he dismounted without his hands and greeted us.

"Good to see you again, Mister Arch. Are you well?"

"Aside from a constant headache, I am. This blue sky is to blame, or my reading with poor eyesight. Who is this beautiful child?"

"You two haven't met officially, have you? Our daughter, Clarinda, and John Rollin, born last March." Arch bowed to the baby and bent lower to meet Clarinda's eyes. He smiled, and she returned his grin, only to dart behind my skirt and peek at him. To her, Arch was a stranger. To me, he was the man who guided me to find a kidnapped Honey, trading his horse to save her life. Time hadn't healed all the wounds made by the Man in the Hat, but the memory scabbed over and brought less pain. I remembered Arch's kind face as clearly as the pale scar on my palm.

"I bring the Word and the post on my way to Reverend Sam's post office in New Echota." Arch chuckled. "Quatie Ross asked that I give this to you." Arch reached into his pouch to retrieve a letter and a small jar of golden honey. The latter he handed to my daughter. She accepted his gift, looking through the glass, changing her world into amber.

I wiped dirty hands over my apron and took the letter. "Thank you. How were the Rosses when you left them?"

"In good health. Chief Ross and his brother Lewis were home. Where is John? I'd like to shake his hand. Ross told me of John's commitment to the passing of the Constitution."

"Not here. He had pressing business with the Creek Council." I suddenly felt embarrassed by my disheveled appearance, not planning on encountering others today. With the back of my hand, I tucked unkempt hair back inside my cap. "When he's home, John spends most weekdays in New Echota with Xander McCoy. They both carry green bags now. Are you planning to stay at McCoy's inn while in New Echota? His wife is so sufficient. She runs that inn entirely by herself." As I complimented Mistress McCoy, I salted a jealous stew. Her husband needed her; I wasn't sure she needed him. Sarah McCoy was the epitome of efficiency and followed Cherokee's old ways, a truly commanding matriarch.

Others demanded so much of John's time that little remained to spend at home. My husband did not need me for much. Arch touched my arm, inferring a sadness I didn't share. "Each Little Spider has knowledge the sweeping eagle doesn't understand. I hope to see you and this beautiful child at services."

"Thank you for the personal delivery. When do you return this way?"

"Saturday, ma'am."

"Come for dinner Saturday night. John might be home, and I know he'd enjoy seeing you."

"I must prepare for Sunday's services on Saturday eve."

I nodded with understanding and said, "God be with you, Arch."

His reply was instant. "I know He is with you."

He mounted his horse with one last grin to Clarinda and rode toward New Echota.

On Quatie's invitation, Major Ridge carried us to Ross' home with a wagon full of cotton to sell. He and Ross, with brother Lewis, would go to the market, and afterward, Major Ridge would bounce us down the Ross Ridge Road for home, faster with an empty wagon.

When we arrived, dense woods hovered behind the two-story, hewn log cabin with a wrapping porch. The house was new, only a year old, so the brown wood had yet to color the cabin's exterior gray. Windows mirrored the morning's sunlight in rainbowed gold, with an iridescent

Yellow Bird's Song

sheen, as if they hid jewels of immense worth from the wandering eyes of passing thieves. On the side of the house, the remnants of Quatie's red and white roses speckled the rusty dirt beneath them, highlighting green leaves above falling brown rose petals.

Standing above a steaming iron pot, Quatie waved and offered us welcome. While she seemed aloof and sophisticated at the Constitution celebration, now she appeared homespun. She must have folded the queen she'd been then into a trunk, awaiting court another day. She looked up from the pot in an apron soiled with brown and pumpkin-colored spots. Her black hair hid inside a solid maroon turban, the shade of her calico dress. At first glance, she appeared to be the house's servant, not its mistress; however, she was suited for the dirty work of candle-making. Then she returned to her stirring stick over the boiling kettle. The air smelled delightful, a harbinger of the season.

"Let me meet your children, and I will introduce you to my girls. We'll have an uninterrupted day to learn from one another."

"I doubt I have much to teach," I admitted.

"Nonsense. Come. I must stir the comb and begin straining. Then we can go inside and dip wicks."

"I must admit, I've never made candles before today." I looked toward the trees, not eager to hear the familiar sigh, acknowledging my inept ignorance.

Initially, Quatie let free an appalled scoff, but it softened into a relaxed expression. "Then, it will be my pleasure to talk you through the task, so you can make them for your home. It seems an ancient tradition, but it is good for our young wives to know how to make candles. Otherwise, our husbands sit in the dark because their wives lack knowledge."

We followed Quatie to her boil of water and honeycomb. The honey's characteristic sweet odor was absent. Instead, only a faint smell of yeast scented the crisp air.

She said, "Last summer's heat brought two honey harvests. My people take advantage of preserving it and the beeswax for leaner seasons. It is a long chore, taking days to drain and boil the comb to remove impurities before dipping wicks. I've been at it all week."

"I think I know how to complete the task but have never taken part in the chore." Clarinda ran to me and grabbed both hands to stop my walking. She pointed her index finger and waved it side to side, then she swatted an imaginary bee from her face.

"Clarinda wants to know where the bees go if their house is boiling in a pot."

Quatie said, "Honeybees live in trees all winter, hovering their wings for warmth. They stay alive eating their supply of honey from the previous season and only venture into the cold to remove waste. In the spring, they build more honeycomb. When it's time to harvest the comb, we blow smoke to keep them calm. The honeybee will sting only to protect her nest, and then she dies."

Whether she meant the information for my daughter or me, I did not know. I made John's invented gesture for the tree, and Clarinda seemed content with my answer. Curious Clarinda's questions brought innovative words to my daughter's mind and new signs for us all to remember. My daughter did not differ from any other curious three-year-old.

Quatie took two large gloves and grabbed the iron handles on the sides of her boiling pot, removing it from the heat. Once placed on the ground, she held a strainer to scoop black sticky goo from the top of the boiler. She skimmed away the most significant clusters.

Quatie stretched the handle toward my daughter, offering her an opportunity to scoop the last bits from the pot onto the ground. Clarinda walked in a careful circle around the burning wood. My daughter held the strainer with Quatie's arm around her waist, ready to rescue her from toppling into the flames.

Satisfied with the texture of the wax, Quatie stretched a thinly woven cloth over clay pots on the ground, wrapping her hands before pouring the heavy pot. She moved Clarinda behind her and filled the pots to the brim and set the iron pot aside to cool. She gathered the straining cloth into a bundle in her fist and rocked the bundle over the bowl, filtering the comb bits from the hot wax.

She looked over her shoulder and said, "Now we wait and talk. It takes time to cool. In candle-making, like most things, the reward comes after the wait."

Clarinda looked at me for translation, as she knew Quatie spoke. I held my palms up and wiggled my fingers. "Wait, Clarinda. It changes colors when it hardens."

"We will have to purify the wax again. But then, it will be ready to dip wicks. Shall we go inside?"

A cry came from the trees. Roosting peacocks, barely visible, with golden-rimmed eyes and teal feathers peeked through the limbs.

We passed Quatie's roses bordering the house. "Oh, they're still flowering. I miss my roses in Connecticut," I said, jealous of her garden's remaining summer color. She pulled a knife from her apron pocket and bent to remove a cutting. "Then we will send you home with this stuck into a seed potato. Next spring, you can grow color of your own."

The open door revealed a spacious cabin holding a stone hearth the

Yellow Bird's Song

length of the wall. In the center of the room, suspended from the log ceiling, a grate rose or lowered from a rope tied beside the door. Six straight-back chairs anchored a large table.

Quatie introduced a young woman, about sixteen, who stirred an iron crock over a well-established fire. "Her father, my first husband, died in the Creek war in 1814."

I did not know Quatie had a daughter of such an age or that she'd been married before. The daughter's graces mimicked her mother's, beautifully tall and slender, with black hair tied in a blue wrap to keep strands from entering the wax.

In the corner, a younger girl, about six years old, tucked dolls into tiny beds in her dollhouse. *"Jane, show Clarinda your dolls while her mother and I dip."* Jane rose from tending faceless cornhusk dolls and took Clarinda's hand to sit beside the dollhouse.

Quatie said, "Come."

I didn't realize that I was still standing outside.

Quatie picked up a wick, stretched it straight, let it fall into the wax, and dipped it repeatedly in the simmer. Her cadence mesmerized me, following the graceful movements of her hands. She said, "Making candles is a task I can do without thinking. It follows a rhythm all its own."

"My mother was not one to dirty her hands making something she could buy," I said, sitting Rollin on my lap.

"We don't have such luxury here. She lives in Connecticut? Not having her close must be difficult."

Mother Susannah must have told her more about me than I knew. I said, "It isn't only that. Sollee and Susannah have such accustomed habits. One threads and the other guides the shuttle. One pulls vines while the other weaves baskets. They meet the other's needs without asking." I straightened in the chair. "My mother commanded, and I obeyed. Watching Sollee and Susannah together teaches me all my mother never did."

Quatie read more in my tone and expression than I intended, but her smile didn't change when she handed the wick to her daughter and touched my hand. She said, "Susannah says you are a wonder with the children, requiring no teaching." She sat facing me and reached her hands for Rollin. "Some think mothering ends when the child is old enough to express their needs. Even with your mother's absence, you understand there is an intuition, a responsibility, that arrives with the child."

Susannah's compliment honored me. I said, "Clarinda's infancy was so unusual. She rarely cried. Just a cheerful baby. But Rollin's temperament is difficult." Hearing his name, he stuck his fist in his mouth. "He cries all night. How can two children from the same parents be so opposite?"

"Does he nurse, or eat smashed vegetables at the table?"

"He only nurses, constantly if he had his way."

"He's growing. Give him something that will fill his tiny belly. Mix rice flour or cornmeal in milk and feed him with a spoon before washing him for the night. During the day, keep him cooler, lay him on his belly on the floor, and keep him awake. He will cry for a day or two but will adjust. You both will sleep better. That is, until he cuts teeth. The top ones will make his nose run."

"And when the bottom teeth come?" I asked.

"Well, it makes for messy nappies."

Quatie's daughter dipped the wick enough times for a slender taper to form and handed me the cotton wick. Quatie sat to take Rollin. I imitated her pattern. Dip and drain, wait for the color to change, and repeat. With each douse in melted beeswax, the taper thickened.

Quatie said, "Once you know the pattern, learn the rhythm; you can dip more wicks at a time. Dip the other side, repeat the pattern until its weight equals the opposite side." She held Rollin's hand toward the ceiling. "When you're through, hang it here, over the metal grate. I dip eight at once with a dowel." She changed the subject. "Forgive me, as it is not my concern, but do you and John plan to build your own house? Or remain living with Mother Susannah and Major Ridge? I can only imagine the space feels cramped with two young children."

Rollin began squirming and fussing. She kissed his cheek and laid him over her shoulder, bouncing his bottom.

"They would not want us to leave. Besides, it isn't my place to ask. What God desires, He will provide."

"God helps those who help themselves. Ask. There can be only one queen in a hive."

"I'm not a queen."

"Cherokee treat all their women like queens." She stood and exchanged baby for wick. "What would your John say?"

I heard his answer in my thoughts. But I couldn't answer her question, direct though it was.

We fed the children a small lunch of apples and cheese as I nursed and changed Rollin. I tried Quatie's suggestion, placing him on his belly atop a quilt at our feet. I had done so with Clarinda; she enjoyed it, while Rollin rolled onto his back and cried. However, this time, he lifted his head and watched his sister play in the corner and found the changing light through the window entertainment enough to keep him awake.

Time slipped from me while making candles and answering Quatie's

Yellow Bird's Song

questions about my upbringing. By mid-afternoon, we'd managed two wooden boxes full of tapers. The sounds of horses pulling wagons outside alerted us to the growing hour. Major Ridge ducked his head to enter the kitchen and collect us, scooping a squealing Rollin into his arms. Clarinda showed him one of Jane's dolls while I thanked Quatie for the afternoon I didn't realize I'd needed. Quatie handed me a box of candles when we readied to leave.

"For your John's late nights." She spoke with a smile. "Until we see one another again... Next time, we'll weave, and you must stay longer." Then, with a wink at Clarinda, and a touch on Rollin's nose, Quatie hugged me and waved goodbye. In her, I'd found a friend.

Quatie's giving spirit marked her as royalty, adorned by kindness like an invisible jeweled crown. After Clarinda waved goodbye, she curtseyed, and made a new sign for Queen Quatie, a crown resting on her head.

Loud voices from the barn interrupted us when we crossed the yard. Another Cherokee, resting a gun barrel across his shoulder, joined Ross and Lewis. They spoke English with such animated gestures, I couldn't help but look.

The gun-toting man spoke harshly, slapping Lewis' chest in frustration. I missed the context, but in broken English he said, "Backing out with the Colonel will cost more. Lavender agrees." Lewis nodded, agreeing with the man's advice.

When Major and I walked to the wagon, they watched us pass. I knew of the man they spoke of—George Lavender. He owned a trading post on Ridge land. He and my father-in-law had a hostile partnership. Major Ridge allowed Lavender, a Georgian, to continue to run the business because it turned a profit with little to no labor on Major's part. But he constantly squabbled with the man. The last argument I overheard was over a dead pig. Major Ridge accused Lavender of poisoning it. God only knew why a man would do such a thing, but there must be reason if my father-in-law made the accusation.

With stern eyes, Major shook his head, implying I shouldn't speak. Then, he occupied his hands, taking Rollin from my arms. He put his other arm behind me and walked me toward the wagon. He lifted Rollin's traveling basket to the seat, hefted Clarinda beside her brother, and helped me climb the wheel.

Major waved goodbye to Ross before joining us on the wooden bench. Clarinda wiggled into his lap to hold the reins inside her grandpa's broad hands. She would drive us home.

"Lavender?" I whispered.

Major Ridge shrugged his shoulders, but the look on his face told me

Heather Miller

he would seek answers for himself soon enough.

As we bumped and tossed on the well-worn path, my mood shifted, and I felt invigorated by the day. I broached the idea of a new house with my father-in-law.

"You may not understand all I say, or you might; I do not know. I do not know whether you will grant the request I'm making of you. I do not know whether asking you and facing your refusal is worse than not asking. It would be a significant expense."

He watched the road ahead but nodded in solitary reply.

"Seeing Quatie today, talking with her, finding her so welcoming reminded me how little I have to share. I have no kitchen to welcome her to. The hearth in our apartment is for warmth, not baking bread. I have no loom or wheel, no plot of earth to grow more than what we will eat this winter. It is vanity, as Quatie said of her roses and peacocks, but growing children are the gifts my God has given me. John and I need our own home." I knew it was unlikely that he'd grant my request, regardless of my volume. "Everything we have belongs to you and Susannah. John and I need a house and land to raise this family. *Owenvsv.*"

"*We are going home; are we not? Daughter, this is the way home.*" I understood most of the distraction he offered, but I wasn't sure he comprehended all I asked.

In the last bend, passing Ridge Ferry, he spoke slowly so I might understand his intent, if not the exact words. I heard "*No,*" followed by each of our names. Major wanted us beside him, especially John, who had become the son his father dreamed him to be.

Clarinda spun around and faced her grandpa. She wove the fingers of one hand through the other, like the joints of log walls, one grooved log raising another, resting their weight on the one beneath. Her dog, Digaleni, leaped with flopping ears to escort the wagon. Major snapped the reins to gather speed while Digaleni woofed until we pulled into the barn.

When Major halted the horses, I thought about what my new friend had said. Queen Quatie believed most things were fostered by the waiting, like winter bees hovering in trees. We, too, must remain here until spring with hopes to build a hive of our own.

CHAPTER 8: "MY LIFE UPON HER FAITH"[1]
John Ridge
Ridge Land, Cherokee Nation Territory
Winter 1827-1828

Vann and I spoke little, so young Peter filled the void. "We just like dem shiverin' honeybees, flappin' our wings, tryin' not to freeze to death."

Undoubtedly intelligent, abundant with common sense, he spoke with a simplicity I'd forgotten. Peter hummed under his breath or told stories lasting for miles, punctuating their endings with wisdom, and laughing at his cleverness. Without overcomplicating matters, his thoughts were as clear as the approaching stars this frigid night.

Vann said, "Peter's right. My legs are warm around this horse, but my teeth won't stop chattering."

We dismounted, spending our last rough night near the Coosa River before following Oostanaula's banks toward Sarah's comfort and my father's judgment.

"I'll get firewood," I said, wandering from my companions, searching downed trees for lighter knot. Vann took care of our horses. Peter followed me, picked up twigs and dried moss to burn for kindling.

When I kicked against a decaying stump, Peter's candor surprised me. "If'n I stay with your people, most be thinkin' yous owns me."

"It may not be much consolation, but you'll know the difference. Slavery is legal in Cherokee Nation, as it is in Georgia." I put my hand on his shoulder. "You'll be safe with us. No one will beat you, chase you with dogs, or force you into labor not of your choosing." I bent over and handed the freed pine knot to him.

He smelled its deep resin. "If'n we find another like this, we won't need another till mornin'." We continued our search, kicking through the thick brush and briars. Peter remarked, "But, even so, I won't be free."

I stopped and let Peter pass. He wasn't wrong. I didn't know how to answer.

Peter stretched his back when his eyes followed a hickory tree from root to sky. He said, "Up there, in Heaven, God don't make the flower dream about the bee—it just blossoms, and the bee come. Freedom supposin' to be the same."

I didn't follow his gaze; I looked at him. "If you do not want to stay with us, I understand. I will provide you provisions for wherever you choose to go, but I hope you'll stay the winter at least."

"Truth is, I's gots no choice. If'n I stay with your family on Cherokee land, it'll be 'cause I don't wanna get caught in Georgia and end up right where I started." He continued farther down the riverbank into the thicker brambles. He turned back. "I 'preciate all you and Mister Vann done. Hard to complain and not seem ungrateful. Just never had no choice before. If'n the Cherokee own slaves and the white man own slaves, there's nowhere close dat's free." He kicked another rotting stump in his frustration. "Like I said, ain't got no choice."

I took a small ax from my belt and hacked down some limbs in Peter's way. "It is a far more dangerous world outside Cherokee Nation for a young man such as yourself." I took a deep breath before asking, "What do you want, Peter?"

He shook his head. "No one ever ast me dat. Drew and me daydream 'bout growin' crops in our own fields. Shoein' horses we be ridin', bought fair and square, with money we earned. Buildin' a ferry pully and chargin' each passerby a dime to cross and a quarter to fish." Peter laughed. "Drew say how we'd need to have da bait ready if we's gonna charge so much."

Hunched over a stump, I found another knot but couldn't get it free. Peter and I switched places, and he pulled, his voice straining with his efforts. "But, with Drew gone, my imaginin's ain't so clear."

"I understand a man's need to prove his worth."

He stumbled back when the knot released and said, "You ain't free neither, is you?"

"Not in the way the Great Spirit intended. I'm trying everything I know to do to keep the land for my people. Peter, you need to know. My family owns twenty slaves. Right now, my wife and children live with my mother and father. But when we build a home of our own, we will be freer to assist you, whatever you decide. My family will welcome you, appreciate you the same way Vann and I have. No one will mistreat you."

Peter smelled the resin in the knot and handed it to me. "Why yous helpin' a runaway? Nothin' in it for you."

"For the same reason you trust me, I hope. You've assisted me more than you know. I'd rather sleep well, with a clear mind, knowing I'd offered you compensation for your efforts, than force anyone into a life they were never born to. If you stay, you'll receive fair pay for your work as a groomsman. And with the money, perhaps improve land of your own, wherever your God may take you."

We gathered more limbs into our arms. Peter nodded, thinking about the possibility. "Peter's Prairie. The Lord do say he make plans for my welfare, not for evil, sendin' hope alongside da rain."

We walked back just as Vann shuffled through cracking leaves,

Yellow Bird's Song

nocking an arrow on his bowstring.

I struck flint to steel, and blew the spark, cupping chilled hands around the budding flame.

Peter called after Vann. "Have more luck if'n you take your gun instead of dat bow. Them dry leaves are like a worn man's clothes." Peter dumped the wood from his arms and sat on his heels, handing me kindling without looking down.

Vann stopped scuffling twenty feet away and waited for Peter to finish. He said, "Like a man, dem bare branches reach toward Heaven—" Peter looked up, "—but with no belt, his crunchin' faults collect round his heels. If'n you want to see what's hidden, you've gots to be quick."

After listening, Vann laughed and returned to camp, collecting the long gun slid along the strap of his saddle. He loaded it and continued down his former path.

Peter kept the sun's hours and quickly fell asleep after eating what provisions remained. I was left alone in my thoughts, interrupted only by the echo from two shots. My successful friend returned carrying two squirrels by their tails. While he skinned and roasted the rodents, he pulled out a recent copy of *The Constitutionalist* purchased from a roadside trading post.

"Headline says Andrew Jackson's wife is a Jezebel. Married to another man when she ran off with the General."

"Don't believe everything you read. A newspaper in Connecticut said much the same thing about Sarah and me. Probably just Adams slandering Jackson, hoping to decrease the popular vote."

Vann flipped to the inside of the paper, and set it to the side, so both hands could pick hot meat from the bone. Between bites, he intermittently spit lead pellets.

I looked at him, raising my eyebrow in disgust.

He replied, "That's why I wanted to use my bow! No doubt I'll be poisoned with lead."

His greasy fingers reached for his paper and began reading another article. "We think it useless, if not dangerous, to hold out to the Cherokees any prospect, save that of departure from their present seats which indeed is the only event that can satisfy the state of Georgia, and the express obligation of the United States."[2]

Vann spit again, more fervently than before.

I said, "After Chief Pathkiller's passing, and Chief Hicks', we cross a tumultuous threshold. Georgia is, no doubt, invigorated with Jackson's populist campaign."

Georgia's Congress was now in session. Governor Forsyth retaliated against our Constitution and took advantage of the lapse in Cherokee leadership, proclaiming the land where my people stood for more than a century, was temporary—our people, cast as mere tenants. Georgia thought they had the power to repossess the land and evict us by any means necessary.

Vann quickened his breath and read further down the column. "The plan to make citizens of the Indians… is chimerical and delusive. In the first place, we doubt whether Indians can be made citizens…"[3] He looked up and asked, "What does chimerical mean? Never mind, I don't care. I don't want to be an American. How about that?" Vann wadded and tossed the paper into the fire's embers.

All the tedious labor to print it disappeared in a searing seam of orange light. Ash fell to the ground as charred carbon. Though the paper's state changed, its lingering threats remained behind. Ignition didn't make the pundit's opinions any less biased or any less plausible.

"*Ah-ni-U-ka-sha-na*. The man is an ass. I'm going to sleep," Vann said. "Staying up?"

"I'm not tired." I lied, knowing I wouldn't rest well until I was home beside Sarah and the children.

Vann turned away, put his hat over his face, and instantly began sleep's deep breathing. I was jealous of his ability to silence his thoughts.

With another day's ride, we'd arrive. And I'd have to tell my father the truth.

What exactly that was, I did not know. Peter's truth was that he could begin again safely away from the Crow brothers. Vann's truth was that he was a wealthier man, regardless of how he earned the sum. But my truth and, subsequently, my political future masked behind Crowwell's incomprehensible whisper. I looked up at the moon, thinking how cold it must be, knowing I stood in a similar darkness, alone on the shadowed side.

From Ridge Ferry, on the other side of the Oostanaula, familiar applewood smoke drifted downwind. At this late hour, Mother would have extinguished the candle sconces in the dining room. The lingering glow from Father's study windows called to me. Our horseshoes clattered against the wood planks of the ferry. Once across, I heeled for speed, passing my companions, to climb the hill behind our house, steering beyond the reach of the study's diamond-shaped light. We rode into the barn, dismounted, and unstrapped our saddles. Ross' horse was there,

Yellow Bird's Song

asleep.

Vann whispered, "I'll help Peter with the horses and get him settled in the hayloft. Then, I'm climbing the stairs and sleeping in your old bed for three days."

I mumbled to myself more than Vann, "He's still up, talking to Ross."

Vann's reply was sincere, "Do you want me to go in with you?"

"Why? Our story is the same." I left the two of them to settle and walked toward my childhood home.

From outside my father's study door, I overheard their conversation. I rapped with my knuckles, not bothering to change or wash. Delivering unwelcome news was the same, whether freshly pressed or dusty with road dirt.

"Come," Father said. Of course, he knew I was home.

Father stood behind his desk and crossed the room to embrace me. *"Sarah, Clarinda, and Rollin have walked the riverbank all week, hoping to catch sight of you."*

In sharp contrast to Father's welcome, Ross' back opposed me. His head was down, pacing in front of the window, investigating the blackening darkness. With the season, the skeletal woods allowed man to see an unaccustomed distance at night, transforming a trail, once memorized, into foreign ground. If Ross sought answers from the river, I doubted he'd find anything I hadn't.

Father escorted me to the chair by the fire and asked, *"How was my friend Yoholo? Give him the tobacco I sent? Any trouble in your travels? How was the council with McKenney?"*

With little in the way of introduction, I retold Peter's tale of the Crows and the Creek's disappointment after Little Prince believed McKenney's false accusations. Ross listened, now seated in the armchair opposite me.

But my eyes followed my pacing father. Tapers' flames leaned toward him after each pass. I'd never seen him this angry, and I, ashamed to be the cause. I ended my story with Little Prince's decision to hand over Creek's 192,000 acres. Father threw his cup across his study, shattering it against the wall, dripping and staining the logs with wine. His boots thumped on the hardwood, glass crunching under his tread with his hands gripped together behind his back.

I hoped Father and Ross weren't questioning my actions, and instead, were contemplating countermoves. But Ross' face turned sallow in the firelight. Father's brow wrinkled, more profound from his shadowed stance. Disappointment radiated from them both, and I lowered my head with their quiet blame.

No one spoke through the uncomfortable silence. Finally, I stood and

86

walked to the window, gathering courage to make eye contact with them. I said, *"The Creek barrier will soon be gone, and Georgia will tighten its noose. Whether McKenney and Crowwell are allies of General Jackson or not, we cannot allow the Crows to continue running whiskey, slaves, and horses through our nation."*

Father sighed and gripped the fireplace mantle, leaning into the heat with his aged head, arching his back to stretch tense muscles. Light from the blaze traveled across his face as he shook his head. Father sank into his seat, trusting the thin chair to hold his mighty frame. He stretched his long legs in front of him and rubbed his temples. He said, *"You did nothing wrong, son. In fact, you had foresight and honesty in the affair. I blame myself for passing the negotiations to you."*

I straightened my spine, accepting Father's faithlessness. My parched throat said, *"I have no proof of the Crowwell brothers' crimes other than the witness of an escaped slave. But Peter speaks the truth. All truthful men deserve choice. I will not return him and force him to face the Crow's justice. We must stop their theft against the Cherokee and prevent the probable death of those walking west on foot."*

Finally, Father said, *"I believe you, son."* Whether he believed in me was a fate he'd force me to face.

There would be no accountability for the criminals in Georgia's court. From Vann's reading of the Milledgeville newspaper, we learned Georgia contemplated banning any Cherokee from testifying against any white man. So, there was little doubt in my mind that an escaped slave would receive a fair defense or justice from a jury of Georgian whites. I knew from last year's council that if Ross had his way, a similar prohibition against runaways would become law in our nation. Ross argued that if Cherokee granted refuge, many would come and seek safe shelter here, angering Georgia's wealthy elites at the loss of property. But Ross' plan was a machination, a political placation, rather than a firm stance on moral grounds.

I shook my head and came from the window to stand between them. Ross stood and faced me. "It was not smart to involve ourselves in the Creek's business. I was worried when you and Vann asked to travel to Washington two years ago. As principal chief, I cannot allow you or Vann to continue interceding in Creek dealings."

His remark almost didn't register with me. So, I didn't shield my gall. "Principal chief? So, the council appointed you in our absence. Congratulations." Ross' contributions to the Constitution and his services were widely known and admired by our people. However, I assumed the role would fall to Elisha Hicks, son of Charles Hicks, our nation's recently

Yellow Bird's Song

deceased chief. Most Cherokee men I knew would have had no qualms about electing Hicks to the position. But to my astonishment, that was not the case. Ross gained the people's confidence, and therefore, their votes.

Ross' white heritage allowed him entry into doors consistently shut against the red-skinned Cherokee. I understood that truth. He and Father had been friends since 1812 and fought beside one another in the Red Sticks War at Horseshoe Bend, sharing a trust validated by battle. So, while America sought to elect the populist Jackson, Cherokee Nation's chief men elected Ross to lead as principal chief, raised higher by gales from Father's political voice.

Ross' brown eyes squinted at my father as he stepped aside, ignoring my presence. He said, "My concern is with Cherokee involvement from John and Vann. Our people will misunderstand their intentions." Then, touting newly elected authority, Ross raised his chin, stuck the pipe in his mouth, and crossed his arms over his chest. He must have seen it as his chief's duty to reprimand me—as if he punished my boyhood self—forcing me to move the woodpile to the other side of the house.

Our chief inhaled deeply before making a declaration, surprising the somber room with his articulate volume. "Publicly, I must censor you and Vann. Of course, you may write a rebuttal—more for white subscribers of the *Phoenix* than Cherokee who don't read. On my order, Elias will print it. You and Vann must resign your seats on the Cherokee Legislative Council." Then his tone shifted to one I recognized, that of the friend I'd once known. Ross said, "Privately, I understand your choice and hold no ill will to your intentions, however troublesome this incident may prove."

Father's face told me he needed no translation of Ross' words, but he didn't utter a word in my defense or question his chief's decision. Instead, Father cocked his head in surprise, raised his eyebrows, and nodded in tenuous agreement. Ross' command took away my stature, like he kicked out my knees, expecting me to kneel before him.

My forceful rebuttal came from a weary place, deep in guilt because I brought trouble to my nation and distrust to the Ridge name. Ross' remark infuriated me. How could we ignore the plight of the Creek when we fought the same fight? I lifted my head to address him, gesturing with a brush of my hand to fan away his smoky exhale.

"So that is your choice. Smoke Ridge tobacco and claim 'I told you so'? That is the Principal Chief's response to his countryman? Let our people believe what they will? Sir, is this how you'll lead?" I tried to exhale such temerity. "Can't you see? Without Peter's testimony, we'd not know of the crimes, illegal by both American and Cherokee law. Knowing the truth may prove fortuitous in our continued battle to hold our ground."

In my frustration, I ran my hand through my hair. I placed the canvas bag of gold coins on Father's desk. *"Take the money. Invest it as you deem necessary or give it to the Cherokee Treasury. With McKenney's assumed report on my integrity in the American House, I cannot build a home, improve the land, or buy cattle and horses. Some will assume Vann and I took a bribe. My assistance offered to Creek Nation, and Yoholo, was never about the money.*

"McKenney thinks his accusations will negate my character. I'm sure he will claim I am a fraud in Washington. But Creek land was never mine to negotiate. I acted only as an advisor, linking Yoholo's wishes to English. I supported Yoholo's desire and protected Creek interests and, in turn, our own."

Father said, *"McKenney must explain himself to representatives we've worked with before, having their own opinion of your integrity. McKenney's misstatements will reveal his eagerness not to be perceived as a failure. His arguments counter what our friends know to be true, requiring evidence he doesn't have."*

Ross returned to the red velvet chair and crossed one leg over the other. With smoke masking his face, he replied, "I will instruct my brother Lewis to move the Light Guard to the west side of our territory. Then, if we intercept whiskey wagons or pony clubs, we will have more proof than this single slave's word."

Nothing could alter the gravitas of this outcome, with few arguments remaining uncontemplated, either from Ross' persecution or my defense. I had nothing more to say except, *"I've offered Peter quarter and shelter here. He requested to continue his trade as a groomsman. With Saul's passing, I saw no need to deny him protection while he decides whether he wants to remain here."* With my back to the room, I turned the doorknob. *"… If there is nothing further, I haven't seen Sarah or my children since returning."*

When I shut the front door, I took a breath. Instead of Father placing his faith in me, he committed his political hopes for principal chief in Ross, a mixed blood, invigorated by his mother's powerful Cherokee clan but gifted in stubbornness inherited from his Scottish father.

These events revealed a side of Chief Ross I'd not seen before: schemes of reputation differing in private discourse from public decree. Although, for now, I'd keep those opinions to myself. I'd learned much from watching white men hide secrets. In Chief Ross' censure, I recognized his two faces—both were pale.

I walked along the border of Sarah's garden, exhaling steam, and leaned my forehead against the outside of our apartment door. I couldn't

Yellow Bird's Song

make myself enter. Four weeks had passed since I'd crossed its threshold, and, for the first time, would do so with regret rather than accolade. The image of Father's hanging head reminded me of the throbbing in my hip, too painful to move forward or backward. Nevertheless, knowing Sarah remained feet away, I turned the knob and crossed, needing to unpack my heart and lighten the saddlebags slung over my shoulder.

Our bedroom was warm, lit by firelight. She sat at her small dressing table in her shift, arm bent at the elbow over her head brushing unbraided red rivers that parted with each stroke. The sight of her unbound my spirit from the shore.

"My good wife," I said to her reflection in the glass while leaning against the door frame, crossing my arms over my chest. She looked exhausted, dark circles sprawling under her blue eyes.

"Not virtuous or capable? Only good?" The same blue eyes shifted to my image and held me captive in the glass.

I bowed my head to her. "Would you allow me the honor of sleeping beside you tonight and every night thereafter?"

The request sounded condescending, even to me, instead of revealing my desperation. Sarah knew better than to believe me. She said, "Surely you have important matters to write. Time better spent in your study, rather than sleeping beside your good wife?" She looked out at the window's yellowing moonlight, turning her ear parallel with her soft silhouette of slumping shoulders. There was no masked coyness, just a breathy sigh, evident of her burdens. She rejected my attempt to retrieve our courtship, a memory lighter than the present one.

"I have a great deal to do tomorrow, but tonight I'd rather rest beside my good wife and delay the inevitable. The view is infinitely better."

"John, just—stop." She inhaled and shifted slightly, taking her image out of the frame. "I'm grateful you are home."

She turned in the seat and looked at me instead of my likeness. When she moved, I saw myself, dirty and broken, with hair overly long, framing severe cheekbones. I mumbled, "I hardly recognize myself."

She turned back to the mirror and tilted her head, examining her sun-blushed skin for freckles. She brushed her cheek with her hand. "Nor am I who I was. More imperfections. Tell me. The land? Does it still belong to the Creek?"

"No," I said. Haughty arrogance brought sarcasm to my lips, speaking louder than I intended. I took off my jacket. "Reporting my dreaded failure to Ross and Father is done." Then, whispering, resigned, I said, "In your face, I see no imperfection."

She crossed the room, and we breathed in one another without touching. I told her of my troubles, the Creek's significant loss, Crowwell's manipulating whisper, and now Chief Ross' revocation of my council seat, breaching each confession with jealousy, pride, disappointment, shame, and betrayal. "Speaking my sins aloud, my good wife, telling you my thoughts reveals secrets I didn't realize I'd kept."

"You knew it wouldn't be easy. Creating a nation is chaotic and brutal. The Earth began in darkness." Quoting scripture raised her faith, not mine.

Anger rose in me again. I walked past her, finding the unlit side of the room. "The fight burns my pride. Is this what Cherokee want? To carve out a purpose, hack it down to the stump, split and burn the wood in our council fires, and then regret the need to set it aflame in the first place?"

Her bare feet crossed the cold wooden planks to find my face with her warm hands, focusing her clear eyes on my watering ones. "So, there's no fight left in you? No reason to continue? Two reasons sleep across the hall. Had you had any light, you may have expected these consequences." I turned away, but she wouldn't allow it. Probing my regret for weaknesses, she questioned me. "Answer me this, what actions would you change? Would you not have helped Yoholo?"

I removed her hands from my face and rested my hanging head on her forehead. For some reason, I imagined Yoholo and Sarah in the same place. I said, "Would that you could meet him."

She was right. I would change nothing, except having to fight the battle in the first place. I pulled my necktie from one end and dropped it to the floor. "My resentment is enough to turn hot coals white. What if I can't find you in all this chaos? What if I lose myself?"

"Step back, stoke the coals. We will find one another."

I said, "The more I discover white man's hypocrisy, their manipulation, the more I fear losing this land. All I can do is rant and blaze against each new incoming threat. Still, nothing changes." Enough of this, I thought. "How are the children? How have you fared in my absence, Ani?"

We separated, and Sarah sat down again, staring into our dual reflection. "We're fine," she said. But her volume exposed her timidness, laying bare her solitude. Sarah wouldn't want to trouble me with matters she deemed trivial, but her solemnity told me there was a great deal she needed to share.

"Tell me," I said.

"Did you know that you were my first real friend?"

"Surely not. What about Harriet?"

She chuckled to herself and turned her head toward the moonlit window. "No, not her. We were together often, but she likes the sound of

Yellow Bird's Song

her own voice better than any other. You were the first to listen to me, to care what I thought. But when you're gone, it's harder to be alone, because I know what I'm missing, who I'm missing."

I journeyed the world with friends in cities near and far. She took to the trail alone, one that I vowed she'd never wander without my hand. I understood Sarah's secrets: the scar over her shoulder, the strained relationship with her mother and father, her jealousy of those she thought more outspoken than her. I watched the homespun girl I courted become a wife, a mother, more thoughtful and caring than I knew her younger self to be. Her heart expanded with patience, endlessly learning signs with Clarinda, and discovering fortitude through Rollin's constant demands for her attention. Her desire to listen to all of us endured—a vow she never broke.

But I had broken the vow to cherish her. I was away more than present, angry more than kind, talking more than I listened. I saw my face in her mirror, echoing an image of selfish guilt I found no words to articulate.

Still, she stood behind me, supporting my every endeavor, no matter her thoughts about their eccentricities. She floated like a leaf on the river, overcoming rock and falling limb, never rebellious to the current drawing her downstream. Even now, being a father, I couldn't understand how she managed such unbound veracious love she showed us all.

But underneath that, the silence she enjoyed, ground once overgrown with seedling and sprout, must feel barren. Tranquility was her luxury. Unlike the sweet-smelling trillium I once gave her, she hadn't broken the soil and lost the blossoming smile I loved. She didn't have time to plant, too busy sewing a life to sleep late under a flowering quilt stitched by her own design.

I knelt beside her, pain from my hip irrelevant, and surrounded her hands with mine. I whispered against her lips. "The heart of her husband trusts in her."[4]

Looking at those healing blue eyes, I swore another vow. "You are my good wife, Ani. My heart safely belongs in you. I have no need of spoils."[5] I rubbed the callouses on her thumbs. "You are the work of your hands, wool and flax, needle and thread. You provide our sustenance from the fields of your labor, the fruit from your hands. Your strength of arms holds our children." I laid my head on her lap, and she arched around me. "Your candle lights our path, our knowledge. And when I sit among the elders in our land, you clothe me in strength and honor." I lifted my head to hers, brushing an escaping tear away. "Many daughters become wives, but you exceed them all. Our children will call you blessed, my good wife, whose worth is far greater than strawberry rubies."[6] I whispered behind her ear, with hands weaving through the hair down her back. "Or lily-shaped sapphires."

She answered me, putting the weight of her head into my hands. "Or emeralds as big as palm fronds..." She pulled the hem of my shirt free. Warm hands pulled me closer. She whispered, "... or a golden set pearl beside violet, amethyst jewels."

I said, "The topaz of Ethiopia shall not equal it, neither shall it be valued with pure gold."[7] Sarah smiled against my cheek.

Philosopher and prophet, shaman and poet knew the remedy to a worrisome man's ills: let go of the reins and hold fast to her beating heart. Othello was right. "My life upon her faith."[8]

CHAPTER 9: BALM IN GILEAD[1]
Sarah Ridge
Ridge Land, Cherokee Nation Territory
Spring and Summer 1829

Carpenters arrived from Tennessee to improve Major Ridge's log home. Ushering in the spring, the sound of grinding saw teeth and smells of rich resin from newly seasoned lumber permeated the house. John drew the plans for second floor renovations, experimenting with architectural design, and oversaw construction. He helped build a beautiful staircase landing with three glass windows, making sure the banister rail was low enough for the children to hold.

Porches extended from each side of the house, as was the country's fashion—a plantation, not a farmer's cabin. The house centered on such a scene of plenty, two stories high with four brick fireplaces warming eight rooms, paneled with hardwood, chinked, and painted white. Thirty glass windows overlooked the budding orchard and the Oostanaula River, framed by walnut trees running beside poplars, lilies, and reeds. With its accompanying plantation, Ridge Ferry was in higher cultivation than most homes in the region.[2] Only Vann's brick mansion surpassed it.

With the aeration and planting begun, my darling Clarinda turned four. For her birthday, Vann sold John his painted mare, Equoni, for the simple price of Clarinda's kiss on his cheek. We gathered at the fence when Peter led the horse from the stable to the paddock gate for Clarinda's first ride. Sitting high atop his shoulders, Major lifted Clarinda to straddle the horse's broad back, so small atop the broad, blue-eyed horse. After mounting behind her, Major draped a leather thong holding a wooden four-hole flute over Clarinda's head. In an endearing gesture, he waved one finger and touched the whistle to her nose. *"Don't take it off, my Clarinda, so we can hear you. Always."*

John and I stood outside the paddock gate. Major looked apologetic and said, *"She can't speak commands. I thought this might do."*

Clarinda learned quickly that the more she blew, the more vibrations she felt. Major held her little frame and captured her attention, holding one finger in the air. Instantly, Clarinda understood and blew hard, piercing our ears with the sound. Then, Major heeled the horse a quarter turn around the ring and stopped. They did this for minutes, stopping and starting. Then, he held two fingers to her, and she responded, while he heeled Equoni into a trot. One whistle for a quarter turn and two for a run through the circle. The horse learned the signals as quickly as she did.

Clarinda interpreted her world with constant questions. She was a child of nature, more comfortable in barked trees than painted chairs. Often, rather than sign, she gathered by the hand me or John, Honey or Grandmother and took us to her question rather than make gestures without sight. My greatest wonder became watching her uncover answers from the fields and river. I watched her think, enthralled by her magical language, enhanced by the lack of hearing.

Mother Susannah arrived at the paddock holding toddling Rollin's tiny hand, who squealed, trying to pull away, crawling under the fence. John picked him up and put him on his shoulders. Mother Susannah protested her husband's fearlessness with Clarinda's new mare. In what, I was sure, wouldn't be the last time, she repeated her warning. *"She's too small for this, Skahtlelohskee. She needs a pony."* As soon as Mother spoke, unexpectedly, Major let go. Clarinda started and stopped Equoni with her whistle, reins, and heels.

Rollin turned two at the end of March. Not to show any favoritism to either grandchild, Major carved Rollin a wooden oxen team, sanded smooth with dull horns matching the giant beasts bringing lumber from the sawmill. Rollin loved to watch them, squealing and pointing when the oxen crossed the river ferry.

Rollin babbled more than he listened. With childhood banter in two languages, John was better equipped than I to understand his meaning. John and Rollin talked while they sat barefoot on the floor. They built towers of wooden blocks and knocked them down with the carved oxen. In shape, father and son were mirror images of one another, with a matching hairline and the same shaped feet, Rollin's toes wiggling in miniature. The two conversed about whether it might rain the next night or whether the trickster rabbit stole the otter's coat. Rollin's bilingual vocabulary grew by the day. He played beside his sister, adding her language to his others, touching his fingertips together to sign that, for one second, he'd let her hold his toy ox.

One morning in late April, Clarinda's quilt was tousled, but she wasn't tucked inside. I had little reason to panic. She and Honey must be with Mother Susannah. I grabbed my dressing gown, hefted Rollin on my hip, and we crossed the short distance to the main kitchen. I assumed I'd find Clarinda's sticky hands next to Honey kneading dough. But when Rollin and I arrived, no one was there. No one had kindled the fire in the hearth since last evening, the air stale. My stomach turned topsy-turvy with worry.

I ran outside to scan the nearby orchard. The heat from Peter's forge pulsed in waves from the open barn door. I overheard Honey's voice and

Yellow Bird's Song

Clarinda's whistles between clatters and bangs of the hammer on the anvil. Clarinda must be feeding apples to her horse. Rollin and I stopped our hurried pace and waited outside with our backs to the open barn door, listening.

The clanging stopped when Honey said, "Whatcha prayin' for? You either be singin' and shoein' or prayin' and fishin'.."

Peter chuckled and replied after a single hammer strike, "I talks to my brother all da time. Never knew a time or a tune without him."

"Where he at?"

"Drew died last fall. We 'smithy together. So's, I keep on imaginin' him carryin' all dem high notes."

"My papa used to shoe da horses, but he wouldn't sing after Mama died. He just grumble. He gone too, a few years back."

"I think it harder to pray for rain than to complain when it falls. Requires faith some people ain't got. See some only have a little cup, and they can't fill it themselves, let alone pour water to the brim for others to drink. Just who they be."

Honey changed the subject. "Let me hears you sing."

Peter said, "Promise'n you won't make fun?" I heard a tool drop to the wooden barn floor, followed by shoes scuffling on hay.

He cleared his throat. "You's ain't givin' it back, is you? Tills I sing?"

"Sure ain't." I imagined Honey's hands on her hips, holding Peter's hammer hostage.

Clarinda's whistle filled the silence in their conversation and set Peter's key like a tuning fork. His voice was deep for a man not yet twenty.

"If you can't pray like Peter
If you can't be like Paul
Go home and tell your neighbor,
He died to save us all."[3]

Peter didn't continue the hymn to its chorus. After the verse, he lofted its last syllable, and said, "Thank you, ma'am."

Honey told him, "You sings so fine. I don't sings no more. No good come from it."

"That's where you're wrong, Miss Honey. It lightens a sadness too heavy to carry alone. Even this mute child makes song, 'septin' it all be the same note."

Honey was brutally honest in two languages. Peter matched her forthrightness. Their voices enriched our daily bread, baked through—but rarely buttered.

And I continued his song, kissing Rollin's sweet head watching the peaceful sunrise. "There is a balm in Gilead to make the wounded whole.

There is a balm in Gilead to heal the sin-sick soul."[4]

Throughout the summer, Clarinda and I rode Equoni down Ross Ridge Road to visit Quatie. Her husband and mine spent the spring avoiding one another, with silence doing nothing to heal their divide. When I asked John if he minded us seeing her, he stopped what he was doing, took Rollin from me, and allowed me time.

Traveling the three miles didn't take long. We met near the bent sycamore stretching over the Oostanaula. When we arrived, Quatie floated on her back. Her shift reflected the summer sun, clinging to her upper body while spreading wide around bare toes. We undressed down to our shifts to join her in the clear water.

She shouted up the bank, "It eases the strain of his weight." Quatie insisted the growing child in her womb would be a boy, and his name would be Jacob, even though she couldn't know for certain.

"What if Jacob is a girl?" I said, holding Clarinda's hand and wading into the trickles over our calves.

Quatie dismissed my question. "Then, I will call her Rachel." She put her arms around her growing belly and replied with assurance. "But this time, I will give my husband a son, a warrior. He stills and grows strong."

"Jacob is a noble name. He fathered twelve sons, leaders of the twelve tribes of Israel."

"As will mine," Quatie said.

Clarinda pointed down the road. Honey found us. How Clarinda knew, I couldn't say.

Quatie sat in the shallows and took Clarinda to her lap while I raised my legs high to step out of the river and climb the brushy bank. When I intercepted her, Honey had tears in her eyes.

"What's wrong?" I asked. "Is someone hurt?"

"No," Honey hiccupped, "nobody hurt."

"Why are you crying?"

Honey shrugged her shoulders and wiped her tears with the back of her hand. She stared back up the road. I touched her face, and she turned back. "You don't have to tell me, Honey, but you may feel better if you do. Come to the riverside. Splash water on your face."

Honey left her dress and shoes on the shore and waded waist-deep in her shift before she stopped sniffling. Quatie released Clarinda, who floated on her back downriver toward Honey. We watched them hold their breath and dip their heads in the river.

Yellow Bird's Song

Quatie whispered, "Do you know what upset her?"

"She'll tell me in her own time."

The two returned to the shallows and floated, stretched their legs and toes on top of the water. They held hands, drifting downriver.

Honey yelled with her eyes closed to the sun. "Sarah, I ain't bad."

I shouted back. "There's nothing you could do to make me think you were."

Honey put her feet down and pushed Clarinda back, who splashed her way back to me. "When I tell you why I's cryin', I don't want you to be prayin' for my soul, thinkin' I've grown into some evil womern, cause I ain't. Since you were here, and there weren't nothin' to do for a time, Peter and I went fishin'. He'd caught a big 'un, and we got excited. Then, dat man grab my face and kiss me!" Honey blurted. "I cried the whole way here, not knowin' what else to do."

Quatie laughed, and asked, "Why would kissing him make you evil?"

Honey mumbled, holding her chin down, "'Cause Peter don't know." She corrected herself. "Doesn't know."

Quatie responded quickly, "What doesn't he know?"

Honey whispered, ashamed. "That I can't give him no babies."

Quatie tilted her head toward the sun and laughed. "Kissing won't give you a baby." Then she wrapped her arms around Jacob, or Rachel, growing inside her.

"I knows dat. Just don't want Peter expectin' more dan I can give, not after them men take me a few years back." Honey scrunched up her eyes.

I put Clarinda in Quatie's lap, waded over to Honey, and wrapped my arms around her.

Quatie asked from behind me, shifting her playful tone to one more serious. "What men?"

Honey shrugged her shoulders and looked to me to find words in her stead.

"White men took Honey a few years ago. Since she was so young when it happened, after her injuries, she may not be able to have children."

Honey said, "Theys took you too, Sarah."

"I know, sweet girl." I took her face in my hands. "Look at me. We survived." She buried her face in my chest. I said, "You're safe. We're safe."

Honey looked up. "But I can't be marrying Peter."

Quatie lightened our somber mood. "Why do you think you have to marry Peter? Because he kissed you?"

I laughed, too, against all my efforts to hold back. I said, "Honey, you don't have to marry Peter, but if you love him, that's entirely different."

"I don't have nothin' to compare to how I's feels. He talk to me like no one else do—close like. Feel him walkin' up behind me 'fore I see him. See him grinnin' when he thinks I don't be lookin'. I'd know his singin' from a barn full of donkeys brayin' and horses neighin'."

Quatie said, "I should hope so. Come sit beside me. My mother and I are of the Bird Clan and mate for life. Sometimes promises come before the feelings. If you're lucky, feelings come before the words, so the promises have something to hold on to." Then Quatie's eyes became unfocused, and she looked behind her. "And then, other times, there are only a few words and no feelings at all."

Honey waded to the opposing shoreline and sat on the bank, gripping her knees, making a tent of her shift. She said, "I want the talkin' and the listen', the singin' and the smilin'." She looked at a rope swinging from a nearby tree branch. "Tender like," she said. "A love that, in time, don't unravel but tighten da knots."

I said, "My mother didn't think it was right for me to love John so much. She forced our separation because she couldn't understand what she saw. She couldn't imagine how love grew between two people so different. So, she sent John home and ordered me to New Haven to stay with my grandparents. It cost us two years of heartbreak to convince her otherwise."

Quatie tilted her head. She said, "That wasn't the way with Ross and me. I was a widow with an orphaned daughter. He married me because I was Cherokee, loaning him my family's heritage. Ross needed a Cherokee wife to give him Cherokee children. Many white men marry Cherokee women. He could provide for us. We made a good match."

She was right. There were many mixed couples here where the husbands were white. But there were only two marriages I knew of where Cherokee men had married white women: Elias and Harriet, John and me. God knows John and I suffered man's judgment for binding our lives together. Elias and Harriet too.

Quatie said, "Many marriages have been built on less. I must love Ross now."

I let her remark go unanswered, thinking she lost her sentiment in translation. Like John, Quatie thought in Cherokee.

Honey spoke up in our silence. "Well, I got them feelin's, but no promise."

I said, "You've got more than you think if Peter kissed you. I wanted John to kiss me long before he ever did."

Quatie remarked with near sarcasm, "All I want is for Ross to want to kiss me." Then she continued, quieter, talking to herself, "Things will

Yellow Bird's Song

change after Jacob is born."

Honey asked, "What should I do? Should I tell Peter 'bout what Lovett and Whitmore did? What if he thinks I wanted dem men to do those things? Mother Susannah said never to tell no one."

I asked, surprised, "The shame was theirs alone, Honey. Was that his name? Lovett?"

Honey said, "I'll never forget that man's name." She spat, "The one with the greazy yellow hair hiding evil eyes under the brim of dat hat."

I cupped water in my hand and splashed my face, washing clean the smell of the man's whiskey breath returning to my nose.

Quatie swam behind me. "You all right?"

I took a deep breath when she touched me, fading my memory's smell. I said, "None of what happened was your fault, Honey. Tell Peter when you trust him enough. You'll know then that he cares for you despite all that happened. But if you don't want him to kiss you again, you must tell him that, too."

Honey looked beyond the trees. "Don't seem right to make him think one thing and gets another."

"Honey, if God wants you and Peter together, you will be. And if He wants to give you a child, He will. It is a truth I trust."

"Maybe Peter be prayin' and singin' for me, and I don't even know." She settled the matter enough. "All right with you if I take Clarinda home? If my hands are busy talkin' to her, Peter won't ask me questions. I's have to be thinkin' 'bout what I wants to say."

I spoke aloud and signed. "Tell Papa I'm with Queen Quatie and will be home soon."

Quatie laughed. "Cherokee don't have queens; we have blessed women, war women."

I said, "Remember you told her about the bees? It's her name for you."

Honey helped Clarinda climb the bank and twisted the bottom of their shifts to release the water before dressing again. The afternoon was so warm, they'd be dry before reaching the house. Honey and Clarinda held hands and passed out of sight while Quatie and I floated in the cool water.

How might I explain to Quatie what Honey only hinted at? She'd be curious, as would I in the same situation.

I said, "Let's swim where it is deep." Our heads rose above the surface. She could stand. I was on my toes, treading water. "John avoids bringing it up for fear of upsetting me. Avoiding the subject doesn't help me like he thinks it does."

Quatie said, "Men are too busy to take our thoughts into account."

John never hesitated to ask for my thoughts. Perhaps Ross was not the same.

Quatie asked, "What happened?"

"No one knows how old Honey is. I imagine she's fourteen or fifteen now, but when the Man in the Hat, Lovett, took her, she was a tiny thing, with blossoms in her hair and a father who thought her more a nuisance than a daughter. Her Cherokee mother died when she was young.

"She followed some white men singing in the woods, too curious for her own good. She was gone an afternoon and a night before we realized she was lost. John and Major were away, so Arch and I set out to find her.

"We found her miles from home, bound, beaten, and raped by three white men transporting whiskey across Cherokee territory. Arch's horse wasn't enough to trade for her life, but I sealed the deal. They released Honey's ropes and bound them to my wrists." I showed her the scars, lifting my hands above the water's surface. She reached out and ran her hand along the indentations in my skin.

I said, "Lovett said he would trade me and the child growing inside me for whiskey with McIntosh. He dragged me behind a horse for miles. I freed myself from the ropes and hid in a cave. Arch brought Honey home and waited for John, Elias, and Major. The four of them tracked the horses and wagon to find me."

Quatie asked, "I don't need to ask how they got you free."

"I didn't see them kill the men. I heard it. Afterward, John called to me through the maze of that cave. When I reached him, he had blood on his hands. When we passed the bodies..." I closed my eyes. "Clarinda was born deaf four months later." Suddenly paranoid, I swam away from her, watching downriver. No one was there. I turned back, admitting a never-spoken guilt. "Clarinda's muteness is my fault. Mother Susannah warned me not to go, but there was no one else."

Quatie was quiet when she climbed out of the water and wiped her face with a cloth from her bag. She faced me. "Honey would be dead if you hadn't gone. You did nothing wrong, except have a heart too big. The Great Spirit gave Clarinda, and you, what you both could manage. Your men followed my people's Blood Law. A life for a life, as your Old Testament says. Although if anyone told the Georgian Guard, they would convict John, his father, and Arch. It would make no difference how right they were."

Quatie's face was kind, radiating light from the inside. Her eyes didn't hold pity or blame. From them, she didn't judge me but understood what Honey and I endured and survived. I followed her, dragging heavy limbs through the water, but my mind was lighter for having told someone. Our shifts clung together when we embraced and squeezed the water from our

Yellow Bird's Song

hair before dressing.

She touched my hair again, as she had done the day we met. "Like copper in the sunlight. Even when it is wet."

I touched hers in return. "Like onyx, smooth, holding every color underneath."

She mounted her horse and called over her shoulder. "Meet me next week? Same day, same time."

"I will," I promised, and we each went down the Ross Ridge Road, traveling in opposite directions. On the way, I filled my pockets with cottonwood buds, rich in resin, to make John a healing balm for his hip. With sticky fingers and full pockets, I sang the hymn where only Jesus listened. "There is a balm in Gilead that makes the wounded whole. There is a balm in Gilead that heals the sin-sick soul."[5]

At summer's end, Mother Susannah woke us in the hours before dawn. When John answered the door, Mother Susannah said, "Quatie is laboring with the child. It is too soon. Her eldest daughter sent for us both. Hurry."

From Quatie's kitchen, I waited through the sounds of bearing and birthing. Quatie's youngest, Jane, sat on my lap. The next morning, Mother Susannah opened the door, releasing Quatie's quiet sobs, held silent behind wooden walls. Mother Susannah held a bundle in her arms and passed the cry-less child to me, face covered in a blanket. Rachel Ross was stillborn in the light of day.

Quatie was not well. She sat straight up, sweat dripping from her face, struck to stillness with the unfathomable emptiness in her once full mother's heart.

I walked outside and looked down the road, expecting to see Ross' horse gallop in, to be by his wife's side. But Ross never arrived. Standing in the doorway, I uncovered the baby's face, eyes closed as if she were a porcelain doll painted in colors too light. I touched her cheek and placed my hand on her still chest. I covered her face again and felt my womb, knowing another heaven-sent soul grew under my fingertips.

For Rachel, four women mourned quietly at dawn. Quatie's body would heal, but I prayed God's healing balm over her spirit.

September announced that summer was through. Quatie recovered, although she tired easily. The last time I visited her, we walked among her peacocks, and she shared how distant Ross had become since Rachel's loss. The father left the mother to grieve in solitude. I couldn't imagine enduring such a heart-wrenching ache alone. After Rachel's loss, time released the tensions between Ross and John, and they talked instead of walking in opposite directions. The more they spoke, John's empathy for Ross' loss brought his forgiveness.

While I hung clean clothes over the line, I overheard Major speaking to John, leaving the back door open to the house. Major's calloused hands stopped my chore. John dropped the shirt back into the basket. Major Ridge turned me by the shoulders to face him. He cleared his throat and spoke, with John's voice overlapping his father's sentences.

"It was you, Sarah, who convinced me—on the ride home from Ross' house nearly a year ago. I heard your heart; it sounded like my son's. Last year, he requested land to improve, to build a home for your growing family. But I told him no. With these improvements, I realized how selfish my reasons were. I could not bear to part with Rollin, Clarinda, John, or you, daughter. Joy fills my life to care for each of you.

"With the profit from last year's cotton crop and the money my son earned translating for the Creek, there was enough to build you a fine home, a mirror of your family's house in Cornwall. Near a running creek, the house sits atop a hill on valley land near my acreage, with ample room to graze horses and cattle. Mountains surround Ridge Valley. To the east, the morning sun streaks the horizon with lavender and crimson.

"With my hands, I built you the most pleasing kitchen porch facing the west, so you can read to my grandchildren before they sleep. Like President Jefferson's Monticello, John has shelves for his law books, a place to negotiate with future American presidents. And for you, my daughter, behind your kitchen stands a hothouse to grow flowers instead of tears."

He signed, releasing the sentiment as he let go of my arms, and grasped the beaded multicolored sheath crossing his chest. *"You've shed enough since coming here."*

Because I knew John, knew him to his core, his emotion stood behind responsibility and obligation. John said, *"There are no words for the honor you've given us, Father. We will make the land improvements profitable."*

He took us both close to his chest with an honest embrace, gripping us with his solid forearms. *"You both make our lives profitable. That is more than enough."*

Too maudlin for such a warrior, Major left us shocked. He crisscrossed through the row in the apple orchard, passing Honey and Peter, who separated their joined hands, putting space between them as he

Yellow Bird's Song

approached.

Major shouted over his shoulder. *"With this gift, I will send ten servants to seed and harvest the fields and assist Sarah in maintaining the house."*

John repeated Major's offer. Before he could escape hearing, I returned his shout. "I will own no one." I sensed John's surprise, but I continued. "They can come if they choose. I welcome anyone's help, but those who come must be free to make the choice themselves."

Before turning my words to Cherokee, John hesitated for an unnecessary moment. His father stopped walking down the path and looked back. Then, with brisk and vast strides, he returned to my side but said nothing. Instead, he reached for my arms, turning me gently by the shoulders toward his cotton fields.

Ridge slaves moved in a silent dance, hearing music coming from the rolling brown dirt that was spotted white with cotton buds. Bent brown backs curtsied and bowed, adorned with seamed straps of burlap sacks full of the fruits of their labor. He showed me just how many hands were needed to do such work.. I understood but would not retreat or cower. He studied me, nodded once, and returned to the barn.

When he walked away, John wrapped his arms around me, lifting me above the ground. He whispered in my hair, "No one else could have convinced him as you just did."

He set me on my feet. I said, "I wish I could talk to my father the same way."

"You will. There will come a time when you must speak so to him."

I said, "Take me home," and grabbed his hand.

Honey approached and took my other hand. She said, "If dem babies is comin', I'm goin' too." I stared at our connection, the contrast of color between our interwoven grasps.

Peter came to John's side and shook his outstretched palm. He said, "This what freedom feel like?" He took Honey's hand.

Our circle was tight.

Peter lifted his head and closed his eyes to the afternoon sun. He sang, "There is a balm in Gilead to make the wounded whole. There is a balm in Gilead to heal the sin-sick soul."[7]

That evening, from the west-facing porch of *Tantarara*, Running Waters, I wove my hands under John's arms and rested my head against his back. He wrapped his hands around mine.

Underneath such rose and gold peace, in colors blended by cloud-like feathers, my faith renewed. The sky's refrain echoed the promise of the land, in a chord overtoned by a passing angel choir.

CHAPTER 10: IT MATTERS
Rollin Ridge
Nevada Territory
September 1850

Disappointment resonated through my monotone. "Nothing ever changes, Wacooli. The man's words may be friendly enough, but what he's charging for provisions makes my eye twitch."

Wacooli and I paced some distance away from Aeneas, who was jawing with the post operator, a man named Jamison, bartering over the price of flour, ridiculous at a dollar and a half. Situated on the Salmon Trout Riverbank, we reached Jamison's trading post after our starved stretch across the desert.

No one had been awake to see us arrive, and thankfully so. Traveling the last twenty miles, I watched Wacooli's face turn from its accustomed brown to sand's muted and dusty shade. All three of us appeared the same, stone-faced from fright, stiff in the saddle, emerging from some Greek and barren Hell, complete with mirages foreshadowing our demise. Whether from dirt or shock, my hair stood straight from my scalp like it was riddled with porcupine quills. Wacooli could have solved long division problems by scratching the numbers in the sweat-caked dirt on his arms. While removing his clothes, Aeneas' pants stood up without his legs inside to keep them vertical. Arriving so late, the only thing we could do was douse in the river and wash sand and smell downstream.

Aeneas tipped his hat to Jamison and joined us as Wacooli took truth to words. "We'll have to sell the mules, or we won't have enough to purchase provisions to get us across the Sierra Nevada mountains, Aeneas."

Wacooli's directness was hard-cracked mud, and his candor was one reason I invited him on this expedition. Wacooli's name meant "where the young thing was found." Peter found Wacooli outside of Fort Mimms near Indian territory. He took the abandoned child into his arms and transformed his grief from losing Honey into love for the child found among the rushes. When I was eleven, the two arrived at Honey Creek, having made the last sorrowful leg of the trail together. Wacooli grew tall beside us, a herd of eight siblings, counting him among our ranks. Wacooli and Aeneas were both seventeen, stuck in the middle of the lot. He fit right in; none of us were white.

Aeneas shook his head, not giving me time to form a thought, let alone argue with him. "Rollin, sell your mule instead of mine. We sold my filly

Yellow Bird's Song

in Salt Lake. It's your turn."

"I will, but I doubt my old mule will yield us over eight dollars. She's swaybacked and bites more than she carries." It was the truth. The only thing I'd regret by selling her was that my horse's load would increase by her absence, slowing us all down.

In Aeneas' heart, he must have known we needed more money. His protest was wasted, but he gave it, regardless. "I don't wanna sell my jenny," he whined. "I helped with her birth, with my arm up to my shoulder inside her mama." That same arm smacked his hat on his pant leg, freeing hidden dust just to emphasize his point.

Wacooli put his hand on his hip, leaned on one leg, and looked between Aeneas' pretty face and mine, both hard with care and weary tired. "Both of you should sell your mules. We've crossed the desert; there are mountains in front of us. We won't survive long enough to make it to California if we don't sell all we can afford to let go. Besides, I'm not cutting and hauling grass again for those beasts." At that moment, I thought how Mama should have renamed Wacooli. Frank was more suited to his nature.

I squinted between the brim of my hat and my bushy beard, looking back to the nemesis of our debate. I offered the only consolation I could. "Jamison told me he's a Mormon."

Aeneas replied with exhausted demand, "What difference does that make? We're half Cherokee. Wacooli's black." Angry and frustrated, Aeneas tromped a toddler's tantrum over to the wagon and unhitched my nag and his beloved jenny. Both mules bawled in protest.

Wacooli and I followed him, and I put my hand on Aeneas' shoulder in consolation. "Think, Aeneas. Jamison should give us a decent price for the mules, being a Christian man and all." But Aeneas scowled. I inferred he wasn't convinced.

Nevertheless, Wacooli continued to try and persuade him after Aeneas handed me the reins. The Lord only knows what Aeneas would say of me after I was out of earshot. Despite Wacooli's vocabulary, it still might not be large enough to encourage Aeneas' forgiveness after forcing such a sacrifice.

Jamison's misshapen hat sat on his head, a pointed end to his body's vertical line, perpendicular against the vast striped canyons paralleling the horizon. I said, "Excuse me, Mister Jamison? My brother said you might be looking for fair trade—our mules in exchange for provisions."

"You and your brother Indian?" Jamison questioned. "I know you aren't related to that slave."

"We're half Cherokee," I countered. "The other gentleman with us is our brother and a free man." His question surprised me and didn't.

He blew air from his nose, deciding he didn't care enough to ask questions. Instead, he talked about only what his eyes could see. "That bluff over yonder..." Jamison pointed a long finger to a jutting rock extending above and beyond the river underneath. "Called Susan's bluff. Last year, a band of Indians killed Susan and her entire family. Scalped her brother, Mike. Gruesome. Indians stole the family's livestock. She survived for a time, but then she threw herself off that rock there. Guess she thought she'd rather decide her fate than be raped and murdered by those Indians. So, folks named it after her."[1]

"That's a shame," I replied. Aeneas' jenny bumped me from behind with her nose, causing me to lose my balance. "How old was she?" I asked, trying to be respectful of the dead.

"'Bout your age, by the looks of you. How old are you? Twenty?" Jamison looked me up and down as if he would only offer six dollars for my own ragged carcass.

Tired of his judgment, I pressed more present matters than the history of the landscape—or tracing my family's genealogy. "Twenty-three. If it matters to you, my white half is asking if you're willing to trade; my Cherokee half wishes no ill will to anyone."

Then Jamison's eyes fell on Kell's bowie knife hanging at my side. After noticing his stare, I pulled my hands away from my body, implying I wouldn't use the blade to gut him, no matter how much he charged for flour.

"Well, it matters," was all he said.

Then, his eyes lifted to my face, studying me to find my mother's Irish skin. He must have seen her in my pale eyes because he took both sets of reins from my hand and walked down the slope in front of me, sliding on pebbles and stones and nearly losing his footing.

Once at the bottom, he looked at both mules from nose to rump. Finally, he offered more than I predicted, a surprising eleven dollars for my mule and thirty-five for Aeneas' jenny. He kept to himself what he thought to propose as compensation for the three ragged souls standing before him.

"We'll take it," I replied. Despite my surprise, Jamison was still a stingy jackass. The irony was he only offered more money, so we'd buy additional sacks of his flour.

We walked across the planked floor of the trading post counter in single-filed silence. Jamison wrote our credit in his ledger. "What's your name?" he asked without looking up while dipping the pen in ink. He poised his hand to write, but I hadn't yet answered. I thought to say,

Yellow Bird's Song

"Cheesquatalawny," just to watch him squirm to spell it. Instead, I said, "Ridge. Rollin Ridge."

He rested the pen's point in the book and closed the ledger to record his next dishonest transaction. Then, finally, he stretched out his hand to shake and seal the deal.

Defiant, I didn't offer mine. I saw it as in-kind reciprocation.

Insulted, Jamison remarked out of the side of his mouth, "Son, shake hands at the end of a deal. Didn't your father teach you that?"

I figured since he'd printed our name in his book, being polite was no longer required. "He did. Don't call me son. As you said, it matters."

We found out from friendly travelers on the road to California that Jamison sold the stock he bought off starving travelers for ten times the purchased price. I wasn't saying what those Indians did was justified—stealing livestock, murdering that family, or taking that girl, Susan. But I can't fathom how what Jamison was doing was any more honest than Indian thievery.[2]

Wacooli loaded up our supplies while Aeneas said goodbye to his jenny mule. I touched the broken seal of Papa's letter when I tucked what little money remained into my saddlebags. After Jamison's arrogance and distrust, I tasted the same sourness Papa must have experienced arguing with arrogant white men.

From an entry in 1829, Papa's journal recanted Georgia's new laws. No Cherokee could claim injustice against any white Georgian hell-bent on stealing our people's gold. Cherokee couldn't refute violent claims in a Georgia court, despite the crime happening on Cherokee's legal ground. In the same vein, no Cherokee could claim any injustice against Ross, not without grave repercussions for daring to blemish his reputation.

Papa and I traveled similar paths, twenty years apart, from opposing sides of North America.

Hell yes, it mattered. No matter how far west we traveled, white men were still swindling.

CHAPTER II: WHITE MAN'S FLIES
John Ridge
New Echota and Turkeytown, Cherokee Nation Territory
September 1829

Our nation's continued liberty and defiance stirred a swarm of white man's flies, a name given to honeybees that followed white settlers with stingers more savage than any queen-less horde. White man's hum grew increasingly louder, broadcast in print from every newspaper in the South, sung aloud by every stage driver from Hiawassee to Savannah:

"All I want in this creation,
Is a pretty little wife and a big plantation,
Way up yonder in Cherokee Nation."[1]

As if the influx of white families were not enough, they'd discovered gold in a northern township. A young Cherokee hunter uncovered a shining *dalonige* rock and sold it to a white peddler, unknowing of its value. From then on, the fertile Appalachian Mountains barely slowed the wave of pilfering white men seeking fortune from luck rather than plow.

My office in New Echota, one I shared with a fellow attorney, Xander McCoy, was a single room encased in an exterior of white clapboard siding. We faced our desks together, with candles on opposite sides, so neither had to move to see the opposing friend's face. That morning, I put down my quill and rubbed my temples with both hands, smearing ink on one side. My head ached. I hadn't eaten breakfast before departing Running Waters in the early morning hours. Nevertheless, I was eager to refute Governor Forsyth's report from Georgia's joint assembly. Xander must have risen early as well, already seated in his accustomed position across from me.

Xander reclined in his chair, placing spotless boots atop his desk. A member of the Long Hair Clan, son to a Cherokee mother, Xander was quite cognizant of appearances. He wore a starched white shirt and cravat, hair striped with temple's gray combed away from his face. Most of Xander's fortune came from his wife's labors and heritage, daughter of Cherokee Chief Charles Hicks. Xander's appointment as clerk to the National Council was undisputed, marrying both daughter and position. With the McCoy family's large inn and stable for travelers, his accumulated wealth increased proportionately to his wife's work and family inheritance, not necessarily from his legal or business prowess.

Xander smirked, licking his thumb to rub a spot from his boots only he could see. "John, why are you holding your head?"

109

Yellow Bird's Song

"It aches, and because of it, my arguments fall apart. The more I build, the less convinced I am of any of my debates holding any water against the Georgia legislature."

Sunlight poured into the windows in our office. Since the day was warm, I rose to open the door and left it ajar to rid the office of the smell of candle-burned wax. Fresh air might do this headache some good. I had only just returned to my chair when a briskly walking Elias left his print shop, darting past his own house, to shadow our open doorway.

"Good morning, Elias," Xander said, with the nonchalance of a man who didn't need to work for bread.

Elias' dander rose with the newspaper in his hand. "Forsyth's arrogance knows no end. No Cherokee can testify against a white man? What if they forge our signatures on deeds? Sell the land out from under us without our consent? Have they forgotten what the British did to the colonists? Forced oppression with no representation or recourse?"

I shoved a chair with my foot. It screeched and skidded across the floor. Elias needed to sit down for this conversation.

Xander placed his hands behind his neck. "From it, I read nothing of note." Both of us knew Xander's casualness was a façade. This morning, he'd poured over the Athens newspaper as diligently as I had.

I murmured, "Hypocritical premises, all." I didn't need to speak loudly to this receptive audience; my pounding head wouldn't allow it, whatever passions I felt.

"What will be the cost of our liberty?" Elias asked.

Xander looked through the gap between his crossed ankles to stare at Elias. "More money than is saved in our treasury." Xander, always eager for lighthearted matters, said, "Does Harriet think you're handsome in that apron? As the mind wanders…"

In haste, Elias untied the strings at his back, pulling it over his bushy black hair, folding the apron's smudges on themselves. He had ink stains across his taunt forearms, freckled like the young fawn of his Cherokee namesake, Buck. Undaunted by Xander's sarcasm, Elias asked, "Must we sell our land to be free?"

Xander stood to stretch his back. For most of the morning, he'd hunched over his candle, reading the source of our collective dismay. "Georgia called the Cherokee matter 'gloomy'. After reading that, I put the article aside." Xander sighed, and his spine popped.

Elias asked, "If we don't belong to the land now, what else could we do to earn that distinction?"

I said, "Didn't the Puritans claim domain over the Massachusetts coast? They believed living on the ground meant that they owned it."

110

Xander chuckled to himself. "I've decided, John. I'll call you Socrates. Promise me you'll keep in mind what happened to that man. You ask too many questions our opponents have no answers to." He grabbed his pipe before winding through the queries tossed over the disarray of chairs. Xander swirled his brown coat behind his back, replaced the pipe in his lips, and put his hat over his graying head. He headed to the door, assumedly to visit his wealthy wife before our departure this afternoon to Turkeytown. My eyes hurt when Xander's retreat renewed the sunlight after he passed.

Elias shrugged his shoulders and raised his eyebrows, as if I had some answer he hadn't yet considered. I didn't.

I said, "They founded America on the same principle. Free families in an independent country united to form a nation. In that case, shouldn't they possess liberty, empire, over the country they inhabit, mindful of the area of their dominion?"[2]

"When can a nation take lawful possession of a country?" Elias wondered what it would take for Georgia to accept our residency as dominion. "We were here first. Is it not a child's argument, John?"

"Our ancestors lie in the ground, interred, to prove our prior claim. It is a disgrace to steal their bones." No one in hearing would question that argument's validity.

Elias offered me a hand up from my chair. "Governor Forsyth would say how the earth should benefit living men. The dead turn no profit."

"You mean living, white men," I countered.

"What's wrong? You look pale." He smugly chuckled at his irony.

"I'm hungry is all. My head pounds."

"Come home with me. Harriet will have warm bread by now. Baby Eleanor wakes the house early."

We walked in silence, single file, down wagon ruts in the road to Elias' home on the edge of New Echota. His wife stood on the porch with Eleanor on her hip. From the bulge under her apron, she was in the family way again. She held a closed fist out to Elias, eager to return its contents. He took her small offering and kissed her hand. He put whatever she gave him in his pocket. Then, she passed their daughter to his awaiting arms.

Harriet retreated, scolding playfully, "You lost an 'S' and some other letter I don't know. Stop leaving font in your pockets all the time; you'll misspell in two languages. Good morning, John. Hungry?"

Elias whispered, leaning down when I climbed his stairs. "Wives can't let husbands lose anything. They see it as personal failure." Elias spoke his sarcastic remark only after Harriet was far enough away not to hear.

I followed Elias toward the dining room at the back of the house. He

Yellow Bird's Song

made faces at his daughter's open eyes while asking, "How much land did the Treaty of Paris allow Georgia? I dare say it is scarcely half as large as what Georgia claims domain over now."

We sat at the dining table as Harriet returned from the kitchen with teacups and saucers, all safely wedged between the fingers of one hand. She left and returned with her teapot, steam emanating from the spout.

I sat opposite him at the table. "The Cherokee were under British command at the time of that treaty. Will we never live past the choice to fight with them against the Continentals?"

Harriet accepted Elias' exchange of baby Eleanor, raising the child like an offering. "Doesn't matter. We'd suffer the same fate now, even if we'd worn blue coats instead of red."

"And what fate is that?" Harriet asked, hearing only a part of the conversation.

"Occupation." Elias' bitter word chilled the tea in our cups.

Elias repoured more of Harriet's blessed reprieve, and I sipped before responding. I said, "All I can say is that the 'gloomy matter' will happen, no matter how many arguments we offer in contradiction."

Immediately, my thoughts traveled to what should be Chief Ross' impediment to Georgia's claim. He was the man whose job it was to refute them. I said, with earnest hope, "Ross will not allow it to happen. None of us will stand idly by..."

Harriet interrupted me, placing a wooden cutting board of sliced bread and a small bowl of butter on the table.

I continued, "Indians secured peace with Washington's administration by treaty, a guarantee of lands, and adoptive measures to promote both civilizations. Great Britain lost any rights to the Indians at that moment. Doesn't it go without saying, if Indians are incapable of making treaties, signatures on previous ones would have been rejected long before now?" I pulled a piece of bread away, dipped it in the tea, and ate, although so many questions still lay on my stomach like swallowed rocks.

Elias asked a rhetorical question. "And, have we become more violent or peaceable during the last half-century?"

Placing baby Eleanor in a cradle in the corner, Harriet drew a chair from under the table beside Elias. Then she sighed, flustered by absentmindedness, and grabbed a jar of preserves from her apron pocket. She set it on the table. "Don't eat plain bread, John. From the looks of you, you need the sweetness."

Elias layered butter before taking ample preserves, spreading them from crust to crust. "Is it possible that Georgia has fallen from the exalted virtue of her ancestors, believing might is right?"

"Thou shall not covet thy neighbor's goods," Harriet whispered. Then, struck by nervousness, she offered, "Would they overtake us by force?" Elias leaned back in his chair and shifted his eyes to his newborn child asleep in the room's corner.

"Depends on Jackson. He needs Congress to vote for war," I said and followed Harriet's advice for jam. "Elias, you ask me what our liberty will cost?" I chewed, swallowed, and took a deep breath. "Land. Avarice has destroyed man throughout the black catalog of infamy. Men like Benedict Arnold..."

"Judas Iscariot," Elias grabbed his wife's hand.

"Perhaps Georgia's Governor Forsyth will join their ranks," I said.

Elias replied, "Well, I have not lost my patriotism and virtue as to fall before such a bribe."

"How many ways can we say, 'Not one more foot of land'?" I recalled my father's words at '23's council fire, confronting another traitor we should add to our catalog, Creek Chief William McIntosh.

I said, "I must get back. We will leave soon for Turkeytown. Jackson's Major Eaton will be there. Colonel Hugh Montgomery plans to make introductions." I stood with a slight nod of gratitude to Harriet, who remained seated.

Elias stood to shake my hand over the table. "Finish the argument, John. I'll print it."

"I was working on it when you barged in this morning, asking all your questions." Then, feeling better, I said, "Thank you, Harriet. My head pain is nearly gone."

Elias delayed my exit from his door with his voice shouting down the hall. "Sign it Socrates. It will take away their ad hominem rebuttal if they don't know who you are."

I opened his door and smiled, looking at the trade and transactions of the bustling New Echota. Then I stepped aside as Reverend Sam entered the Boudinot home with his arms full of Bible and parchment. We nodded a greeting as I held Elias' door open for him.

Chief Ross and Father stepped into my office shortly after I returned to work. To be on time for tomorrow evening's meeting, we'd need to ride hard between villages this afternoon, spend the evening rough, and at daybreak follow the Coosa on horseback west to Turkeytown.

Xander was late. But refusing to delay our departure, we mounted without him. Father commented on how *"Xander knew the way"* and galloped ahead, eager to renew his acquaintance with Eaton, now President Jackson's appointee.

We walked our horses into every circle of every occupied village along

Yellow Bird's Song

the way, persuading citizens to resist Indian Agents' sly temptations: large lump sums for land improvements.

Father's grand entrance gathered the women first. Their husbands and brothers followed closely behind. Father gained their eyes and bowed to Ross to begin his speech.

Ross recited the same words each time. "First, men in military coats will offer you gold, an amount to exceed the profit gained from years of corn harvests."

Father interjected, *"But the coin comes at a steep cost. You and your families must move West, away from family and clan, and travel the direction of the setting sun, never to return."* Each warning, each seed of defiance, planted by Ross' presence, fertilized by Father's eloquent words, created a tangible sprout of resistance, uniting a people.

Xander joined us to hear the last speech at dusk, remarking on the gathering crowds. He said, "No matter their poverty or class, progressive or traditional, they cry out—defiant."

After leaving the village circles, we heard whooping war cries, loud enough to be recorded by newspapermen in Milledgeville, repeated to Savannah's coastal plains. Cherokee raised bow and tomahawk, and shouted, *"We will not move!"*

My father sat between Ross and me around our evening fire. I asked, "What kind of man is Eaton?"

Ross looked over at me to answer, "Link my words, so Major fully understands, yes?" I nodded to confirm I would, even though many stories lost their drama in translation.

Ross continued, "Let's just say gaining land is the single topic Eaton feels most comfortable discussing. I met him years ago, before we both served General Jackson against the Red Sticks, although I doubt that he knew it was me he met."

He told the beginning of his tale to the fire, staring across the flame to an empty spot, an absent fifth party.

"I couldn't have been much older than you when it happened. Kalsatee, a linkster, and another, a slave, stocked my longboat. We set out to trade west down the Tennessee River. We hit rapids at Dead Man's Eddy, the Suck. After days awake trying to navigate the rough currents, we stopped to trade the longboat for a keelboat—easier to steer. We broke our backs, switching the cargo from one boat to another. But it could have been worse."

"*It always gets worse,*" Father remarked with disembodied wisdom, faceless under his hat.

Ross continued. "I didn't know so at the time, but a band watched us travel from the shoreline. I couldn't see them, but one distinctive voice said, 'Damn my soul if those two aren't Indians.'"

Xander asked, "Loaded with so much cargo, surely they intended to rob the boat."

Ross said, "I lied to the men on shore, said my companions were Spaniards." He dug his heels further into the dirt and leaned forearms against his knees. "I thought none would be the wiser—until the men on shore asked to hear each man speak Spanish."

Father's hat spoke again. "*See? Worse.*"

"My slave spoke Spanish, but our translator, Kalsatee, could not appease them. Understand, many tribes sided with the British at the start of the war. But I rather doubted they would assess Kalsatee's loyalty before deciding whether to kill him. And since we could only move downstream, I anticipated an ambush."

I said, "As anyone would."

Ross continued, "I steered the rudder to the opposing shore and sent Kalsatee on foot to follow, traveling across land alone to meet us at the trading post. I passed as a white man. They'd have taken no notion of my servant. But Kalsatee had little chance of survival if the men boarded our boat."

I asked, "Did Kalsatee arrive?"

Ross said, "He did. The man walked thirty miles on foot. I can see his face as clearly now as when I asked him to leave."[3]

That was who Ross stared at across the flames.

Ross shook the image from behind his eyes. "I believe it was Eaton who led those men. When I returned the following year on horseback, near those same rapids, I met John Eaton on his way to meet General Jackson. There was something familiar about the man's voice."

I couldn't stop my thoughts. "If so, that explains Jackson's choice of Eaton for the appointment, his proven agent on the ground."

Father removed his hat, laying it in the nearby dirt. "*A conniving, insistent man Eaton is. John, tomorrow, link my words exactly and watch his face. Tell me your impressions when we retire in the evening. I trusted Jackson at Horseshoe Bend and joined his ranks to triumph over a common enemy. But now, sitting across the table from his man, Eaton, I cannot say I expect the same mutual regard.*"

"*I will.*" His reminder was unnecessary, and it stung, swelling my pride already stretched thin.

Yellow Bird's Song

Father, Ross, and Xander fell asleep. I lay on my side and watched the fire dwindle beside the snoring men. So, by his own admission, Ross denied Kalsatee, shunned a fellow Cherokee to lonesome cold, and placed his life in danger because he feared some scorching words from shore. To Ross, was the cargo worth more than Kalsatee's life? Or instead, was he saving himself, pretending to be a white man with no Cherokee connection?

Turkeytown's only inn was rectangular, with two second-story staircases built on the exterior to keep the proprietor's property taxes low. After boarding our horses, we entered the tavern's dining room. Pewter chandeliers lit a white woman wearing a striped skirt, tied in knots at her knees, delivering drinks to blue backs guarding their cups.

Colonel Hugh Montgomery, a plantation owner on the Chattahoochee and pro-removal Indian Agent for Jackson, sat in a Windsor chair across from a man, assumedly Major John Eaton. Both men puffed cigars. Sprawled coins piled in the center of the table. Each man held four playing cards close to their vests with one card facedown. Neither looked up from their hands when our quartet entered the inn, even after Father had to bend low to pass through the doorway and avoid knocking his head.

Eaton won the hand and dragged the pot before they saw us. He said, "Don't fret, Montgomery. You'll have it back before the end of the evening." However, Eaton's snide remark didn't change Montgomery's sour sulking expression. Eaton ignored his grumbles and stood.

Ross outstretched his hand. "Pleased to renew our acquaintance, Major Eaton. It has been nearly twenty years since you ordered the Cherokee brigade to swim across the Tallapoosa River and steal Red Stick canoes."

"It wasn't my idea to do so," Eaton remarked, stepping aside from Ross to address Father. "From what General Jackson said, I believe it was this man's strategy." Eaton stretched his hand to Father. "Major," Eaton said, raising his inflection with the second syllable.

I repeated my father's greeting while he shook Eaton's hand. *"Major Eaton, you appear as formidable now as you were then. This is my son, John, speaking my mind and his own today."* Father placed his broad palm against my back as a reminder of his request.

After finding seats at the table, the server returned with brandy instead of ale. Only Xander and Ross drank from the glasses placed in front of them. Tavern guests busied themselves, attempting to appear uninterested, but their penetrating eyes over their shoulders told me they heard every word spoken.

Major Eaton shuffled the cards in his hand. "We have toured the ground of complaint, sir, founded by the ignorance of your ancestors and their fondness for the chase. We object to how much land the Cherokee claim dominion over, too much for your people's numbers."

Father stood after I linked Eaton's remarks with the most direct translation. His hands balled into fists. Father's reply was conciliatory, but he clarified Eaton's objection and made no gesture, only stared into Eaton's eyes. *"You are mistaken. The case is reversed, and we are now assaulted with the menaces of expulsion because we have unexpectedly become civilized. We have formed a constituted government."*

Cherokee sarcasm isn't subtle, with its intentional verb tense. I found it difficult to smooth Father's sharp edges. He continued. *"It is too much for us now, to be honest, virtuous, and industrious. Because then, we are capable of aspiring to the rank of Christians and politicians, which renders our attachment to the soil stronger and, therefore, more difficult to defraud us of possession. Disappointment inflicts the mind of the avaricious white man, mortified by delay and with the probability of the intended victim's escape from the snares laid for its destruction."*[4]

Nervous Montgomery interceded, turning the conversation from our land to its people. He stood and waved his hands as if he were swatting imaginary flies. "Sir, let me assure you. Your civilization pleases us. The land to the west of the Mississippi is where your people can maintain their culture, spread out, claim dominion over the prairies, and govern yourselves."

Father's reply was stoic, despite being affronted with terms of emigration rather than Cherokee statehood. Father became ironically graceful. I hoped my translation did the nuance justice. *"If the country to which we are directed to go is desirable and well-watered, why is it so long a wilderness and a waste, uninhabited by respectable white people, whose enterprise would have induced them to monopolize it from their poor and unfortunate fellow citizens? From correct information, we have formed a bad opinion of the western country beyond the Mississippi. But if the report was favorable to the fertility of the soil, if the running streams were as transparent as crystal, and silverfish abounded from their element in profusion, we should still adhere to the purpose of spending the remnant of our lives on the soil that gave us birth—rendered dear by the nourishment we receive from its bosom."*[5] Father whispered, *"Pointless,"* and turned to leave the tavern and talks.

Ross and I followed, only to intercept a tardy Indian Agent, John Crowwell. The short man had no trouble entering with his hat still in place.

Yellow Bird's Song

I knew his face, the same White Crow who refused to shake my hand, the man who shot Peter's brother in cold blood, who whispered manipulations in bloated McKenney's ear. None there had informed us of the man's invitation, and again, I could not see in the dark.

Crowwell said, "An apt argument, sir, except you omitted one fundamental precept. The Cherokee have no choice, as our relationship with the Creeks has proven. General Jackson's administration will not compromise."

He angled himself and made a graceful bow to Ross. "Chief Ross, your choice remains violence or emigration. Hardly leaves room for redundant debates such as these."

I translated the rebuke.

Father lunged at Crowwell, knocking several empty chairs to the floor. After White Crow's scathing reply, Ross attempted to barricade my father behind him—a dangerous and futile obstacle. Father didn't hit Crowwell, although the two stood toe-to-toe.

Ross responded, trying to calm the situation. "An intimidating adversary is only as strong as his ability to stand outside his own argument." Chief Ross turned his head behind him toward Eaton and Montgomery. "Unfortunately, it appears only one side here deserves recognition."

After the taut impasse, we took to our separate rooms. I stepped outside to stretch my legs and check on our horses for the night. Father retired upstairs, I assumed, to pace a white streak on the floor. Below, I was positive the white men continued drinking brandy, discussing Father's outburst, and laughing at Ross' inability to offer more than English philosophy. Xander remained, I hoped, to lessen the tensions our party left as souvenir.

I wished Sarah could have witnessed the audacity of the men. My recollection may not do their derogatory words justice. What did Crowwell think his threat might produce? Angering my father to the reaches of violence so Eaton and Montgomery could smear it in newspapers across the South that they had bettered the unchristian and violent Major Ridge?

Or rather, was the mention of the Creek for my purposes? Spoken to entrap me and discredit me further? Or was Crowwell simply a narcissist, hell-bent on staring at his image until death? After walking through the yard, and thinking too much, I turned the corner to reenter the candlelit tavern. I stopped and used the exterior stairs rather than crossing through the dining room. The last thing I needed was to be accused of speaking to the men alone, suspected of making some claim to the government's negotiators without witness.

When I entered our bedroom, Father seemed calmer, stretched upon a corn-husked mattress with fresh sheets. However, the ropes needed tightening because it sank under his weight, and the mattress folded around him. He spoke with his eyes closed, arms behind his head, and boots dangling from the edge of the bed. He asked, *"Do you remember how the honeybee earned his stinger?"*

Surprised by his topic, I said, *"Of course. The Great Spirit gave the bee a stinger as a weapon against man's desire for more honey. But because of the bees' anger, they only get one sting and die."*[6]

He opened one eye and said, *"After revealing my temper, if I don't wake in the morning, tell your mother I'll wait for her in the Nightland by the great council fire."*

I laughed and walked toward the window. *"Mother would say you're more bear than bee."*

Before Father could respond, we both heard Xander's voice on the stairs outside. I glanced out the window, and then, placed my back against the wall, so he'd not see me. Xander met a waiting Eaton, Montgomery, and Crowwell. They entered the stable to retrieve their horses. Why would Xander leave with the enemy? It felt wrong to be so suspect, but I could think of no reason for all of them to leave together.

Seeing what I had, Father said, "Follow them." He could not go. They'd recognize his graying head and height with a single glance, but I could find them. Tossing my buckskins from our bag, he said, *"Don't be seen. Take your pistol."*

I followed the single line of horse tracks until nightfall brought shadows too deep to discern prints. I closed my eyes and smelled smoke. Light from their fire blurred the tree line near the river. I'd found them.

Since their horses would warn them of my presence long before they heard any crackling leaf or snapping twig, I hunched low, moving in a wide perimeter, downhill toward Terrapin Creek, and entered the water. I approached their firelight from the downhill slope. I dug my feet against the steep bank, into the sandy shallows, and listened to the men speaking above me.

Xander said, "I have a large inn, ample stables, outbuildings, many cattle, and half stock in the Coosawatee Ferry between New Echota and Vann's plantation."

Eaton replied, "Substantial and worthy holdings."

Montgomery offered, "It would be worth thousands more for you if you set an example, persuading other leading families, like Joseph Vann, to emigrate West."

"I'm not saying we will go. My wife's family—" Then Xander stopped short and asked, "How much would you estimate as the worth for such holdings?"

Greed overcame Xander's loyalty. I couldn't hear the offered sum, but whatever was quoted made Xander cough. The three white men shook hands with promises to renew their acquaintance, leaving Xander alone to stomp out the remaining embers. When their horses were far enough away, I smelled dirt-tainted smoke. Xander must be putting out their fire. I knew it was time to call out a traitor.

If I rose from the crouch, climbed the bank, and circled behind him, he'd never see my shadow. I had to have silent feet. If he saw me, he'd slink into the forest's shadows, like a scared animal, eyes shining in the black. But if he never felt my gaze, I could wedge him between his fate and his fire. No escape. Capture.

He turned to go, and I was there. In what light remained, I scrutinized his face, holding him to account like the moon judges its subordinate stars. He looked away, reeled, appalled, affronted. I rolled my neck, pressing down the tense muscles in my shoulders.

Xander stuttered, "What did you hear?"

I reached for his cravat, pulling him to me. "Enough."

He didn't offer any witty retort to deflect his accountability. No explanation could redeem him from such duplicity. Excuses would only thicken the humid air, made denser under this midnight moon.

Xander took the long road home. He left that same night but arrived in New Echota two days later than us, in no rush to face Chief Ross. In council the following month, Xander admitted his betrayal. For his disloyalty, the council took swift action, dismissed him from his post as clerk, appointing me to complete his term.

I regained Ross' trust and Father's approval at the cost of Xander McCoy's reputation. I didn't know whether to feel guilty or relieved. I desired the appointment but wanted to earn the position rather than Ross granting it to me. Perhaps in uncovering Xander's betrayal, I had earned it. Xander accepted his consequences, blaming himself. And because of his forthright admission, Xander spared his own life.

No measure or law would rid the land of so many white man's flies, stealing more honey than one man could eat alone. The Cherokee believed honeybees swallowed briars to preserve their hive against such greed. But with only one vicious sting, Cherokee honeybees surged into battles they couldn't win, and, overrun, committed suicide with each brave assault.

CHAPTER 12: A GARDEN OF THREE SISTERS
Sarah Ridge
Running Waters
October 1829

If cold enough, October was the month to slaughter hogs. Honey and Peter prepared by sharpening long knives and gathering boiling kettles. The sun set while they worked, so Peter lit a small fire and gathered a chair from his smithy so Honey could press the petals while he sharpened knives against the spinning grindstone.

She shook her head. "I like da sweetmeat. Sarah drips maple syrup over the ham. But don't get me wrong now, I like them beans salty."

He took the knife off the blade and blew across its sharp edge before touching it with his thumb.

"Miss Honey, if'n you add salt to the fatback in dem beans, you'll have to make more trips to the well for da thirst it brings. Cookin' green beans with fatback makes 'em salty enough."

My mouth watered from listening to their hum. I continued churning butter on the porch, smiling. I wondered if she'd let him kiss her again. None of my business, so I didn't ask, but I couldn't help but notice how at ease they argued, all the time, agreeing with one another. Together, Honey and Peter were the same savory blend of salty and sweet.

The following morning, Walking Stick began the tremendous and time-consuming task of butchering. One of the newer hands at Running Waters, Walking Stick arrived with the Major shortly after we moved our belongings to our new house. Major led a cattle herd on horseback, driving eighteen heads the six miles from his fields to ours. Major stopped to round up a straggler, but he intercepted a roaming Walking Stick riding toward him with a lasso around the stray. As the story goes, Major talked with him from one end of the massive beasts to the other, and they instantly took a liking to one another.

When John and I met Walking Stick, he remarked how he preferred the company of cows to most people. He said his wife's mother regretted allowing her daughter to marry him, and shortly after, both women shunned him and placed his tools outside. He didn't seem troubled by the separation. If he was, he never said.

Walking Stick stayed on as a cowhand and brought firewood to the kitchen door every morning. He worked in exchange for shelter, bacon, and biscuit. Most times when he brought wood, he'd walk in and walk out, saying nothing.

Yellow Bird's Song

Honey was skeptical and scrutinized the Cherokee cowboy. She studied him when she crunched red apples straight from the tree or picked green beans off the vines. She watched him cross pastures, tracking him by the sunlight reflecting off his metal armband or the turkey feathers embedded into braids, towering over his head like a church steeple.

Last July, on a blinding bright day, Honey and I held our hands above our eyes to shade the sun, staring at him in the field across from the house. She said, "He just tell them cows where to go, and they go. He just ask politely, and they gather." She reentered the house, walking down the narrow hall beside the stairs. She said, "He must be a-talkin' through the Holy Spirit to them cows." Afterward, Honey threw her hands to the ceiling and resolved that Walking Stick perhaps wasn't "… as knotted up as I thought." After that, Honey stopped tracking him and included him in her circle of worry. She'd punch her fists into the dough and say, "I don't understand why his wife didn't want him. Walking Stick ain't lazy. Least slackin' man as I've ever seen."

I said, "Maybe they had words with no feelings."

Honey said, "Two folks should warm up first, before they talk the vows. Don't make no sense in the other direction."

Heavy with child, I sat through much of August's heat when Laughing Water and his son, Will, arrived, asking for work. Will and his mother suffered from smallpox last winter. She passed, but Will recovered, with scars across his cheeks and throat. After her death, most of his mother's clan emigrated from Tennessee to Arkansas territory. But the father and son didn't follow. Instead, they traveled southeast, seeking work in New Echota with their wagon full of farm tools. We were lucky they passed Running Waters.

Rollin took an instant liking to Will, a young man who didn't think it unmanly to play with a toddling boy. He put Rollin on his shoulders and walked through the tassels of the summer corn. It was a beautiful sight, hearing Rollin shout "Mama," with his head bouncing above the golden silk bursting through green corn husks. Even though Rollin's hair was dark and thick, among the corn tassels, the sight reminded me of his Cherokee name. His warbles mixed with belly laughter, trilled high from Will's shoulders.

Today, I'd risen before the sun, before John, too uncomfortable to sleep beside his tossing and turning. He'd woken me, speaking Cherokee, still asleep. So, still dark, I went downstairs to occupy my mind.

The downstairs parlor became my refuge through many dawns. Clarinda and Rollin were still dreaming in Paradise's colors, with heavenly names their souls still remembered. At dawn, God spread His golden glow onto the raspberry-red textured wall coverings, with matching toile de Jouy draperies depicting romantic courtship scenes. The circle of my spinning wheel made its own shadowed sun, slanting across the wooden floor. Pearlware stretched its blue-eyed chinoiserie, gleaming in the sunlight from behind the corner cabinet's walnut-framed glass doors.

Shortly after my morning's solace, John dressed and came down the stairs, still mumbling in Cherokee.

"Do you want something to eat?" I asked. He shook his head and fixed his tie. I said, "Stop worrying. It will follow as God intends."

He cocked his head. "Why are you up so early? Go back to sleep."

"Don't go yet. I have something for you. Ordered it months ago. Walking Stick picked it up for me in town the other day." I handed a cane to my husband. "I know you hate to lean, but since they are so distinguished, I thought you might not mind."

His eyes traced the dark cherry wood and brass handle in his hand. "Even if I lose today, I've won more than I deserve, Ani, *Gvgeyui*."

"*Gvgeyui, Skahtlelohskee.*" I straightened his lapel. "Worrying about the vote won't change it. You've done your best. What else could the council ask of you?"

He studied the cane in his hand and tilted his head. "They could think I took bribe money from the Creek and sold their land from underneath them."

"Yoholo wrote to Ross. He knows what you told him was the truth. Slandering you and Vann was part of McKenney's plan to get the acreage. It was a lie meant to persuade the Creek and prevent you from helping them. McKenney couldn't manipulate them when you and Vann were there."

"I know you're right. Regardless, I never want to feel such shame again."

He walked to the end of the room using the cane. He turned around and said, "If I must make a tough decision regarding our land, I don't want other council members to think I'm motivated by greed."

"Those who know you—couldn't."

I followed him to the stables in my dressing gown while he readied his horse. Once he strapped the saddle around the horse's girth, he slid his walking cane through one strap. He mounted, rode outside the barn doors, and studied the trees at the edge of the woods.

"Tell Walking Stick, although he'll know, to expect rain later today. They'll have to work hard to finish the butchering before it comes."

I looked up. "The sky doesn't look so now."

Atop his horse, he said, "The poplars are showing their silver."

Yellow Bird's Song

"I wish I could go with you. Without word, I'll worry."

"I'll be home tonight if I am unelected. But if I am appointed secretary, I'll be home tomorrow. For once, Ani, pray I'm late." He smiled with his characteristic one-sided grin and donned his hat.

"I know," I said, squinting up at him with daylight in my eyes. "You said so in your sleep."

He touched my face. "I leave my heart to beat for you and the child growing inside you."

I gripped his hand and held my growing womb with the other. "Take care of mine while you're gone. I'll guard yours with my life." I stayed until his horse found the trail northward to New Echota. He didn't look back, only around him, seeking advice from the bent trees he knew like the lines on his palm.

It was then I realized how much I loved him. My husband sowed the fertile ground under my feet, washed me with the waters of the Oostanaula, and cooled my head by blowing his breath through my hair. I could stand still because he moved.

After seeing him go, Honey and I woke and dressed the children. Honey arranged a quilt on the floor in the kitchen for them to play while we awaited Quatie's arrival. I'd written to her, asking for a recipe for cracklings and pig liver. She returned a note, saying she would come herself and spend the day with our hands in raw pork, rosemary, and thyme.

I leaned against the kitchen doorway while the men gathered near the fire. Peter filled each vessel with rainwater from the barrels and placed it on the iron grate above the white coals. Steam poured and blossomed into the blue sky above the smokehouse. Quatie rode into the barn when Clarinda and I were headed toward the henhouse.

Quatie blocked the light coming from the doorway of the chicken coop. She wore orange, with her black hair in braids over her shoulders. She put her hands on her hips and took a deep sigh. When Clarinda saw her, she pulled on my skirt and made a crown, separating thumbs from her joined fingers in a circle, and placed the shape on her head. I put the eggs inside Clarinda's basket and met my trusted friend, holding the strain from the backache with both hands.

We embraced outside the chicken coop. She looked surprised, placing her hands on the child in my womb. Quatie tilted her head and looked questioningly at me. She didn't know. In my weakness, I didn't have the strength to tell her.

"I didn't want to cause you any more heartsickness. The baby is due this month."

"Been too long since we've seen one another. I am glad for you and John. That man loves you."

"He better. And Ross? How are you both?"

Quatie didn't speak but bent to see Clarinda. She touched my daughter's nose and imitated a child in her arms, saying, "You'll be a big sister again soon." Then she reached behind her to give Clarinda a peacock feather. Clarinda waved the teal and golden plume before us as we took hands and walked to the kitchen. When we passed under the shade of the broad oak trees, I glanced at Quatie's changing face. She dropped any forced effort to smile.

Peter shot the pig, and we jolted, hearing the report while Clarinda continued unfazed, taking careful steps not to crack the fresh eggs laying in her basket.

From the kitchen corner, Rollin stacked blocks on his blanket. Quatie scooped him from the floor and rested his weight on her hip. She kissed his nose. She placed him back on his feet to hand him another peacock feather. He rubbed the kiss away before it dried and waved the feather in the air.

Quatie said, "He still smells like a baby even though he walks."

I chuckled at her remark. "He runs. He's only been awake for half an hour. Give him a few minutes, and he'll either smell like he's worked in the fields or rolled in cow dung. As you know, it doesn't take long." I redirected my attention from her to Rollin, who reached for buckets on hooks beside the kitchen doorway, intentionally placed higher than he could reach.

I looked down at him. "Yes, it's your turn now, Rollin. Let's go milk the cows." I asked Quatie, "Come with us?"

When we walked outside, Walking Stick stepped away from the circle to lift an iron pot of boiling water and douse the pig carcass. After, the men removed the animal's hair with metal scrapers. Large swatches and tufts of brown hair gathered around each of their feet.

"The smell sours my stomach," I said, pointlessly turning my head in the opposing direction.

Quatie said, "You look pale. You must eat." It was the same advice I'd heard from all I'd encountered in the last few days. Without stating the obvious, I was paler than everyone around me.

"I have little appetite," I said.

Rollin announced our entrance into the barn by stating the obvious. "Cow. Cow." He pointed his little fingers toward full udders swaying in the stalls. Quatie grabbed a stool near the doorway and hoisted her skirt to sit.

Yellow Bird's Song

"I'll do it," she said. "You'll tip over if you sit on a stool."

Rollin wiggled between her legs. She reached around him to place the bucket under the cow. The first squirt spread cow milk on Rollin's face and made him laugh.

I asked her, "What is the news from town? John only tells me of the men's business, not the women's affairs."

"Harriet Boudinot and Sophie Sawyer have become fast friends. They both talk of little but book learning and saving everyone's souls. Harriet ministers by playing hymns all afternoon on the piano forte her parents brought her."

"Yes. We dined with them when they were here."

Quatie smirked. "Not everyone needs saving, Sarah." She settled on the stool under the second cow. "Speaking of being saved, Ross aligned himself with the Methodists."

What might John think of Ross crossing politics and faith? Man's history records more wars fought by their union than by their separation.

"Does he think doing so will persuade Christian Cherokee not to leave for Arkansas?"

"I could only assume. Ross didn't say. I overheard Reverend Worcester and Elias Boudinot speaking about their New Testament translations, and one of them said Ross' name. By the way, they've translated through Luke."

She was so cynical today. I guessed rather than knew its cause. "Is Ross' eternal soul on your mind, or are you upset because he didn't tell you?"

She held her breath, then exhaled. "He should have talked to me before making such a decision. Now, I hear it from others. He must be losing the war, asking everyone and anyone to help the Cherokee cause—but me." She chuckled under her breath to add, "And I wither under his heat."

Curiosity overwhelmed me with candor. "Why, do you think?"

She looked me in the eye. "Because he's terrified of being ordinary and unremembered. He's too Cherokee to be respected by whites and too white to be respected by all Cherokee."

Rollin sang a squealing song, experimenting with his voice in long and high-pitched moos. Indifferent cows swatted rogue flies with their tails. He reeled backward, falling into Quatie's chest. When she caught him, I heard her laugh for the first time this morning. Quatie imitated my child's invented music, straightening her back and shoulders and lifting her chin to moo as loud as Rollin had.

She squeezed him and spoke in his ear. "You will be a speaker someday."

126

We returned up the hill to the kitchen with full buckets. Clarinda sat on Honey's lap at the table, writing on her slate. Clarinda showed me her work when Quatie and I placed the milk buckets beside the door. Clarinda's English letters for horse was missing the silent "e". Clarinda pointed to her word with one hand and made a gesture, signaling the flap of the horse's ears.

Quatie asked, "What is she signing?"

"The same word she's writing."

"What a wonder." Then, Quatie wiped her hands on her dress and asked, "How does she think? She wouldn't attach meaning to words like other children."

Honey spoke in my stead. "Clarinda turns her thoughts to pictures. She understands all she sees and fixes da row of letters in her mind to name da thing."

I said, "John teaches her when he's home. She sees in both languages."

"So, Clarinda understands she has two clans," Quatie gasped, astonished.

"Why wouldn't Clarinda know she is both Cherokee and English?"

I grabbed a sack of corn ears from the floor and lifted it to the end of the table. The strain pulled my belly muscles, and I wrapped one arm around my stomach, hunching over. It took me a quiet moment before I replied. "Clarinda is more like John than me, with so many gifts of understanding."

"What don't you understand?" Quatie asked.

"Most Cherokee talk too fast for me."

Walking Stick entered the kitchen to hang an iron pot full of skinned pork fat on the hook above the hearth fire.

When he left without a word, Honey said, with sarcasm, "Good morning, Walking Stick." I imagined she wanted to ask him how he could walk through a room and not greet those standing inside.

She looked at me with wide eyes. "He may not be lazy, but he won't use what's in his head. Did he not see us all standin' here?"

After Honey's remark, Quatie followed him to the doorway as Walking Stick joined the sounds of grunting men and rattling chains. Looking toward them, Quatie said, "The slaves must be ready to brine."

"Not slaves," I clarified.

She faced me with eyebrows raised and shook her head in bewilderment. "How can this farm profit without slaves?"

I passed behind her and poured three cups of cider from the jug. I handed the first to Honey and the second to Quatie. After sipping mine, I said, "Each person at Running Waters is here by choice, earning their

Yellow Bird's Song

wages in trade or coin. They profit from the same sun, water, shelter our family does."

"The Cherokee have taken slaves as far back as I remember." Then, thinking but saying no more, Quatie grabbed a hickory paddle to stir the cracklings.

I said, "The poorest—those separated from family and land, including freed slaves—deserve the liberty God has given them. It is not my will to take it from them."

Quatie raised her tone and her eyebrows, adding pepper to season the boil. "Is this John's way or yours? His father owns slaves. Thirty, I believe." She continued, "Your John listens to you?"

I said, "At first, there was nothing we could do to change anything while we lived with Major and Susannah. But after meeting Peter, he saw slavery from a different perspective."

She replied, "But my husband decreed no freed slaves could live on Cherokee land. Permitting so would only cause more to come and anger whites at losing such property."

"People aren't property, Quatie. You know that. Let people believe what they choose." I began shucking corn, placing the husks inside a muslin sack to dry.

Honey snapped beans in her lap into a wooden bowl. She kept her head bent over the work of her hands. Quatie hadn't addressed Honey during the conversation, and I couldn't fault Honey's need to speak.

"No one says I can't lives where I want or says what I want. I stay at Runnin' Waters with Peter, Brother John, Sarah, and des chillern, 'cause I'm needed. They love me, and I love them. Been taken 'fore. So's has Peter. We looks out for one another, keepin' the lot of us safely in each other's sights."

I dropped more husks in the sack and placed another ear of corn on the growing pyramid. "Quatie, no one can stand alone."

Quatie didn't stop stirring. She said, "Even if I wanted to advise him, Ross would not listen. I'm the woman who could not bear him a breathing child." Quatie's voice wavered, making light of what she said. "He neither forgives nor forgets. Perhaps the Methodists can teach him." Then, she faced us with the hickory paddle still in her hands, dripping melted fat on the floor. She shrugged her shoulders. "He doesn't eat or sit at my table. He loves his children and writes to them when he's away but closes every door to me. Punishment, I suppose."

The fat crackled behind her, so she returned to stirring while I shucked corn.

I couldn't see her face. She said, "I miss my mother's time when women decided important Cherokee matters and attended council to talk to their warrior husbands away from battle. Or they took up guns and fought beside them, like *Ghigau*, the blessed woman, Nanyihi.[1]

"Her name meant 'wanderer'.[2] After her husband, Kingfisher, fell to a Creek bullet in a battle, she took his musket and fought in his stead. Some thought her actions were treasonous, but most respected her as a war woman, a blessed woman. Our elders asked Nanyihi to distribute the black drink and advise councils at Old Chota.[3]

"My mother attended one council where Nanyihi sent a letter. Her daughter came with her mother's cane and spoke on her behalf. Nanyihi was old by then. They listened to her words like a sacred mother. She advised them not to part with our lands but to enlarge our farms. Grow cotton, and after the harvest, women could weave cloth. *Her desire was for our people to make peace with the whites. I don't know that I agree with that.*"[4] She apologized over her shoulder. "I'm sorry. The memory is in Cherokee."

"I understood enough."

Quatie stared into the fire beneath her. Her dreamy tone stirred her thoughts, searching the iron for generations of Cherokee women past, staring into the firelight for further advice from the matriarch, Nanyihi.

"And da menfolk listened to Nanyihi?" Honey brought Quatie back to the present with her question.

Quatie answered, "It's an old way, but better. Ross would listen if I were stronger." She faced me, twisting her neck over her shoulder. "Whites own slaves, so Ross does. His law says no freed slave can hide on Cherokee land. If more knew, they might overrun farms like Running Waters, with too many seeking food and shelter."

"We try our best to serve all who come to our table."

"Nanyihi dreamt of a future, one I hope will never come to pass. She saw a great line of our people walking. Babies in their mother's arms, fathers with small children on their shoulders, and elders with bundles on their backs. In her vision, they marched west with white soldiers behind them, tears dripping onto a trail of corpses."

The hypothetical tragedy she spoke of invigorated her resentment, and she stirred with renewed fervor. "What would Nanyihi say now about making peace with the whites? What would our living mothers advise? Those who bake, cook, sew, and garden? What would they do if their husbands fell? Are they courageous enough to pick up the guns and fight, as Nanyihi did? Or sit idle and wring their hands and pray. Our mothers' wisdom cannot be ignored behind closed doors."

I had no answers to offer. I walked to her and stopped her hands. I held

Yellow Bird's Song

her for as long as it took to feel her arms around me. I wouldn't let her suffer her trials alone.

I said, "Our husbands will keep that from happening."

She held me at arm's length. "Your compassion doesn't come by force, making others believe as you do, like Harriet Boudinot or Sophie Sawyer."

When we separated, her tearful eyes found my quiet daughter sitting beside her noisy brother. Quatie knelt beside them and touched Clarinda's red hair. She looked at me, saying, "It comes to you like Clarinda's words —by sight. You shelter the squash, so its leaves don't shrivel from heat. You allow bean vines to wind your stalk, so they don't rot, lying on the ground."

Rollin chose this inconvenient moment to toddle toward the open door. He tumbled headfirst down the single step out. I doubted he was hurt, but I hurried to the doorway when he cried. I raised him above my head and into my arms and felt piercing pain. My ears rang. I felt dizzy and swayed on my feet.

Quatie rushed to take Rollin from me.

Honey dropped her bowl of beans to the floor and came to my side. She grabbed my arm and touched my forehead. Her touch was so much warmer than I felt.

Quatie took charge. "Honey, get Sarah some water?"

Honey bent over me and said, "You're paler than white corn. Stood too long today."

The kitchen walls were spinning. Quatie spread her fingers along the tightness of my belly.

"We're fine," I told the hovering room. "I just moved too quickly, is all."

I drank Honey's water and waited for the pain to ease after each quiet sip. It didn't.

"We have so much to do today," I said.

Quatie's natural smile returned. "I believe we've added a task only you can finish."

Honey called Walking Stick, who came to the doorway, wiping his hands on a cloth. After surveying the room, he and Quatie lifted me to stand. Then, with one on either side, they placed their arms underneath mine as we walked toward the stairs.

When I picked up my skirts to step up, the water sack surrounding the child burst, and its liquid soaked my petticoat and stockings. The pool wasn't clear. Red streaks smeared my white stockings. I closed my eyes and bent forward, gasping with breathtaking pain.

130

CHAPTER 13: BROKEN STRINGS
Rollin Ridge
Placerville, California
Spring and Summer 1850

I could no longer feel my legs after riding so long. When we arrived in Placerville, wide-eyed, we took in the town's sinful sights and human smells. Near a hay yard, a large white oak stood with branches strong enough to hang guilty and innocent alike. Underneath, a hunched man sawed away on his bow and fiddle. He played a dandy tune, as fast as his fingers could hold down the strings. Pale bow hair gathered around his bent wrist like willow branches. Then his music halted while he examined the instrument's curved wire, a snapped and broken string.

Aeneas said, "He's playing 'Arkansas Traveler'. Well, he was. Guess we'll blend right in."

We tied our horses to a hitching post in front of the El Dorado Saloon and Hotel at Quartz and Main. Filthy prospectors packed into wagons like roosters in a coop too small. Their faces were similar, flat and frowned with no shine to their skin. Bodies smelled of campfire smoke, salt, dirt, and rust. Miners rode in wagons, holding collapsible canvas tent sticks, sitting on top of overturned iron cooking pots and wooden sluice boxes. Picks darted across the main street, slung over men's shoulders, with handles peeking through their grips. Their travel stirred the dust, burning our eyes, making it challenging to see four feet in front of us. Yet, through the haze, we smelled their tainted anticipation, a clammy thrill emanating from gripping drooping canvas bags held closely to their sides. Their gray bodies meshed into a lengthy line at the bank, each praying gold prices remained high.

Wacooli pulled his hat lower to hide his face. He looked back toward the quiet fiddler under the hanging tree. He said, "Hope no one concerns themselves with me being dark. I need a bath something awful."

I offered what consolation I could. "California is a free state. Look around. Everyone is brown in mining towns."

Wacooli's concern for his appearance continued. "Maybe," he said, and changing the subject, estimated our expenses. "It'll cost us, but we need new clothes."

Aeneas' next remark remained muted under his bandana, keeping dust hanging in the air from his throat. "It won't be a warm bath, that's for sure. Saw an advertisement in Salt Lake for a mining town named Bath. I wonder how far it is. Bet they got hot water there." He looked over his

Yellow Bird's Song

shoulder back in the direction we came.

I put our priorities in order. "Let's find a couple of beds first. Then, we'll find the trading post and buy three clean shirts. After, we'll find the barber."

"I don't want no haircut, Rollin. Mama would never let me grow it long. It's past the ugly stage."

"How would you know? You haven't looked at yourself in a month." Wacooli stepped back and evaluated Aeneas from top to bottom. "Can't rightly say I agree."

"I'm the prettiest child; Mama said so."

Wacooli and I spoke in unison. "Believe what you like."

Aeneas pouted, speaking under his breath. "I'm the funniest too."

Wacooli and I walked a few paces onto the road before Aeneas caught up. Then, finally, he asked, with all sincerity, "Rollin, why do we need a barber?"

Wacooli laughed over his shoulder at Aeneas' ignorance of the many benefits of a proper barbershop. He said, "Did Mama Sarah say you were the smartest? If so, it was the only time she ever lied." Wacooli's sarcasm was inevitable, correcting Aeneas' misconceptions about how a barber earned his living.

I hadn't laughed so hard in miles. It felt good to think of Mama without seeing so much sadness on her face and renewing the anger I hadn't found time to unpack. I told Wacooli, "I hope she said you were the brightest. There's no doubt in my mind."

Wacooli's tone turned serious. "Mama Sarah doesn't show no favorites. Let me tell you, I wouldn't mind if I needed further arithmetic lessons to add up all the gold we find."

He turned his attention to Aeneas, who eyed the El Dorado Saloon's upper balcony. Scantily clad women leaned over railings, weighed heavier by breasts blossoming from their corsets. Aromas of cheap perfume wafted below, mixed with the alcohol pumping through their sweat to sour the scent. Aeneas couldn't have cared less about the smell. He removed his hat to show off his overly long, reddish locks. Like Clarinda, he had Mama's hair.

Aeneas said, "Who's thinking about arithmetic?"

Wacooli said, "Carry the one, Aeneas."

I laughed too loud. Aeneas didn't hear Wacooli's remark, distracted by his voice shouting compliments toward the female employees of the El Dorado Saloon. In English, the hotel's name meant "The Golden". I hoped its name predicted our good fortune.

I struck my gawking brother's chest, still transfixed by the beauty above him. "Say nothing to them, Aeneas. We can't afford it."

To Wacooli, I said, "I'm getting two rooms for two days." I tried a further bargain. "I'll sleep beside Aeneas tomorrow, if you will tonight." It took Wacooli two tries to gather enough spit in his hand to shake and bind our deal.

Aeneas said, "Rollin, you and Wacooli go in. I'll guard the horses. My view is finer than frog hair."

I looked up, following Anee's gaze. "If she leans out any further, you'll have to catch that frog with your measly arms."

"I'll catch her. The one with the big—"

Wacooli interrupted him, "What would Mama say?"

There were no quips left to deter my brother from smiling an ear-to-ear grin. I had little desire to do so. With only the two of us for company, I couldn't blame him for staring at more female skin than he was accustomed to seeing, even with sisters.

Drinkers and gamblers crowded the saloon's interior this afternoon. Sunlight beat in the windows and heated the curtains, releasing last night's cigar smoke. Round tables covered men's boots, stretched like overlong draperies across the scarred floor. Various shades of brown darkened the room, the same hue as the half-full glasses on their tables. Mismatched kerosene globes cast pale colors along the paneled walls with no determinable scheme.

I crossed to the attendant and asked for two available rooms. Wacooli leaned his back against the counter, surveying the clientele with his hat in his hand.

"We normally don't allow his kind here. Stirs up the southern guests."

Wacooli looked at me and said, "See? Tree stands in the middle of town for a reason."

I pulled one of our last silver dollars from my pocket and held it in the light from the attendant's lamp. I turned it in my fingers. The hotel clerk's eyes followed my gesture.

"If we aren't allowed, it'll rest easy back in my dark pocket."

The attendant passed through a muslin curtain to speak to his superior. When he returned, he jotted down our names in the hotel's guest book. Guess silver was more important to this establishment than any other hue.

"Want clean sheets?" the clerk asked.

Wacooli turned his chest toward the clerk but kept his feet facing the door. "How much more is it?"

"Quarter a room."

Wacooli answered the man. "Worth it."

I dropped the coins in the man's upturned palm and asked, "How far is

Yellow Bird's Song

the closest barber?"

"Depends. You want the cheap barber or the expensive?"

We both replied, "Cheap."

The clerk's eyes didn't leave his registry book. He said, "Might need to ride a stretch to Sacramento. Mike Murphy's contraption only costs two bits, and it's mighty cold, but at least you won't have to wash in someone else's dirty water."

"Thank you kindly. And the postmaster?"

The clerk attempted to step behind the curtain. His voice mumbled. "Man named Thomas Nugent, down Main Street a stretch."

Wacooli turned and said, "One more, the closest trading post? My brothers and I need a fresh start."

When Wacooli said "brothers," the man turned around, with eyes darting from Wacooli to me, trying to reason out our relations. We'd become accustomed to such looks. Our blended family was none of his business.

He answered only after he gave up, unable to make sense of our fraternity. "Only one brick store in town, owned by Colonel Bee and his brother."

I thanked the man. "Appreciate it."

We wove through the day drinkers and prostitutes to meet Aeneas, still gawking upwards. Wacooli dragged him down the street to our first stop, the brick store. Inside were stacks of gold pans, sluice boxes with metal grates on the bottom, horse tack, and liniment canisters of all designs and colors along the back wall. An older gentleman reached for one with a pole, raising gartered arms with shirtsleeves rolled to his elbows. After dropping it to his hand, he charged the customer two bits for snake oil in a can.

He turned to greet us before seeing us. "Hello, gents." Guess he didn't care what color we were if we toted coins to exchange.

I said, "We need some fresh shirts, maybe pants too, depending on the expense."

Colonel Bee asked, "Where do you plan to wear them?"

Aeneas said, "Gold mining, sir. Durable, not fancy."

"Weather out here stays the same unless it's the rainy season, but that won't hit us for months. Days are warm; nights bring a chill. Flannel is cheaper and will serve through both conditions."

He led us to stacks of shirts in every size and color. Wacooli and I also bought gray trousers—Aeneas said his skins could hold out another month. When we stepped out of the store into the sunlight, Aeneas complained, "Bet even the small won't fit me. Collar's ugly."

134

Wacooli couldn't stop himself. "Don't be a dandy like Cousin Boudi. Quit your fussing."

We stowed our new clothes, mounted, and rode thirty minutes to the outskirts of Sacramento where miners were few. The air cleared. A river ran through the city, blue as the sky, with trees releasing a freshness I hadn't smelled since we crossed the prairies. Here, elegant gentlemen and ladies strode through the streets with matching clothes and parasols above their heads. Fine horses led carriages down wide main streets. Four-story buildings touched the blue horizon, with chimneys like sprawled fingers. In Sacramento, my memories collided, blending a landscape such that I hadn't seen since my studies in Massachusetts. While Aeneas and Wacooli scanned the street signs for a striped pole, I imagined Lizzie wearing a fine dress strolling these streets on my arm.

"Know why the pole has red stripes, Aeneas?" Wacooli taunted him.

"No, why?"

Wacooli grabbed his arm and surprised him. "It's because that's where they suck your blood with leeches."

When we found it, Aeneas wouldn't go inside.

Murphy said, "For three showers, that'll be six bits, including soap and a towel." Without pause, Wacooli handed over the money. I'd rather sit in a hot tub till the water cooled than be doused in cold water.

From behind his establishment, we approached three holes in the ground with barrels inside. First, we shucked our filthy clothes, flopping them in a pile. Then, naked, with lines creased on our arms and necks from skin exposed to the elements, we closed the makeshift drapes. Inside was a lofted, teeter-tottered, red kerosene can with holes in the bottom. At our feet were two slick wooden pedals.

Aeneas yelled beside me, "How do you make it work?"

Wacooli yelped. Then he shouted, "Shift your weight, Aeneas, one pedal to another." Soon, our yawls joined his.

Soaped up and rinsed clean, my brothers and I shivered while we dressed in new clothes smelling of bitter dyes. I buckled my belt, tying Kell's knife to my thigh. I'd used the blade as often as hunger beckoned but kept my promise to Mama that it would never kill another man. Yet, with the familiar arrowhead under my thumb, so returned my urge to slice Ross' throat.

We rode back to Placerville, and after an expensive meal of pot roast and vegetables, none of us could keep our eyes open. We retired to our rooms for a night's sleep. I had one more task before finding sleep's oblivion.

Yellow Bird's Song

My Darlin' Lizzie,

Today, we arrived in Placerville, California, although those native to this region call it Hangtown. Wacooli assumed the reason. We arrived worse for wear. Our heads looked like mops used to scrub floors from time immemorial. Combs were useless, impossible to draw downward. If we had ridden into Fayetteville, astride our bony mounts, we would have caused such hilarity among the townspeople. Small boys would follow us, hooting and taunting. You might have to gaze at my ragged countenance for a time to recognize your husband, wooly with a beard and hair to my shoulders, ribs and hip bones protruding under fraying clothes.[1] Aeneas, Wacooli, and I could only laugh at ourselves and aim to recover our health with a shower (in the coldest water west of Salt Lake), fresh shirts, and a meal of anything other than salt pork and dried beef. We plan to sleep for days, God willing. Writing to you will be my last task to this perpetual day.

Packers passed us on the road (names the miners are called), whose appearance was so exhilarating that I leaned back in my saddle and nearly killed myself with laughter. We've passed many a poor ragged devil who began the journey with meager attire under the expectation of becoming wealthy in California. He passed us riding a gaunt old steer, fully able to run a race with a snail, drubbing the poor old beast at every step to "get along". I confess my mirth was such that gods and men envied me. Poor humanity! To what miserable passes will it put itself in for money? [2] I, too, am guilty of the crime.

Aeneas, Wacooli, and I plan to set up mining operations here. However, from our brief time in this region, we've learned that thousands dig at every little hole for six miles up and down the creek. From what little energy I've spent scouting, the terrain appears challenging, with so much unforgiving work just to figure out whether a place has enough gold to balance the labor it takes to mine it. We shall find out soon enough.

For many to have traveled here (on a steer, no less), there must be an immense amount of gold in the hills. But the few miners we've talked to say it is hard to find in large quantities. There is no certainty of discovering it, with no more luck than playing a hand of cards. They cover expenses with what they find, which isn't much. But we've suffered enough to try our hand.

When we arrived today, we heard a fiddler playing 'Arkansas Traveler'. After he broke a string, he couldn't finish the tune.

Since then, all I can hum is the unheard end. I hope it isn't an omen for our fortune, or lack thereof, as we head to the rivers and mountains.

> A stranger in a strange land,
> Too calm to weep, too sad to smile,
> I take my harp of broken strings,
> A weary moment to beguile.
> And tho' no hope its promise brings,
> And present joy is not for me,
> Still, o'er that harp I love to bend,
> And feel its broken melody
> With all my shattered feelings blend.[3]

After weeks of getting our boots stuck in knee-deep mud and finding no more gold than would yield us four or five dollars each day, we moved on, conversing with fellow travelers from Springfield, Missouri. They dressed like us, smelled like us, and had the same pain-riddled expressions we'd adopted, a combination of somber and weary. But, eager for company, our bands rode beside one other through the short miles between the Cottonwood and Trinity Rivers.

One man, too hunched and infirm to consider mining a profession, said, "People say a season can yield a man fifty thousand, but I've never seen it. One man said he made twenty, but he could have been lying." Despite the giant wad of tobacco under his lip and the amber spittle dripping from his mouth, I understood.

His traveling companion overlapped his partner's mutterings. "Only one in a million digs his fortune from California rock. Where are you headed?"

I responded with the truth, despite my suspicions they intended to follow. "Farther upriver, toward Whiskey Creek, under Mount Shasta."

"Fine gold there," the older man responded, spitting spent tobacco in a wad on the ground, wiping his mouth free of brown spit with his gray sleeve.

I said, "I hope so. Let's hope it isn't so fine we can't see it."[4]

We split at the fork at Whiskey Creek, named for the only item sold there. With fewer miners than near Placerville, we hoped for more gains with fewer hands in the pot. Miners pitched tents around a communal cookfire. So, I raised ours, completing the established circle. After a supper of slapjacks and pickled pork, Aeneas and Wacooli went to test a

Yellow Bird's Song

few pans in the river, seeing what they could uncover before the moon stole the remaining daylight. I stayed behind to guard our belongings.

I wasn't alone, though. Worn boots shrunk inside a neighboring tent, replaced by an older black man's grin, carrying his hat full of holes. His curly beard was gray at the roots and made paler by pounding rock dust. He climbed from his tent on all fours and stood with painful groans, holding whatever ailment he suffered at bay with broad palms against his back. He walked a few paces to throw more river driftwood on the common fire, dulling the light I borrowed for writing.

When he turned, his face revealed thicker eyebrows, denser than the patch of boisterous hair receding from the crown of his head. Although few here had anything significant to smile about, the man's cheeks lifted in a grin as if he remembered the punchline to a story but had yet to share the humorous tale. My first impression of the man was from his subdued laughter. Although, nothing struck me funny.

He wobbled, stepping on one leg, and dragging the other behind him as if it tingled from numb nerves. Then, finally, he asked, "What you writing?"

Infected by his smile, I returned his lightheartedness and answered his question. I squinted, blinded by the setting sun behind his back. "Uninspired at present. Just a letter home."

"Don't have a soul to write to. Name's Spencer Hill." He reached out his hand to shake mine.

"Rollin Ridge." Copper and black hands shook with the new acquaintance.

He drank from a flask in his vest pocket and passed it alongside another question. "Where are you planning to send it?"

"Fayetteville, Arkansas. Writing our troubles to my wife and mother."

"Nice to have women at home. Gives a man something to dig for. I'm from Arkansas too, near Little Rock."

"Been there, flat as a slapjack." More eager for conversation than retelling the same woes, I corked my pen, and rose to offer him a bit of what measly food we had. Our cast iron pan was still hot. "You hungry?"

He nodded, rolled pork into the hot cake, and ate it in two bites. Then, with his mouth still partially full, he stared at the vast mountain range in the distance. He said, "Hear tell from some Digger Indians nearby that a Sky Spirit lived on that mountain once." He looked at the peak of Mount Shasta, covered in purple shadows from the setting sun. "Wind blew the Sky Spirit's daughter from that peak. Swans caught her and flew her down here, with us hairy bears, who walked on two legs." He thought the image funny and laughed, tearing his eyes away from the snow-capped mountain

138

side. "Can you imagine?"

He returned his upward gaze. "When the Sky Spirit came down to look for his daughter, he found her in love with one of those bears and met his half-bear grandchildren. You'd think he'd be overjoyed, but nope. Mighty angry he was, so he forced the bears to walk on all fours and took away their ability to speak."[5]

I blew the air from my nose and put my hand on my hip. "My father's people believe we come from one union too. When I was a boy, Papa's stories seemed so real, difficult to tell what was true. Hard to know where you're going, not knowing where you've been."

"Bet that mountain knows. Been here longer than any man. What it must have seen." Spencer shook his head, then caught my eye to clarify such wonder. "What it's yet to see. Can you imagine how far a Sky Spirit, or a man, could see, standing so high?" Spencer Hill reached into his pocket and offered me a bit of his tobacco stash.

He held the rolled tobacco between his lips and squinted one eye to keep the smoke from making him tear. Then he sat on the ground. He used both hands to take off each of his boots and return their captured pebbles to the earth. Afterward, he replaced the boots over filthy socks. I couldn't judge him, with mine just as wretched.

I said, "Man could see time and change. All those things he works through, but rarely recognizes until they've passed. He'd have perspective."

He chuckled and flicked ash. "You sound more poet than miner. Bet a man could take a deep breath up there, and then, he'd be free."

An eagle appeared, gliding above the peak. Spencer saw it, too, and pointed his finger to follow its broad-winged flight.

I said, "If a bird can find enough air, a man could too."

Spencer said, "Wasn't enough air for me in Arkansas. Bound to wheatfields and man, earning nothing from the harvest but another day's work. That's why I'm here. Digging gold to buy a plow and tack and turn dirt on a claim I own in this here free state of California."[6]

I said, "I had that once. A wife and daughter, growing corn and wheat near Springfield. Family close. Couldn't see what was in front, gripping too tightly to what was behind. Gave up my chance to choose my life."

I'd seen slaves working in the deeper mines downriver but knew freed blacks and immigrants sought some version of an American dream under Shasta's rocky face. Spencer sought opportunity, like the rest of us here, but his ambitions weren't lofty like mine. He sought only a plow and a horse, a roof over his head. When I had those and more, I wasn't as grateful as I should've been. Now, I'd lost what mattered, searching for an

Yellow Bird's Song

abundance I'd yet to find. It was the want that drove a man insane. Didn't matter for what: wealth, justice, respect.

I told Spencer, "My father and grandfather fought for my people's right to be free—to grow corn from a piece of earth they knew as well as the back of their hand. A place to ride across untouched pastures and chase the sun. Ride across the wilderness without being shot in the back. Where a son could bury his father and not feel the ground tremble from white men riding West with a new treaty in tow."

"You hiding?" He looked at me with a raised eyebrow but dropped it when I didn't answer. I couldn't, not without accepting failure by speaking it aloud.

Spencer said, "Back in Arkansas, the man who owned me, name of Tucker, clutched his heart sitting on his horse, fell, and crushed his wheat. Neither the wheat nor the man stood back up. He had no living wife, no family I'd ever seen. After he died, I flew like that eagle there. Free to remember how I'd changed. Old enough to recognize the time I'd lost."[7]

The eagle disappeared behind Shasta's rock moments before Wacooli and Aeneas returned from the river. Ascending the hill, they dumped the remaining swell from their pans against their pant legs, dotting them with oblong water spots. When my brothers approached, Aeneas tilted his hat toward Spencer and me.

Aeneas said, "Night, Rollin. Had enough today." My exhausted baby brother entered his tent. Shortly after, Aeneas threw out his dusty boots. One landed on the bottom, ready to put back on in the morning. The other lay on its side, too tired to remain standing.

Wacooli took a damp handkerchief from his pocket and wiped his face. "All we found was some dust. Maybe ten cents' worth. We can't keep this up. We'll starve before we find a run that turns a profit."

I looked up at him, holding my knees. "We owe it to ourselves to try. If we don't find a streak, suppose we could stand the boredom of city life? Go back to Sacramento. Find work?"

He nodded his head, confirming his thoughts echoed mine.

I introduced him to my new friend, Spencer Hill, and they shook hands. Listening to them exchange pleasantries, I wondered what Wacooli's fate might have been if Peter had not found him. Would whites have forced him into slavery?

Wacooli said, "Rollin?"

"Huh?"

"Let's give this plot a month. Then we'll decide. I'm beaten up tonight."

Spencer said, "Guess I'll turn in too." He gestured toward the

140

unfinished scribble beside me. "Finish that letter. Safe bet those women are impatient to hear from you three."

"Thank you kindly, freeman Spencer, for the tobacco—and perspective. Best of luck to you."

"To you as well, Cherokee Rollin."

In the many dawns that followed, I took great pains for numbness. Lit the candle mount on my hat with clay-stained hands. Followed my lantern underground, tracing lingering sulfur air singed from blasts of dynamite. I followed the stench willingly, hand braced against embedded veins of iron ore. Work too brutal for shale so brittle.

With pickaxe supine, I heaved the miner's tool in relentless rhythm against ribs of bedrock. Amidst such brainless work, my memory sparked in flashes against the limestone and gneiss.

Tragedy struck.

I woke again that dawn, heard the banging of the door, the clank of the broken lock, the scuffle of men's feet across the wooden floor. Overlapping cries, some in anger, some with fear. Papa's *"Wait."* Mama's "No." And in drops like the sweat down my back, the warriors steadily spit their threats. *"Treaty,"* they said. *"Traitor,"* they said. *"Trail,"* they said. *"Tears."*

Man against nature, in tedious monotony, I rose, hands sliding to grip, overlapping, and thwack. Axe teetering at the fulcrum point then, the collapse. First, a chink, then, the fall of sharp severs that buried my boots. Rocks rang as I bellowed, "Let him go. Leave him be." No one heard me then; no one heard me now.

I threw my axe underfoot and grabbed the drill rod and hammer. Shadows and sunlight. Men against man, the war party carried him outside. Mama's hands held me behind her. Mask and kerchief kept her from him.

Beat and turn. Arms pound and burn. They stabbed. Twenty-seven. Twenty-eight. The arrowhead on the bowie knife. Twenty-nine. They stole his breath, walked single file across his body. Mama in blood-soaked white. Papa raised himself to speak. Air escaped. No words.

This man warred against his thoughts. My mind couldn't separate Papa's visage in life after seeing him pale with death. His blood oozed through a winding sheet and fell, drop by drop on the floor. By his side sat my mother, with hands clasped in speechless agony. Bending over him was his own afflicted mother, with her long, white hair flung loose over her

Yellow Bird's Song

shoulders and bosom, crying to the Great Spirit to sustain her.[8] I lost time to such futility. With buckets in tow, I surfaced, tracing limestone serpentine toward the sun, sonless.

At the time, we scarcely knew our loss.[9] The same day Papa died, Grandfather was ambushed, shot in the back. Uncle Elias' head was beaten in by lying men.

After so many voiced condolences and unvoiced threats, Mother sent me away. And my life sped behind never-ending coach windows, taking me to my grandparents' house, the Northrups in Massachusetts, to study Latin and Greek in Great Barrington's classrooms. Years later, another coach returned me, much slower, to Arkansas, to Washbourne's lawbooks, to Lizzie and her mountain lion. Canoe rides. Our wedding. Holding Alice. Erecting cabin walls. Planting corn, wheat. Killing Kell. Papa's letter. Mama. I hacked through it all. But more rock lay ahead, despite all my efforts to touch the golden reprieve on the other side.

Inside my mind, their faces remained, not the books I'd read or the places I'd lived. Papa's letter said he wished to live for his own sake, his wife and children's sake, and for the sake of his race. He'd said the sacrifice of his life was the consequence of his choices; he had already put his life in danger and contingently given it up. Must I learn the same lesson, realize the same, and die searching for repose and refuge? My pan was still light, even after sifting endless piles of rock for specks shining under the muted earth.

I wanted to fly like an eagle on top of Mount Shasta and glide above the world. Maybe there, I would find the truth, held out of reach of mortal's hand. From the ground, all I'd uncovered was that reason remained as elusive as unfound riches, despite all it cost me to look. Gold mining was not why I was born. My purpose remained insurmountable, like Mount Shasta—my birthright: the Ridge legacy.

Like a tall, wise father, Mount Shasta recited what had already passed. With a child's ears, I heard the mountain's sublime consolation. With the remaining firelight, I uncorked my pen and transcribed the Father's voice.

> And well I ween, in after years, how
> In the middle of his furrowed track, the plowman
> In some sultry hour, will pause and wiping
> From his brow, the dusty sweat, with reverence
> Gaze upon that hoary peak. The herdsman
> Oft will rein his charger in the plain and drink
> Into his inmost soul the calm sublimity;
> And little children, playing on the green, shall
> Cease their sport, and, turning to that mountain

Heather Miller

Old shall of their mother ask: "Who made it?"
And she shall answer — "GOD!"[10]

CHAPTER 14: MERCY
John Ridge
New Echota and Running Waters
October 1829

Behind the mountains near New Echota, the sky's mouth mumbled its warning before the storm. Its cloud-hazed countenance drooped with heavy eyes. Despite such foreboding, chiefs from our eight districts traveled to New Echota and filled the inns. Since construction of New Echota's council house—two levels, with shuttered glass windows and a second floor for executive meetings—there was no need to endure poor weather for annual business. Thankfully so. Many gathered inside before thunder burst forth with rain slung sideways. Wind wrapped the council house from all directions.

Seated on the backless bench, I stared as raindrops swirled on the window's glass. Each droplet blurred with the next with no clear vacancy. In contrast, behind me, candlelight shimmered over silver and gold gorgets worn by colorful chiefs with tattooed necks. Reds and yellows covered bare chests and shoulders, interspersed between buck-skinned jackets adorned with multicolored beading and shells. Unbuttoned military jackets, some in American blue, others in Britain's red, broke patterns of green and black frock coats filling the honored white bench.

Since I was on the ballot, Sleeping Rabbit counted the votes. He shaved his head close, with a large tuft of black hair extending from his crown, adorned by a spread of turkey feathers. Golden bracelets adorned his biceps, matching the three-tiered gold gorget at his neck with earrings dangling from his lobes. His chest was bare, covered in tattooed lines forming diamonds touching at their peaks. The pattern hid on one side, draped by wool-dyed red.

I recognized the painted cross symbol resting between his collarbones. Reverend Daggett, my teacher at the Foreign Mission School, recalled how the Christian Templars wore the same symbol during the Crusades. But to Cherokee, it stood for the balance of the four elements carried inside each man.

Father called Sleeping Rabbit to the podium after completing the tally. He rose from the gallery, wove through the aisle, and stepped over fellow clansmen's capes pooling on the newly sanded floor.

Father read the announcement and with humble gratitude I stood. The people had elected me for the position. I breathed a deep sigh of relief, knowing I'd earned their trust by merit. Five men's votes were missing from the total. Absent was my own, of course, and my father's, as well as Foreman and Hicks, the other nominees, who abstained. Who was the fifth man?

Ross did not rise, not until my father extended a proud hand to shake his. Dismissing thoughts as envy more than suspicion, I returned to the chair at the secretary's desk and took up my quill. Father returned to the speaker's podium so we could conclude business discussed, but without a recorded vote.

Thunder cracked, but it did not interrupt. Father said, "*As a nation, we cannot speak frivolously nor react without thought. There is too much to lose.*"

Lightning's arc distracted me, and I lost my place.

Father continued, "*We must continue to protect our ground from disillusioned Cherokee, who dismiss the severity of the conflict at our door.*" Before voting in the Blood Law, Father concluded his remarks. "*If any citizen of this nation should treat and dispose of any lands belonging to this nation without special permission from the national authorities, he shall suffer death.*"[1]

Chief Womankiller stood, hunched from a lifetime of carrying his clan. His white head was high, hands free of cane or stick. Foxtail fur arched around his shoulders, keeping his creased neck warm. He held a hand to stop Father's call for the vote and addressed us all as his children.

"*I am an old man and have lived a long time watching the well-being of this nation. I love your lives and wish our people to increase in the land of our fathers. The bill before you will punish wicked men who may arise to cede away from our country contrary to the consent of the council. It is a good law—it will not kill the innocent but the guilty.*"[2]

He lifted his arms above the heads of those seated near him. "*Those who have passed to the Nightland, my youth's many companions, men of renown in council, now sleep in the dust.*" He gestured to my father on the platform, saying, "*They spoke the same language as Ridge does now. I stand on the verge of the grave to witness their love for the country. My sun of existence fast approaches its setting, and they will soon lay my aged bones underground. I wish them laid in the bosom of this earth we have received from our fathers who had it from the Great Being above. When I shall sleep in forgetfulness, I hope you will not desert my bones.*[3]

"*I do not speak this in fear of you, as the evidence of your attachment to the country is proven by the bill now before you. I am told that the United States government will spoil their treaties with us and sink our National Council under their feet. It may be so, but it shall not be without our consent or by the misconduct of our people. Of that, I am certain.*"[4]

Yellow Bird's Song

Father said, *"The vote is open and made public."* I tallied, calling each council member's name, as hands raised and lowered. After Chief Womankiller's words, the bill passed unanimously. And so, the Blood Law found its way from tradition to bill to practice.

I shared Chief Womankiller's worry that Georgian boots would stomp out our legislative fires. We knew Georgia set an end date of June 30th, 1830. At that time, Georgia voided all Cherokee laws. By this time next year, if the state had its way, no Cherokee could assemble within Georgia's boundary lines, and her emissaries would annex our land and hold lotteries to remove us from our homes. We barely had six months to file a federal injunction, hoping to persuade our Georgian opposition to reconsider. If it came to blows before that time, we'd request federal mandate to bring in the U.S. Army's bayonets and keep Georgia at bay.

Cherokee's representative democracy worked in the way Yoholo's didn't. Creek chiefs threatened the thoughts of one another, following the old ways. Our head men debated, listened to one another. And the majority ruled.

Father's voice filled the room. *"Chief Womankiller is correct. We are attached to the land in which we are now in possession—it is our fathers' gift—it contains their ashes; it is the land of our nativity and intellectual birth. We cannot consent to abandon it for another far inferior, and—"*

Before he completed his thought, a high-pitched whistling wind sounded from the opening doorway. All turned at the interruption. Outside, a tall man and petite woman stood at the foot of the stairs. Black hair whipped, striping their faces. Rain saturated her dress, a yellow-and-black calico sewn into a pattern of stars. Although highly irregular, Light Guard warriors waved them inside, but they refused to enter and chose to shout through the rain.

I translated the man's declaration. *"I am Noochawee, a criminal condemned to die this day by the Aquohee District Court."* He gestured to the woman at his side. *"Her name is Ahtseeluhskey. I killed her husband, Ahmahyouhah."*

Undiscernible whispers stretched between nearby ears. I watched Ross scan the crowd for Ward, council member for the same district Noochawee named. Ross squinted and condemned Ward, not only for this interruption, but held him accountable for this prisoner's escape.

Ross waved for the Light Guard to escort the disruptors upstairs to the privacy of the executive room. Neither appeared to have the desire to enter the house. Noochawee must have assumed that by bowing his head to enter, the guards ensured he wouldn't leave without chains.

Ross crossed the aisle and spoke to me. "Adjourn council. I don't care for how long."

I didn't question and did as he asked, giving an hour's retirement.

Ross' brothers, Lewis, and another brother, Andrew, followed Ross upstairs. Ward never took his eyes off Chief Ross, waiting for an invitation to the interrogation, one Ross never offered. Each council member quietly recessed, with lingering looks to the self-proclaimed convict and the unspeaking woman waiting beyond the executive door.

Once the bottom floor was clear, Father and I ascended the staircase. My hands carried parchment and quill; he gripped his speaker's gavel. When we knocked and were granted admittance, Noochawee handed Ross a petition. *"Fifty signatures ask that my life be spared."*[5]

After a glance at the damp paper in Noochawee's hand, Ross handed the signatures to me. Otherwise, Ross' unflinching eyes never left the prisoner's face.

Noochawee nodded his head in the woman's direction. *"She has no tongue to speak. Georgian guard cut it from her mouth. Her husband, Ahmahyouhah, was my friend. The court convicted me of his murder."* He turned his body away from Ross and singularly addressed my father. *"I knew you would listen. You know the old ways and the new.*

"Ahmahyouhah could not protect his wife from the white men with guns. The court believed I took his life, but that is only a partial truth. The soldiers cut the tongue from her mouth, so she could not bear witness to their crimes."

Father spoke up, *"Where was this?"*

"Near High Falls, close to McIntosh's tavern. In a Cherokee settlement near old Saunders' place."

Ross spoke to brother Lewis, "Aren't there near twenty homes there?" Lewis knew the territory well, as he was part of the Cherokee Light Guard. Ross promised he would enforce a stronger policing presence there after I told him Peter witnessed pony clubs and whiskey runners.

Lewis Ross said, "As you know, those who already emigrated to Arkansas have abandoned many homes. Apparently, this woman and her husband remained."

The woman, without a tongue, grunted in protest and raised her fist, moving it in the air, signaling she wanted to write. I arranged the paper on the desk under the window, opened the ink well, and outstretched my quill to her. The men in the room watched her pass, streaking the pale floors dark with rainwater dripping from her skirts. When I held the chair for her, she sat and dipped the point in ink. I stood over her shoulder and read her testimony aloud. She scratched the symbols of Sequoyah's syllabary with a shaking hand.

Yellow Bird's Song

"*My husband burst through our cabin door, far too early for him to come in from the fields. He said officers led by a white man stole our horses. From the back pasture, he told them to stop, but they chased him back home.*

"*Ahmahyouhah grabbed the musket off the mantlepiece and told me what happened while he loaded powder from the horn. At first, I didn't believe him, but he looked at me with eyes I trusted. He told me he loved me while opening the door. He promised to escape and find me. His last words were to run. 'Find the Ridge.'"*

Those in the room looked toward Father. The woman re-dipped the quill and moved her hand to the left side of the page.

"*I ran through the back door, but a white man wearing a blue soldier's coat stopped me. He grabbed my arm and drug me behind the house, where the trees met the grazing field. I screamed, tried to pull away. I kicked and scratched, tore the sleeve of his soldier's coat. He stopped when we heard a single shot fired from the opposite side of the house. After the blast, the wind carried angry voices. Ahmahyouhah's answered, so I knew he was still alive. But Ahmahyouhah only spoke Cherokee. The guards spoke English.*" She shook her head, filled the feather's point with ink, and added commentary. "*Words don't matter when both sides hold guns.*"

She continued. "*The soldier must have wanted to see what happened. So, he pulled me around the house and threw me next to a dead soldier's eyes. A fat white man in a black coat commanded the soldiers. They grabbed my husband and pulled him down the stairs. They tied Ahmahyouhah to the tree with his head pointed toward the earth and his bare feet toward the leaves.*"

Tears overwhelmed her. They dripped onto the page, adding salt water to the symbols. She sniffed, held them back, and retook the ink.

"*Another soldier raised his gun to his shoulder and shot Ahmahyouhah's knees. His screams made me retch on my captor's boots. I wrestled free, ran toward my husband. I needed to be beside him. If he was to die, I would travel with him to the Nightland. But I gained little ground before the soldier grabbed my waist with one hand and held my arms down with the other. He picked my feet from the ground.*

"*I couldn't understand what the white man said to the other soldiers. But after, they pulled blowguns from their saddlebags. Two of them sat on the ground and laughed when they blew darts into Ahmahyouhah's chest. They cheered as each dart stuck, while my husband writhed against the tree. Blood dripped in lines down his chest, red streaks through a maze of darts, falling into the dirt beneath his shoulders. Then, the soldier dropped me hard. I tried to scurry away, but he grabbed my ankles. They laughed. I could not kick free. Another soldier lit a torch. He bent to my husband's face, spit in his eye, and lit the darts."*

She dipped the quill again as her lines became too thin to read.

"Ahmahyouhah screamed from the burning. The soldier drug me over rocks and twigs to take me where Ahmahyouhah could see. The soldier put his knee on my head and cut out my tongue. I couldn't breathe gagging on blood. Pain took my spirit into the underworld, even deeper when he forced himself into me."

I put my hand on her shoulder. *"Your husband was still alive?"*

She confirmed it with a single nod. *"When the soldier's seed slipped from him, he left my body alone. My mind cursed him—a rodent burrowing in the home of another."*

Behind *Ahtseeluhskey*, the Ross brothers whispered. Andrew Ross spoke. "What could have motivated such an attack? Why make it appear that a Cherokee war party committed the crime, hanging the man upside down, and setting blow darts on fire? These are old warrior methods, no longer used by the Light Guard and never used by Georgians."

Lewis repeated his brother's suspicion. "They made it appear Cherokee warriors were responsible. Why would they bother? Few whites would care whether Cherokee murdered one another."

Pacing behind the woman, I said, *"Newspapers would care. The more violent they report the Cherokee, the easier it becomes for Georgia to declare us enemies to settling whites."*

She wrote that the white man gave the commands, not an officer in uniform. When the question of his identity surfaced, I assumed who it was. I asked her, *"Did the guards steal your horses?"*

She affirmed my suspicion with a nod.

Kneeling at her feet, I took her hand. *"I curse the Black Crow who flew past your door."*

Ross and Father had heard Peter's story. They both should have understood. But only Father looked up with recognition. He squinted his eyes to dam the rising anger behind them. He made white-knuckled fists at his sides knowing we'd need a great deal more evidence before accusing a powerful white man of murder on top of theft. Georgia's courts wouldn't listen otherwise.

Either Ross didn't hear what I said or didn't follow my connection between events.

Reverend Worcester knocked at the door; his arms were stacked with blankets. Worcester nodded to Chief Ross, saying, "I'm sorry for the intrusion. Standing Rabbit said there was need." After Worcester saw the

Yellow Bird's Song

woman, he wrapped her shoulders in a blanket and knelt to dry her feet with his handkerchief.

Noochawee filled the ensuing silence. From beside the warming fire, he whispered. *"Shots echoed across the valley. Took me until dark to reach them. Had it not happened during the full nut moon, I may never have seen that Ahmahyouhah was still alive.*

"Circles of blisters with burned darts embedded in his skin. I watched his shallow breaths until I found enough courage to end his suffering. After my gunshot, a sob rose from the grass. I found Ahtseeluhskey there, bleeding from her mouth. I took her to my wife's mother for healing. And by the harvest moon, I sat trial for Ahmahyouhah's murder."

Ahtseeluhskey wiped her tears with the back of her wrist, pushing her eyes back along with a memory she could never unsee.

Ross paced the room, staring out the rainy window. "We must protect this witness, but I cannot do so." He turned his head halfway toward us. "Georgians come and go from my home. Quatie and I could not assume such a risk."

I addressed *Ahtseeluhskey*, "the flower" in Cherokee, as it was her decision. *"You can stay with my family at Running Waters. It isn't a long journey. We have an empty cabin where you could live. We will protect you."* She nodded and stood. To the room, I said, "Sarah and I will take responsibility for her."

Ross put his hands on his lapel and stepped toward Noochawee. His mercy could decide whether the man lived or died. "I will explain your request to the council and encourage a vote to rescind your sentence. You will not die this day for saving this woman's life and ending her husband's pain."

Noochawee attempted to hold his emotion, but a single tear fell from the relief brought by Ross' compassion.

Then Ross called my father's name with the deeper tones of an order. "Major Ridge, what I ask of you will take you back to the warrior's ways of your youth. Although, it is necessary. Go to her home. If you should meet the Georgians who did this, take heed to bring them here to our authorities. Do not kill them."

With Ross' command for revenge, Father loosened his fists. He turned toward the door to prepare for his task, quieter than I expected him to be. It was a dangerous weight Ross' confidence placed on Father's shoulders; however, I had little fear of Father's ability to carry out the task.

Then Ross called my father's Cherokee name to stop his long strides toward the door. "Joe Foreman will assist you and lead the Light Guard. Take only those with discretion. Build a war party of those you trust—

150

those who can see far in the distance."

With a single glance over Father's shoulder, his familiar eyes found mine, and mine alone.

CHAPTER 15: LILY OF THE VALLEY
Sarah Ridge
Running Waters
October 1829

Less time passed between birthing pains and rooted me to the bed. Behind me, Quatie leaned my body forward. I breathed through the contraction, trying to distract myself by looking out the window. This afternoon's storm melted into a foggy night. This weather would delay John's arrival even more.

Quatie broke the tempo of raindrops tapping tree leaves outside. "Have you eaten speckled trout in the last few months? If you did, this baby will be covered in freckles and birthmarks." She intended a distraction to help me breathe. I laughed, exhaling all the air held in my lungs.

I said, "Then, she'll look like me."

Quatie said, "Was your mother fond of fish?" Then she fixed her eyebrows in pretend sternness. "Have you eaten black walnuts? Tell me. I must know."

"Is that bad?" I asked.

"Only that your son will have an enormous nose."

Mother Susannah entered the bedroom and spoke with her pipe wedged between her teeth. "Let's call this baby down," she said. Susannah brought with her a basin of steaming water, cloth, and the baby basket. Sheathed in leather across her chest rested her familiar blade.

She'd called many a baby down, chanting prayers in each of the four directions. East and west to bring a little boy.

As she moved toward the northern corner, Honey entered and interrupted Mother Susannah's smoky chants. *"Might as well just stay there. That osdi is going to be a baby girl. Sarah been eatin' sweets for weeks."*

Quatie asked Honey, "Has Sarah eaten rabbit stew? Surely, even white women know what that means."

Honey tilted her head, confused by Quatie's question.

Quatie said, "If Sarah has eaten rabbit stew, this baby will sleep with its eyes open. It's how Sleeping Rabbit earned his name."

Mother Susannah came to my bedside. She held my hand through another pain, comforting me with humming and whispers. If Major Ridge had a gift of calming horses with his voice, Mother Susannah did the same for expectant mothers. She put her hand on my constricting belly and whispered to the child underneath. "Four mothers await you, little one,

Heather Miller

with gifts of loom or blow gun, whichever you choose."

Honey said, "Where are the papas? Walking Stick should be back with them by now."

Quatie said, "Fathers don't bring babies into the world." She turned to me and said, "That nightingale in the oak is telling us the storm has passed. Can you hear it?"

Mother Susannah lowered my back when the pain subsided and took the cloth from my forehead. She doused it in the water basin and wiped my face. Afterward, she placed it on the back of my neck. I exhaled with the momentary calm its coolness brought. I rested my head on Quatie's chest, closed my eyes, and breathed. "It is late in the season for them. It's singing in the rain."

Honey came to my bedside in a shuffle of skirts. Quatie brushed my hair and began braiding it.

Mother Susannah said, *"Birds know much we do not."* Quatie repeated the message in English.

A little time passed before another pain pulsed, tightening the skin across my belly. After Mother Susannah raised the quilt to check on the child, she gave a busy and nervous Honey something to do. "Go to the kitchen and prepare Sarah some honey water. Make plenty. Steep some yarrow and shepherd's purse from my bag."

Honey nodded, and, for once, closed the door behind her.

Quatie asked, "What is the tea for?"

My incoming pain stopped Mother Susannah from explaining. Behind me, Quatie's chest raised and lowered. She said, "Breathe with me." The quiet whirl of her hair brushed across my shoulder. I tried to follow her lead. Instead, with the gripping pressure, I clenched my teeth, squinted my eyes, and held tight to the air in my lungs.

Quatie said, "It doesn't serve you or the child to tense."

I moaned and rolled to my side, holding my belly. Mother Susannah kneaded her fists into my lower back, pushing against the tense and tired muscles. Like unraveling an old knot, it was difficult to find purchase enough to set it free. I asked, "Where is he?"

Quatie said, "The child will not wait for its father. No matter. I wouldn't let him near you now for all the world. Men have no business with babies after seeding the field."

I said, "With Clarinda and Rollin, John was here."

Mother Susannah gently rolled me to my back and pushed my knees apart. Her warm hands touched me. When she rose, she folded the quilt covering me over my thighs, and her face told me more than her words. She said, *"It's nearly time."*

Yellow Bird's Song

Quatie responded in Cherokee, but whatever she said made Mother Susannah's face fall.

Speaking of the blood scared me more than thinking about it. But I knew this pain was more complicated than other birthing pains, with sensations more like tearing, rather than only tautness. Everyone stopped speaking when I said, "Save the child."

Mother Susannah nodded, understanding my request in English. But such a choice brought a thorny stillness into the room.

Quatie moved from behind me. In her absence, I prayed.

Men find their faith with sight, ever altering like moonset's arch toward sunrise. He praises God for fortunate rain but curses the same God for sending a sun-scorched drought, baring a single breath between. Women's sorrow doesn't exchange blessing for curse. Her faith doesn't shine blue light like the transient moon—but pulses from unseen rays under her skin. A mother's faith glows through anticipating and enduring the unforeseen, recognizing whatever comes as God's will.

The nightingale's song called, with swelling breast under brown feathers.

Honey returned with two cups. After drinking both, I shook. The instinct to push told me to bear down, but after laboring all day, I had little power to do so. My muddled vision smudged dark like the snuff of candle smoke.

Quatie's troubled face blurred. I heard Honey beg to delay. Mother Susannah's hand touched my forehead, across my taut belly, and between my legs. When I opened my eyes, Susannah raised a red hand in front of her face.

The nightingale warbled.

Mother Susannah called my name and commanded, "Wake. Push."

Mother's blessing, not Eve's curse.

The pulse inside me. Bearing down.

The nightingale whistled.

With a gasp, I was no longer in any pain. With an unblemished sight, I saw Jesus' mother, Mary. She knelt on a stone floor before an open window, hands clasped in prayer. She was bound to the earth by streams of moonlight. We both heard the resonant voices of angels, speaking with the same dissonance to follow the ringing of bells.

Mary put her hand on her swelling womb. When she conceived the Son of God, she could not see Him, even though she sensed His presence, one ordained by God's will. At first, only the stretch of muscle or push of bone let her know of Him. In time and without warning, Jesus swirled in her womb. His effortless touch reassured her He was alive.

154

Nightingale's bottomless song filled my ears.

Blind to distant sounds. Underwater. Holding my breath.

Minutes seemed like hours. Tightening. Constricting. Bearing down. Baptized with blood.

When I opened my eyes, I floated, a pulsing silver cord attaching my spirit to my body.

I smelled animal musk and dry hay from an unfamiliar barn. Joseph comforted Mary and held her hand as she felt for the Son she couldn't yet see. Jesus' earthly body filled Mary to bursting, wretched in painful sorrow, believing her heart enough to hold Him. God trusted Mary with a gift only known to her. With angelic midwives, Mary gave birth to the Son of God. And He breathed. Even in infancy, He cried for the sins of the world.

Tugged. A suck of air. Awake. A child's cry.

The knife. Separation. Mother Susannah said, "Daughter." The child was alive. Then, I felt the flow of rivers in bright red blood.

The nightingale's warble turned into squawks and shrieks.

John's scent overwhelmed me. He stopped in the doorway and then rushed to my side. He lifted my body, cradling the weight of my head on his arm. He begged his mother. Then, I couldn't feel his warmth or hear his voice. I floated above. His lips said, "Do something!" Mother Susannah didn't answer, couldn't.

A stranger, a woman dressed in yellow calico, entered with a lit candle shining up on her face. Loose hair hid her sunken cheeks. She raised the candle toward my spirit. When no one else had seen me, she did. She set her light beside the stained bedside and touched John's shoulder. He lifted my body, bracing my back against his chest.

Without words, the stranger moved Quatie's and Mother Susannah's hands to hold my ankles and feet tight. Her hand entered my womb and pulled the bloody cord from me. Her other hand pressed my womb from the outside, palpating.

The silver cord retracted. The softest touch was unbearable. When she tugged, my senses returned. I screamed in agony.

My heavy body shuttered once more and stilled. I floated again, with no silver cord attaching soul to body. Calm.

John's voice caught, and he rocked me closer to him. Indigo light emanated from his forehead, between his eyes, and draped like robe's sleeves over his arms. Faint pulses of teal, the color of Quatie's peacocks, rose from the crown of my red hair. Each hue absorbed into his skin, making his color deeper, richer.

John tilted my limp head to his. His voice shook, stopped, and started

Yellow Bird's Song

again, interrupted by weeping breaths. "I will not—give your heart back—I cannot. It's too late." I understood his thoughts without need for speech.

Mother Susannah reached bloody hands behind her and slid down the wall to a waiting chair. Quatie reached for her hand, a tear falling down her face.

There was no need for tears.

John said, "Do you remember when you held my heart in your hands? The night we went to water?"

I could never forget it.

"The Great Spirit came to us through the river. He took your heart and put it inside me, took my own and placed it in you."

We knew He did so even though we couldn't see the work of his hands.

"Since then, I've heard it beat—your faith in my chest. I know its rhythms by heart as you know mine. We are only half ourselves without the other."

He shook my body and then, with sudden serenity, accepted what was.

"I'll tell our children how much you loved them each day. You held our lives dearer with every breath. I will hold them close so they can feel your heart beating against their cheeks."

With each of his promises, his strength, the purple light, seeped from him and dissipated. The turquoise light emanating from my spirit faded into blue ether.

My spirit floated toward the open window when the woman raised her hand. The yellow of her dress had turned russet orange with my blood. Her black hair became a sunflower's collection of seeds. White light emanated from her eyes, as if she held her face to an invisible sun.

I sent my thoughts toward her, asking her to allow me to stay. I said, "Mary's faith manifested in her arms, nursed with love, swaddled in hope, for the babe she'd loved but never seen. Through faith alone, she was reborn."

The woman, a sunflower, nodded her head with understanding. She opened the door and gathered my baby from Honey. No others moved in the room when she exposed my breast and guided the baby to latch.

At first, John wouldn't release my body, wouldn't allow her to touch me. When he recognized her intent, he relaxed his arms.

With the familiar tug, I opened my earthly eyes. The child suckled and stared at me with golden hues under their infant blue. Tufts of black hair covered her pale white head.

"I'm right here," I said.

Honey sobbed. Mother Susannah fell from the chair to her knees.

Quatie's hands dropped from her mouth. John's eyes, full of tears, held us both, mother and child. And the beautiful sunflower angel stood over us, smiling.

I awoke to morning sunshine. From the chair next to me, John held our daughter's hand above the blanketed swaddle resting on his forearms. He stood, gently laid the bundle in my arms, and kissed my forehead. He was never more than an arm's reach away.

During the night, Quatie must have returned home. Honey changed the bed and helped me change into a clean shift. Mother Susannah forced me to drink her tea and honey. And the sunflower angel, that I didn't know was real, stood as sentry and stared out the window.

We admired the morning's grace, a sky's array of gold and rose, like quartz infused with rose-clouding crystal. While my daughter suckled, the tender soreness in my womb returned. Her healing saved my life. The holy ache was a reminder of the miracle I'd been granted. With my sacrifice of blood, our daughter brought me visions of Heaven. That quiet morning, we named her Susan—the lily of the valley.

In Cornwall, Reverend Daggett once called the flower's white blossoms "Eve's tears," shed when God banished her from Paradise in sinful shame. Reverend Sam called the same flower "Mary's tears," cried under Jesus' cross. Susan, too, was manifested by faith.

The nightingale no longer hovered outside the window. The Greeks believed the bird sang of sorrow: a piece of hidden music sung by a broken-hearted woman transformed into a bird.[1] Later poets imagined the nightingale's song accompanied the lover's waltz, a tune for those who'd rather tryst among the sage, dreading their inevitable separation when the cock announced the morn.[2] My mother believed the ladybird cried, searching helplessly for a mate to care for her.

But Mother was wrong. They all were. The nightingale's song comes from the male, trilling until dawn, calling his love down in the hours before day, hoping they'll reunite under his protecting wing, safely on the ground.

CHAPTER 16: TOO IMPATIENT TO WAIT FOR GOD
John Ridge
Running Waters
February 1830

Sarah embroidered and rocked Susan's cradle with her foot, although there was no need. Our child breathed deeply in slumber. Firelight flickered on one side of Sarah's cheeks as she focused her eyes on the needle and thread in her lap.

What I was about to tell her would take away the peace we'd known this winter. I set aside my copy of the *Phoenix* and wove my fingers together to keep them still. I had procrastinated telling her, knowing she wouldn't want me to leave.

"Father asked that I go with him to Sunflower's home tomorrow. White families will soon occupy her village. Well, families of the Georgian Guard. But the abandoned cabins belong to Cherokee. We cannot allow the squatters to stay." Under my breath, I added, "It is more cost-effective for Georgia to give them our property rather than pay the soldiers. But they don't own the land they offer as payment."

She stopped sewing but didn't meet my eyes. Sarah stowed her needle in the hoop and rested her hands in her lap. She sighed. "And when they retaliate?"

I tried to console such unnecessary worry. "Twenty-eight other Cherokee ride with us. We'll outnumber the soldiers."

Her volume elevated, more high-pitched. "An entire war party?"

"We won't kill them." My remark offered her some consolation, but it didn't damper her fire.

She said, "The white men will not take the time to interpret your intention."

I couldn't fault her logic. She made perfect sense.

"We've tried evicting the invading settlers with the law. I've written pleadings to Hugh Montgomery, but he stands on the outskirts of the argument, choosing not to get involved. He said the federal government shouldn't take sides."

She stood with quiet fury and paced over the rug. She crossed her arms, thinking aloud. "Doing so keeps the government's alliances on all sides." Then she looked at me as if some sudden thought reached her toes and halted her feet. "Did Father ask you—or tell you that you must go?"

That was not what I expected her to say. I separated my hands, placed them above my knees, to stand. My eyes surveyed the doubt emanating from hers. I said, "What difference does it make? He trusts me, asks me to lead. I speak English; the Georgian Guard will not speak Cherokee. Father understands tribal justice, although my presence dampers that instinct in him." I took a deep breath and reached for the arms crossing her chest. She must understand. "I owe a great debt to Sunflower; she saved your life. The least I can do is bring her some semblance of justice."

My reasons did not appease her. She said, "Is Sunflower's fate what you want for me, for us? What would I do? If the guard kills my husband, my children's father, and grandfather on this journey for justice? Have you considered that?"

"Of course, I have." My response was weak. Sarah's empathy for Sunflower's story made her nervousness clear and more relevant. Such fears were genuine. After all, the Georgian Guard had little remorse when murdering Cherokee.

Sarah shocked me. "You don't want justice for Sunflower." Sarcasm, not sincerity, elevated the temperature in the room. "Tell me. Are you going to play these deadly games with white men who do not care whether you live or die? Those in command want nothing more than to take your voice out of the debate."

"I will be careful." It was a promise yielding little faith if her prediction came true.

She scoffed, walked past the arch into the hallway, and turned back. "How does one do that? Leave your head on a swivel, constantly looking behind you, hoping soldiers don't shoot you in the back, or tie you upside down and shoot out your knees? Cut the tongue from your mouth? No one will believe your accusations if they catch you or any member of this war party. So, what stops the Georgian Guards from killing you and going on about their day?"

"If we interrogate the Georgian Guard already living there, perhaps we will find out whether Black Crow ordered Sunflower's husband killed. We hope to bring in the man who hurt her. Someone must be brave enough to stop them."

"I see," she said. "So, it isn't only for justice. You also go to prove your courage. You want the Cherokee to love you as they do your father. It isn't only from gratitude that you make this journey. It is for your own satisfaction, with something to prove."

I took one step forward, but she stopped my forthcoming promise with her upturned palm. She countered, but I interrupted her and raised my voice, insistent. "Nothing will happen to me!"

Standing apart from one another, in distance and belief, she confirmed, "There is nothing you or your father can do to guarantee that. This is an

Yellow Bird's Song

unnecessary risk you take with your life."

"I cannot sit here and abide, asking Cherokee to risk their lives in my stead. A lieutenant doesn't ask his soldiers to gamble anything he doesn't also risk."

"A lieutenant, then. You go to make a stand and earn respect from the Cherokee warriors riding beside you."

"It isn't only that, but yes. I must go. Other than Vann and Peter, I'm the only one who can identify that Crowwell brother. We must confirm his stake in these crimes."

Sarah said, "Won't he recognize you?"

"A chance I must take. When Vann and I met Thomas Crowwell before, we dressed as natives and didn't speak English to him. But his brother, John Crowwell, would recognize me. He was the one who wouldn't shake my hand, who tempted Xander. He is too proper to tow the evidence and risk being caught. I doubt White Crow will be there. But his brother, Black Crow, might."

Sarah retorted, "All the better for the Georgian Guard. Witnesses to your execution. Go if you must. You won't listen to my warning. If your father demands your presence, you must."

I didn't think before I spoke. "Sarah, you are being irrational."

Affronted, she closed the distance between us and looked into my eyes so quickly that I felt a warm breeze pass between us.

"I'm not the one headed into the lion's den, John. I see you like no one else in this world. Your desire to be respected gambles all you've won, spent to outwit a white man. You were the same in Cornwall, railing against Samuel's bullying, against the fire-toting mob when we married. Now the battle has shifted south, onto your ground."

I tried to help her understand. "Don't you see? If I can catch them in the crime, I'll have enough evidence to back my claim. Georgian courts cannot deny my charge with indisputable facts. Trust me; I know what I'm doing."

She crossed beside me and gathered Susan, who whimpered at our loud voices. Then, with our daughter cradled in her arms, Sarah whispered, "Georgia can and will deny you simply because of the color of your skin. They won't hear you because they don't see you as an equal, and they don't care enough to listen."

Her slicing words shocked me, even though I knew their truth. Then, exasperated, I placed my hands on my hips and looked away. "Sarah, this is bigger than us. You're asking me to choose where my loyalties lie. One is as much a part of me as the other. Please. Don't do this."

I knew she'd be upset, but I couldn't have predicted so much fury.

Once, she stood behind my every endeavor. Now, she'd rather I remain safe at home.

From the foot of the stairs, she caught my eye. "It is not your place to seek God's vengeance for the white man's sins."

Claiming my obligation, I refuted her. "Then, who will go in my stead? I've placed my bet. I must show my hand." In an accusation I didn't mean, I replied loud enough for her to hear. "You aren't listening either."

She heard all that I said and all I didn't. I couldn't force my tongue to tell her she was right, see her side, and still go.

From the top of the stairs, she said, "Just because I don't agree with you doesn't mean I'm not listening."

I stood before the fire, transfixed by its embers. What difference would it make if she was right? As she said, I still would go, and constantly look over my shoulder. As much as it pained me to admit, when I shared our plans with Elias, he begged me to cast aside my vengeance. Regardless, my soul was ill-equipped to supply mercy for those who stole joy with cruelty, arrogance, and greed.

In the hours before dawn, Sleeping Rabbit beat his drum to call my father's men. Once gathered, we stared at our reflections in river water, painted our eyes black, and adorned our heads and bodies in regalia of feather, bead, bell, and shell. Then, we joined Father in the circle. Each man armed himself with a war club in one hand and gripped the handle of a tomahawk or bow in the other.

Father began his call with a resounding whoop, exhausting all the air in his lungs. The sound bellowed against the hills, waking and warning our enemies sleeping beyond. In unified answer, we repeated Father's terrifying scream. Sleeping Rabbit continued the rhythm of his drum and steered our feet with his repeated chant. Father's bells clanked, taking the war dance's first steps.

The jingling reminded me of another time he'd left for battle. With his clansmen, Father screamed then as he did now, turning and treading the earth before fighting uprising Creek Red Sticks in 1814. I was sick then, fevered, and could not come down to study him. But my mind recollected the sounds as clearly now as when I listened and watched him from my window. With buffalo horns on his head, Father danced, pounding imaginary renegade Creek warriors under his moccasins. Even from that height, I remember the vengeance in his eyes, the same eyes that cared for me, wiped sweat from my forehead, and rubbed my back through

Yellow Bird's Song

coughing fits. He was all I ever wanted to be, fiercely free and robust, his voice regarded by others. The years had changed nothing.

But beside him now, his bells rang with the wild abandon I felt. Father's war dance imitated how we'd stalk our foes, observant and muzzled through the pines and oaks. Our feet stomped forward in a circle, never backward in retreat. We beat the ground to Sleeping Rabbit's pace while Father sang sage advice across the roaring fire, nearest the circle's center.

"Our wives and children should never mourn. If we die, we bring victory to our nation."[1]

We echoed his cries, acknowledged his direction by imitation, and swung our wrists, gripping knife handles with blades extending from our palms. There was no resistance swiping through the air. Yet, in our minds, we sliced our enemies' throats. Testing our strength, we raised clubs to dent their skulls until their brains seeped from their ears. Sleeping Rabbit increased his tempo; we stepped with his speeding rhythm. We bent low again, saw the victims in our minds, bled the throats of invaders, and beat their blood into the Creator's earth with our feet. War dances offered no mercy.

After his ending cry, Father led us to water. Each of us was out of breath, but invigorated, infused by images of blood seeping between gripped fingers. As we followed one another down the hill, the Creator's power rose in me, lifting my body hair like earth predicting lightning's arrival. Powerful and intoxicating, all my years of reason left me. I became instinct itself.

We doused our bodies from the Oostanaula's shallows in bone-numbing, icy water. After submerging and emerging, a throng of us stood behind Father, facing west. Steam rolled from our bare chests in one predestined swell.

Father shouted to the west, defiant against the Cherokee's direction of death. He said, *"The Cherokee are a civilized tribe."* The other men and I repeated in unison, and the trees shook at the vibrations of our voices.

"We cannot take the scalps of those who tortured Ahmahyouhah and raped and maimed his wife. We cannot dress for war, arm ourselves with club and blade, and ride through the night to kill those who stole Cherokee lives and homes—despite stomping the war circle.

"We must show them mercy while they showed none. Hide your warrior hearts behind white man's clothes. Wipe free your eyes of the black masks. Sheath your blades. Even though we load our pistols, we cannot fire. In the coming days, we teach our enemies that we know they deserve a dishonorable death but will not grant it them."

Heather Miller

No one spoke, but all looked south, confused. Father spoke behind us. *"General Jackson, the American president, says we must negotiate with General Coffee and Colonel Montgomery. But they are weak and will not act. They prefer to stand and watch, eager to report us as savages from their printing presses. Chief Ross believes we must bury our instincts to kill. Yet those trespassers must leave our land. We will burn the homes they stole and show the whites Cherokee honor through mercy."*

As a conclusion to Father's command, we turned north, submerged, and reemerged, feeling the cold vanquish the violence of the dance, stowing it inside our bodies. Father was calmer, but his voice resonated off the banks; no man had trouble understanding his imperative.

"Let the families go free. Bring the soldiers to New Echota to face justice in Cherokee court. We must keep our wits. No whiskey must dull our senses."

We faced southeast, the direction we would travel. Father said, *"This day, we ride to Beaver Dam and Cedar Creek. Georgians might forge our names on deeds, but they will hear our testimony today. Only then will they know they cannot steal our horses, rape our women, and live on our land."*

As the sun crept over the treetops, we emerged clean and dressed in frock coats and ties as he commanded. Each man packed his skins while arming himself with gunpowder and ball inside hidden pistols. With the Cherokee warrior barely under the surface, we looked like a proper delegation, as Father said—civilized.

Once we mounted, we left Ridge land in two regiments. Father chose me to lead the smaller second group, riding beside Vann, Chewoyee, Mills, Waggon, and Rattling Gourd, traveling in plain sight up the public road. He, his old friend Sleeping Rabbit, and Joe Foreman leading the Light Horse Brigade, wove south through the woods on horseback. We'd planned to reunite near the village so we could survey Georgia's numbers. It would take us until dusk to arrive.

Vann and I rode most of the morning in silence, still reeling from the effects of Father's commanding war dance. As we rode, I heard Father's powerful chants above Sleeping Rabbit's relentless rhythm, matching the sway and steps of my horse.

Vann ducked under a nearby branch, swiping away a limb with his hand, and spoke to me. "I'm sick of your quiet. What's wrong? Is Sarah well enough for you to be here?"

His question returned my thoughts to home. "She is well, but angry with me, even after I told her this journey was on behalf of Sunflower."

"Sounds like you regret coming. I know your father. Doesn't take much to understand why you could not refuse him. My wife, Jenny, has no use for this journey. She called it a waste, showing Cherokee weakness if we didn't kill the squatters."

"Sarah said vengeance belongs to God, not man." Saying her words aloud to Vann replayed the argument. Sarah flared, too warm to sleep beside. I didn't stay and rode to my father's house in the night.

Vann said, "Well, call me impatient. We don't have time to wait for God."

We approached Old Saunders' place near Beaver Dam with stealth. With hobbled horses behind us, not to give away our position, we reunited the two branches of our war party. We scuttled to the edge of the clearing and counted how many soldiers claimed residence in the village.

But smoke came from only one chimney. We'd planned to surround the house, call forth the family, anticipating that any others present would make their presence known. After allowing them time to load their wagons, our warriors would burn the houses to prevent them or anyone else from returning. If we didn't, they'd circle back and unpack before our war party made it home.

The warriors crawled back first. Father and I remained under cover, watching.

"*Son, my eyes are not what they were. Tell me, how many men do you see?*"

"*Only the Georgian soldier filling his arms with firewood. Wait. There's a woman and a boy child, maybe eight years old.*"

"*This would be more pleasant without the presence of women and children.*"

"*True.*"

"*You wish to interrogate him?*"

"*I do. I speculate he's part of Crowwell's outfit, traveling from McIntosh's tavern to Fort Stewart, selling their liquor stock before heading west to sell the ponies and slaves.*"

"*Don't ride in first. Remain in the rear until I've secured the house.*"

"*Why? If we set a perimeter guard, we'll know if his friends attack behind our backs.*"

"*Command Chewoyee, Mills, Waggon, and Rattling Gourd to remain and guard the four directions. Keep Vann beside you; that's why he's here.*"

"*Vann speaks English. Knows Crowwell. If I needed protection, why did you ask me to come? He could have served you in my stead."*

"That is not true. You are smarter than Vann, cannier, and have more experience negotiating with whites. Vann reacts first and thinks second. You think ahead. I'd rather Vann hold the pistol and you ask the questions. Son, lead us to the men responsible."

He scuttled backward on his forearms and knees, cleared the rustling brush, and left me to my thoughts. Over my shoulder, I watched him zigzag through the pine trees, and remove the restraints from his horse. Such confidence in me elevated my pride, to be sure, but I didn't know how to take his admission. Was Vann's life any less valuable than my own? I touched the drawing on my chest and remembered saving Vann's life from a snakebite. Father knew Vann would repay the debt with his own life. After closing my eyes, I cursed myself for not trusting. Father asked for the same blind trust he had when he'd watched me through the sound-filled night I journeyed from boy to man. Then, as now, he wouldn't leave me alone.

I commanded my four men to ride the outskirts, relay from one to another, covering the ground in each direction. Father reminded the war party of the rules of engagement. He unwrapped a cloth soaked in pine tar, and the men followed his lead, wrapping the ends of their torches. Father gave his last command. *"Light these with the fire in the white man's grate."*

Shaking ground warned of our arrival before our enemy could react to our galloping band. We stopped twenty-five feet from the occupied cabin door. From his porch, a soldier, armed with a British Baker rifle, crammed the muzzle-loading flintlock into his shoulder, aiming straight for my father. He'd have only one shot alone to take down thirty Cherokee. The numerical odds were in our favor, proven by the sheer number of cocking pistols responding to his singular threat.

He knew so too, based on his panicked expression, gritting his rotten and missing teeth.

Father said, *"Put down your weapon. We do not shy from a single ball."*

Vann rode forward to link my father's words to the soldier, who after hearing them, begrudgingly laid his gun at his feet. How did Crowwell expect this single soldier to defend this village against attack? Even though I knew there were Cherokee stationed in the woods, I couldn't help but wonder whether the guard hid their reinforcements. So, from the rear, I did as Sarah said, looking behind me more times than I could count.

Once he was unarmed, I rode through an opening in the warriors. His eyes tracked me as I dismounted and walked to the bottom of his stairs.

Yellow Bird's Song

The soldier thought he could afford sarcasm. "Who are you? Some limping Cherokee dressed as a dandy?"

I ignored his insult at my expense. He spoke with audacity and undeserved privilege. I asked, "How did you tear your coat, sir?"

Sunflower ripped the soldier's coat who attacked her. She described him as a heavy man, not agile, with a cloud over one eye. She wrote how the middle-aged man had forgotten how to run and drank too much. This man met her description.

The soldier said, "What are you talking about? What difference does it make?" He brushed aside the fraying tear, clearly visible with his white shirt poked underneath the gap in blue wool.

"I asked you, sir, how did your sleeve tear?"

He looked toward the tree line, telling me exactly where the crime had happened. Then, he lied, saying, "Caught it on some briars. Happened months ago."

"And your wife didn't repair it? Hard to believe." I stepped forward and rested one foot on his bottom stair. Behind me, Vann cocked his pistol.

"Wife just got here." The soldier thought to retreat, but the same wife and son came through the cabin door and blocked his exit. Foreman had ordered the Light Guard to surround the house.

Father said, still mounted on his horse, "*Ask him where the others are.*"

"Are there other families who live here?" I asked.

Before he could answer, his wife made a tear-filled gasp and covered her son's eyes, holding his head against her waist.

The soldier said, "Arriving any minute now. Georgian Guards and their families." With mock confidence, he boasted, as if reinforcements would show by his command. He looked to the road, expecting to see the cavalry.

After translating the soldier's warning, I approached my horse, hoping he'd think his bluff effective, and we'd leave. But I stopped and turned back. "You are sure that coat wasn't torn in some struggle?"

"No Cherokee to fight since last fall—until now."

After his inadvertent confession, I rejoined him, closer by two stairs this time. "I wonder why your supervisor would leave you and your family to survive the winter alone. Trespassing on Cherokee ground, no less."

He stepped back. "My commanding officer awarded my service with the charge here."

I said, "I doubt you know the meaning of the word. Too bad you won't reap the benefits of your labors. Truth is that your commanding officer left you to tend to those stolen horses there." I pointed toward the grazing pasture. "Just until he could return and gather them for the trip west."

"You don't know what you're talking about. This is my land, my horses, given to me last fall for my service on special assignment."

"Oh, I'm sure killing a Cherokee man, raping his wife before his eyes, and living in their home is ample reward for dutiful service."

"I don't know what you're talking about." After his denial, he shoved his wife and son inside. At least he feared for their lives, but his reaction was another admission of guilt. He realized we knew of his crimes, unknowing how we would seek retribution. When the innocent entered, I took the last step to reach his porch and kicked his rifle away. We stood, my brown eyes to his muted green. I knew I stared into the face of Sunflower's rapist. A cataract haze covered one of his eyes. I pushed the soldier down the steps to the yard in front of the house.

Vann grabbed him by the front of his damaged coat and asked, "Which tree was it? Where you shot her husband? Do you remember, or was your flask too empty by then?" I linked Vann's words, so our warriors knew what he said.

When Vann mentioned the flask, the soldier ironically reached for it. From behind him, I grabbed it from his pocket and kicked the back of his knees, forcing him to kneel.

I spun the top of the flask open, smelled it, and dumped the last of the fire whiskey onto the ground beside him. Four warriors dismounted with torches in hand and surrounded the soldier. He cowered with his hands above his head, thinking the approaching warriors would bash in his brains.

I said, "Who gave you this land? Who offered you whiskey and this home as a reward for murder, horse theft, and rape? Tell me his name." I spoke through gritted teeth, not recognizing the gristle in my voice.

I grabbed his shirt, pulling him forward, tilting his head up so he could see my face. "Tell me where this man is. Now."

Overpowering dread made him talk, despite doing so with arrogance. "He rides with a wagon full of the same whiskey you spilled. Black Crow will know you've been here if you take the horses. When he sees our bodies rotting in the grass, with our homes smoking to cinders behind us, he'll know."

I said, "I don't plan to wait that long to intercept him."

One of the Light Guard set down his torch and gathered rope from his belt to tie the soldier's hands and feet behind his back.

"Who is Black Crow? Tell me his real name, or your wife and son can watch you burn. It's your choice." Never ask a question without already knowing its answer.

I'd never spoken so cruelly to anyone in my life. My lungs ached to

Yellow Bird's Song

find air enough to taunt and threaten him. I knew I was on the edge of a line I dared not cross. But I reminded myself we were playing the white man's game, and his rules were more savage than ours. I didn't translate the threat, embarrassed I'd made it. We wouldn't take the soldier's life, but he didn't know that, so I played on the fear of smelling his own burning flesh.

Vann grabbed him by the collar and slapped him. Once. Then twice. When Vann let go, the soldier spit blood from his mouth before stating his admission. "Thomas Crowwell. He runs the tavern out of Fort Stewart in Alabama. His brother is Colonel John Crowwell, Indian Agent to the Creeks."

Vann looked at me in surprise. I said, "I'm acquainted with both men."

Father approached me from behind. *"It is as you suspected? I heard the man's name. Call out the woman and her son."*

I did so, and she came only half a shoe's length over the threshold. "Mistress, we will not harm you, but you and your son must leave in the morning. Take with you only what you can pack in your wagon. You will travel south at first light, off Cherokee land, never to return. Your husband will stand trial in New Echota. This home does not belong to you. Your husband earned it by mutilating and raping one of our women. Then, under Thomas Crowwell's command, your husband's brigade strung her husband upside down, shot out his knees, blew darts into his chest, and set them on fire. He left them both to die, bleeding, to suffer the wolves alone. All to steal horses. Tonight, we'll burn each of these homes, all but yours. We'll save that fire for cooking breakfast."

Four Light Guards entered her house around her, ducking under the cabin's short doorway. They filed out as fast as they entered, torches lit from the soldier's family fire. I called out to Vann, the last to enter. *"Lift the loose floorboard under the table. Bring me what you find there."* This confirmation would be the last evidence I needed to prove the man's guilt.

Vann nodded.

From the ground, the soldier asked, "You're not gonna kill me?"

"What purpose would it serve? 'If any citizen of the U.S., or other people not being an Indian, shall settle on any of the Cherokee lands, such a person shall forfeit the protection of the U.S.' The Cherokee may punish him or not, as they please. Sir, treaty law is on my side."

Behind me, the warriors' spirits came unmasked, escaping them in overlapping war whoops. Their horses galloped down the row. With fire lofting from their hands, riders thew burning torches through the windows of abandoned homes. The heat from the inferno warmed us, kindling orange light in all directions.

Vann stood next to me, watching the flames grow, listening to falling timbers and the crackle of burning pine. In the smoky swirls, he handed me the bag. Although it wasn't my place to do so, I loosened the ties on the canvas. Inside were two locks of black hair bound in a leather thong, wrapped in a piece of wedding-white blanket.

CHAPTER 17: NOT SEEING, I HAVE SEEN
John Ridge
High Falls Tavern, Middle Georgia
February 1830

Our party arrived at Indian Springs to the sounds of a gristmill cascading water over the large river rocks beneath. In the center of town, McIntosh's Inn stood, famous for its medicinal waters. Guests paid a steep price to soak in hot baths during the day any play cards, billiards, and drink brandy each evening, defeating the day's healing with nightly intoxication.

In his eagerness, Chewoyee pulled his reins beside me. He said, *"Are we all going inside?"*

Behind him, Rattling Gourd shook his head no. He said, *"If the man you seek is at the inn, his whiskey wagon will be nearby."*

Waggon asked, surveying the open landscape, *"Where would he hide it?"*

Despite little sleep, my mind reeled with clarity. *"Someplace high. Wandering thieves are less likely to spot it there."*

Vann said, *"We will look for flat rock under shallow river water, hidden under tree cover. It's where I'd hide it."*

Waggon asked, *"Whiskey isn't illegal in Georgia. Why not just keep it at the inn?"*

Vann said, *"If it's worth stealing, it's worth hiding."*

I pointed north. *"Ride the high paths. Investigate anything unusual. Sleep in turns if you must. You know how important this evidence is. Vann, find me in the tavern when you've got it."*

Mills said, *"Even if we find the wagon, we won't be able to prove it is his. If the cargo is so valuable, there will be guards."*

Chewoyee said, *"John, even if you could get him to confess to owning it, all he must do is deny it later in court. Cherokee cannot testify against a white man without white witnesses."*

Chewoyee wasn't the only one worried about the many contingencies in this plan. Best scenario, we arrive home with evidence and jaded guards ready to testify. Worst, we didn't make it home at all. I said, *"I'm hoping his white guards won't take kindly to not being paid if Crowwell doesn't return. There are our witnesses."*

Mills looked at me and shrugged his shoulders. *"If the guards move it, should we let them go?"*

Mills, more so than the others, was eager for blood. But more likely, he tested the differences between my command and my father's. I said, "*Yes, but follow them if you can. When Crowwell comes for it, he will follow the same road we traveled, back to the village, to pick up the stolen ponies.*"

Rattling Gourd asked what the others thought. "*Then what was the point?*"

"*Information,*" I said, "*and evidence worthy enough to convict the Crowwells, or at the least, terrify them into bartering to escape consequences.*"

Rattling Gourd said, "*This will come to nothing if we don't find the wagon.*"

Chewoyee asked, "*What will you say? Bluff him? Convince him we have it already?*"

I didn't know what I'd say and didn't offer any answer. Given the circumstances, the five in my charge had the easier task.

When I approached the hotel, my first thought was its opulence, and the expenses needed to build such a fine establishment. I learned from Yoholo that McIntosh funded it with shady deals with white politicians he called cousins and friends. In '25, McIntosh's signature, penned in the treaty room at this very hotel, sold Creek land to the federal government without unanimous tribal consent. Afterward, the government felt emboldened to evict the Creek and encroach on Cherokee land.

The tavern was grand, with a wrap-around porch extending off its clapboard white walls. Slave quarters lined the back behind two stables as white as the house. Lit tavern windows revealed movement within the front parlors. Shadows of passersby dimmed the kerosene lamp light which brightened after as they passed. I hoped one silhouette belonged to Thomas Crowwell.

I entered and paid my fee for the night, although I didn't plan to sleep under any roof built by McIntosh. Invited into a back parlor by the evening's host, he escorted me down a paneled hallway to a brighter room. McIntosh's portrait hung above a lathed fireplace mantle. In the painting, McIntosh's signature smirk flashed between a plumed crown and a chest covered in tartan plaid. I recognized the artist. Charles King painted McIntosh a decade before I sat for a similar portrait. King had put a quill in my hand, painting me in occupation. Too bad King didn't have a color on his pallet that would reveal a man's deception. If such had existed, McIntosh's portrait would have been monotone in hue.

At the tables, finely dressed white men sat smoking cigars and lifting brandy snifters to their noses and lips. Passing slaves refilled glasses beside long-fingernailed women of the evening trailing their hands over the shoulders of men whose naïve wives slept upstairs.

Yellow Bird's Song

To be sure, this room was enemy territory. Few noticed me, which gave me uninterrupted moments to observe the many receding hairlines gambling in the room. I recalled the features of the man who dashed our chess match, the same man who chased young Peter through the woods after shooting his only remaining family.

I checked my pocket watch. More than an hour had passed since our party separated. I hoped my men searched in the darkness with as much awareness of their environment. If the Georgian Guard captured them, we'd lose all we'd wagered.

I walked the room's perimeter to avoid attracting attention. A man sat across the room, scratching a hound dog. He turned his face into the light. It was Thomas Crowwell with his scar-pitted pale cheeks. Long salt-and-pepper sideburns, shaved close, touched the corners of his lips, masking most of the cheek's defects. Crowwell revealed an As Nas hand to a gentleman seated across from him. Three As, aces, queen high. With a chuckle, he gathered the substantial pot across the walnut table.

"It is a game of chance, not skill," Crowwell remarked with a relaxed grin, exerting only enough energy to smile from one side of his mouth.

The gentleman who'd lost the wager scratched his chair legs against the hardwood floor. Even after Crowwell's consolation, the loser left the table, not inclined to play any further hands.

My memory of Crowwell's sarcasm returned after hearing him speak. I was certain he was the man I sought.

As Nas required little skill beyond that of a stoic face. When we played at the Foreign Mission School, there were always four players with others huddled close by, awaiting their turn. Each player was dealt cards and risked coins to bet whether they held the highest-ranking hand. I learned to play the Persian game from the only Hindu student in our class. Abdul's family traveled to America via France. His parents spoke Arabic and guttural French, so he struggled to make English phonetic sounds. Regardless, he had little difficulty staying awake all hours, teaching us the game and its characteristic phrases. Despite the language barrier, exclamations from winning and groans from losing crossed oceans, and all sounded the same.

Because he lacked another player, Black Crow finished the brandy in his snifter. So accustomed to liquor's numbness, he didn't react to swallowing the firewater.

He saw me standing by the window. "Latecomer," he said, "fancy a game?"

I turned from the window and said, "Don't you need four players to play As Nas?"

172

Heather Miller

"So," he said, "you are familiar with this game?" He stood, helped by his resting hand on the tabletop and, with the other hand, gestured to the cards piled on the table. "Join me?" It was the invitation I both hoped for and wanted to avoid.

I nodded and took the offered seat. I could play him for information, only if he didn't recognize me from our chance encounter in the Creek's woods. My best tactic was to delay long enough for Vann to let me know the men discovered Black Crow's contraband.

"It has been quite some time since I played. Sir, please remind me of the rules."

"I'd be happy to assist your memory—after your initial contribution to the pot." He drew a half-cent from his vest pocket and slid it across the smooth table surface with the "liberty" side facing upward.

The cost was not much compared to what I could learn. I could afford more if it purchased evidence of his crime, its origin and means. And if his substantial brandy consumption assisted such talk, so be it. I was content to pay to listen.

"Where did you learn to play?" he asked, studying my resting hands more than my face.

"From a foreign classmate. He was originally from Persia and spoke terrible English, but he adored this game." Keeping to the truth might help me keep the lies clearer.

He spread the cards face up to reacquaint me with the deck. "See here? The artist depicted the four As with a horse and a mountain lion locked in the throes of battle."

I asked, "Who might win, do you think, in a true battle of such beasts?"

"The wild cat, surely."

How poorly acquainted Crowwell must be with how ruthless a startled horse can be.

"Next are the kings sitting on their thrones. Look. Each representation has subtle differences."

The artist had elegantly painted the four kings, absent of any other obvious demarcation. The second king's card carried a smirk the first didn't have. A scepter was present in the third but was absent from the fourth.

Underneath the row of patriarchs, he flipped the queen cards over, with her regal crowned head holding a young prince seated atop her lap.

"Beautiful artistry," I said.

He placed the last four cards in a row closest to me.

"Soldiers in various formations of battle," he remarked.

Yellow Bird's Song

"Correct me if I am wrong, but I remember there is the fifth row depicting, shall we say, ladies of the evening?"

"To add in the whores, we'd need two more players."

I nodded as he retrieved his cards, bridged a shuffle, and dealt both of us two cards facedown. He returned the remaining cards to the table and raised the corner of his overturned cards. Overly confident, he retrieved another liberty dime from his pocket and put it on the table. Then, he studied my face to see whether he'd dealt me beast or man. I didn't reach for my cards. My hands stayed on the Windsor arms.

He cleared his throat and asked, "There is something familiar to your face, sir. No doubt you are native, but I asked you into this game since you dress as a gentleman of worth."

I leaned forward and offered him my first thought. "Is a man's attire the only depiction of his savagery?"

"His talk reveals his true nature as well." Black Crow adjusted his posture, more erect than before. He coughed as a distraction. Finally, he asked whether I would look at the cards in front of me.

"Not seeing, I have seen," I said, just as Abdul taught, and matched his bet.

"It appears your memory of the game has returned. Have we met before this night?"

"I do not know. Do you spend much time in Cherokee Nation, sir?"

The twitch of his eyelid marked his response, and his following gesture attempted to rub the annoying muscle smooth again.

"When I must. My brother is a colonel and runs a fort in Alabama. Crossing through Indian territory is a necessary evil." He grabbed the deck again and dealt two more cards facedown, adding mine to an array I'd yet to touch. "I wouldn't call it a nation, no matter what documents their Chief Ross has written. I have business dealings on both sides of the Cherokee's invisible lines. Easier to go through than around."

Under the circumstances, his vagaries were not a confirmation of guilt. Many white men traveled through our land rather than spend days to take the lawful detour. Black Crow sipped from his brandy glass while a servant with a carafe stood by, waiting to refill his glass. He gestured to me, implying she should also bring me a snifter. But I waved her off. He watched her leave as I asked, "Do you find your travels dangerous?"

He didn't answer the question. "I cannot shake the familiarity of your face. Are you Cherokee or leftover Creek?" Dealing another round, he examined his new card, leaning back in his chair, resting his hands on the sides, and adjusting his stocky frame in the seat.

My hesitation made him nervous. Again, Black Crow asked, "Aren't you going to look at your cards?"

"Not seeing, I have seen." I reached into my pocket and felt the first coins that touched my finger. I placed two liberty dimes in the pot and raised the stakes.

Black Crow declared, "Either you have some assurance of luck, or you are foolish beyond belief."

"So I've been told."

He met the bet and dealt one last card to each of us. He smiled and gestured to the unrevealed cards in front of me. "One last opportunity to know your fate."

My response stayed the same. "Not seeing…"

At that moment, Vann stepped out of the dark hall into the tavern room and whistled, calling the hound, who rose from Black Crow's feet and lumbered to greet him like an old friend.

"… I have seen."

Black Crow recognized Vann at once and placed us both in his memory. I looked quite different now, dressed in a white man's finery. I spoke English, clearer than most. "Weren't dress and speech your two requirements for civilization?" I asked.

Vann joined us, pulling a chair from under the table. "White men are too concerned with appearances," Vann said, petting the dog as he had done when Peter covered himself in manure to avoid Black Crow's whip.

Black Crow was cornered, and none had yet to reveal his hand.

More confident with Vann by my side, I asked, "Sir, if I may ask, how exactly do you run whiskey, pony clubs, and slaves across Cherokee land, Mister Black Crow?"

In reaction, he stuttered with spit-filled sounds and no understandable words.

"Perhaps a side wager?" I wove the fingers of both hands together, and with them, covered my mouth and chin. "If I win, you answer my question." I lowered my hands to rest on my unseen cards. "If I lose, we leave. Keep your confession and the pot to yourself."

"I'll take that wager. Without evidence, it doesn't matter. It isn't as if you can testify against me. Besides, your chief wouldn't allow you to try."

His last remark took me aback as I tried to squelch my reaction to his taunt. What could he mean? Did Black Crow know Ross?

With a deep chuckle, he returned to his cards and revealed one at a time from the sprawling fan face down. His first card was a king, followed by another. Then, a soldier, another king, and an As. Three kings, As high. Black Crow's hand was lucky, that was certain. But I'd watched the man closely and didn't suspect him of cheating, regardless of his other

Yellow Bird's Song

exploits.

"Excellent hand." I nodded to him, conceding my probable defeat in this wager.

Fate might offer me three lowly soldiers, the lowest-scoring cards within the deck. To best his hand, I would need to hold the unlikely trio of three As.

Vann cocked his pistol under the table, pointing at Black Crow's overly large belly. After hearing it, Crowwell's expression changed from arrogant to sinister, neither expression showing any intimidation.

I turned one card over. It was As. Next was a lowly soldier. The third, a queen, the fourth, an As. If the fifth card were the last remaining As, the last ace in the deck, tonight would have been worth every deception. I overturned the last card.

His mouth hung agape, staring at my hand, and then, he returned my smirk with a bitter stare.

He hastily stood, eager to remove himself as Vann's target. He shrugged his coat over his shoulders. I thought he'd leave without answering, but a smile spread across his face. Before departing the table, he said, "I travel freely with my cargo across Cherokee land because Chief Ross earns five percent from every sale. The Cherokee Light Guard, led by a man named Foreman, directs his men on patrol the other way."

CHAPTER 18: A NEWSPAPERMAN'S SHOES
Rollin Ridge
Sacramento, California
August 1852

I replaced Papa's playing card in my pocket, hoping age hadn't deterred its fortune. Up and down Sacramento's main street, I dodged trotting carriage horses, run-off dogs, cowboys leaning against porch railings, wild pistoleers with arms hanging on the shoulders of prostitutes, and miners who looked lost among this sinful mass of humanity. Observing the multitude bordering the streets, passing one another without a friendly acknowledgement, all were strangers in this new world. None cared to know his fellow man.

Despite such indifference, I persevered, annoying as many business-men who would take in my rugged countenance and hear my request for employment. I entered each shadowed storefront and exited back into the sun after a brief conversation. With a single glance at my face, each merchant made short excuses. If I didn't find work soon, like the prodigal son, I'd be sleeping with pigs.

Aeneas and Wacooli remained in Placerville, selling the mules, and looking for work as teamsters. With his fire for adventure smothered, Aeneas wanted to travel home after saving enough to go by steamer. Wacooli told Aeneas he was foolish to travel alone, but I knew the real reason Wacooli would leave with him. He missed his father. Wacooli had had his fill of horseback and white men, deciding he'd rather farm the prairie and cut hay for the rest of his life than dig for gold one more day. I didn't begrudge either of them their desire to return to Arkansas. I felt the same pull, but for me, returning to Lizzie meant strife instead of serenity.

I paid in advance for a week's room and a meal each day, so at least I'd eat and sleep a few days more. With a dollar's worth of half-dimes in my pocket, and feeling sorry for myself, I passed through the doors of the nearest saloon and planned to drink until I passed out or ran out of nickels, whichever arrived first. It was not a well-thought-out plan, not wise, but I was sick of being responsible and thought to quench my thirst for stupefaction by the fastest means.

Craftsmen stained and sealed the bar to appear as if it were made from expensive cherry wood. The only other drinker at the carved counter sat behind an innocuous white coffee cup. The contrasts in color drew my attention more than the stranger's features. Slurping aromatic steam, the sober man reminded me of an eastern politician walking down a street in

Yellow Bird's Song

New England wearing a tall top hat, escorting some cameo-pinned woman. Such couples didn't labor for their livelihoods and led a life of leisure.

I reached into my pocket, took out the first half-dime, slid it across the bar, and quietly said, "Whiskey." As soon as the barkeep filled my gill, I tossed it back. After the alcohol's heat radiated down my arms, I sat beside the sober man. I ogled him after noticing his examination of me.

"What are you looking at?" I asked with a bitter tongue from the day's futility.

He said, "I find it fascinating to see human nature in all its wildness. You, my good man, appear less than tame. Except for those shoes. When you walked in, at once, they attracted my attention."

"They were all I had that didn't have a hole in the sole." I laughed at my rhyme and the honesty revealed by the phrase.

"Ahh, a punning poet. I, too, lean toward the satiric. My name is Alonzo Delano, writer for the *True Delta* and author of frontiersmen sketches," he said and extended his hand.

I took off my dusty hat and set it on the bar. I wiped my hand on my pants, a pointless exercise, and returned the grip of his hand.

"Rollin Ridge," I revealed.

He leaned in. "You might know me by my pseudonym, The Old Block." His inflection rose at the end of his declaration as if he'd asked a question. Then, when my face didn't change, he asked, "Haven't heard of me?"

I raised one eyebrow. "Should I have?" My retort offered him little consolation. "Maybe you should ask someone else here. I've been out of circulation for months. Mining gold. Little luck. Thought I'd venture into town in search of a job. Know anyone that's hiring?"

"Well, you're not likely to find any employment worth doing, wearing the clothes you've slept in for the last three months. Have a trade, other than mining?"

"I'll do anything that's honest,"[1] I said and placed another coin on the bar to toss back the second gill, finding it less challenging to swallow than the first. After it soaked in, I had fewer inhibitions to ask for a third.

"A vagabond poet with elegant shoes and a conscience. A man who wears different disguises but most disguised when showing his real features."[2] Then he said, "That's good," and scribbled the phrase in his sketchbook. He looked up and said, "Ridge isn't an alias for Murieta, is it?" He leaned into my side and whispered, "If you are the infamous Mexican bandit, I'll write your story, and tell no one of your mask."

"You read too many of your own newspapers. I'm not the man, although I have heard of him. Robbing from the rich. Offering his stolen

178

booty to the poor." He side-eyed me, not yet convinced of my answer. "I promise," I affirmed. "My name is Ridge from Arkansas, not Mexico."

He seemed a man pleased to discuss himself, so I changed the subject. "You're a writer? Is the *True Delta* a newspaper of note?"

He nodded his head. "You must be a fellow scribe if you use the word 'note'. A man of letters yourself?"

"Only the kind one posts home. You wouldn't believe it to look at me, but I studied the detestable occupation of law. Before that, I attended the Barrington School in Massachusetts."

"A mysterious, disguised, but distinguished traveler, then. You would make a great sketch."

Freedom's abandonment followed my next gill. "How would you describe a man such as myself?" I asked, my joints feeling looser, although my arms and legs seemed heavier with the infusion of alcohol.

He walked around my stool with both loathing and interest. He picked up my hat from the bar, examined it, and replaced it. His eyes lit up with quiet questions when he looked at Kell's knife on my hip.

He reached to touch the sheath.

I grabbed his wrist and twisted his hand away from my body. "Don't," I growled.

He saw the bone handle protruding from its hand-beaded sheath and made an obvious observation. "It looks wicked," he said.

I let go. "You couldn't know how much."

In response, he made another assumption. "You're a long way from Indian country."

"I'm aware," I said and ordered another, slamming a half-dime on the bar.

He resumed his original seat and began scribbling in his journal. Before the bartender tilted the bottle to fill my glass, the gentleman held his hand for the barkeep to hold his pour. Obviously, Delano didn't want me too lost in my cups to hear what he had written about me. I watched over his shoulder as he scribbled with his modern pen. Finally, he capped it carefully and angled his knees toward me.

"Ready Mister Ridge?" he asked and cleared his throat.

"Tell me all about myself," I shouted, waving him on, certainly feeling enough of the alcohol's effects to pause a minute before swallowing.

He cleared his throat and held his journal at eye level. "His dress was unique and added much to his personal beauty."

I scoffed and put my hand on his book, pulling it down to reveal Delano's crook of a nose. I said, "That's not a very masculine adjective. Call me handsome if you must."

Yellow Bird's Song

Delano scratched it through. "You're as good as an editor. May I finish?"

I dismissed him with a wave to continue. Delano held open his journal with his thumb and pinky to read his own words. "He was crowned with an old weather-beaten hat, filled with holes, from which locks of black hair protruded, the only thing keeping it from falling from its elevated position. He wore a faded red flannel shirt, which buckled around his waist with a leather belt, from which was suspended a murderous-looking butcher knife. His nether limbs were encased in a soiled, greasy pair of leathern unmentionables, while to cap the climax of his outré appearance, a pair of glistening patent-leather shoes covered his feet."[3]

Delano continued, "The man described told me he was willing to do anything honest, never having been brought up to steal. He could never do that. Even to this day, with all the luminous examples set before him— indeed, he never held office under any government, which may account for such obtuseness."[4]

I laughed heartily, not only because of the alcohol. "Not bad," I said. "To confirm your assumption, no, I haven't worked for the government." I gestured to the barkeep, who listened to our conversation. Delano waved to the man to complete his waiting task. When my glass was full, Delano and I toasted. Our cups made no sound before I downed the whiskey.

"My father did." I exhaled the burn, and said, "There are a few politicians with noble intentions. Unfortunately, most don't cover their faces but hide their thieving black hearts behind satin-lined lapels. Unlike that Murieta fellow, they don't deliver the funds they steal back to their constituents."

"How right you are, friend."

The barkeep walked away. There was a brief hush before Delano cracked, "It's your turn now."

I cleared my throat. "To do what?"

"Draft a sketch. Let's see whether your education gave you a vocabulary for the news. If you've studied the law, hyperbole and exaggeration must come second nature."

I nodded and turned my back to the counter, surveying the room for a subject.

None of the men had histories particularly challenging to predict. But then, two bandoleros entered the bar, pushed inside by a blast of evening sunlight. I squinted when they entered, but after my eyes adjusted, my gaze followed them to the darkest corner. As discreetly as possible, using Delano as a shield, I studied the smaller man of the two through the open space of Delano's arm. After sitting, the larger man swirled three cards with a paw missing two fingers; his ring finger and pinky were gone. Light and quick, the smaller man pointed and stopped the center card. From the shadows, he eyed the room with what I interpreted as ever-increasing boredom.

Delano's eyes followed them too. I whispered, "What game are they playing, do you think?"

He said under his breath, "Monte, it looks like."

I stopped the teetering room by leaning my back against the bar, facing the mysterious men. "You ready, Delano?"

"Fire at will."

"His complexion was neither dark nor light, but clear and brilliant, and his countenance exceedingly... handsome."

"Diction duly noted," Delano replied. "Go on..."

"... exceedingly handsome and attractive. His large black eyes kindled with the enthusiasm of his earnest nature. His firm and well-formed mouth, his well-shaped head, from which long glossy black hair hung down over his shoulders, his silvery voice full of generous utterance, and the frank and cordial bearing distinguished him, making him respected by all who engaged him."[5]

Delano said, "Brilliant. But I must ask, why did you choose 'respected'?"

I turned back to the bar, placed another half-dime. "I wouldn't want the man's fate who didn't offer that stranger respect." Courage overcame me. To confirm, I needed to approach my subject. "I'm going to play a hand with them. See if I'm right."

Delano said, "Right about what? Foolish to test his patience. Stay here with me."

Before he finished his command, I stepped forward.

Another man played cards with the stranger in the dark. He stood and left the table, appearing to have won the hand, shaking coins in his palm. As the winner wove past me, I staggered and found his empty chair still warm.

"Mind if I take a turn? What's the ante?" I asked, holding the chair's arms to slide myself under the table.

"We could start with a half-dime. You had plenty of those at the bar."

So, he too was observant. I looked back and found Delano eyeing me, furiously writing in his journal with a fresh cup of steaming coffee in front of him.

"What's the game called?" I asked, reaching into my pocket for his price.

"Find the Lady." His accent was Spanish, not that of a native English

Yellow Bird's Song

speaker. He leaned forward to the round table's surface, resting his arms. He held out a single card in front of me, the Jack of Diamonds.

It took effort to focus.

"He, my friend, finds riches for his king."

He placed the card on the table, flipped another from the deck, and held it still for my eyes to study.

"The King of Clubs is a noble, battle-ready royal."

He did the same with the king, placing it facedown. Finally, he scanned through the cards for his third choice.

"Ahh, the Queen of Hearts, a lady forced to live alone. If you can find her, you can keep her, and win the game."

He laid the last card facedown and leaned back in his chair, handing the remaining playing cards to the three-fingered man. He leaned forward, taking each hand's pointer finger and applying pressure to slide the hidden face cards, circling one card around the other. I followed the queen with my eyes. When he stopped spinning the cards, I knew exactly where she was.

"Do you know where she hides?"

"I do."

"Up your bet, then. Double your money." I was right about his silvery tongue.

In my spinning head, I couldn't think, didn't think, and put all but two half-dimes beside the cards on the table. He easily matched the bet.

"Where is she?" He stretched his words.

I pointed to the center card, too drunk to question myself.

He turned over the card on the left, the Jack of Diamonds. My chance of winning just increased by a third.

He turned over the card on the right, the King of Clubs.

"You found her, my friend."

Unnecessarily, he flipped the queen over.

I put my arm across the table to drag the coins away, but the large man, who hadn't spoken, placed his three-fingered paw over mine.

The dealer said, "Give me a chance to win my money back, friend."

I removed my hand and watched as he flipped the same three cards over again to hide their images.

This time, he spun the cards faster. With my focus distorted, I lost the queen a few seconds in.

"She's escaping your grasp. Can you find your lady a second time?"

I leaned forward, studying the backs of the cards for an answer they wouldn't reveal. I pointed to the card on my left.

"She will be so disappointed if you lose her."

I didn't speak, only nodded.

He flipped the card on my right first. The Jack of Diamonds. He flipped the center card, and, staring back at me with drooping eyes, was the queen. I'd lost my hand.

The three-fingered man put his mangled paw on the coins, ready to draw them back to the table's edge, when the dealer said, "I'd be willing to let you earn back your losses with one more game. Bet that knife at your side."

Defeated, I said, "You wouldn't want it. I can't separate myself from it without enduring madness, while keeping it ensures the same. I don't think I could let it go if I tried."

"I understand a man's attachment to his blade. No matter how often it's covered in blood and washed in a river, something of the dying stays behind. Cold because it has touched death."

"This knife killed my father." I unsheathed the blade and held it above my head to catch the light. Then I stood, flipped the edge downward, and slammed its point into the center of the wooden table, cutting a hole in the king's face.

The three-fingered man stood and pulled his pistol, but the smaller man didn't rise, didn't flinch. Although the other stinking men in the saloon did. After my show, our dark corner held their undivided attention.

"This man means me no harm, Jack," the small dealer said. "I think I understand. Which tribe did the killing? Which tribe did the dying?"

"Cherokee." I belched. "Both."

"I know only a few Cherokees. Their instinct is to kill first and justify the reason afterwards. The Tejon Indians of California are cannier."

"I'm half Cherokee. Both my halves know the difference between reasoning and killing." I heard my voice slur, distancing itself from my thoughts. I belched again and tasted whiskey mixed with acid from my empty stomach. Then, with one last effort at appearing sober, I pulled the tip of the blade from the king and sheathed it before falling back into the chair. I said, "Don't make assumptions about the whole based on knowing a few of its parts."

"Wise words, my friend. People say the same of us Hispanos, whose land became the white miner's California.[6] You understand, no?"

"I do."

"Might I hold this cursed blade?"

I don't know why I trusted the man, but I felt assured he wouldn't steal it in front of witnesses, so I handed him the bone with its arrowhead handle.

Using both hands, the stranger summoned its power. He looked down its line, held it sideways to measure its stability, and returned it, grasping the tip of its blade.

"Too bad it isn't balanced. I could employ a man who knows how to toss a weapon like this, cursed or not, if his bone outweighed his blade."

Shelled as I was, his offer was tempting, although I knew that whatever he asked of me would require me to break every vow I'd ever made. I said, "I'm honest, if little else."

Shrugging his shoulders, he dropped the offer of a job and another game. He and his three-fingered companion left me seated behind the table. The smaller pistoleer came around to my side. "What is your name, Cherokee friend, in case I happen this way again? We might play that last hand."

Why not tell him? "Rollin Ridge," I said.

He offered me the sliced king and leaned to my ear while handing me the card. "I am Joaquín Murieta."[7] And the duo left the saloon without another word.

Delano walked me back to the hotel as excited as Christmas. "He said that was his name?"

All I could say was, "I lost the queen." I stopped walking long enough to yell, "Delano, how could I lose her? I had to leave. She had to stay behind."

He returned to my side and urged me forward down the street. "It happens to the best of us. The entire game is a swindle."

I grabbed the man by his swanky lapel. "Not the cards. Lizzie."

"Who is Lizzie?" he asked, waving away the smell of my breath.

I stumbled forward while he waddled to keep up. I said, "Don't you see?" When we entered the hotel, I misjudged the distance between my shoulder and the doorjamb. "Ouch," I said. "She was my Queen of Hearts."

"I'm sure she still is," he said, placating me.

"There was a time…" I stopped walking.

He walked back to me, motivated by my fragment. "A time when what?"

"When no white man could come between us. She wouldn't want me now if she knew what I've become." I tripped on the stairs.

Delano sat beside me. "Describe her to me."

"Sweet eyes of blue, soft silken hair. Beautiful waist, and bosom of white—" I reached for her, touching the apparition of my stolen white girl

"—that heaves to the touch with a sense of delight."[8]

I couldn't be sure, but I thought Delano rolled his eyes.

He helped me stand. "There are things I don't need to know, Lizzie's delights, for one." He put my arm over his shoulder when I stumbled up the stairs.

Each door looked the same. "It is number five, I think. I can't remember."

"Here, give me the key." He propped me up against the wall while he opened the door. "In you go," he said. I entered only to fall, face first on the bed.

He closed the door and spoke under his breath. "I hardly know you, and I'm in your hotel room." Then he resumed his louder tone. "I can't believe you met the illustrious vigilante, Joaquín Murieta. Wait. Do you think the man was lying? I heard Murieta's gang was in Yuma, not here in Sacramento."

"That's how the man survives. People think he's one place, but he's already moved on," I said, kicking off the patent-leather shoes of Delano's fascination. I rolled on my back and put my hat over my eyes to block the kerosine lamplight. I could still see him through the holes. Delano sat beside the lamp and opened his sketchbook again.

"What exactly did Murieta say? I might have a chance of finding him again tomorrow. Surely, he's staying in town. Maybe you could pretend you've changed your mind about joining his gang and bring me the inside story."

"If I did," I mumbled, "I'd write it. Not you." I sat forward, holding my head to stop Delano's image from levitating. Then, I remarked, "And, I wouldn't say he had beauty."

Giving up on me, he closed his book and tucked it in his coat pocket. I watched his feet walk to the door and heard it open but not close.

Delano said, "Meet me downstairs in the morning. I'll buy you a new suit and introduce you to Colonel Grant from the *Delta*. You own a pair of newspaperman's shoes already."

The knocking woke me. I crawled to respond. Delano looked where my height should be but found me hovering a foot above the red carpet. Finally, he said, "Up and at 'em, Ridge. Colonel Grant is already barking downstairs. Looks like you'll have to meet him as you are."

My first thought questioned why he used "barking" to describe this man, but when I heard Grant speak, I knew Delano chose the right word.

Yellow Bird's Song

The backs of the standing crowd reached the waist of the man wearing a white coat and eccentric red tie. He spoke not to those standing beneath him, but loud enough to be heard by those walking across the street. His efforts weren't wasted. A stream of future readers found their way to stand at his feet.

"Buy a subscription to the *True Delta*," Grant bellowed, making my head pound in tune to his tempo. "Eight dollars for a year's worth of political commentary, polite humor, and news from these United States. It is, by far, the best Atlantic newspaper ever sent to California. Buy a subscription, and I'll offer you a canister of miracle paste that whitens the teeth for no additional charge."

After collecting several names, addresses, and coins for the paper and the paste, Grant recognized Delano and, by proximity, eyed me standing on the edge of those filing away. He seemed a man whose joy was proportionate to the jingle of coins dropped in his pocket. He approached and shook Delano's hand.

Delano said, "This is the man I wanted you to meet."

I offered him my hand then stood in profile, staring across the street, waiting while Colonel Grant took in my ragged self.

Grant remarked, "You're a strangely attired fellow, good-looking under an honest day's dirt. Delano here says you are in search of employment?"

"I'll do anything honest." I picked up a canister of the paste, thinking Grant must be a scam artist to sell baking soda in a can and call it a miracle. But at eight dollars per subscription, he needed to keep coins in his pockets. This must be the way he fills that need.

"Can you write? By your appearance, one might guess the contrary."

"I did some writing back home," I said, not boastful but true.

"Where's that?" he asked.

Might as well get this out of the way. Most men ask. "I was born in Cherokee Nation in the East, then removed to the West, to Indian territory. After my father died, we lived in Fayetteville, Arkansas. Had a farm in Missouri."

"Hmm," Grant said. "Well, Delano can recognize talent from a mile away. So, for him, I'll do this for you. Write me a piece for the *Delta* and bring it back tomorrow morning. I'll read it, and if it has merit, you'll have found a career writing and selling the news."[9] After making me the offer, both men walked down the street together, assumedly to feed themselves after the morning's exertions.

With a pound in my head and in desperate need of a bath, I sat on Grant's barking box and gathered my thoughts. I had one remaining dime.

186

Heather Miller

I needed something to write on, so I walked in the opposite direction to find the closest trading post. From my saddlebags on the hotel room floor, I retrieved the pen Mother gave me. Unable to think inside, I found a tree on the outskirts of town, and sat beneath its shade. What I'd write, I did not know.

The sun set before I corked my pen. I'd penned a travelogue inspired by experience.

The following day, when I handed it to Grant, he stood atop his box and shouted my words down the street.

"The plains lay so level and open in which to ride with speed, and the mountains so rugged with their ten thousand fastnesses, in which to idle." After the first sentence, he stopped screaming. Instead, he continued with a wondering tone, holding the sheet closer to his scanning eyes. "Grass was abundant in the far-off valleys which lay hidden in rocky gorges. Cool, delicious streams made music at the feet of the towering peals or came leaping down in gladness from their sides."[10]

People gathered as they had the day before, more strolling over after each phrase. Grant spoke so soft that the people standing beneath him strained to hear his illustrious voice, an uncommon volume for the man.

"Game abounded on every hand and, for nine unclouded months of the year, made a climate so salubrious that nothing could be sweeter than a day's rest under the tall pines or a night's repose under the open canopy of Heaven."[11]

Grant left the listeners wanting more and stepped down from his barking box. "I cannot pay you what it is worth. But it is the best thing I've read on the subject and deserves more than my means allows me to pay. I will give you eight dollars an article for this and all equal to it. I shall gladly secure you as a correspondent for the *True Delta*."[12]

When he outstretched his hand, I smiled genuinely for the first time since meeting Spencer Hill and leaving Mount Shasta. After he walked away, I pulled Papa's faded card from my pocket. The battle between the cougar and the horse raged on, but I sighed, thinking how some of its good fortune remained.

CHAPTER 19: WORLDS COLLIDE
Sarah Ridge
Running Waters
March 1830

"Beef won't cure with luck." Honey yelled from the kitchen to the parlor. "We're nearly out of sugar, too. Yeast won't rise without it."

"I know," I whispered while making a list of things to purchase in New Echota. Besides Honey's request for salt and sugar, I added coffee and a tea block to my list. We'd gone without for weeks. I needed to collect the post from Reverend Sam Worcester, purchase supplies, and hopefully meet Harriet and Elias' new son, William Penn, born just last month. John usually brought supplies to Running Waters, but in his absence, the necessity and responsibility fell to me. Mother Susannah remained in a nearby village, caring for a fevered elderly cousin. Quatie couldn't rattle along in the wagon, as she was expecting to give birth soon. So, Clarinda and I would go.

Peter came to my parlor and said, "I'll take you." I folded the list, placing it in my petticoat pocket.

"There's no need, Peter, not with so many chores here." I passed him in a flurry and headed to the kitchen.

He followed. "Work can wait. I'm not comfortable with you goin' alone."

I didn't look at him while I wiped Rollin's face smeared with jam. "And I'm not comfortable with you so far from Ridge land. I'll be perfectly safe. There's no choice."

Peter said, "Mister John wouldn't want you to."

I told Peter what he already knew. "Well, he isn't here."

I sighed, exhausted from the truth and restless because of the same. I'd wilted a bit more each week since John left. He might have understood why he needed to stay if I had understood why he felt so compelled to go. But, after berating myself, again, I could think of nothing more that needed doing except taking coins from the box in the bottom drawer of John's desk to pay for the needed supplies.

When I opened the door to his study, my husband's scent pushed me back: pine sap, black pepper, ink, and saddle leather. Even in his absence, his essence hovered in the drapes and white walls, inside the pages of his books, among the fibers of the sapphire rug. I felt guilty for being here without his permission.

My father's study was a forbidden place. Papa said, "A man's room is no place for silly girls." My family's housekeeper, Jane, was the only "silly" female allowed beyond the door. Only when he was gone could she dust or collect empty cups and saucers. Then he wouldn't have to listen to her prattle on about the cost of things or her tasks that remained unfinished.

I usually didn't enter John's study, not because he shunned me, but because I didn't want to disturb him. I selfishly missed the peace knowing, just beyond the door, John sat writing or reading.

Two weeks ago, Honey, the children, and I had dinner with Major and Susannah. But the father had returned without the son. No one had seen John, Vann, or the others. Honey translated Major Ridge's words, who remained confident of John's impending arrival at Running Waters. While momentarily assured and offering him a brief smile, a small voice in my head didn't believe him. If I listened, the voice made me panic, as if cornered in a stuffy room, too hot from so many people breathing.

I silenced the voice by beginning a task noisy enough to drown out its sound, easy to do on a farm with children. But here, alone in John's study, the cautionary voice returned, warning how John might not return. The voice sounded like my mother's.

My parents' house was only loud when something was amiss, brought in from the outside, like when John arrived so ill. To them, silence equaled happiness. In Mother's insistent quietude, she was a passive participant in her life, shut-up and buttoned-up, standing quietly behind my father's work, presenting the image of a dutiful wife, sinless and respectable before Cornwall's hypocrites. She lived a life of obligation, not choice. To others, she appeared happy, so much so, that when she spoke, all she could think to say was to repeat my father's words.

But after marrying John for love, I found the opposite to be true. Happiness isn't a quiet dependency, but a trusting partnership between best friends, between lovers, between souls who hear the other's heartbeat. Arguments, laughter, echoes through caves, whispers in candlelit bedrooms broke such silence. Happiness isn't living in separate rooms on separate floors. Love is loud.

I wanted to go back to the night John didn't kiss me goodbye and shout from the top of the stairs, "Can't you see? I live for you."

With prayerful determination to send him home faster, I walked to his desk and opened the bottom drawer where he kept profits from the ferry. Borrowing his quill, I dipped it in ink and wrote the amount I'd taken and its purpose on a small sheet of paper. I dated it and placed it inside the box beside the household's remaining coin. When I left, I slammed the door

Yellow Bird's Song

shut behind me, reminding myself how loud love should be.

Clarinda was excited about going to New Echota. She turned the doorknob to the front door and nearly stepped on her dog. Taking her hand, I said, "No, Digaleni. Stay home today." I barely had time to kiss Rollin's bushy black hair before he and Digaleni ran behind the house. Digaleni's long ears dragged to the ground when his nose found trails from skittering squirrels or rogue opossums. He and Rollin would run them off their territory.

Clarinda and I climbed into the wagon and settled on the bench seat behind her Equoni. I looked at my sweet girl in her blue bonnet and swung my arms left to right, asking if she was "ready". After she nodded, I put two fingers to my mouth and breathed out, pretending to whistle. Clarinda pulled the leather cord from her gingham dress, retrieved her whistle, and blew once. Equoni pulled, and we jolted forward.

Most of the horse-backed travelers on the road tipped their hats and nodded with friendly gestures. However, when no one else passed, I felt an uneasiness, a sixth sense someone followed us. I squeezed Clarinda closer to my side and snapped the reins for Equoni to move faster.

Behind us, horses whinnied over the sounds of shoe clops along the path. I twisted my neck to see two white soldiers in blue military coats, horses led in single file. Ten miles separated us from the well-populated New Echota. My small voice returned, reminding me of the last unfamiliar white man I met in Cherokee territory. He dragged me behind his horse and tried to exchange my life and that of my unborn child for whiskey.

I tucked the reins under my leg and signed to Clarinda. If anything should happen, she should run as fast as she could for home. Trying to be as discreet as possible, I reached under the bench seat for a tool, something I might use as a weapon, preparing for the worst scenario I could imagine. Underneath was a small mallet used to repair a wheel and a wedge to split firewood. An attacker would need to be close to use either.

Equoni followed a bend in the road, and for a moment, I couldn't see the white soldiers following us. Then, I recognized our hound's deep bawl. Around the blind turn, horses whinnied, and in the commotion, cruel shouts preceded pistol shots. I put my hand to my mouth after the first report, shuttering after the one that followed. Equoni sped ahead, and it took all my strength to stop the wagon. As soon as the hint of sulfur smoke reached us, twigs snapped after their horses broke into the opposing trees.

With another look back, flopping ears bound toward the wagon with another low-rumbled woof. The soldier's bullets missed our beloved dog. I got down and opened the back so Digaleni could leap inside. "Good boy," I said and rubbed his head, grateful he'd chosen to protect us instead of

Heather Miller

napping in the sunlight. The soldiers detoured, but my paranoia didn't fade, expecting their sudden reappearance.

Without further incident, we arrived in town, greeted by a wave from Xander McCoy from the porch of his house. He wasn't wearing his lawyer attire but an open shirt with no waistcoat, sitting on the porch while his wife gathered dirt with her straw broom. They hadn't packed and moved. Staying reaffirmed his loyalty.

We pulled past Elias and Harriet's house, the print shop, a smithy, and a boot shop. We stopped first at the point farthest away: Reverend Sam's residence, where he performed not only his ministerial duties but also served as New Echota's postmaster.

I took a deep breath, relaxing only when we stopped at the house of a friend.

Reverend Sam stepped onto his porch and wiped his hands on the white, ink-stained apron tied around his waist. "Good to see you, Mistress Ridge. So glad you came. I have letters for Running Waters."

I waved and answered back, "I hoped there might be."

Digaleni woofed his greeting. Before I could get down from the seat, Clarinda climbed to the ground and grabbed the stair rail. She stood before Sam with her hand outstretched to shake his. They'd met before, but she was too small to remember.

"Hello, Miss Clarinda," he remarked, forgetting she couldn't hear. Stepping from the wheel to the ground, I watched their exchange. Reverend Sam bent over his enormous feet, steadying his tall legs. God pieced that man together, straight up and down. He sat on a bench to study Clarinda's hands as she signed.

Reverend Worcester asked her to make the gestures again. "Slower?"

I signed for Clarinda to repeat her name, but asked her to sign each letter, one at a time, so Reverend Worcester could "practice".

He quickly mastered every letter, repeating each back to her. "What is the gesture for thank you?"

I showed him. "Touch three fingers to your chin and extend them to the person you are thanking." It was logical, straightforward.

He looked astonished. "She is a miracle, and I am a student again. Sophie Sawyer, our teacher, must meet her. My girls are with her now. Could I walk you both to school?" He redirected his attention to Clarinda and spelled her name instead of saying it aloud. I couldn't tell him how much I appreciated including her in his invitation.

John and I protected Clarinda from outsiders. In a world that thought the deaf were feeble-minded, our care was necessary. We didn't want anyone to make her feel inadequate, as she was so bright. But undoubtedly, from a missionary teacher, Clarinda's feelings would be unharmed.

"Yes, but before we go, would you gather the letters, please?"

"Of course. God's miracle, this child, distracted me."

Clarinda and I followed him into his office. There were many shelves holding framed slots, with another sitting on the floor. Letters and newspapers overflowed some, while others remained empty. Next to them sat a stained desk with a dark ring in the corner from repeatedly spilling overfilled teacups. Ink spots traveled from the well to where the man's papers sprawled along the desk's surface. Spent candle wax ribboned down from the taper's stub, unlit in its pewter saucer.

He scanned the boxes. While he looked, I asked, "How is Ann? I haven't seen her for quite some time."

"We can go see her if you'd like." He looked over his shoulder through a glass window toward the back of the house. "She's outside with her hands in soapy water."

"We'll see her another time then."

"Have you met little William Penn yet?" he asked.

"Not yet," I said. "I hope to do so today."

Reverend Sam said, "Elias named his son to honor Reverend Jeremiah Evarts, with Evarts' pen name. Just last week, he was printed in the *National Intelligencer*." Reverend Sam didn't recite Evarts' words from memory but shuffled through newspaper scraps on his desk. He found the issue he sought when it fell on the floor. He bent his long legs to stoop and squinted his eyes to read the fine print. "'Removal of any nation of Indians from their country by force would be an instance of gross and cruel oppression.'"[1] He looked at me and remarked about how John would agree.

"Wholeheartedly," I said.

Reverend Sam reached atop his desk with his long fingers for his eyeglasses. He found them and wrapped the ends around his ears. He stretched to full height, nearly touching the ceiling, and continued to read the quote with clearer sight. "'All attempts to accomplish this removal of the Indians by bribery or fraud, by intimidation and threats, by withholding from them a knowledge of the strength of the cause, by practicing upon their ignorance and their fears, or by vexatious opportunities, interpreted by them to mean nearly the same thing as a command—all such attempts are acts of oppression and therefore entirely unjustifiable. '"[2]

Reverend Sam replaced the paper on his desk. "When John returns, I need his counsel. Georgia wants me to pledge my allegiance to follow their laws while I preach and live here. But I think it a betrayal, no matter what Georgia threatens. I follow God, Cherokee law, and the directives of the Foreign Mission Board, not the political dictates of selfish men." He took off his apron with a furl, retrieved and donned his black frock coat. "John will know what I should do."

I wondered whether I should tell the Reverend about the white soldiers who followed us. But then, considering the demands made upon him already, I thought my worries better kept to myself.

He passed us, assuming we'd follow his lead. He bounded through the exterior door and to our wagon seat and snapped the reins to move Equoni into his barn. When he returned, our lop-eared hound walked beside him, where we waited by the foot of his stairs.

"Let's walk, shall we? Will be good to stretch."

We traveled to the center of town to Miss Sawyer's schoolhouse. Sam didn't knock before entering the classroom but opened the door with one hand while holding the other behind his back, acting as both observer and authority.

"We're at a schoolhouse. Where children learn from a teacher," I signed.

Clarinda asked me whether the teacher inside knew more than her papa.

I shook my head to the contrary. "No, not more than Papa, I imagine." And the voice in my head repeated his name. I looked across the town streets, hoping to see him ride to Elias' house. Then, from my imagination, John looked across the walking crowd and found me standing where I watched him.

My daydream faded when I heard Miss Sawyer instruct her pupils to complete the arithmetic lesson on their slates. Both boys and girls responded in unison, and she and Reverend Sam stepped down the stairs, leaving the door cracked to listen for any misbehavior.

Sophie Sawyer was a sharp woman with squared features, except for her smile. She had a teacher's heart. "Good morning, Mistress Ridge. It has been ages. Reverend Sam says there's someone here I need to meet."

"This is Clarinda, our daughter. She just turned six."

Miss Sawyer gathered her gray skirt and knelt so her eyes would be level with Clarinda's. Our daughter curtseyed and studied Miss Sophie's kind face.

Sam gestured at Clarinda's hands and said, "Watch."

Clarinda looked at me when she saw their lips move. I spelled Miss Sawyer's name. Clarinda reciprocated by introducing herself as she had done before.

Miss Sawyer said, "What did she say?"

I made the signs and spoke the letters "C.l.a.r.i.n.d.a." A horizontal

193

Yellow Bird's Song

wave signified the mountain ridges denoting our surname.

Miss Sawyer put her hand to her chest with glee and asked, "Does she read?"

"Yes, in both syllabary and English, but only simple words and phrases. So, I spell slowly."

"Truly a gift from God," Miss Sawyer remarked.

I confirmed, "She is. Entirely."

Sounds from a gathering crowd interrupted us. Two Cherokee on horseback rode into town. Immediately, people abandoned their chores and their porches to surround them. We could no longer see anything, but the resulting disarray brought by their arrival. Xander McCoy ran from the collection of people toward Elias' house.

Reverend Sam followed their increasing noise to find out what caused such trouble.

Miss Sawyer said, "I must return to the children. We will pray all is well."

I nodded our goodbye and took Clarinda's hand to follow the continuously building crowd.

"Sarah!" Harriet called, watching us pass the open yard. Elias ran past her, down the stairs toward the fray. Harriet cradled William Penn in one arm and used the other to call us over. Clarinda and I followed Digaleni, who flopped up the Boudinots' stairs without urgency.

We embraced, and I touched the infant's cheek, speckled with milk spots. "He's beautiful," I said, but the increased shouting caused us to look up from the baby's face. Several men caught a wounded warrior sliding from his horse. With his hands held to his bloody chest, the others needed to carry him into the McCoy's inn.

I asked Harriet, "What could have happened?"

She responded with another question. "Has John returned home?"

"Not yet. Why?" My volume matched my panic. "Were these men with John?" My worst fear, spoken by my mother's voice inside my mind, overwhelmed me. I sat in Harriet's rocking chair and reached out for Clarinda to sit on my lap. I needed to hold her. For however long we sat there, beside the uproar, seeing the injured man, I too became mute, deaf to the world beyond my fear.

Reverend Sam and Elias whispered together while they returned to the porch. Harriet stepped aside so her husband could see us. Elias didn't hesitate and kneeled to take my hand.

"Sarah," he said, looking at Sam over his shoulder.

"Was John with them?" I asked once and then repeated myself. The first, too quiet to be understood, and the second all too demanding. If Elias

194

didn't answer, I knew the worst to be true.

"John and Vann were not there when this happened." I breathed in relief, but knew Elias had more story to tell, or he wouldn't have continued to hold my hand.

He looked for silent advice from his wife before continuing his story. "The men found a whiskey wagon. John sent them to bring it here as evidence. But on the way home, they stopped and opened a cask. Chewoyee drank more than his companions, and they tied him to a tree to shut him up. And, in his cups, he made so much noise that he attracted over twenty Georgian guardsmen tracking the smoke from the burned village. The men fought. Guards beat Chewoyee in the head. The butt ends of their rifles mangled his body. According to Rattling Gourd, all four of them were arrested, bound hand and foot, and led toward the Carroll County jail. Now sober but wounded, Chewoyee fell from his horse. When the guardsman dismounted to tie him to his saddle, he realized his prisoner was dead. Without care, the guard left Chewoyee's body where it fell."

Reverend Sam added, "The three fled. But only Rattling Gourd and Waggon escaped. Waggon has a large knife wound in his chest. Assumedly, Mills was rearrested, and held in jail."

I found Elias' eyes. "But John and Vann weren't with them? You said they weren't with them."

Elias' eyes first looked pitifully at Clarinda, who burrowed under my chin. Then to me, he said, "No one knows where John and Vann are."

Harriet said, "I pray the evil brought on by these days will leave us."

Elias stood beside a waiting Reverend Sam, both expecting tears. But instead, I said, "Two white soldiers on the road followed us here. They tried to kill Clarinda's hound when he chased them."

Elias looked with telling eyes toward Reverend Sam. He said, "The guards can't find John and Vann either. They're watching the house." Elias rubbed his forehead, then held the bridge of his nose. After taking a deep breath, he said, "I'll dispatch quick word to Major Ridge and Chief Ross. I'm sure the warden at the jail interrogated Mills. Mills knew Major Ridge followed Chief Ross' orders to burn the village. We must send the Light Guard to protect them all."

I said, "Quatie cannot feed soldiers now. She's expecting."

A familiar voice surprised me, one I was grateful to hear. Arch stood at the bottom of the stairs. He said, "I'll take the messages to Chief Ross and Major Ridge after I drive Mistress Ridge and Miss Clarinda to Running Waters. I'll protect them."

Sam said, "Let me go tell Ann. I'll go to Vann's cabin at Cave Spring."

I put Clarinda to her feet and took her hand. "I need supplies before we

Yellow Bird's Song

leave." The request seemed silly, left over from who I was earlier this morning.

Arch held out his hand to help me down the stairs. He said, "Hurry, Little Spider." Every time he called me so, it reminded me of the power and worth held by the smallest of God's creatures. I squeezed Clarinda's hand tighter.

Reverend Sam called after us. "I'll bring your wagon round the front of the store."

I embraced Elias and whispered in his ear. "You'll let me know if you hear anything more?"

"I'll ride to you myself with any news."

I couldn't cry and alarm Clarinda any further. I'd not signed a word. Seeing adults, those she trusted, talking with serious faces would scare her enough. So, I lied and signed, "Everything is fine," and smiled. She stopped our walking and slapped her leg, so Digaleni would follow.

I bought our necessary items quickly. Arch hefted the cloth sacks into our wagon. I lifted Clarinda into the back. Digaleni hopped in beside her, and they sat together on the sacks of salt and sugar.

Arch slid a musket under the seat before snapping the reins.

It was a mile or so out of town before he spoke. "I'm leaving this gun with you, loaded and ready to fire when I ride on to warn Ross and Major."

I said, "There's no need."

"There is genuine need."

"I don't know how to shoot it."

He reached for my hand and squeezed. "Aim and squeeze the trigger."

I didn't let go. "John never taught me."

"He will." Arch didn't say any more, nor did he let go of my hand.

Once home, I told him, "Saddle Equoni. Go to Ross' and Major's house."

"Keep the gun beside you. I'll return with more men."

"I could never kill anyone," I said.

Arch insisted and handed me the gun. "Never say never. Don't answer the door."

I informed all at home of the situation. Peter and Honey rocked on the front porch, humming hymns with Arch's rifle resting between them. Laughing Water and Will patrolled the outbuildings, the kitchen, my hothouse, the corncrib, the smokehouse, and the barns. Walking Stick, armed with more throwing knives than I cared to think about, remained mounted and rode the boundaries of our grazing fields.

Night fell before Sunflower and I put the children together in the parlor, making their beds near the fire. Neither of us would sleep.

Sunflower lit the candle tapers in the sconces on the wall before sitting near me and twisting vines. Her hands moved so fast I could not follow the pattern of her weaving. Opening my eyes from constant prayer, I stopped her hands with mine, hoping to borrow a shred of her courage.

The mantle clock marked the passing time. I sat in John's armchair, rocking Susan's cradle with my foot. I made absentminded stitches in one of her dresses, thinking how soon she'd grow out of it. But my attempt to embroider was pointless, pulling the needle free and un-threading every stitch I'd just made.

I paced with my hands on my back. If John and Vann were close, I didn't want them to come home, not tonight, not with soldiers patrolling the woods. I clung to the hope that John and Vann, wherever they were, were together and safe—not in some jail cell like Mills or, worse, lying dead on the road. I couldn't allow myself to fixate on such conjured visions.

Several shots echoed beyond Ridge Valley. Our bodies shuttered. Hearing it, Sunflower bent over with a sob. Her reaction came from her memory, from her barren heart. My cup was empty of any comforts to offer. I'd spent such faith on hope.

Riding in a full gallop, Major Ridge led a band of four or five other painted Cherokee, whooping and screaming as they approached. Their lit torches circled the house, leaving riders stationed at intervals. Arch stopped his horse near the front door, and withdrew a long gun from his saddle, holding it across his chest. My father-in-law, with all his might, dismounted beside Arch.

He opened the door and closed it quickly behind him. Large boots made wide strides down the hallway, stopping after seeing his sleeping grandchildren on the floor. I put my finger to my lips before he gestured for us to come to him. Sunflower and I were safe, held tight against his chest. But we had no way of letting John and Vann know they weren't.

He and I walked to the kitchen, where I offered him food and water. Before he could sit down, he unstrapped an arsenal attached to his waist and chest and laid the weapons of metal and bone across my table. He leaned back in the chair, stretching his long muscular legs in front of him, and sighed.

I wrapped my shawl closer around my arms, angry at his calm demeanor. "Aren't you worried?" I spoke. "If he can get home, he'll ride into a trap."

Major said nothing. What that meant, I couldn't fathom.

Frustrated by his silence, I said, "I can't stay closed in here another minute. I'm going outside." I nodded toward the door, so he would

Yellow Bird's Song

understand. He gestured, granting his permission.

Alone for the first time in hours, I glared toward the tree line, imagining the worst hiding under it. John's family never failed to protect my children or me from dangers they could and couldn't see. I knew this, although Major's insistence put John in danger. As I paced to one side of the porch, I blamed him, and walking to the other, forgave him. Peace in the middle ground remained elusive.

There was little space to feel gratitude for all the despair in my heart. Trembling hands touched my flushed cheeks. I didn't know what to do with all I felt, not able to walk it off or climb the hills to ease whatever in my body made my heart pound. I dropped my shawl, picked up my book from the seat of a nearby chair, and threw it into the yard with all my fear and frustration, anger and anxiety. I grabbed a pot of seedlings on the edge of the porch and threw it behind the house. The pot shattered. Tears fell from my eyes, not in grief or sadness, but in helpless rage. I never considered what trouble the sounds might bring. I grabbed another larger clay pot of dirt and hurled it with both hands into the mess. After each heave, I looked around my feet for something else to throw.

I ran the short distance to my hothouse and closed the door, trapping myself inside. Clay pots covered the table with apple and quince tree seedlings I'd started last winter. I didn't care how well they'd grown. I picked up the first and hurled it against the fireplace's stone. It hit and shattered against the iron pot used to boil water to steam the room. I grabbed another and held it with both hands above my head, ready to smash it to pieces against the rock floor.

It fell from my hands and split in two. Someone snatched me by the waist with one hand and covered my mouth with the other. I thrashed and kicked, trying to free myself. The man pulled me back against the glass windows, entrapping my arms. I bit his hand and the man's tight grip released me. I opened my mouth to scream, but before I could gather air, he turned and kissed me, stopping any plea for help from escaping my lips.

My captor's face was half-covered in black ash and bear grease, with handprints made from the same paint across his shoulders. He held his hands away from his sides, implying I was in no danger. I stepped away and saw the tree roots tattooed on his chest. His smell filled my senses: the bitter tangs of pine sap and black pepper mixed with oil used to soften saddle leather.

He took one step forward. He whispered, "Don't be afraid."

I touched him, examined him for bullet holes, as well as the light would allow. "Did the guard shoot you?"

John said, "Sarah, stop. I'm not hurt."

His fingers crawled up my back, and he stared at my lips. "Walking Stick shot twice in the air, a diversion, nothing more. Guards rode toward the gunfire and allowed warriors to circle me while we rode to the house. I never thought of disguising myself as who I am might save my life." His grin took my lips.

Another crash of clay pots broke against the river rocks covering the hothouse floor. We collided. My legs surrounded his waist as his arms lifted me onto the table. Flames from the warrior's torches outside lit his golden eyes. They flickered amid the shining black paint. He tasted the skin over my neck and my chest. I brought his face to mine, whispering, "I'm sorry I didn't listen."

He raised and brushed the hair away from my face and looked puzzled before saying, "I'm sorry it took so long to get home."

I needed to see the eyes of the man I loved underneath the color. With my shift, I wiped away the shadows around his eyes. The warrior's paint unveiled his adoration. Devotion replaced sorrow. Blame forgave. He rested his forehead against mine, breathed in my breath, and opened his eyes again.

I saw myself there, not helpless but fearless, not disregarded but treasured, not cursed but enchanted. His want became my need. Our heart sounds found their pulse, a beat we shared, familiar and known.

He rocked into me. Our covet of the earthly ground fell away, and we rose to a tremendous and limitless sky. Neither of us was bound to solitude any longer. Fiery sun and icy moon shared the night sky. *Nvdo walosi ugisgo*, the eclipse.

CHAPTER 20: FEATHER, GOBBLE, STRUT, AND SPUR

John Ridge
Running Waters
Spring and Summer 1830

Sunlight poured into the windows of my study while I read two months of newspapers stacked on the floor. Each word from Athens, Augusta, Savannah, and Milledgeville declared "War in Georgia". Yet, no one had seen the elusive Georgian Guard for weeks. Those men who'd stalked Running Waters, Vann's Cave Spring cabin, my father's house, and Ross' home must have returned to their forts or farms at the command of superiors who thought to save soldiers' lives by encouraging more white settlers. The vicious state didn't care who removed the Cherokee if we were gone. After reading too many articles, all with similar slander, I hoped their lies never became the truth.

After the burned village, newspapermen wrote falsehoods, calling my father a savage killer. Their columns said Major Ridge was "painted red for battle and wearing a war bonnet." Cherokee don't wear war bonnets, whatever they are. They said: "he led his war party waving a tomahawk against innocent white homesteaders, killing helpless women and infant children, and burning their homes during the coldest winter on record."[1] My father carried a pistol and did nothing of the kind.

The article failed to mention that the burned cabins were Cherokee homes on Cherokee land. Unmentioned too was Sunflower's rape and her husband's murder. No mention of pleas to Colonel Hugh Montgomery months before and his continued refusal to remove the soldiers. Sensationalism. Mistruths written to provoke white settlers to seek vigilante justice for savage murders that never occurred. All to vilify the Cherokee and justify the whites' further theft of our land.

I walked to the fireplace, lit a switch from the fire, and touched the flame to the candle wick on my desk. I tossed the switch back into the popping pinewood burning in the grate. Redundancy at its finest. After, I snapped the curtains closed and blocked daylight. I sat again and grabbed another paper, flipping it in both hands to extend the next series of lies beyond the crease.

President Jackson believed in the power of propaganda. The *Augusta Chronicle* expunged Jackson's generous proposal for Indian removal. Jackson's speech reported a "happy consummation" between him and the Congress who'd elected him, concurring that the Indian's "speedy removal" was imminent. Wholeheartedly, I doubted the truth of the

200

remark, knowing full well I'd signed no treaty forcing my people to move. According to the article, only one unnamed member of the House disputed Jackson's endeavor. Who was the solitary protestor, I wondered.

Overall, Jackson's speech abounded with rhetorical questions, asking but already knowing how the representatives would respond. I read Jackson's quotes aloud, alone. "'The waves of population and civilization are rolling westward, and we now propose to gain the country occupied by the red men of the South and West by a fair exchange and, at the expense of the United States, to send them to land where their existence may be prolonged and perhaps made perpetual. Doubtless, it will be painful to leave the graves of their fathers, but what do they do more than our ancestors did or than what our children are now doing?'"[2]

I gripped the paper and paced the room's perimeter in contrary consternation. Jackson spoke with a forked tongue. He poorly constructed a weak line of reasoning, imitating, like snakeskin, a ridiculous pattern of fallacious claims. Jackson's apathy encouraged Georgia to allow an invasion, with no treaty granting the thieves access. It mattered not. We had limited avenues to counter dishonest men. I said aloud, "Whatever treaty terms they can't negotiate, they take by force."

We were legally and morally right to defend ourselves. But by doing so, Chewoyee died, and Mills hung in prison. However, with the Georgian Guard ever present, Black Crow's illicit deal with Ross was destroyed. For the time being, there'd be few undiscovered routes to transport stolen horses, whiskey barrels, or slaves that would pass unnoticed.

Still, I couldn't think of how best to use the knowledge of Ross' betrayal, gained at such a steep cost: Chewoyee's and Mills' lives. Since returning, I couldn't sleep, seeing Mills swinging from the logs in the jail and, when awake, plagued by my suspicion of Ross' dirty financials.

I needed to be elected to a higher office to assess the treasury reports. Suppose Ross was opportunistic enough to risk Cherokee lives to increase his fortune. Wouldn't he also steal from the annuity paid our nation? If so, how could I call him to account without destroying our people? Georgia would capitalize on such a weakness. Newspapers would report the implosion of our infant government. We couldn't unite and fight President Jackson if scandal divided us from within.

Jackson's speech asked another question. "Can it be cruel, in this government, when, by events which it cannot control, the Indian is made discontented in his ancient home to purchase his land, to give him a new and extensive territory, to pay the expenses of his removal, and support him a year in his new abode? How many thousands of our own people would gladly embrace the opportunity of removing to the West on such conditions!"[3]

I held the paper to my pounding forehead and scoffed. Had I sat among the American representatives, I would have shouted my answer to his stupid question across the Capitol floor. "Send your people West—instead of the Creek, the Seminole, the Choctaw, the Chippewa, and the Cherokee. We're fine where we stand."

From Elias' *Phoenix*, he countered so many "mistruths" published in the white man's news. He offered an exact account of events and reported how Colonel Hugh Montgomery's incompetence led the charge by refusing to remove settlers. When refuting Jackson's bill, Elias too asked rhetorical questions, appealing to the common sense of his paper's northern subscribers. "When do we have an example, in the whole history of man, of a nation, or a tribe, removing a body from civil and religious means into a perfect wilderness—all to be civilized?"[4] In ironic contradiction, Elias' acknowledgment of Jackson's senselessness was apt. And I was glad my cousin was brave enough to print it.

People believed what they wanted. With the welcoming hand of the federal government, Georgians felt little empathy for "ignorant tribes," no matter how civilized. It was against their interests. While President Jackson and Georgia's Governor-elect Lumpkin bought and paid for newspapers to report white "progress," they charged Cherokee Nation the cost of the paper.

I rested my elbows on my desk and rubbed my temples. I heard a knock behind me before a little hand turned the knob. Rollin ran across the floor to show me turkey feathers he held in his hands.

I picked him up and sat him on my lap, picking seed spurs stuck in his hair.

"Yellow Bird, where have you been? I've been looking for you all day." Of course, I knew exactly where he'd been. I was jealous of his freedom, running free under the sun.

He handed me one feather and answered my question. *"Clarinda found them, Papa. In the field, near the stream."*

I asked him, *"Why do you have them then? The Great Spirit sends the feather to the person who finds it."*

He said, *"Mama said she had to share."*

I'd seen thousands of turkey feathers in my life. White horizontal streaks settled through speckled deep brown strands. I ran my hand down the plume and rested it on top of the mound of newspapers. Then, Rollin's beautiful mama appeared in the doorway.

She called Rollin to her, who slid from my lap, running across the floor.

"I'm sorry. I know you need quiet to read."

"You and our children should interrupt me more often." I stretched my open hand to her to come and stand beside me, while I couldn't help but squint my eyes at the bright light entering the room behind her.

I must have appeared sallow because when she got close, she touched my forehead and asked, "Are you well?"

I took her hand away and rested my heavy head on her waist. "My head hurts. Too much tiny type with no good news."

She turned to leave for the kitchen. "I'll make you some tea," she said, but I pulled her back.

She kissed the top of my head. Her palms raised my eyes to look at her. "You need light, fresh air. The sun is out. Go hunting; take Rollin with you." She looked over her shoulder to the doorway after saying his name. "Since his birthday, all he does is argue with me, saying he wants one thing, only to decide he needs another."

I turned to the papers on my desk, sneering and blowing quick air from my nose. "I've been reading of similar complaints."

"Then stop. For today, at least. If you spend all your time in the house, what is the purpose of fighting for the land? Strap Rollin to your back or ride with him to get your father. The guards are gone."

"A good idea, my philosophical wife." When we stretched our arms apart, I held onto her hand.

"Don't go yet." I opened the bottom drawer, retrieved the household money box, and pulled from it the note she'd written. "I need to talk to you about this."

She looked guilty for no reason, as I knew she would. I asked, "Why did you write it?" and handed her the scrap of paper.

She set the note back on the desk, staring at her script. "You were away." She shrugged her shoulders. "I didn't want you to think I'd take anything for any unnecessary reason." She took a breath. "I wrote it the same horrible day they forced you to sneak home."

I bent to see her eyes. "Sarah, you don't need to account for anything." I pulled myself from her. "Truth be told, I need to turn the running of this house and its finances over to you entirely. After reading the news, I will have little time to manage heads of cattle or corn and cotton prices." I tore her note and slid its pieces into the pocket hidden in her petticoat. "I'll teach you how to manage this summer. And after that, keep me informed. You'll make these decisions in my stead. I trust you."

She stepped back, slighting my intentions. "I couldn't. I don't have the skill. Trust Peter or Walking Stick to do it. The children fill my days. My father never would have entrusted my mother with so large a task."

Sarah's parents' voices were never completely absent from her thoughts and reappeared at the most inconvenient times. "How many times do I need to remind you? You aren't her. I'm not him. You already take care of everything here when I'm gone." Before she escaped the room and worried her mind with newfound responsibility, I stopped her from leaving. "You must, Ani. If something happens to me, I won't leave you unprepared. You must."

"After reading all this," I gestured to my desk's disorganized mess, "we need another delegation to travel to Washington, one that gets the ear of Chicken Snake Jackson, regardless of whether Ross wants me to go."

She said, "Snakes don't have ears." She made me laugh. "Why would Ross not let you go? He trusts you."

I hadn't told Sarah about Black Crow's deal with Ross. When Ross learned what I knew, our trust would be severed. Unfortunately, so must Sarah and Quatie's friendship.

She asked, "Do you think he'll speak with you?"

"Ross?"

"No, not Ross," she laughed, "Jackson. I can't imagine it a simple thing to get an audience with the president."

I picked up the feather off the desk and replied, "Sometimes, one must be the loudest bird in the yard."

I followed Sarah's green gingham to the kitchen, where she broke a bit of tea from the block and put it in one of the cups her mother sent. I walked to the open doorway of the kitchen and looked out, leaning into the frame with my arm. "Mistress Ridge, I have improved upon your idea."

"Which?" she asked without looking.

"While the children sleep this afternoon, I'm taking you hunting instead of Rollin. His squeaks will scare away the birds. And you need to learn to shoot." After she poured hot water into the cup, I turned her around and kissed her forehead. "I am suddenly hungry for turkey."

Sarah walked behind me, studying the ground. I'd already seen their tracks, three-pronged indentions with talons pointing in dry dirt. She followed them, walking in whichever direction they led, but all she did was crisscross.

I put the musket's barrel over my shoulder, walked back to her, and said, "I love you more now than I could ever say."

She smiled. "What makes you say that?" Then, with barely a breath between thoughts, she studied the turkey tracks. "Where did they go? They stop here."

"Watching you think fascinates me. Turkeys fly, Ani. Not far, but they do."

"And snakes have ears. Of course, turkeys fly. What did you think I was thinking?"

"Are you being sarcastic, Mistress Ridge? Surely not." I laughed. "When men bring home a bird, all the women can think about is all the feathers to pluck. The hunter has the harder job. He must stay out of sight. Far enough away the turkey won't know he's there, but close enough to hit the biggest one. If we find a rafter, we watch for the gobbler with the largest spread and longest beard. Then aim for the smallest part of his body, his head."

"Where did the turkeys go that made these tracks, my philosophical husband?"

I put the gun barrel toward the ground and grabbed my wife's waist, pulling her to me with my free hand. "They roost in trees. I don't remember you being so witty. When did this happen?"

She said, "In childbirth. So, turkeys roost like Quatie's peacocks. If you don't let go, I'll be with child again before we leave the woods, with or without a bird for dinner."

I kissed her quickly, released her, and took her hand. "Yoholo's wife would agree. I don't know if I could give you another child right now. I'm starving. Come on."

At the edge of the field, behind a downed log, we lay beside one another, with our shoulders together and our ankles intertwined. I was on Sarah's left, watching the open field where Clarinda and Rollin found the feathers earlier this morning. I whispered in her ear, "Shooting a partridge is about patience and stealth, but when a turkey gobbler spreads his tail feathers for the hens, he doesn't care who knows he's there."

Sarah whispered back, not taking her eyes from several females who scratched through leaves, looking for seeds. "Would I be wrong to assume that men behave differently?" She put the rifle in the socket of her shoulder and looked down the sights.

"Don't shoot the hens," I warned. "Watch and wait for the gobbler." A jake bustled into the group and strutted in a circle, fanning his feathers, eager to boast about his spread.

"Hold on. Let's see if that jake brings a gobbler."

After a few minutes of entertainment watching the jake flaunt his feathers, a deeper gobble drew our attention to the right of the field.

I pointed. "That's the one you'll shoot."

"But if I miss, they'll all fly away."

"That is true, and we'll eat salt pork for dinner, but what a story you'll have to tell."

The jake and the gobbler fanned their feathers, circling one another. The young male flapped his wings and threw a spur to the gobbler, while the gobbler proved his dominance by throwing his own. After considerable flapping, their sparring escalated, and the gobbler wrapped his neck around the smaller jake's, trying to drop him by pushing his head down.

The turkeys' fight for dominance mesmerized Sarah.

I whispered, "Brace the gun into your shoulder and don't think about missing. You'll hit him. You didn't miss when we practiced shooting all those clay pots you broke."

She lifted the rifle to her shoulder, staring down the barrel, and closed one eye.

"Don't close that one. Close the other eye."

She switched eyes. "Right."

"The gun will kick, but you know how that feels. Take a deep breath and let half out before pulling the trigger."

"Stop talking to me."

When the smoke cleared, her bird was down. I took the gun from Sarah and helped her stand. She wiped her hands on her dress and said, "I wasn't sure I hit it. I couldn't tell through the smoke."

"You killed it. That means I must pluck it." Sarah took down a bird so old, Rollin and Clarinda would have feathers to spare.

Summer drought followed spring's bounty. When I rode down the path toward New Echota, miles of bent and shriveled stalks gripped dry husks curling around barren cobs. Cotton prices skyrocketed. With slave labor, Ross profited from his cotton more than even Rich Joe Vann.

With Sarah's frugality, those living at Running Waters suffered only from our labors in the heat watering the primary gardens. The orchard crop was thin, but planting corn close to the stream meant we'd keep the crib full enough to sustain ourselves and our animals.

My father's cotton fields suffered, but with his field hands, he managed a thin crop, selling it for more than it was worth. We prayed thanks for such bounty and shared as much as possible with those less fortunate nearby.

But instead of a joyful family affair, July's Green Corn Ceremony was full of drunken games and viciousness. Cherokee clans traded flasks and chanted through the turkey dance, singing, "We are living in one cove, a flat and level cove. We are scratching, spreading leaves in just one cove. Tail feather spreading first on one side, then the other."[5]

During that dry summer, many Cherokees lost their coves, and each singer's defeat was palpable. Stand spoke to many a visiting farmer pushed from their land. One disheveled man asked why he should plant, work the ground, and allow Georgians to reap from his labors. Stunned into an uncommon silence, Stand had no answer.

Before the following day's council, elders waved large turkey-feather fans over Chief Ross, lending him the bird's pride. They fastened cock spurs to his boots. More turkey feathers hung from the long stem of a pipe smoked between him and the councilmen.

My father took the pipe first, inhaled, and sucked the smoke back into his nose. Father began a story while studying the pipe in his hand. *"The diamond-backed turtle conjured to win the race with magic, hiding secrets he still won't tell. On his journey home, the turtle stopped to drink from the river. He dipped his face and got his scalp wet, the war trophy he carried around his neck."*

Father passed the pipe to Sleeping Rabbit, who added to the story, *"Behind him, a large turkey gobbled from his kernelled neck and startled the thirsty terrapin."* Then he puffed from the feathered pipe and passed it to his friend, James Starr.

Starr said, *"The turkey challenged the turtle. He said, 'I don't think that scalp looks good on you.'"* He inhaled from the feathered pipe and laughed, which made him cough. He passed the smoking end to Chief Ross.

Ross puffed with small inhales but exhaled a single stream of smoke. He didn't continue the story, just passed the pipe. Ross fully understood Cherokee but spoke our language little. His matriarchal line made him one of us. However, he still hadn't spoken the language of the people he represented.

Elias took the pipe from Ross and said, *"The turkey challenged the terrapin for his trophy scalp."* Elias puffed his chest and changed his voice to talk as he imagined a turkey might. *"'That scalp drags on the ground when you wear it that way. May I see it?'"*

Stand elbowed his brother and took the pipe from him. *"The terrapin made the mistake of his life. He took off his scalp, handing it to the gobbler. That sly turkey threw up his spur, hanging the war trophy around his own neck."*

Stand patted my back with one hand and handed me the pipe. I said, *"The turkey ran away from the slow terrapin. Called him gullible, gobbling, 'How does it look on me at this distance?'"*

I switched to English and traced our fire's circle. I honored Chief Ross with the last smoke. "The turkey stole the turtle's beard. The turtle could never move fast enough to catch the robbing gobbler."[6]

Chief Ross looked puzzled, put the pipe to his lips, surrounded by a beard of his own, and inhaled.

Georgia's ban on tribal assembly went into effect two weeks before the Green Corn Council, but we risked holding it in New Echota one last time. Stand shook my hand as we walked inside. "The paint on our beloved council house has barely had time to chip before Georgia forces us to abandon our capital."

When we took our seats, I told Stand, "Ross recommends we move future councils north to Red Clay."

Before Stand could answer, our chief took to his podium and began, "I am not your enemy; American President Jackson is. To fight against his Removal Bill, I plan to secure American attorney William Wirt of Baltimore. I've appealed for the aid of Georgian attorneys Underwood and Harris. According to Secretary Eaton, the President will not intercede when Georgia surveys Cherokee territory to prepare for the lottery. Therefore, we must hire lawyers to dissuade Georgia's premature and unlawful initiative. They agreed to aid us, but at significant cost."

I felt the wind from Ross' wings. He made the situation sound desperate enough that the council would have no choice but to hire Wirt.

Ross recognized me to speak. I spoke first in Cherokee and then following with English. My people came first. *"This is the same Eaton who believes Cherokee are no more capable of being educated than wild turkeys. Can we afford such costly representation?"*

Ross stared at me. I waited for his explanation, trusting my intuition.

Ross countered, "We'll solicit support from our northern allies to cover the costs."

His reply was weak, embarrassed by our nation's lack of funding. I followed his remarks with another question. "And if we do not receive enough money from their kind donations? A trip North for delegates would be expensive. Cherokee Nation cannot afford such noteworthy attorneys and pay room and board for delegates in Boston, Philadelphia, and New York."

Ross had yet to tell the council of General Eaton's further sabotage. So, I asked another question. *"What if Jackson follows through with his threat, as Eaton said he would? To pay the annuity to each Cherokee family instead of granting the lump sum to the Cherokee Treasury. We are less likely to afford such expensive council if Jackson pays individual men."*

I wasn't disputing Ross. We both knew Eaton would do so, having met the boisterous man. But with no large deposit, the treasury would be penniless to afford expensive attorneys. Jackson and Eaton threatened with intention. Why would President Jackson allow treaty payments, paid by the American taxpayer, just so Chief Ross could sue the American government and use the money to pay expensive lawyers to argue against them? With Americas coffers still recovering from the War of 1812 and the inflated price of new land acquisitions, the American purse was far from overflowing.

Still, it was a great deal to ask poor Cherokee families to travel a week for their portion, a mere five dimes, no matter how great that sum might appear to drought-starved farmers. The money and the choice needed to belong to them.

Ross cleared his throat. "The council should sign its districts' power of attorney to me, so I may claim the annuity on behalf of the treasury."[7]

I wanted to ask him to repeat himself, fearing I didn't hear him accurately. Ross' words felt like a spur scratching against my chest. How dare he assume the council would allow him all the power and all the money?

I covered the imaginary wound with my hand and sat down as councilmen rose to their feet. Men talked over one another, some agreeing to Ross' request, seeing the benefit. Other hands pointed across the aisle, accusing men of theft who'd been friends the night before.

James Starr walked down the aisle and asked Ross for permission to speak. Starr turned to his fellow chiefs and said, "I nominate John Ridge as president of the National Council. We need a man who's not afraid to question our chief. John brings us information we didn't know. He should oversee the treasury. However, I agree with Ross. Our nation needs lawyers to fight President Jackson."

Vann seconded the motion. Xander McCoy walked and stood beside me, picked the quill from the desk, and said, "I will finish John's term as clerk, if council grants its consent."

This might be the only way Ross' request for the attorneys might pass. After my nomination, Ross had to decide whether toallow an uncontested vote for me as president of our National Council or deny it, and appear a money-hungry tyrant. With only two choices, neither good for him, Ross called for the vote. Father abstained and followed me down the quiet aisle outside while Xander recorded the hands.

Yellow Bird's Song

I turned left and paced at the foot of the stairs. Father stood still. Being in motion helped me think. Once the doors closed behind us, I said, *"Surely Ross knows he can't hire attorneys without enduring eyes on the treasury."*

Facing similar circumstances during British oppression, Hamilton, Jay, and Madison wrote *The Federalist Papers*: the checks and balances of government.

I stopped and faced my father. *"What must a chief do to save his nation? How much will it cost?"* I crossed in front of him and stopped on his other side. *"Why does it always come down to handing over the coins of our liberty, our rights, to a king?"*

I crossed again, farther away, talking to myself. *"The wealthy hold riches and therefore the power but can be blackmailed because they do. The poor have nothing to steal except the ground beneath their feet."*

At the Foreign Mission School, in Reverend Herman Daggett's Constitution class, he taught us *The Federalist Papers*. Most of my peers stared out windows or doodled on their slates, holding chins in their palms. But Elias and I were attentive. I remembered Madison's particular phrase in English. "Knowledge will forever govern ignorance, and people who mean to be their own governors must arm themselves with the power such knowledge brings. The abuse of liberty may endanger their liberty, but also by the abuse of power."[8]

Remembering, I shook my head and passed my father again, stomping the ground more adamantly than before. *"Even if I am not granted this position, I cannot, will not, with a clear conscience, sign away the rights to their money, unchecked."*

He stopped my stride by pulling a turkey feather from his coat pocket. He brushed it across my face and handed it to me. *"Leadership and loyalty have found you, my son. All any nation's people can ask of its chiefs is to speak and to serve."*

I sat on the council steps with my head in my hands when Father resumed my pace. We heard them before McCoy opened the double doors. Friends and brothers poured through, overwhelming me with handshakes of congratulations.

Over their heads, Ross and I saw one another. He twisted his neck, straightened his head, and acknowledged my victory with a solitary nod. If the council granted Ross the right to spend the Cherokee's annuity on lawyers, they'd asked me to stand directly behind him and follow their money.

CHAPTER 21: "OUR LIBERTY—MOST DEAR"[1]
John Ridge
Washington City
Winter 1830-1831

Washington City was a dirty place, especially when winter bared the poplars lining the streets. Rain turned to snow when our carriage approached the corner of Pennsylvania Avenue and Sixth. From my view through coach windows, stray dogs barked at horses pulling wagons as they passed elegant carriages transporting mysterious, hidden dignitaries. Ambivalent to class, indifferent carriage wheels dropped into icy ruts in the road, splashing half-frozen mud on pig or statesman alike.

I used the cane Sarah gave me to exit the carriage in front of Brown's Indian Queen Hotel, between the Capitol and the President's home, neighbored by the General Stage Office and the Centre Market. The hotel was a federalist white, four stories tall, with twenty glass windows on the bottom floor. Dormers on the roof created a platform between them for a balcony promenade.

Our driver delivered our bags to a bellhop, while the hotel's proprietor, Jesse Brown, greeted us. Despite the season's bitter cold, he met all his guests at the door. He stood beneath the colorful sign depicting the Indian Queen, Pocahontas, with her bow and quiver, loaning the establishment its name. Naturally, Brown took a personal interest in checking in with every guest. However, how he informed his manager of his random room assignments, I couldn't say.

"Dinner is served in an hour, gentlemen," Brown boasted when he opened the shining brass handle to ample lamplight from the hotel's lobby. Under a framed lithograph of the hotel, my attention was directed toward chiming sounds. A formally dressed clerk bowed to us after handing a note to a bellhop. Behind him hung a vast wall of bells, answering what must be the persistent needs of the hotel's temporary but famous tenants.

After a brief repose, we dressed for dinner and walked toward the renovated dining room. Husbands, wearing white waistcoats, held chairs for their adorned, elegant wives. Across the hall, bachelors hovered in parlors in small groups, standing in front of papered, epic scenes of Greek battles extending from chinked ceiling to hardwood floor. Others smoked cigars behind the anonymity of winged, jewel-toned chairs with faceless hands tapping cigar ash into trays resting atop shining mahogany tables.

I was joined by Coodey, Ross' observant nephew, and two others: Taylor, with his pessimistic and pensive face, and Tahunski, an elder.

Yellow Bird's Song

Tahunski's mind was quick, well-informed, responding to his counterparts with a quick tongue. Some might say the same about me—my father, for one. But I had learned to offer silence as the less offensive answer. When Tahunski spoke, I feared what he might say. The man shuffled his chair close to the table, while Coodey sat last, taking the dominant chair at the end.

I sat next to a fellow southerner, or so I assumed, overhearing his banter to the gentleman seated on his left. The southerner's long hair parted down the middle, although his fashionable sideburns framed a clean-shaven chin. His eyelids folded over his lashes, with a sharp nose above a gracious smile.

He noticed me when I lifted the napkin onto my lap. He leaned to my side and gestured toward the end of the table. "Here comes Brown in that white apron of his. Seems we are to have ham for dinner."

The weight of the smoked ham required two servants to carry the large platter. After the meat's grand entrance, Brown held a large fork in one hand and a slicing knife in the other. The entire table applauded when he cut into the meat and served the first guest. Then he continued to plate while servers arranged cutting boards of fresh bread and bowls of seasoned and roasted vegetables to fill and color the white tablecloth.

Tahunski mumbled, "There's enough food here to feed New Echota. White man's excesses." After his remark, he snapped his napkin open and placed it on his lap, begrudgingly following the rules of European etiquette.

"When in Washington—" I replied.

The talkative white man to my left passed me a serving bowl and said, "Take these. I've lost all taste for sweet potatoes."

I spooned a helping onto my plate, asking, "Why is that, sir? Do you not care for their sweetness? Perhaps it is the texture that turns you from the root."

"Neither. Ate too many of them once, starved after eating corn mush for months."

He spooned a serving of stewed greens onto his plate from another serving dish and passed it to me.

With the exchange, I asked, "Did you serve in the militia? My father refuses to eat corn mush for the same reason. Although he has no aversion to sweet potatoes."

"Yes, in a volunteer regiment from Tennessee." He cleared his throat. "During the Creek Wars, under Jackson's command." He took up his fork and continued his tale, "We took a Red Stick village of mostly women and children. It was the day I decided I'd rather meet my maker with a clean conscience than fight any longer under Jackson's command. Some other volunteers and I tried to leave after the slaughter, but Jackson threatened me with a lead bullet at close range. So, we unstrapped our blanket rolls and stayed.[2] Under one of the burned Creek huts, we found a hole filled with sweet potatoes, enough to feed the men for a month. We were too hungry to ration them. So, we roasted and ate them all in one sitting. After that, I lost my will for slaughter and any taste for sweet potatoes."[3]

I said, "My father fought under General Jackson, leading a Cherokee brigade against the Red Sticks at Horseshoe Bend. Your stories remind me of his."

"You couldn't be." The man scoffed and replied, "Then again, I can see the man in your face. Would you be Major Ridge's son?"

"I am. John Ridge."

He put down his utensils and extended his hand. "Nice to meet you, John. Feel like I know you already if you're anything like your father. How is the Ridge?"

I rested my fork handle on the edge of my dinner plate and shook his hand. "If you were to ask him, he'd say he's as young as ever. But, of course, my mother might offer you a different answer altogether."

"We'd still be fighting barricaded Red Sticks if it weren't for your father. Name's Crockett, congressman from Tennessee."

"Your reputation precedes you, sir," I replied.

He resumed his dinner with a bite of the steamed greens. "Has to. Reputation is necessary for politicians, regardless of its truth. Just last week, I had a portrait made. Instead of representing myself as a dignified congressman, I donned my buckskins and threw my musket over my shoulder. An hour before, I'd gathered some stray dogs off Pennsylvania Avenue and had them painted sitting at my heels. My constituents expect the frontier Crockett, and I intend to give him to them."[4]

Crockett continued, "I received a letter of appreciation from your Chief Ross. He thanked me for standing up to Jackson. Your chief could have just written thank you, but he carried on for four pages. Unfortunately, a once direct man seeking public office loses his aptitude for simplicity after they count the votes."

I took my knife and sliced two pieces from the bread loaf. Handing one to Crockett, I said, "Then I'll just offer my thanks. It is no common thing, especially for a southerner, to oppose President Jackson's Indian removal and stand against the democratic majority."

"Well, I'd rather be politically buried than hypocritically immortalized."[5]

I handed him the butter dish and gestured toward our delegation. "We

Yellow Bird's Song

seek audience with Secretary Eaton and President Jackson."

"You all might need one of these." Crockett held his knife into the light and studied its edge. "We call Jackson 'Sharp Knife' for a reason. The man is uncompromising. Speaking against him for your people has likely ruined my political career. But our Constitution gives Congress the power of the purse, not the executive. So, I couldn't see the point in violating such an honorable document to provide this President control over the sum it would take to buy out the Cherokee." Crockett shook his head and buttered the bread held in his hand.

Tahunski overheard our conversation and offered his thoughts. "Shame we didn't just kill Jackson at Horseshoe Bend. I didn't know you then, but I would have shot back if Jackson had threatened my service in a volunteer militia. Taken the man down then if I knew he'd cause my people so much trouble."[6]

I said, "If General Jackson gives us an audience, we plan to make it clear how the entire holdings of the Second United States Bank would not be enough to persuade us to move. Nor do I believe America's tax-paying citizens would agree to such an offer."

"Agreed. I learned that same lesson from a man behind a plow. Said he wouldn't vote for me. Course I asked him why. He said I'd voted for an unconstitutional bill, twenty thousand dollars to aid women and children left destitute after a fire in Georgetown. Some of the hardest work I've ever done, putting out that blaze. When I saw the poor state of the victims with my own eyes, I voted to relieve their suffering with federal dollars.[7]

"But that farmer, Horace Bunce, wouldn't budge. Finally, after offering me a convincing argument, I agreed with him and acknowledged my error. I promised him I'd never vote for such again. Many suffer across this nation, homes ruined by fires or floods I know nothing about. As Bunce said, it was the principle of the thing. Bunce taught me it wasn't the federal government's task to offer charity to some and not all."[8]

Crockett sliced into cold ham with the knife in his hand. He continued, "The Constitution outlines the responsibilities of government: protection of personal rights and the rights of each state, establishing and maintaining laws, defending against foreign invasion, and regulating trade and tariff." He speared and took a bite. After swallowing, he said, "Like Bunce said, the rest is just usurpation."[9]

During the meal, our conversation attracted the attention of the man seated to Congressman Crockett's left, who introduced himself as Bluff, a correspondent for the *New York Observer.* He said, "I attended a dinner here at the Indian Queen last April, honoring deceased President Jefferson. Jackson's dander was up when he and Vice President Calhoun debated whether states had the right to override federal laws after South Carolina threatened to nullify the administration's tariff demands. Jackson dominated the first toast, saying, 'Our Union—it must be preserved!' Calhoun, not to be outdone, stood and raised his glass after Jackson's toast. 'Our Union—next to our liberty, most dear!'"[10]

I responded softly, and my two new acquaintances leaned in to hear. "Had I been in attendance, I would have raised my glass only after Calhoun drank from his."

The three of us poured glasses of wine and set about toasting, "To Liberty—most dear."[11]

Congressman Crockett filled our days with introductions. We met a congressman from Kentucky who supported our cause and another, Frelinghuysen, from New Jersey, who last session filibustered six hours against native removal. Another man, Senator Edward Everett of Massachusetts, spoke two days concerning Cherokee's struggles on the Senate floor. He warned us to burn the treaties made by America's fathers, saying they no longer retained their power.[12] The senator concluded his fine speech by saying Jackson's disrespect disgraced the memory of Washington and Jefferson. "If the attitudes of the present administration stand, then the Cherokee should secure no further agreements with the American government."[13] His honesty overcame me, so moved by emotion, I had to cover my eyes.

During our first month at the Indian Queen, I slept well with such optimism. Everett's words fell upon my ears like soft music of other days when the administration of the general government observed sacred regard for subsisting treaties with our nation, maintaining the faith and honor of a united America handed down to them from their great revolutionary ancestors.[14] Jackson's Indian policy was deservedly unpopular. It met with opposition at every stage whenever Congress had to supply funds.

I wrote to my father with the same mind. I was the first to admit my surprise at such a welcoming reception. These representatives were influential in vote and eloquent in voice, morally sound white men who became our friends. The more I engaged with each of them, the more I felt Cherokee earned favor with a vast majority, especially from northern abolitionists who equated ending slavery with their fight against Indian removal.

I knew I wouldn't sleep much after our meeting with Jackson's Secretary of War, John Eaton. The last time I'd seen Eaton's face was at

Yellow Bird's Song

the Turkeytown tavern when Father delivered his defiant speech and nearly punched the smirk off Crowwell's graying face. That was the same night Xander secretly met with Crowwell, Eaton, and Montgomery, three worthless scoundrels, offering him appraisal for his land improvements in New Echota.

I laid in bed, recalled how directly I spoke to Eaton. "Will the federal government intervene if Georgia moves its force to possess our land? We have the right to a frank answer."

Eaton's response was indifferent. "We will decide on the matter when the crisis arises." He refused to give any small verbal consolation. Eaton's tactic was delay, procrastination, equivocation, which I thought of as salty avoidance, like placating a hungry baby, offering it a pinky.

No amount of optimism could squelch my suspicion of Eaton. It grew each day and continued through this restless night. My mind replayed the day's conversation whenever I closed my eyes. No doubt, Jackson, the head of the snake, controlled Eaton's moves, both awaiting the Supreme Court's decision on our injunction against Georgia.

I was exhausted yet so restless. I turned my feather pillow over and planted my head in its center. Still, the tension in my neck was unrelieved. Although I couldn't see in the dark, I stared toward the ceiling.

President Jackson's desk was covered in empty brandy glasses holding down corners of maps of the continent.

Coodey never let me forget Ross' directive, that he was the only man allowed to speak with Jackson. With subservience and metaphor, Coodey tried to persuade "Old Hickory" not to divide the annuity and allow our treasury to distribute the funds. Jackson did not appear to be even mildly entertained by Coodey's complements and condescending speech.

I put my arms above my head after suddenly becoming too warm. If I had taken the opportunity to speak, I would have addressed treaty issues with Jackson instead of finance, requesting federal troops to prevent Georgia's further violence. I knew leadership began with prioritizing perspectives. But unfortunately, that was another area where Chief Ross' opinion and mine diverged.

Jackson didn't respond to Coodey as he walked around his desk and stood before me. We were the same height, of similar build, except his age and risk streaked his hair white. Jackson's pale eyes met my brown. He looked at my cane and examined my attire from shoe to head. His eyes studied my face with a quizzical brow before stretching, reaching full height by lifting his chin.

"I believe I rewarded your father with the rank of major for his service in the Creek Wars. Am I correct? You are nearly as tall as my Cherokee friend." His stern tone masked such a personal remark.

I said, "Yes, sir. Out of respect for his general, he adopted the rank as his first name." I knew Jackson preferred the title general to president, which said something of the man's hubris. To engage him was to flatter him.

To engage me was to respect my father.

After a thoughtful moment, he said, "The Ridge." Those were his only words.

I said, "He remains the man who walks on mountaintops, Kah-nung-da-tla-geh."

Afterward, Jackson simultaneously dismissed Coodey and our delegation with a wave of his hand without further commentary on the future of the annuity. He walked behind his desk and retook his prior position. General Jackson didn't look up from his maps when he said, "Sirs, your audience has ended. There is nothing more I can do for you."

Tahunski and Taylor left the room first, donning their hats after exiting the doorway. Coodey bowed and walked backward before King Jackson, perhaps a more apt title. After he left, Jackson addressed me with a nod. I reciprocated and offered him the same respectful gesture before I passed Eaton, who closed the door behind me.

The air in my room became overly warm. Restless and irritated, flat on my back, I pulled my arms from underneath the red quilt and flopped them at my sides, searing myself inside the bedclothes. If I couldn't stop my mind, sleep's blessed oblivion would never come.

With sudden realization, I opened my eyes and spoke aloud. "Guns." If Jackson enforced his act via militia, my people would have no choice but to fight or flee. I flipped to my other side and pulled the sheet over my shoulder. I closed my eyes again, but all I could see was smoke from musket shots. All I heard was cannon fire.

Would it be necessary to outfit our nation's warriors with weapons? Call those who'd emigrated West back home to fight a revolution. Make alliances with other civilized tribes and go to arms? Fight General Jackson, who, riding his white horse, would lead thousands of federal troops into Cherokee Nation? The man defeated the British in New Orleans with far fewer men at his disposal.

Sleep would never find me with a revolution raging in my head. Crockett and Father, Ross and Yoholo witnessed what Jackson considered proper warfare with Indians—absolute and total slaughter. How much oppression and violence could we withstand before Cherokee history recorded its own Lexington and Concord?

It would take unlikely alliances to win—Cherokee banding with

Yellow Bird's Song

remaining Creek, Choctaws, Chippewa, and Seminole. More than a decade ago, Tecumseh tried joining bands of Indian nations to fight the Americans. His Shawnee militia tried to keep settlers from Kentucky and Ohio by aligning with the British against the Americans. Father knew the British would betray the Shawnee warrior. That's exactly what happened. Tecumseh died next to his vision of an Indian Confederacy. The bullet ending his life came from Harrison's American gun.[15]

Lesson learned—a point where I imagined Ross and I would agree. There could be no war for Cherokee independence. Our only avenue was to argue in the American courts. However, the attorney costs made us bleed treasury gold rather than red blood.

Wirt had concluded his arguments before the court. While we spent ten minutes in the President's company, Wirt expostulated the Cherokee case against Georgia to the justices until three o'clock, condemning Georgia's violations of our sovereignty.

Rightly so, I thought. Wirt declared us a foreign nation and equated our treaties as binding as those between England and France. Therefore, Georgia's laws were unenforceable as we were a separate country. His syllogism was apt, his claims, proper.

Abandoning the idea of restful sleep and suddenly chilled, I rose and put more wood in the fireplace. I warmed my hands, struck by an idea. I lit a switch and guarded its flame against my hurry and rush. I lit the wick and recited President Jefferson's honorable words to the dark.

"'When a long train of abuses and usurpations, pursuing invariably the same object, evinces a design to reduce them under absolute despotism, it is their right, it is their duty, to throw off such government and to provide new guards for their future security.'"[16]

I nearly fell to the ground trying to put on my pants. Instead, I wrapped the quilt from the bed around my shoulders and sat at the desk. I grabbed a piece of parchment, dipped my quill, and wrote: "In vain, appeal after appeal has been made to the present Executive of the United States, invoking the kind interposition of that authority which treaties and laws have invested to save from oppression and the forcible expulsion of the Cherokees from the land of their nativity."[17]

I dipped again. In my rush, ink spots dropped along quill's path. I didn't look up when I rang the bell. At two in the morning, I requested a copy of the *Declaration of Independence*. I had to ask twice, so the night manager understood my request. Brown might remember me as the Indian Queen's only guest to request America's founding document in the middle of the night. It took more than an hour before a knock sounded. I snatched the paper from the bellhop's hand and closed the door without thanking the poor soul.

I needed to review the document's structure. Jefferson listed colonial grievances before declaring finality with his noteworthy and well-remembered "therefore".[18] I would write a similar catalog of Georgia's "long train of abuses and usurpations" and reaffirm Wirt's argument that Cherokee Nation was a "free and independent state".[19]

I needed the summer to complete my people's *Declaration* and seek its approval from our council in the fall. Meanwhile, Ross must take steps toward furthering Cherokee capitalism with independent markets and establish trade rates for corn, tobacco, and cotton. He could lead us into a self-sustaining economy, where treaty annuities were not our only sustenance, but existed only as a line item on our national budget.

Then come winter, I would return to the Indian Queen and deliver this Declaration of Sovereignty, a memorial, to Congress in its next session.

Suppose we could hold Georgia and the American military back another year. In the meantime, we might win this injunction and lobby our northern friends to choose Whig's Henry Clay to replace war-mongering Jackson. In that case, we could seize the time by declaring our liberty—most dear—and force the government to recognize Cherokee sovereignty before Jefferson's same "candid world".[20]

CHAPTER 22: CURSED
Sarah Ridge
Running Waters
Summer 1831

William opened the kitchen door with scrapes on his cheek and dirt embedded in his eyebrows. He dropped split wood from a broken plow handle at his feet. He shut the door and slammed the latch closed, resting his back against it. "There is a *tsgili* nearby."

"A witch?" I asked while spoon-feeding Susan. "There's no such thing."

"How else," he asked, "could I explain the rock in the middle of a field I've planted many times before? Why didn't the mule see it? The blade hit a deep rock and pulled me over the handle. It snapped and sent me straight into the clods."

"Come. Sit. Tell me why you think it was a witch."

"When I got up from the ground, I felt her eyes on me from the woods, but the only animal I saw was a *dewa* twitching her tail, staring at me from a high pine branch. Sweat dripped into my eyes. When I wiped it away, the squirrel disappeared."

I said, "Squirrels move quick, Will."

I rinsed the cloth in water from the basin and sat beside Will to clean his cut. He turned his head away, not in pain, but in dismay that I didn't panic like he did. He believed wholeheartedly in what he was saying, shivering, even though it was July.

"Everyone should stay close to the house. A broken plow is an omen."

"Quatie and I planned to ride to New Echota today."

"Don't go." Will stood and retrieved the pistol from the top shelf and began loading it. "Something bad is coming."

When he set it on the table, I lifted Susan from her chair and put her on my hip. "There's no need for all that."

Honey came into the kitchen, tying her apron behind her back. Will's serious look stopped her movement. He said, *"There's a tsgili in the woods."*

"Aww, Lawd, no," she said. Then, in a rush, Honey took Susan from me and went into the front parlor. She stared out the window, guarding the children. My mouth hung open, amazed at how seriously the two reacted to the word *tsgili*. Such superstitions were astounding. Will picked up the broken plow handle from the doorway and left the kitchen armed.[1]

It would be an hour before Quatie arrived. We planned to meet Mother

Susannah and tend to Ann Worcester through her impending childbirth. With the time, I sat at John's desk and began a letter addressed to the Indian Queen Hotel. It had been a month since I received word from him. The delegation lived in Washington these last six months. Honestly, I hoped he'd never receive this letter, already aboard a steamer for home. Every time he left, I waited longer for him to return. I dipped the quill and placed its tip on the parchment.

> My dearest,
> Rollin misses you a great deal. Your father taught him to ride, and he cannot wait to show you how well he sits a horse. Clarinda has sprouted, her head reaching my waist. Little Susan sits up to watch her brother's and sister's antics. I prop pillows around her so when she belly-laughs, watching them argue with their hands, she doesn't hit her head when giggling and falling to her back.
> It eases my loneliness, hearing their laughter. When I miss you so much, think I can't leave our bed for selfish sadness, the children wake. I pray my gratitude for God's gift of healthy babies. He answers in their voices, granting me the will to rise another day.

I refilled the ink, thinking how Rollin's voice was so like John's, albeit spoken in higher tones. Their cadences were the same. I noticed it the most when Rollin argued with me at bedtime. But after quieting each night, in the silence, I brushed away the thick black hair from his eyes.

Clarinda inherited John's eyes and keen sight. She spent more time with Mother Susannah, learning herbal remedies. When Susan coughed so last spring, Clarinda found bishop's weed. We pounded the leaves for their oils. I rubbed the mixture on Susan's chest, and she breathed easier because of her sister's efforts. I rubbed honey on Susan's gums and let her drink more with lemon in the water. It helped tremendously.

Whenever John left, his essence remained on the faces of our children. Taking care of them and this farm was all I could do to take care of him.

Lost in the letter and my thoughts, Quatie called from the kitchen. Hearing her serious tone, I knew finishing John's letter would have to wait. When I found her, Quatie stood beside an elder Cherokee woman, hunch-backed with white, unkempt hair matted around her shoulders and eyes set so deep that her lids covered the whites of her eyes. Underneath them, skin pooled, resting on her cheekbones. Her skin was like leather from years spent laboring under the sun.

Quatie turned the old woman by her shoulders and showed me whip

Yellow Bird's Song

stripes along her back, each crusted with dirt and dried blood. I gasped, staring at the results of barbarism and cruelty.

Quatie said, "She came to me this morning. I didn't know what to do except bring her here. Her name is Marz."

"Does she speak English?"

"Yes," Quatie affirmed.

I asked the woman, "Who did this to you?"

Marz didn't answer, but Quatie did, flushed with indignant anger. "Who else but the white soldiers? She said the Georgian Guard evicted her. When she refused to leave, they drove her away with whips!"

Quatie helped the injured old woman sit. Marz whimpered when I twisted water from a cloth and began dabbing her wounds. She arched her back at my every touch and moaned in pain.

I called Sunflower, who came from her cabin into the kitchen. "Help me?"

Sunflower shuttered, as if overcome with cold, as Will had done before. Clarinda came into the kitchen from the main house and stopped in the doorway.

The old woman cooed at Clarinda and reached out with long and dark fingernails. Sunflower moved the puzzled child by the shoulders toward us. When I handed Sunflower the bloody cloth, she traded places with me and continued cleaning the wounds.

I signed to my daughter, "Help me find some herbs?"

Clarinda answered by grabbing her basket from the hook on the wall and my hand. She pulled me toward the running water. From the base of a poplar tree, we gathered wild ginger root with its broad, green, circular leaves.[2] She smelled the plant before pulling it from the ground, like Mother Susannah taught her to do.

Clarinda signed, "Goldenseal, Mama."

I nodded and reminded her, "Yes, white and red berries with large soft leaves."

She signed, "Squirrels eat it. It grows in the shade."[3]

Clarinda blew her whistle. I found her hunched over, smelling the red-spurred flower pod in the plant's center. After gathering what we needed, we hurried home.

Sunflower steeped cherry bark tea for pain while Clarinda and I ground the plant leaves to an oily paste. "I'll take her to my cabin." She took a deep breath before she said, "The head men must make this stop." One palm hit the other with insistence as she exclaimed in signs.

Quatie sighed and said, "Ross would never have allowed Marz to stay with us."

"Why ever not?" I asked.

"Important men and high-ranking officers meet with him. Stay for days at a time. He wouldn't want anyone to see her."

"Why? In case they recognize their handiwork?" I couldn't keep the anger from my voice while I tore bandages from woven strips of cotton.

Quatie said, "I don't want to anger him. Since George was born, Ross has been different."

"How so?" I asked.

"Tender," she said.

In Sunflower's cabin, the three of us moved in silence. We covered Marz's back with poultice and bandages. We cleaned her face and hands, dressing her in a clean shift. Sunflower brushed her hair. She thanked each of us with a squeeze from her long-nailed hand, and fell asleep, safe and in less pain. Sunflower kept watch from the bedside chair.

Quatie and I promised the Boudinots and Worcesters we'd come.

When we reached the forest surrounding New Echota, she said, "Hunters have taken all the game."

Looking like an outpost settlement, canvas tents covered the heads of Cherokee women left idle with no fields to plow or bread to bake. Whiskey barrels had found their way in, toppled and empty, as medicine for broken hearts and stolen homes. Pony clubs had stolen nearly five hundred head of cattle and horses. White settlers, the impatient but fortunate lottery drawers won the land, and further assisted by Georgian soldiers, evicted more Cherokee families.

Quatie followed my stare. Men gambled near campfires as their shoeless children chased one another through the encampment. She said, "Ross said Georgia disbanded the Light Guard. Unemployed officers are finding their fortunes bringing whiskey wagons, selling cups for cheap."

I said, "No one benefits when fathers drink, and gamble away what they've saved from last year's crops. We must feed these people."

Quatie said, "They won't accept a white woman's charity."

I replied, "It isn't charity, Quatie, it's humanity." When families lost ground, they discarded hope, like seeds, along the roads they sojourned. Harvesting nothing, in abundance.

When we arrived at Reverend Sam's, cavalry officers surrounded a wagon. Whispering onlookers ogled from a distant perimeter.

Last March, Reverend Sam refused to sign his allegiance to the state. They'd arrested him but released him a month later, because he was

Yellow Bird's Song

postmaster and paid with federal funds. The last time I saw Reverend Sam, he hunched over his horse, carrying a boulder's weight in certain guilt, knowing that staying home placed his family in danger. Were the soldiers here to arrest him again?

Elias and Harriet came to us from across the street, hand in hand. Elias said, "Georgia's Governor Gilmer asked President Jackson whether he considered missionaries servants of the government. Jackson said no. So, after that, Georgia restricted all mail coming into or out of the nation and dissolved Worcester's postmaster position."

I asked Harriet, "Is that why they're here? To arrest Worcester? What about Ann? Would they have so little Christian mercy to arrest a father so close to his child's birth?"

Harriet said, "Of course they would. They draw surveys of the land and invade the gold mines, prosecute with vigor with authority of their Christian governor. Every day, the Cherokee cry robbery. All to no avail."

Elias pulled his wife close. "We are denationized."[4]

All movement forward ceased. Whispering voices hushed when Sam walked down the front stairs, pale and silent. His hands were bound behind his back, escorted on either side by two soldiers gripping his elbows.

Soldiers held hitched horses still while they stationed Sam behind the wagon. Already inside sat Missionary Butrick and another man I didn't know, both bound and gagged.

Chief Ross hurried past us to intervene, arguing with a blue-coated officer whose shoulders were adorned with golden epaulets. I couldn't hear what they said, but he held up his hand to deny Ross whatever mercy he'd requested.

Behind us, another guard cursed and taunted minister and physician, Doctor Butler. "Get over there, you Indian savior."

The prisoner lost his footing. The soldier dragged him by his coat across the road toward Sam and the awaiting prison wagon.

The schoolhouse door opened. Sophie Sawyer shouted, "Let him go! You cannot do this! He is a doctor, a man of God!"

Ross shouted, "Stop!" Waiting horses twisted their harness chains, frightened by his stern command.

Sophie Sawyer ran too close. The soldier let go of his prisoner, turned his gun, and hit her with the butt end shoved into her chest. The blow pushed her to the ground. Then, a smirk, evidence of his little remorse for striking a woman, the soldier grabbed Doctor Butler's coat only to throw him forward to tumble at Sam's feet.

Quatie, Harriet, and I ran to Sophie's aid. She panted and held her chest, stupefied at the guard's cowardly blow. There was nothing we could

224

do but watch as the soldiers took the ministers. If Elias and Ross were powerless to stop them, we could do nothing. To the militia, we were just a spread of skirts, colors arrayed against a dirt road.

The commanding officer ordered one cavalry soldier to dismount and handed him two trace chains, one for Doctor Butler's neck. The other he strapped around Sam's throat. No smith ever forged horse tack for use on free men.

The soldier gathered the chains by their loose ends. He fastened Sam to a horse and Doctor Butler to the end of the cart. The soldier driving the wagon released the brake and snapped the reins. The prisoners lunged forward, while another soldier prodded them from behind with his bayonet.

Chief Ross shouted, "Where are you taking them?"

"To prison or to Hell," the officer said as if the scene were a play, a comic skit rather than a somber-telling prologue to a tragedy.

The commander ignored his subordinate's sarcastic remark and said, "They'll face trial in Lawrenceville, a week's walk from here. It's where they'll be prosecuted and hung."

Chief Ross asked for another mercy from the commander. I couldn't hear what he said, but the commander refused. "No. They'll walk," he said. Without another word, the commander mounted his horse, passed prisoners and wagon, and led the charges through town.

Sophie gathered enough breath to say, "With wounded feet. Chains of thorns. Carrying their own crosses."

An unnecessary fife and drum led the wagon around the next bend, as if the gallows were feet instead of miles away. None nearby could turn their eyes from the scene; the music was unwarranted.

When we could no longer hear the march, Ann Worcester stepped to her porch in shift and shawl. She held the child in her womb, and another infant in her arms. Tears dripped into the babe's pale hair.

That evening, Harriet played hymns on her pianoforte. I sat on the Worcester's porch steps, drying my hands on a towel. Sophie Sawyer closed the door and sat beside me.

I said, "Amazing Grace. God knows we need to hear it now."

Sophie said, "New Echota looks nothing like it did when Harriet's parents visited a summer ago." She placed her hand over the sore place where the soldier's gun bruised her chest. "They brought her that instrument at great expense. They spoke of you and your family when they were here. You two grew up together?"

"Yes." I focused on the damp dishtowel in my hands. "My parents just left Connecticut for Massachusetts. After John and I married, my father's position at the Mission School was threatened. After all, he and Mother raised such an immoral daughter. Then, after the town's hypocrites burned effigies of Elias and Harriet down Bolton Hill Road, the school's doors closed for good."

I scoffed and silenced nearby crickets. "When the Golds returned North, they reported to my mother and father how influential their son-in-law's paper had become. Until Mistress Gold told Mother how well we were, how successful John's law practice had become, I think she still believed we lived in a mud hut and scraped our dinner from barren fields. My mother thinks her grandchildren believe in witches roaming the woods. She's never met them."

Sophie hummed a harmony to the hymn's final chorus over Harriet's accompaniment seeping from the open window. After the final note, the window went dark.

Sophie asked, "What would she do if guards came for Mister Boudinot? I fear it only a matter of time."

I said, "If Elias were jailed, if he died in prison, I think she'd take their children to her parents. Put them in school and move forward as if their Cherokee half didn't exist."

"And you?" she asked. "What would you do if the soldiers arrested your husband? Go to Massachusetts?"

My mind replayed the cavalry's fife and drums, blending into the pianoforte's lingering key. "No," I said. "Not even if John died. I'd do the only thing I could. Remain on Cherokee ground, seed the fields, protect our children, and never let them forget their father's sacrifice."

Baby Jerusha Worcester, another girl, was born a day later, but only survived the week. She failed to thrive, wouldn't suckle, losing blood in her nappies. Her imprisoned father didn't know he should grieve.

Georgia's Supreme Court sentenced both ministers to four years of hard labor in Milledgeville prison. While nine other arrested ministers signed their commitment to the state, Reverend Sam and Doctor Butler continued to refuse any offers of clemency.[6]

CHAPTER 23: CHASING THE SUN
John Ridge
Ridge Valley, Cherokee Nation Territory
Fall 1831

By mid-September, I arrived in New Echota in utter disbelief. Men gambled over dice, unabashed and unashamed of their drinking. Homeless families riddled the streets, idle among tents and campfires popping under iron cook pots. Children ran barefoot up and down the roads. Considering there was safety in numbers, I couldn't blame them for congregating here. What could we do? The Cherokee Treasury didn't have the resources to move them, build new cabins for so many.

This town, once a dream my father called the new Baltimore, looked more like a military encampment. Years ago, Sarah and I stopped here on our journey South. We imagined buildings before Cherokee carpenters had time to erect them, daydreamed of a life we'd yet to experience. So many families' dreams had been stolen while they hovered in New Echota, hoping the government they'd voted for would save them.

Where was their chief? How was Ross leading our nation through this catastrophe? Were Ross and his brother still profiting from our people's suffering, as Black Crow said? Was this how he coerced Cherokee obedience? Otherwise, how could our people have fallen so fast? People must see his weaknesses sooner rather than later.

Elias approached us and assisted the stage driver with removing our trunks from the coach roof. He looked through eyes surrounded by dark circles, with his back hunched low in weariness. He managed the *Phoenix*, translated the New Testament into Cherokee syllabary, held examinations for school children, and offered sermons to a diminishing congregation in Sam's stead.

Coodey, Tahunski, and I said our goodbyes before they set off on the last leg of their journey home. Once alone, I embraced my cousin. *"I can only imagine what you've endured. Give me a task."*

Elias made one request. *"Wirt lost the injunction case. Convince Ross not to hold council here next month."*

I said, *"What? He wanted our last council meeting moved to Red Clay. Why change his mind now? When we face arrest? Georgia will never allow us to assemble here, not when they have the upper hand."*

My mind was riddled in Ross' contradictions. He must believe our government would crumble if we allowed Georgia's bullying to continue. But I knew of his selfish intent. If our nation fell apart, he'd lose all voice

Yellow Bird's Song

and therefore all power.

Elias said, *"Soldiers watch day and night."*

"What does my father say?" I asked.

We walked to the steps of his house before he answered. *"I haven't spoken to him yet."* Elias pulled a folded flyer from his pocket and paused long enough for me to read it. He said, *"After Worcester and Butler, council members would rather resign than risk arrest."*

I looked at my watch: four o'clock. I said, *"We have sunlight until eight. Want to go see Ross now? We'll take Father with us."* Changing Ross' mind wouldn't become easier with time. I said, *"Stay at Running Waters tonight. Return tomorrow."*

Elias went inside to tell Harriet he'd be away. In the meantime, I walked to the stable behind his house and hitched horses to his carriage.

On the ride to my father's, I said, *"There's something I need to tell you. Should have long before now. Don't print it."*

I shared my burden, a secret I'd held for a year. I told him of Thomas Crowwell's crimes and how he paid Ross to ignore them.

Elias pulled the reins to stop us and reacted the only way I knew he could. *"So, the people suffer while Ross profits from their misery? Surely Foreman knows. He's Ross' lackey."*

I said, *"He does. In Georgia's eyes, livestock theft isn't criminal if the victims are Cherokee."*

Father talked with Stand under the orchard trees, picking ripe fruit from the branches. If I ever wanted to know what the younger version of my father looked like, I did not need to look any further than Elias' brother. Though Stand was shorter than my father, both were stout and commanding men. There was something similar in the set of their shoulders and how their heads bent in consternation, tilting in the same direction. Stand looked more like Major Ridge's son than I did.

Stand said, *"Glad you could join us, Brother Buck. Who is this stranger you've brought down the road?"*

I laughed and shook his hand. *"I haven't been away that long. We have a great deal to tell you both."*

Father said, *"I got your letter. Had to ride to Red Clay to pick up the post. No more mail deliveries. General Jackson is unbending?"*

I said, *"He's a hickory. But I remain undeterred in my continued attempts to convince him."*

The four of us strolled away from servants' ears, while I recounted my meeting with Eaton and Jackson, the memorial, and Wirt's loss. Then I told them the reason for Ross' lack of culpability for those suffering under Georgia's iron grasp.

Stand scoffed, kicking up dust with disbelief. Father put pieces together with information I didn't know. He said, *"Sarah and I overheard a conversation between Foreman, Ross, and Lewis. I had nothing to connect it to, but it makes more sense after what you've said."*

I asked, *"What did they say?"*

Father said, *"Something about breaking a deal with a colonel."*

Stand looked upriver with his hands across his chest. *"That makes Crowwell's words more true than false."*

Elias said, *"Do you think Ross allows the people to drink because he's still profiting?"*

I said, *"Keep the voting populace drunk and dependent. It assures he keeps his authority. It is a similar manipulation to what Jackson holds over Congress. Keep them fearful of retribution, and they comply with his demands."* Crockett taught me that.

I'd rarely heard Father so quiet. Stand walked down the path with his head in his hands. Elias and I looked at one another. I said, *"Is that why Ross risks holding council in New Echota? Does he hope they will arrest and silence us, like Worcester and Butler?"*

Father nodded for me to follow him, steering my shoulder. *"Son, why did you keep this from me?"*

I stuck my courage and told him the truth. *"Because you didn't defend me when Ross commanded me to resign my appointment on the Legislative Council. I had to bring you more proof to discredit the chief you chose over your son."*

I looked anywhere but Father's brown eyes.

I'd have changed nothing. Not my friendship with Yoholo, not helping Peter escape, not my behavior after Little Prince banned Vann and me from Creek business. Nothing. *"I was angry. You made me feel a shame I hadn't earned."*

Father listened while walking further down the path, gripping his hands behind him.

I continued, *"In time, I thought about why you didn't defend me. You expected me to speak for myself instead of letting your voice command mine. It was a hard lesson, but one I've used in every negotiation since."*

Father returned, crossing the distance in three strides. *"You deserve an eagle's feather."* He continued, *"Rollin is young, so you won't know this for some time. But the shift from father to friend is a most challenging battle. I know you no longer need me. I didn't realize I could feel so much pride."*

No matter how old I was, as both father and husband, I never grew tired of hearing those words. Father hugged me hard and patted my back.

Yellow Bird's Song

I said, *"I am who I am because of you."*

Father held me at arm's length. *"We have much to do."*

Father called Stand and Elias to us with commanding urgency. *"We must convince Ross to move the location of the council. I will never see the man again with yesterday's eyes."*

Ross was in his barn of plenty sharpening a blade on a wheel. He stopped what he was doing and waved at our approach, calling out, "The delegation has returned, I see. Tell me how the news of Worcester's arrest has spread to Washington. What do our northern friends think of Georgia's gall? Wirt appeals on their behalf. Worcester versus Georgia."

Ross shocked me when he put his arm around my shoulder and walked me to the house. Father, Stand, and Elias didn't speak, but I sensed them following behind.

I paused with Ross' obvious façade. "Our delegation met with President Jackson a second time, after Georgia imprisoned Worcester and Butler."

Ross asked, "What did Sharp Knife say?"

"Little, honestly. Jackson's deep cough interrupted his condolences that we had pilfered our treasury funds to hire Wirt and his team of schemers. He assured me the lawyers would fleece us. He reiterated his friendship with our people but insisted that he wouldn't interfere with state laws. When Eaton shut the President's doors to us a second time, we decided our delegation's influence had passed and made for home."

When we passed over Ross' threshold, Quatie sat weaving with her daughters. She rose and gathered a crying child from a cradle.

Ross left the door open. Elias began, reiterating his request, "Sir, I've taken pains to find out the sentiments of the General Council. Unfortunately, some of them would rather resign than risk their lives meeting in New Echota."

Father said, *"We cannot serve the people behind bars."*

Stand linked the sentiment as Ross sat and gestured for us to do the same. Elias, Father, and Stand took chairs, but I walked to the other side of Ross' study. In my thoughts, I compared the similarities between this room and Jackson's office. Ross displayed a framed sword on his wall. Jackson did the same, although the President's wall held more lethal weaponry. I couldn't understand using weapons as decoration, trophies of man's ability to kill his fellow man. I didn't hang my bow on the wall. To me, it was far better to be surrounded by books instead of blades.

My mind was on such when Ross asked, "John, do you concur?" When he called my name, I turned around, shocked he addressed me in their debate.

230

"I concur with Elias, Stand, and my father. However, based on what I saw in New Echota, further degradation will come to my people if Georgia takes the entire council as prisoners and forces us into a cell."

Ross stood and walked around his desk. He faced me, putting his hand on my shoulder and said, "Not your people. Our people. But, as mine is but a single opinion, I am one against four. I'll do this, gentlemen. I'll invite members from both our chambers here. We'll meet as private citizens and discuss the practicality of assembling in New Echota. We can find out whether avoiding interaction with Georgia's Guard is useful or self-defeating."

"Quite a risk," Elias warned. My father nodded in agreement.

Ross said, "That is my decision." Then, he escorted us to the door, nodding at each of us as we passed, single file down his hallway. Our footsteps stamped the hardwood floor.

I was the last in line. I stopped to address Quatie. *"Your husband is a determined man."* To what end, I kept to myself.

Quatie looked up from the still-crying child held in her arms. *"Are you so different?"*

Elias stayed at my father's house, knowing how long it had been since I'd been home. Without sending a rider ahead, I traveled six miles to surprise my children and their mother. On the way, I understood why my father rode his acres so often. He was memorizing them. From tree root to rock, everything in his watchful gaze marked time. I followed in his footsteps.

My path along the running waters ensured no one would see me. I crossed the sheep's pasture to reach the barn from its backside. Inside, Peter held the reins while Rollin sat on an Appaloosa pony.

Peter scolded my slouching son. He said, "Rollin, horses have eyes. Look between his ears so you can see where you goin'."

I startled them, still atop my horse. I said, *"Cheesquatalawny, where'd you find such a fine Appaloosa?"*

Peter spun around. Rollin's posture improved, lifting his chin, and raising his chest. "Papa!" Rollin shouted.

Peter grinned from ear to ear. "Your missus gonna be flyin' higher than the mistress in de moon when she sees you!"

"Let's keep it a secret for another few minutes. Rollin, Mama said you'd learned to ride. I thought it was my job to teach you."

Peter laughed, "Well, when da Major tell you he's gonna do sumfin, you just get out da man's way."

Yellow Bird's Song

"Wise," I said. "I've learned that lesson many times, often the hard way."

I steered my horse parallel to Rollin's pony. *"Who gave you such a horse?"*

Rollin started his answer in English, "Grand—" With my look, he changed his response to *Eduda*. He put his tongue between his teeth, thinking, and then decided on words. *"Eduda horse Clarinda gift she four."*

I understood what my Rollin meant. His Cherokee was close enough.

Rollin held his arms up to me, and I shifted him from his pony to sit on my horse. "You're heavy. What's Mama feeding you?"

"I've been growing while you've been away meeting the President." He smiled over his shoulder.

"Peter, would you mind putting Rollin's pony into the stall for the night? Rollin and I are going to chase the sun."

Peter nodded and spoke to the horse's brown eyes. "C'mon, Dick. Hay's awaitin'."

Rollin asked, instantly excited, forgetting Peter's valuable lesson, "Does that mean we're gonna go fast? Eduda makes me ride in the fence."

I winked at him. "Eduda isn't here." I wrapped my free arm around his waist and clicked my tongue to move the horse outside the barn. There was no better homecoming than running the pasture with my son.

We took the horse on a simple walk to the front of the house. I took the reins from Rollin and pulled them to stop. *"Cheesquatalawny, where might we find the sun?"*

Rollin pointed. "That way," he said.

"Which?"

"West."

"Right you are. Keep your eyes between the horse's ears, and never let go of the saddle horn. If you fall, you could get hurt. If that happened, Mama would make me sleep in the barn on my first night home. So don't let go."

Rollin said, "Papa, sleep with me. I'll move over."

"That is very nice of you, son." I imagined Rollin and myself sharing his small bed, with my feet hanging off its end. Grinning, I tossed my hat to the ground, feeling heat trapped underneath escape my hair. I wrestled to pull off my coat and untied my tie, feeling instantly calmer. I undid the clasp on the saddle holding my bag, and let it drop beside the other articles in front of the door.

"We don't need the extra weight holding us down. Horses give you wings you weren't born with." Rollin wiggled and bent forward, preparing for flight. "Lean back against me. *I won't let you go.*"

I took the reins and heeled the horse to a trot.

When we cleared the fence, Rollin asked, "Can I yell it?"

"Please. We'll never make it in time if you don't."

With Rollin's "hiya", the gelding unleashed its might. The horse flew, galloping down the hill and parting the pasture grass. Cows ran, darting out of our way. Rollin's hair lifted against my chest. Horse hooves beat against the ground, throwing dirt clods against our legs. I heard the wild abandon in his thrilling squeals, a sound I would never forget for as long as I lived.

I squeezed my son tighter when we slowed and stopped near the lower stream. Our gelding blew from his nose with sudden exertion while Rollin's quick breaths came from exhilaration. When he calmed, we looked toward the setting sun. He squinted and stretched his arm toward the glowing orb bordering the Appalachian ridges. I traced his line of sight and held out my hand. With nothing but air in our fists, together we held power enough to hold night at bay.

"Rollin, you're becoming a fine rider. I'm proud of you."

Rollin grinned, still amazed. He said, *"Papa, we caught it!"*

Out of the mouths of babes, I thought, while we stopped the sunset one moment longer.

CHAPTER 24: RIDING BLIND
Rollin Ridge
Sacramento and Yuma, California
Fall 1853

I gripped my stomach. My liver suffered bilious complaints after drafting article after article covering the sightings and sudden disappearances of the notorious California thief, Joaquín Murieta. Some writers drank coffee, like Delano. Most newspapermen I knew sipped whiskey while drafting a story and drowned themselves in the bottle after ending it. It was the same with California politicians. Brandy loosened the tongue and made government men lose their stutter, so their lies flowed easier. My pay from following bandits and politicians kept me in cheap whiskey, although it ran this already poor newspaperman afoul. After gambling my lot, I doubled the morning's hangover, tripling the previous night's regrets.

To rob rich politicians and businessmen, Joaquín needed money and horses. These he could not get except by robbery and murder, and thus he became an outlaw and a bandit on the verge of his nineteenth year. He walked into the future, as a dark, determined criminal, and his proud nobility of soul existed only in memory.[1] Armed to his teeth, on a quest for justice for his people, the iron in his fist merged too deeply into his soul for him to stop.[2] Most said he was only fit to grace the gallows, for his merits certainly entitled him to such distinguished elevation.[3]

Sitting at the bar, I saw Joaquín's face in my glass of brown liquor. Had Fate chosen not to send me to California, had my mother not kept so many secrets, I may have been the Joaquín Murieta of Cherokee Nation. If I hadn't left, I might have masked my face, robbed Ross and brother Lewis, and returned so many stolen coins. They belonged to my people, after all. After the tragedy of the trail, the debt was owed to them, paid in full, with heartbroken tears from dispossession, disease, and death in the snow. Murieta's motivation, like my own, was why I became so fascinated by the Mexican bandit's Robin Hood schemes.

Sitting at the bar, I finished my drink and made my way through the dark saloon to the daylight to meet my editor. Colonel Grant lived in his shabby office above a restaurant. Newspapers from across the country stacked on his floor in tall piles, with the most recent on top of decade-old copies stuck to the hardwood floor. Sitting at his desk, he was boxed in by the news.

His desk wasn't much more organized than the floor, with an overly full ashtray of cigar butts, small glasses, scrap receipts, correspondence, and submissions. The room smelled of molding paper and the tang of stale smoke.

Grant sat behind the desk and didn't lift his head after hearing the ringing bell over his door. A single clock hung above him, left unwound forever. Every time I was in here, it read 8:52. Papa's watch said it was past noon. I stood before him for more than a minute as he scribbled at the bottom of a page. His handwriting was unreadable to anyone other than the author.

I coughed. Colonel Grant made what I assumed to be his last mark, threw his pen on his desk, and leaned back in his chair, putting his arms behind his head.

"Ahh, Rollin, you're a welcome sight, haven't seen your face in a month. You still have that nobility about your eyes. I dare say, in your new suit, you're the handsomest man I've ever seen. Bet you have no trouble attracting attention from every female you pass." He gestured for me to sit. Before I could, I had to remove Grant's characteristic white coat, several newspapers, and a case of the paste that he swore whitened the teeth. He might sell more if he used his own product.

I sat down, saying, "There's only one I want, and she's in Arkansas."

In a hurry, Grant asked, shuffling papers on his desk, "Why did you come to see me today? I have places to be."

He was a complex man to catch, so I took advantage of the opportunity. "I'd like to request an assignment, but I'd be away for a while. I want to begin a series. Maybe turn it into a novel. Bottom line is this. Joaquín Murieta's been spotted in Yuma. I thought of aligning myself with the Indians nearby and tracking the bandit. I know what he looks like. Our readers might find vicarious adventure in 'The Celebrated Life of Joaquín Murieta'. Just a working title."

Grant said, "Write that down somewhere, 'vicarious adventure'. You know, many have tried to get close to him."

"Delano said once the man was most disguised when showing his genuine face."[4]

"Aren't we all," he mumbled and reached out his hand for his coat. "It is a wild goose chase. Paper after paper say they know his hangouts between here and Mexico, but no one can nail him to one spot. If you heard he's in Yuma, he's long gone by now." My hands shook while handing him his coat.

"You feelin' okay?" he asked.

"Why wouldn't I be?" I put my trembling hand between my knees. "With your consent, I'd still like to try."

"That's right. I nearly forgot. You don't look very native wearing that suit. Although that blade you wear is a dangerous reminder."

I said, "To myself more than any other. If you give me your permission, I'll post pieces every two weeks. I've got responsibilities. Who knows? I might follow James Cooper's lead. Pen a novel."

Grant headed for his door. "If you want to capture the real Joaquín, you need to show him you'd write him as more than an outlaw. Like Cooper, you'll have to turn him into a hero on a quest to avenge his country's wrongs—washing out the disgrace forced upon his people with the blood of their enemies." He held the door open for me, implying he needed to go to some appointment or another. Impressed by his own turn of phrase, he said, "That's good." Then, he said, "Write that down."

We left the office, ringing the bell again. I said, "I will. Thank you."

He left me standing there alone as he walked down the street, shouting over his shoulder. "Every two weeks, Ridge. Don't be late with those submissions, and don't get scalped. Your wife might be upset if she shows up in California, and you've lost all that dashing hair of yours."

I took a swig from the flask in my breast coat pocket. The tasteless whiskey no longer burned my throat but calmed the shakes, which returned if I didn't imbibe. I was eager to change out of this suit, pack my belongings, and ride to Yuma. I threw my new black coat on the hotel bed, undid the tie at my neck, and let it fall. I left the cap off the whiskey bottle and grabbed paper and pen to write Lizzie and Mama.

Fiction was easier than lies. Clumps of paper cluttered the desk and the surrounding floor, with each draft decreasing the liquor in the bottle. Neither Mother nor Lizzie would condone such a journey, riding into a gang of thieves and murderers. Mother would fear I would become what my father hated—a dishonest man. Lizzie would say I chased the cattywampus, bound to lose my mind. Neither was entirely wrong, but Joaquín was no wildcat. He was a horseman, too. Still, I wasn't so far gone as to be senseless. I chuckled to myself and thought how that was what all drunks believed.

I tipped another whiskey back with my scripted salutation and placed the empty cup beside the letter. I lied to them, saying I would not write this next month because I was in bed with stomach complaints. Not entirely a lie. I'd retched once tonight and surely would again before sunrise. I read over the deception. Such brevity seemed believable. So, I leaned back in my chair, deciding it was a waste of time to pour the whiskey into a glass, and finished the bottle's contents straight from the source.

Southern California country was full of lawlessness and desperate men who bore the name of Americans but failed to support the honor and dignity of that title.[5] Without jury trial or proper conviction, the sheriff and local townspeople offered: "$5,000 Reward for Joaquín Murieta."[6] The printer used his largest font for the declaration, "Dead or Alive." I chuckled at the common phrase, knowing the law could only deliver him in one of those two states. Such a high dollar amount was likely propaganda. But, if the local citizenry wanted Joaquín's head on a platter, they'd have to pay.

They posted flyers on every hitching post and postmaster board. The crude drawing underneath didn't match the man's face. The sheriff watched me ride in, hidden under my duster with my hat tipped low. I tied my horse to the post near the jail and climbed the stairs. The sheriff bent his head to examine my face. Then, he said to another man seated in an old weather-beaten chair, "Nope. Ain't him."

I couldn't help myself. "Who'd you think I was?"

"That Mexican, Joaquín Murieta. Nope. Don't look nothing like that renderin'." He pointed at the wanted poster. "You're not as dark as he is. But you've got the copper. You Indian?" After his question, he slapped the seated man's chest, gathering his attention, before adding, "Better hold down our hats, deputy, or we might lose our scalps."

Prejudices of color and the antipathy of races are stronger and more bitter than the ignorant and unlettered. It could not be overcome.[7] White man wouldn't change because it afforded them such a convenient excuse for cruelty. Telling them so only wasted my time.

Instead, I asked, "Do you think Murieta would turn himself in to collect his own reward?"

"Probably not." He introduced himself. "I'm sheriff here in Yuma." He gestured to the bored man next to him. "This here is my deputy. What you need, Indian?" He broke apart the words, tucked his chin low as to make his voice monotone, and stressed every syllable.

The sheriff was gullible, stupid, and not likely to catch the infamous bandit with only those qualities at his disposal. But rather than tell him of his asinine ignorance, I asked for his advice.

"You've seen Murieta? I'm Rollin Ridge, writer for the *True Delta*. I was told he made his presence known in Yuma earlier this week."

The sheriff said, "Damn my eyes if I saw him. I was busy letting down a corpse. I hate a horse thief."

There was a sentiment where we both could agree. I asked, "How'd you know he was here?"

"Follow me. I'll show you."

Yellow Bird's Song

As the sheriff opened the door of his jail, I stepped out of his way. A rancid smell hit me. Had to be why the sheriff and his deputy sat outside. A drunkard repeatedly dry-heaved into a wooden bucket in one of the two holding cells. The sound of his hurling, the image of him throwing his head forward, doubled the putridity.

The sheriff quickly took a paper from his desk and passed me, stepping back to the porch. I followed, toward fresher air, while the sheriff reached around me, grabbed the door handle, and pulled it shut.

It wasn't my place to say, but sympathy motivated me to speak up for the fellow sinner inside, heaving his humanity behind bars. I said, "Should let in some air. Get that prisoner some water."

"We tried. Hurls it right back up. That's why we're out here. Giving him time to vomit his livers and sleep off the whiskey."

"Ahh," I said, reminded of how I had done the same after writing to Lizzie. It was the reason I left a day later than I intended. Shaking away memory's burn of the bile in my throat, an aftermath accompanied by guilt, I returned my hat to my head and changed the subject. "So, Joaquín?"

"Look you, right here." He handed me a copy of the flyer, wadded up and flattened again. This one wasn't as brown and weathered as those hanging down the street. This paper was soft with oil stains on the corners where dirty hands had creased the page.

I asked, "What makes this one so special? A hundred more on the way here."

The sheriff poked his finger toward the bottom of the page. He recited the tale as if he'd said it a thousand times. "On Monday, see, we'd had us a hanging, so there were plenty of people in town. But fewer than a dozen saw that young Mexican ride in. He got off his black horse and walked right up to it to investigate the wanted poster. Then, to beat it all, he took a pencil out of his vest pocket and scribbled on the bottom of the poster. Look. Right there."

Underneath the "$5,000 Reward" the bandit wrote, "I will give $10,000. Sincerely, Joaquín."[8]

I couldn't stop myself from laughing, no matter how much I pursed my lips.

"Man was bold enough to ride into town with his compadre, Three-Fingered Jack, double his reward, and ride back out before anyone figured it was him."

"Did you and he," and I pointed toward the deputy studying a stretch of empty road, "track Murieta and Three-Fingered Jack?"

"Got as far as the mineral springs on the Colorado. But there was no sight of them so, we turned back."

I stepped down the stairs and untied my horse from the post when the sheriff lifted his voice. "You a bounty hunter? Going to track him for the reward?"

"I told you, I'm a newspaperman. I'd rather talk to him, write his story, and survive the encounter."

"You'll never find his camp. If you do, you'll never get close enough without being sniped by one of his gang. Won't see the shot that kills you. Guaranteed to meet your maker. Murieta will kill you for knowing where he buries his gold."

Taking the reins, I put my boot in the stirrup and swung my leg over the saddle.

"Then, if I can find his hideout, I'll ride in blindfolded."

"How are you gonna see where you're going?" he asked, assuming the same of me as I regarded him—an idiot. The lawman and I kept our opinions to ourselves.

"Horses have eyes," I said, and turned my sorrel toward the Colorado.

I'd ridden an hour or more, following the river bends, anticipating the echoes of gunfire at every passing moment. Still, I heard not so much as a breath of wind careening between the bluffs. So, I dismounted on the river trail, now wide and straight, aged by time. My hands shook; my thigh muscles ached. Walk it off or down a bottle; either would cure my ills.

I dismounted near a makeshift cairn with dead fern bouquets and bound sticks placed underneath three towering rocks. Its shape struck me as unusual because it defied gravity, balanced on its thin base. When looked at it from the right angle, the boulders created the profile of a hunched old woman guarding the entrance to the cliffs nearby. My horse wandered, and I squatted at the foot of the formation, retrieving the flask from my pocket.

No sooner did I put its metal spout to my lips than I heard a voice from horseback speak above me. "This is a place to pray, not to drink."

With the stranger's interruption, I threaded the cap closed and raised myself from my squat on boot heels. I said, "Then I'll be on my way."

The young man steered his horse to scale the rock shelf beside the old woman. He was bare-chested and barefoot, with not much more covering him than his breechcloth. There was a single feather in his hair, which stretched halfway down his back. He swung his leg over his horse. "Didn't you stop here to pray to her for a safe journey?" He gestured at the meager

Yellow Bird's Song

gifts already at the old woman's feet. "Many before you have done so."

I said, "My people's Great Spirit stopped listening to me fourteen years ago."

"But still you ride?" he questioned.

I turned my feet away from the late afternoon sun and looked east. I told the stranger, "Just in the wrong direction."

He laughed. "Ahh, a funny man. He goes where he doesn't want to go. If you no longer talk to your people's spirits, how do you know which is the right direction?"

"The ghosts tell me."

The Indian said, "How can you hear ghosts if you don't pray?"

I looked away from his curious face, replying, "I manage."

He knelt under the old woman's feet and lowered his head for a silent moment. Then, ending his prayer, he looked me in the eye. "I have had dreams of a coming traveler. A selfish, lost man who saw too many choices and refused to decide. Stared to the east but couldn't see. Dove through water but couldn't feel. Dug in the ground but couldn't find. He walked west on living land but listened to those who'd passed beyond. Couldn't sing with the spirits. He hadn't yet learned their songs."

He touched the hard spot under my coat, where I'd hidden my flask. "This will take you West too soon. You won't have liver enough to make it to dawn."

"Are you a shaman? My sister sees beyond, although it was never a gift the Great Spirit granted me."

"My people believe if I speak of my gift, our spirits will deny the power I have."

"Shaman, your dreams are simple to predict. Most people are from the East, displaced miners looking for some other way to make money."

"Is that what you're looking for? Money? Gold? Ahh, I remember you now." He gestured to the old woman. "She was in my dreams, too. Called you by an odd name—*dalonige*. You know such a word?"

His remark made me shudder, and I stepped backward from such a prophecy. In Cherokee, *dalonige* means yellow. Both awe and its antithesis stunned me. My mind whipped backward. Hearing my father call my Cherokee name, tousling my hair, smelling the earth and ink on his hands. I squinted so his vision might dissipate. I couldn't allow myself to be so affected. Not now.

I said, "I'm looking for a gang led by a Mexican robber who rides beside a thick man with three fingers. Law's chasing them. These bandits might stay away and leave horses grazing for long stretches. Seen anyone like that?"

"Some men, like those you speak of, build fires near Rock with a Crevice. The Old Ones walk the same trail. If you travel there, you must throw a stone on top of the cliff to honor them."

Then, addressing the old woman again, he pulled wildflowers out of a satchel slung across his chest and added them to the gifts previously laid underneath her. He grabbed his horse's reins to remount in one seamless dance. "Under the cliff, you'll find what you seek. It is a powerful place. Let its strength pass over you, under you. It will turn back the yellow in your eyes. You will hear the Great Spirit's stories again. Stay here tonight. Pray to the old woman. Tomorrow, she will lead you where you seek, if you are sober enough to listen."

He rode up the path into a canyon and left me alone with my chaotic thoughts. I circled the holy formation to gather river driftwood and threw some grass at my horse. My temptation to down the flask's contents remained constant. If I did, I'd numb the Yuma shaman's words and Papa's memory, swallowing both away. But the old woman's eyes followed me, judged me.

And I was guilty. I punished myself. From its hiding place inside my vest pocket, I undid the cap on the flask and poured its contents into the dirt between my boots. My cure was gone, but the disease urged me to ride back into Yuma and visit one of its tiny saloons.

Inside my saddlebag, matches spilled from their casing, and I had to reach deep to remove a few. Pulling my hand free, Papa's journal fell among the gifts left under the old woman's altar. I retrieved it. Holding it in my hand, I knew that opening its green and gold binding meant I'd be forced to listen. Listening would anger me. Anger would make me turn back for Yuma, and I would solve nothing. I'd never find Joaquín if I was too drunk to look. I returned Papa's journal to my saddlebag and hid it beside another clean shirt and sundry supplies.

Unable to sit still, feeling the need to occupy empty hands, I squatted and began stacking the found kindling for a fire, and lit the match on my boot.

After sunset, cold crept along the lowlands under foreboding rocks and sparse trees. From the ragged clouds, stars struggled to shine their dim light. The blanket around my shoulders didn't ease the trembling. My head chased echoes, bounding, and retreating, that called my name. "Cheesquatalawny." Perhaps it was the voice of Yuma's old woman; maybe it was Papa's.

I gathered Papa's journal from my saddlebag. It was the only way to suffer the night, avoiding whiskey's cure for insomnia. Midnight, with its dangers and troubles, would find me regardless, protected solely by the

Yellow Bird's Song

voice keeping watch at my flank.

In 1832, Papa changed his mind, standing beside the banks of the Potomac. After condemning removal to its most staunch advocate, he accepted that Cherokee's survival depended on moving the people West. When he left the riverside that day, he dedicated his life to preparing a safe place for his people to begin again.

I read of Papa's anger, recognizing my tones in his similar phrases. He wrote of Ross' continued machinations in '33 and '34, his outrageous request of Congress for twenty million in removal money, and Congress' expedient laughter, then of their outrage, and their final denial.[10] Then Ross presented another ridiculous alternative, moving the Cherokee to Mexico.[11] Papa said Ross' pleas were those of a desperate man.

Papa's uphill battle began by building the Treaty Party on a solid foundation, convincing many to support him as chief. Ross and his men delayed elections and shut down Elias' free press. The problem was, many Cherokees who'd supported removal had already packed their families and traveled West, taking their votes with them.[11] Ross' authoritarian control over the people deterred any who might consider an alternative.

After closing Papa's journal, I read a letter from Brigadier General Arbuckle to his commanding officer. In it, Arbuckle chronicled Ross' attacks on the old settlers, friends of the Treaty Party. Arbuckle reported that duringd the Double Spring Council, Ross' principal men planned Papa, Grandpa, and Elias' executions. This general presented a substantial case that Ross' hired guns were to blame.[12]

Everything I suspected was true. Everything I knew to be true became real. So, I pulled paper and ink from my saddlebag and wrote Stand.

> I am tormented by the folks at home whenever I talk about returning to the nation. They urge me in their letters not to venture to Arkansas with my family. I am resolved to quiet their fears by providing for my family in this country, to place them above all want. Only then, I will be at liberty to follow the bend of my mind, leading me back to my people and returning to my country. It is only on my mother's account that I have stayed away for so long. It was on her account that I did not go back in the spring of '50 and risk trial. I am not afraid to do so, provided my friends will back me. But let that be as it may. I intend someday, eventually, to plant my foot in the Cherokee Nation and stay there, too, or die. I would rather die than surrender my rights. You recollect there is a gap in Cherokee history that needs filling. Boudinot is dead, John Ridge and Major Ridge are dead, and are but partially avenged. I

don't know how you feel now, but there was a time when that brave heart of yours grew dark over the memory of our wrongs. But we will not talk about it because I believe you feel right yet, and I admire your prudence in keeping so quiet.

I want to preserve the dignity of our family name; I want the memory of my distinguished relatives to live long after we have all rotted in our graves. I want to write the history of the Cherokee Nation as it should be written, and not as certain white men will write it. They will tell the tale to screen and justify themselves. All this I can never do unless I get into the proper position to wield influence and make money. Don't you see how much precious time I waste in California? Instead of writing for my living here, I should use my pen on behalf of my people and rescue from oblivion the proud names of our race. Stand, I assure you, this is no idle talk. If there was ever a man upon earth that loved his people and his kindred, I am that man.[13] I will write their justice.

Yellow Bird

By the time I finished the letter, the horizon lit, turning the sky the color of steel. I went to water. After dousing, I dressed to ease dawn's cold and was again bound to the leather thong holding Kell's bowie knife sheathed around my thigh. After fasting to prepare my mind for the day ahead, I mounted and rode the singular beaten path to Rock with a Crevice.

At a distance too far for bullets, I wrapped the kerchief around my eyes and tied it tight. Chilled by the shadows, I knew I was under the cliff that the Yuma shaman spoke of. I swung my leg over my horse and touched the rock-ridden ground. I held the strap around my horse's girth to bend and retrieve a handful of stones. When I stood, my hand found the saddle horn, and I steadied the horse and myself.

I tossed one rock, and it hit my hat. I tried again with the same result. The third hit the horse, and he skirted away. I tossed the fourth with my left hand, stretching wide and bending my wrist to flick the stone toward the cliff. The fourth didn't fall. My fifth attempt must have reached the outcrop too. Trusting that my gift satisfied Yuma's Old Ones, I felt for the stirrup, placed my boot, and mounted again. Although, if Joaquín's henchmen were here, the stones would announce my presence. If so, my horse carried us both into simultaneous suicide.

Papa died before my initiation of the long night, the trial for a Cherokee boy passing into manhood. Better late than never, I thought. I'd never ridden blind. Every imagined sight triggered my ears, keener, more

Yellow Bird's Song

apt to search for sound. A hawk cawed and announced the metal ticks of cocking pistols. Blood pumped and set my veins on fire, but it made me feel better, more alert than I'd been in weeks.

Boots approached. My horse whinnied and snuffled. Momentum ceased, and as a result, I lunged forward. Someone grabbed the reins and a familiar voice spoke with an accent born south of the Rio Grande.

"Ahh, Knife Slinger. Have you come all this way only to lose at cards again? Dealt by the notorious bandolero, Joaquín Murieta? I would still like to win that blade from you, or, better yet, take you and your blade into my service."

"I am no knife slinger; I wield a pen. Call me Yellow Bird. The bowie knife, I cannot bet. Its curses and blessings are mine." I said, "Joaquín, I have a proposition for you."

He said, "I'm listening, my sober and sightless friend. Take off your mask."

CHAPTER 25: BRONZE EAGLES
John Ridge
Washington and Boston
January 1832

Behind me, Greek columns surrounded the arched half-circle of the House chambers, with no head or foot. Unable to take a full breath, I held onto my lapels to occupy my clammy hands.

When I turned to face the House congressmen, a bronze eagle hung above a nearby fireplace. To my people, the eagle symbolized strength and power. *Uwohali*, the eagle, carried two twin feathers on its tail. If only native nations and America could steer side by side and embrace the continent's future together. If Congress vetoed Indian removal, it would return our faith in American justice.

I unfolded my memorial and set it on the podium. I didn't need it, having rewritten the words so many times. Without grand gestures, I raised my voice in sincere solemnity.

"My people have suffered great injury and loss of property, disposal of liquors and the insults which Georgia prided itself in heaping upon the unprotected victims of their rapacity. Congress must look with sanguine hope and offer us its shield of protection.[1]

"We pray for the return of a happy day—when the dark clouds which lower upon the habitations of Cherokee Nation's citizens will be in the deep bosom of an ocean buried, and the patriot's heart throbs with feelings of good faith and friendship."[2]

Every Christian congressman should vote his heart. If he didn't, he needed to ask himself who was the savage, the heathen. Could the honest part of the world dominate over Indian nations while my people, and many unresisting tribes, suffered such trials?[3]

I laid my copy on the table and recessed down the aisle. I joined Coodey, Martin, and Elias, and we crossed into the foyer. We breathed only after the doors shut behind us.

From Pennsylvania Avenue, I looked toward the dome. Coodey and Martin strolled ahead, but I stopped walking and grabbed Elias' arm.

He looked up the three flights of grand stairs. "Such great sums spent to renovate the building after the British burned it to the ground."

I replied, "Money would have been better spent saving native nations from ruin."

When we walked back to the Indian Queen, I thought how Jefferson, Franklin, Washington, Hamilton, Adams, Monroe all attempted to create a utopia, a realization of what the first immigrants called their "City on a Hill." If half of what America's forefathers envisioned became a reality, then the world would look to this continent as an example, where its people voted their fate.

The following month, Elias and I left Coodey and Martin in Washington and traveled north to Boston's "sanctuary of freedom." Bells on the exterior of the Old South Meeting House struck ten when our barouche driver stopped near the front of the brick, steepled building.

We were to speak in the same place where colonial rebels cried out against British oppression. From Elias' stillness, he appeared to be affected by similar throes.

I said, "From its pulpit, Samuel Adams rallied colonists against King George's Intolerable Acts. From this street corner, they led the walk toward the harbor. Can you see it? In your mind's eye?"

Elias said, "All I see is a herd of white men dressing as Indians, screaming war whoops, carrying crates of tea on their shoulders."

I laughed. "Well, that too."

Elias didn't even smile. "How soon these Americans forget."

Inside the meeting house, chinked, plastered walls held stained molding, in dark shades. The sanctuary contained a maze of boxed pews under a single balcony carved with indented filigree. So many arched windowpanes let in the day's natural light.

Elias and I sat stoically while the meeting house pews filled with mumbles.

Elias asked me if he could be the first to speak. I'd memorized his speech after repeated hearings, but this time, he held my attention anew. The congregation rested in his palms.

"I ask you, shall red men live, or shall they be swept from the earth? With you and this public at large, the decision chiefly rests. Must they perish? Must they all, like the unfortunate Creeks, go down in sorrow to their grave? They hang upon your mercy as a garment. Will you push them from you, or will you save them? Let humanity answer."[4]

The crowd stood in silence, unwilling to break tradition of not applauding in a house of God. As he concluded, I listened closely. Gasps and sighs signified the audience's acceptance, their sympathies. Such feelings defined hostility by antithesis.

I took the podium after Elias returned to his seat. Absent reason, my heartbeat was steady, without the nervous acceleration I experienced in the

Capital. Here, history granted me the camaraderie of its compatriots. In front of me was a bronze eagle, holding a large clock with Roman numerals to denote the time.

My passions rose. So overcome, I didn't conclude with words I'd prepared. To make this moment count, I spoke with fervent will.

"You asked us to throw off the hunter and warrior state; we did so. You asked us to form a republican government; we did so—adopting your own as a model. You asked us to cultivate the earth and learn mechanical arts. We did so. You asked us to learn to read. We did so. You asked us to cast away our idols and worship your God. We did so. Now you demand we cede to you, our lands. That we will not do."[5]

An elderly man in the back stood first, followed by his younger neighbor. Across the aisle, another. Toward the front, a fourth. Three on the balcony stood together. No one remained in their comfort by the time I returned to Elias' side. We looked at one another, fulfilling a dream we shared: to be heard as men not perceived as savages. Once, we'd been viewed as mere spectacle, but these men saw us as revolutionaries. The money and miles traveled became worthy of such expense.

We didn't realize that outside there were multitudes waiting to greet us. We placed a copy of my memorial, in place of a petition, at the head of the receiving line. Each man shook our hands, offered prayers for our cause, and signed his name on the document. The day gathered six thousand names, not marks.

A graying gentleman and his younger companion waited their turn to speak to us. I recognized them as the first two to stand in the sanctuary. The eldest held the brim of his top hat and bowed graciously.

With charismatic Boston vowels, he said, "I have never heard of a people more self-reliant than your Cherokee Nation. Mister Boudinot, I am honored to make your acquaintance. I subscribe to your *Phoenix*. Today, gentlemen, you fired my blood and roused the indignation of all those who listened. Like the Cherokee, I am no stranger to God's voice in the trees and mountains. I heard its voice again, today, from you both."

"Thank you, sir," Elias said. "To rise from the ashes, one has to burn."

The elder said, "Then I hope for a quick revival. Your people presently stand in the heat."

Invigorated by his overwhelming support, Elias credited his Lord and Savior. "The Holy Spirit walks with us on this journey out of bondage."

The elder continued, "Our darker brethren walk a similar path." After equating slavery with removal, the gray-haired man introduced himself as Ralph Emerson, a reverend and philosopher, a man of headwork. At his side stood his apprentice, Henry Thoreau. With such a dark complexion, I wondered whether native blood flowed in his veins. But with so much facial hair, he must be of European descent. The younger wore a wrinkled homespun suit, countering his freshly pressed mentor.

Thoreau said, "The white man's honeybee stung the red child's hand, a forerunner of that industrious tribe that came and plucked the wildflower from the race by the root."[6]

I said, "I sincerely hope, Mister Thoreau, God sees fit to alter your vision and sees to it our people remain safely at home."

Elias continued. "At least now, it is apparent to all who heard us today which side is right, and which is wrong.[7] Slavery and removal are moral issues and should not cross into politics. The Constitution leaves such matters to state sovereignty."[8]

Emerson said, "Trust yourselves, gentlemen. Every heart vibrates to that iron string."[9] With that, both men traveled down the street toward the bay, holding the brim of their hats with harbor winds in their faces.

When the Supreme Court returned to session, rooms at the Indian Queen were scarce. Newspapermen filled the halls each night, but were absent during the day, congregating, waiting for the court's decisions. If they wrote faster than their competition, their reward for such diligence brought increased sales.

The press collected in front of an exterior podium when Justice Marshall arrived to read the decision in Worcester's case. Our attorney, Wirt, and the Cherokee delegation were granted no special seat or private room for hearing such a pivotal decision. Hopefully, the court freed two noble men, and by extension, a noble race from Georgia's constitutional illegalities.

In his robe and wig, Justice Marshall addressed the waiting crowd. We stood at the back, straining to hear. Whatever it would be, we must remain calm, absent exclamation or groan, without elation or cry. Nearby, newspapermen spotted us with pens at the ready to report such reactions.

Justice Marshall said, "Cherokee Nation is a distinct community, occupying its territory in which the laws of Georgia have no right to enter, but with the assent of the Cherokees. Every legislative act against their people by the state of Georgia is consequently void."[10]

I asked Elias, "Did he say void?" I couldn't be sure I heard.

Elias looked at me with tearful eyes and replied with an astonished whisper. "Our prayers have been answered." Among the press, we kept stoic, but walked taller when returning to the Indian Queen.

Behind closed doors, we clapped our hands and shouted praises to Heaven. We recited the ruling repeatedly, in all its glory. For so long, each defeat after each escalating defeat, we'd faced more challenges, climbing unceasing hills with the elusive summit always out of reach. The Cherokee topped the precipice, the pinnacle, in united victory. Nothing could remove the smile from my face. The ruling elevated us to constant jubilation.

Elias said, "A great triumph on the part of the Cherokees, so far as the question of our rights. It will no longer be a question between Georgia and the poor Cherokees, but between the U.S. and the state of Georgia."[11]

"The judiciary prevails," I said. "Such a win sets a righteous precedent. Georgia's laws over our people are null."

I was glad Elias was with us to celebrate. His editorials supported such a win. He deserved to feel the dignity of his success, achieved without violence, misdeed, or mistruth.

In my heart's human selfishness, I wished I could be the one to tell my father and feel his gratitude and pride. My vain ambition wanted to be the one to tell Ross. I imagined his face when I would say, "I was here, pleading our case. Elias and I spoke in Massachusetts, collecting signatures and donations for our cause. I acted on behalf of the Cherokee Nation. Not you."

The next morning, I packed such arrogance beside my clothes. I could not wait to make the long journey home and tell Sarah all that transpired. She'd be revived, glad I could stay home.

But nothing travels faster than bad news. At breakfast, we'd heard rumors of Jackson's reaction to the high court's decision. Murmurs spread like wildfire how Jackson denounced the ruling and sided with the dissenting opinion. One reporter imitated Jackson's sarcasm and reported that Jackson said, "John Marshall has made his decision. Let him enforce it—if he can."[12] Rumors in other newspapers took the report one step further, saying Jackson called the court "stillborn."

Our people again crossed one peak only to find another mountain.

I waited for our steamer's departure in the silence of my room, scouring newspapers for confirmation of Jackson's words in the dark. Then, the Indian Queen's bellman knocked and delivered a letter. The post held only my name scripted where the address should be. On its back was the seal of the Office of the President. Jackson requested my presence for "private discourse" the next day.

Why would Jackson want to see me alone, without the others in our delegation? I knew better than to converse with him without witnesses. McKenney's accusation taught me that. However, the president could not be denied. I knocked on the neighboring doors and reported Jackson's strange request.

Coodey said, "I should go in your stead."

"No. There must be a reason he asked for me." I said, "It's past time for Chicken Snake Jackson to crawl and hide in the luxuriant grass of his nefarious hypocrisy."[13]

That evening, instead of attending the crowded dining room for supper, I requested a plate brought to my room, and unpacked.

My appointment at the White House was at five in the afternoon. I arrived early, but Jackson's aides did not leave me to linger on the nearby grounds alone. Instead, they escorted me up a grand staircase lit by a crystal chandelier to the second floor and down a wide hall near Jackson's private residence.

This room was extravagantly decorated, with ceiling-to-floor green tapestries smelling of kerosene lamp oil mixed with the stench of hand-shaken secrets. My guide called it the Audience Room when I stepped onto the green carpet, the same hue as the papered walls. The white fireplace mantle was the centerpiece of the room, engraved with a prayer attributed to President Adams.

"I pray Heaven bestow the best of blessings on this House, and all that shall hereafter inhabit it. May none but honest and wise men rule under this roof."[14]

I doubted whether my present opposition was a man of such integrity, "honest and wise," as President Adams hoped. Above the mantle, two portraits hung, one of President Monroe and the other of his wife, Elizabeth. Since I was alone in the room, I spoke aloud to Monroe's fixed gaze. "Do you remember me? I was the student who wrote to you about the Cherokee's war for liberty. The enemies I fought then are the same I battle now."

While waiting, my eye caught a sheen of gilded bronze, eagles nesting in the window's cornices. I whispered, "*Uwohali*," when Jackson stepped inside, shutting the door behind him.

"What's that you say?" Jackson asked.

"I was just admiring your eagles, General, the *Uwohali*."

His body seemed thinner than when last we met. General Jackson made his way to me and shook my offered hand. Afterward, he gripped both his hands behind his back. He wore no frock coat. White sleeves rolled at his elbows, bordered by a maroon vest, and a black tie girding his neck. He appeared even more formidable with his graying bushy hair brushed neatly back from such a stubborn forehead.

"I ordered those," he said. "The room needed something to break up all the green. Don't you think?"

"Of course, sir."

He rocked on his heels and stifled a cough. "You've never hesitated to disagree with me before. Do you think them gaudy?"

I shook my head and said, "No, sir. Just noting the coincidence. In my last months, I've seen many such bronze eagles."

"My Rachel would have loved this room. She didn't live long enough to join me in the White House. Died at the Hermitage of a broken heart after the death of our Creek son. Then, my political opposition attacked her character from the pages of every paper."

"My father told me of your son. I'm sorry for both your grave losses. I've read the propaganda, sir. My wife and I too faced slander when we wed. Although our experience doesn't compare, I know the sting of hyperbole." It was all I could think to say, knowing how dearly the man loved his deceased wife.

How ridiculous, I thought. We avoided the reason for this meeting. I meant to present myself with more fortitude. That must be Jackson's plan, to disarm me.

He gestured toward the armchairs. I set my hat and cane on a nearby elaborate mahogany tabletop. Its craftsman had inlaid golden threads under its transparent surface. How frivolous. Gold's worth sealed under white man's brandy glasses. I unbuttoned my coat and sat in the seat General Jackson offered.

He rested his hands where the side arms met the wings of the chair. I didn't know what to do with mine.

He gestured to my cane. "How'd you get that limp?"

"Childhood illness, sir. I do not have my father's constitution. I was sick when he left home to fight with you, leading the Cherokee brigade at Horseshoe Bend."

"How old were you then?"

"Twelve. Attacked my lungs. My hip still swells and aches from the residual illness."

"I wasn't much older than that when the British killed my mother and brother. During the war, I ran messages across battle lines. They caught me. Held me captive for months. Caught smallpox in their prison."

"Your hatred of British occupation and oppression is widely known, sir."

"Yes, it would be. Thought I'd die for certain. Didn't much care, except that I was defiant enough not to give the Redcoats the satisfaction

Yellow Bird's Song

of burning my corpse. I recovered. America and I had our revenge in New Orleans."[15] Jackson asked, "Do you have children?"

"Yes, sir, three. My wife and I are expecting again."

Why did he avoid the obvious reason for calling me here?

"After suffering the pox, Rachel and I never could have a child all our own."

He didn't finish his thought. Instead, he packed a pipe, shuffled through a nearby cylinder for a switch, lifted the golden fireplace cover, and lit his pipe.

I still did not know why I was here, alone. Surely, it wasn't to turn an enemy into a friend.

He leaned back in the chair. "We both have scars. Some seen. Some unseen."

I broke the promise I made myself. Restraint. I asked, "Are what the papers report true? You will not enforce the Supreme Court's decision? You will refuse to send federal troops to Georgia?"

He puffed and exhaled. "You're a direct one. I like that. No, Ridge, I will not. More than that, though, I cannot. The law gives me little room to act against Georgia. Americans would see any federal intervention as turning the army's weapons against its own people. I will not oppose providence, expansion. How could I? I'm its staunchest supporter."

I responded quickly. "The president's authority as commander in chief would deter Georgia's attacks against the Cherokee."

He retorted just as fast. "Such an order would imply war is my intention. Last year's Creek rebellion proves it. Settlers will come. Invade Cherokee land regardless. They covet the fertile ground."

His abrupt honesty took me back. I had no words to counter such a prediction.

Jackson asked, "Surely, at home, you've witnessed the effects of four hundred whiskey shops bordering Creek Nation.[16] Heard about the smallpox epidemic plaguing the Creek?"[17]

"My people suffer under the same yoke, sir. But unlike the Creek, our government would never trade our sovereignty. Not with only federal assurances of removing white encroachers."[18]

"Why not?" he asked, letting the question hang in the air like a disease.

"As you aptly said, whites approach regardless. If one white man leaves, ten more take his place."

General Jackson's stare urged me to further forthrightness. I said, "Last year's treaty destroyed Creek sovereignty. The federal government divided and conquered them."

He said, "Think. Why hasn't Ross agreed to a similar treaty? Are your

252

people not desperate enough? Could there be some other reason?"

I answered without thinking. "If Ross signed such a one-sided treaty, he'd have to relinquish all power. The man revels in it. Reveres it."

Unsurprised, Jackson leaned forward and held his pipe between his hands. "Answer me this. Has Chief Ross' policy of passive disobedience deterred Georgia?"

"No," I said, offering Jackson the same honesty and directness granted me.

He advanced his reasoning. "Does your National Council seek to declare war on the settlers? Support warriors who'd provoke Georgia into outright war?"

I said, "Our numbers are too small. Such a sting would mean mass suicide."

He said, "You've seen what Georgia's papers report about warriors evicting settlers? I've read of your father's troubles. Georgia's governor told me his version of events."

I rebuked him. "They accused us of what they do: theft, rape, and murder. What the paper printed was an utter mistruth. Georgia was the one who captured and beat some in our party to death. My father knew we took a risk, but there was more at stake than you know."

"Your father was a sensible man. I assume he still is, with all his faculties?"

"Very much so. I am grateful. He is my strongest confidant."

"Then, tell your father the only hope of relief is to abandon the country and remove to the West. I am a powerful man, but not powerful enough to keep greed at bay."

He put his pipe to his lips again. "I offer Cherokee sovereignty at a safe distance from those who cause your people harm. I do not want my loyal friends to see their livelihoods stolen. For this, the American government will pay their way West and sustain them the year following. Despite what you may think, I do not wish for the demise of the Cherokee Nation. How could I? I may be many things, John Ridge, but I am loyal to my friends. Friends like your father. Not that scamp, Ross."

I felt the need to defend Ross after Jackson's slanderous remark. But, instead of rushing to speak, I raised my eyebrow. After seeing it, he gave his reason for the insult.

Jackson said, "Your principal chief may align his political pursuits on behalf of your people, but I believe he's vested more in his personal financial success through his real estate dealings."

"Our people admire him." When that remark did not move Jackson, I said, "He and our National Council fight to save the land of our ancestors.

Yellow Bird's Song

Land where we've grown and hunted our sustenance much longer than the invading Americans. How could you speculate as to Ross' intentions?"

Jackson tilted his head, as if, in his mind, he debated whether to show the last card held in his hand. He lowered his voice. "I know because Ross negotiated a treaty in 1819. It guaranteed civilized half-breeds the opportunity to become wealthy American citizens. For Ross' efforts, he received six hundred and forty acres in the Tennessee Valley, land ripe for cotton. I know because I sat at the other side of the table and wanted to buy it. In 1819, your chief sold Cherokee land to the government, denounced his citizenship, and profited from the cotton grown there."[19]

My conclusion spilled from my lips with abandon. "So, Ross is an American when it suits him and Cherokee when it lines his pockets. He makes money either way."

So much of what Jackson said aligned with what I already knew. Ross refused McIntosh's bribe because it proved him faithful to the Cherokee. He married Quatie for her family's political heritage. With her as his wife, even if he were entirely white and American, she could hold the land and all its improvements under Cherokee law. It made sense—the story about Kalsatee, the man abandoned on the way to trade in Tennessee. Ross' arrangement with Black Crow.

As if Jackson read my thoughts, he asked, "Have you had the misfortune of meeting former Indian Agent Colonel John Crowwell? Eaton said the two of you shared words."

"He and Father nearly came to blows. Yes, I have had the misfortune of his acquaintance and that of his brother, Thomas."

Jackson said, "Did you know Agent Crowwell resented Chief McIntosh's control over goods bought and sold in Creek Nation? After McIntosh's murder, he redirected buyers and sellers through his brother's business. Important to keep affairs in the family, wouldn't you say?"

I remarked under my breath, "Some of McIntosh's and Crowwell's business associates assaulted my wife." How much did Jackson know?

Jackson leaned back in his chair. "No need to ask how they were punished. Deservedly so, I might add. Would have done the same had they taken my Rachel."

Since Jackson offered an exchange of trust, I reciprocated. "In a fortunate hand of cards, Thomas Crowwell told me how he ran pony clubs and sold whiskey and slaves. He paid Ross a percentage of the profits to redirect our Light Guard, granting the thieves safe passage. With Georgia's soldiers evicting so many, I hoped Crowwell's business venture ended."

Jackson tilted his head into a slight nod. "I doubt it. Crowwell's horse racing is an expensive hobby, often incurring handsome debts. Crowwell and his brother bet more than they breathe." General Jackson crossed his leg. "Ross' involvement doesn't surprise me. You'll be pleased to know I dismissed Colonel Crowwell of duty, effective December 31, 1832."[20]

I covered my fist with my other hand, holding both over my mouth. After Ross' involvement with the Crowwells, the man sought control of our treasury. New Echota was in ruin because Ross paid white attorneys rather than feed those evicted from their farms. I saw why he prioritized the lawyers, but at what cost?

When I looked up, I couldn't stop my tongue. "My people are destitute. With so much homelessness, the civilization we've pursued for decades has become all for naught."

Jackson said, "Your people are as weak as Ross wants them to be. Control the story, garner the funds, and control the population. Keep them poor, or worse, drunk. It makes them needy, seeking answers from their chief."

I whispered my thoughts. "Ross delays."

"He's trying to wait out my presidency. Truth is, I have no reason to believe the people won't reelect me. Not only as the incumbent but as America's war hero, offering land to meet the needs of an increasing population. During my next term, we reach the Pacific."

General Jackson would relocate or kill every Indian nation from here to the ocean.

But now, my nation took priority. I said, "I have enough political standing to bring articles of impeachment for Ross' crimes. But I'd risk a great deal by doing so. The men in his service are loyal, and the Cherokee people believe everything he tells them." Prosecuting Ross for fraud would divide our nation and make it easier for Georgia to move their belongings into our homes that much faster.

Jackson admitted, "I've thought of killing him myself. It would shift the chess pieces on the board, so to speak. But the war sure to follow would end the Cherokee. If you impeach him, Cherokee judges will serve better justice than making him a martyr in the hands of a federal court. His punishment shouldn't come by government lead but by Cherokee tomahawk—if you will. Or you could run against him. Rally your people's emotions. Make them see a better alternative. They must change their minds about Ross. You are your father's son, are you not?"

Comforted by that truth, I said, "I am. Thank you for your honesty." I knew I needed to talk with my father and stood without asking Jackson's leave.

General Jackson shook my hand and retook his seat to smoke his pipe. He coughed after inhaling but gathered enough air to stop me from turning the doorknob. "Young Ridge, despite what you may think, the American eagle stands for liberty and justice for all."

With pipe smoke lingering above his head, my reply was immediate. "*Uwohali* reminds us of our people's strength and power."

Jackson's smoky haze chuckled above the wingback chair. "John Ridge, they are the same thing."

On the shores of the Potomac River, I sought escape from Jackson's words. But in their place, my doubt lingered. Had I become what I hated, like dishonest McIntosh bargaining with land he had no power to sell? It was entirely possible I would die because I considered changing my mind. I knelt by the bank and removed my glove, hoping the water's icy numbness would wash such thoughts away.

River branches travel from the same source, flowing north to south. Through its travels, it bends, above and below ground, and never stops. Would that I could follow at such speed. Make my way home in days instead of the long month aboard steamboat and coach. I yearned to return to its peace.

I reached for the head of my cane and used it to stand. Jackson spoke the truth, in all its ironic contrast. Chief Ross squandered the people he'd vowed to raise. To find their strength, the people must see how Ross leads their desperation.

My people must choose between our sovereignty and our land. Either we negotiate removal on our terms now or die, wallowing in debt and destitution, bleeding from bayonets gripped in the hands of blue-clad soldiers.

CHAPTER 26: THE SHEPHERD
Sarah Ridge
Running Waters
June 1832

Watched over by clear blue skies, we tended sheep. Honey cut the fleece with sharp shears while Peter held the docile two-year-old ewe against his chest. The sheep had a pleasant expression on her woolly face, enjoying cool freedom from her matted mess. The wool we cut today would take two days to wash and the same number of days to dry before Clarinda and Rollin could brush it through. Marz, Sunflower, and I would fill quiet summer evenings, spinning the fleece into yarn.

In the field, Rollin and Clarinda danced with last winter's lambs. Sunflower held Susan's hands and lifted her by her arms through the tall grass. Each time Susan flew, the grass tickled her bare feet. She laughed with her entire body, as only young children can. Susan's delightful squealing led us all to mimic her laughter.

A wagon lumbered up the road. A somberly dressed Sophie Sawyer drove the horses. While her attire was never extravagant or store-bought, she wore a dress of black and a matching bonnet. For her to make such a trip alone, wearing the darkest dress she owned, I feared she brought no good news.

I held my hand up to shade my eyes when Sophie stopped the horse and shifted the brake. She climbed down the wheel and began her short ascent to our front door.

She wouldn't see us in the fields. I called, "We're just here."

Recognizing my voice, Sophie followed the beaten-down grass to the fence gate and closed it behind her. She'd only made it halfway before I gathered the four corners of the quilt, keeping the wool in place, and met her near the oak.

"Good afternoon, Miss Sawyer. I hope you are well?"

"Yes, thanks to God."

"Come inside out of the sun." I gestured to the house.

Whatever reason brought her so far from Worcester's and the school, I expected we'd be far more comfortable in the private light of the parlor than standing under June's sun. I wiped the sheep's lanolin from my hands and untied my apron to appear more presentable.

After I opened the door, Sophie said, "Such unlikely color companions." When I gestured for her to enter the parlor, she said, "Such comfortable furnishings. I have not seen the likes since Vann's picnic."

Yellow Bird's Song

"Thank you. Most afternoons, toys and slates, shoes and caps are usually scattered on the floor. But since we've been in the fields, the hardwood is free from hazards. Please sit and make yourself comfortable. What brought you from school in the middle of the week?"

"Most children don't attend school this season with fieldwork requiring all hands. Besides, my work is in vain, with no one to offer examinations. However, I didn't come here to complain. Sad to say, I come to tell you of Brainerd Mission's recent heartbreak."

"Has something happened to Reverend Sam and Doctor Butler in prison?" Most expected it and that would account for her dark clothes. Elias told me that despite the Supreme Court ruling, Georgia's governor had not yet pardoned or released the ministers from Milledgeville prison. I prayed Governor Lumpkin would listen to the public's pressure to free the missionaries. Even the newspapers said it was past time for him to send the men home to their wives.

But if Reverend Sam passed, I could only imagine the insurmountable grief Ann would endure. Seven months passed since I'd seen John's face. Letters were no substitute for having him here. But I recognized God's blessings on our family. My worries were few compared to Ann Worcester, who each day couldn't help but imagine her husband in chains, like Job, sleeping on a bare floor.

Sophie ran her hand along the soft surface of the sofa between us and pulled a handkerchief from her sleeve. As if mustering power to tell me her news, she nervously gathered the embroidered white cloth in her hands, stretching it between short-nailed fingers.

"Worcester and Butler live. No, the news I bring may cause you personal distress. Arch passed and is now with our Lord and Savior."

Shocked to stand, I couldn't believe it. The further my heart sank, the more my words mumbled, and I said them aloud to believe them. "How could that be? He was well when last I saw him. He'd often check in on us and stay for dinner."

"He suffered from dropsy since February, with only a brief reprieve from the illness earlier this spring. His body swelled horribly, and as a result, his skin tightened, and his limbs ached because of all the fluid. His head ached so, but in the end, it was his heart that stopped. He died on the evening of the 18th, surrounded by Mr. Chamberlain from the mission in Athens, Tennessee, and his mentor, Reverend Butrick. They both spoke so eloquently at his funeral."

I wish I had known. Mother Susannah might have eased his pain. Sudden grief stopped my words. I stuttered, "Wh-what did they say?"

"Reverend Butrick called him the Cherokee's shepherd. The flock relied too much on him. Bringing Cherokee to the Lord's plentiful table would be more difficult without him. Minister Chamberlain spoke of the man's piety. His Christian character contained no stain of vanity or pride."[1]

Many would feel his loss. But in my selfishness, all I could think of was my own. It was true; Arch was a shepherd. Those following his crook remained ever in his protection.

She reached into the pocket of her dress, pulled a weather-beaten book bound with a leather strap. "One of Arch's last wishes was that I deliver this to you."

Arch had written a spelling primer, in syllabary and English. On the inside of the cover, in pencil scratch, it read, "For Little Spider's children, present and future." After reading his dedication, a tear escaped my eye. Even from the grave, God's shepherd led the lambs. I had no words.

Several days later, in mid-afternoon, I sat with Rollin and Clarinda at the kitchen table with their slates and chalk, absorbed in Arch's book. Short Bible verses taught the children to spell. "Behold the Lamb of God, which taketh away the sin of the world."[2] As they practiced, Peter opened the door and angled a heavy trunk through the frame.

Peter said, "He looks like rain clouds dumped their wares all over him."

Rollin stopped writing and signed to Clarinda, "Papa's home!" The children broke their chalk when it rolled to the floor. They sped through the open doorway to the stables. I didn't follow. I hurried up the stairs to gather Susan from her nap. Brushing black hair from her closed eyes, she barely woke when I picked her up and nestled her head under my chin. "Papa's home."

I hurried around the corner of the hothouse. My husband stepped into the sun from the barn's shade. Rollin sat high on John's shoulders while he gripped Clarinda's hand. I heard him before I saw him. He asked Rollin, "Where are your mother and baby Susan?"

Rollin replied, "Susan isn't a baby anymore. She runs wherever she goes. Mama's making my brother in her belly. He'll run faster than she does."

"How could you know if it will be a brother or sister?"

Rollin's sternness was unmistakable. "Because it isn't fair. I already have two sisters. Time to even things up."

John laughed and said, "Fairness has nothing to do with it, Yellow Bird."

Yellow Bird's Song

Susan burrowed into my neck to keep her eyes from the light. John lifted Rollin and set him to his feet. Without words, he stretched his free hands to hold Susan. She looked at him and, absent any fear, reached back. Susan's calm demeanor waylaid my fears. I worried she might cry, thinking her papa was a stranger. John missed the end of her infancy.

He removed her tiny white cap and cupped her black hair. "She still smells like my baby."

He stepped closer and put his cheek against mine. He whispered, "I dreamt of you. You sent me a lock of your auburn hair woven in hemp tucked inside a blue ribbon. I wore it on my lapel. Then, the vision was replaced by us walking through an unfamiliar cornfield." He stopped rubbing Susan's back and pointed toward the tasseled stalks. "We pulled husks from some of the first fruit and roasted ears for the children.[3] I have so much to tell you of the world, but my poor education lacks words enough to put the thoughts into words."

I brushed the hair from his face, held his cheeks in my hands, and kissed him. "Talk about the world later. Let's see if the corn is ready."

We did as John's sleeping imagination dictated. Honey and I prepared roasted chicken with vinegar and tomato marinade sweetened with honey from Running Water's beehive. And after supper, we roasted corn ears next to a bonfire. John winked at me when he took Rollin and Clarinda to the barn. In no time, the three rode out. Clarinda on her mare, Rollin on his Appaloosa pony, and John atop Saloli. They sped down the hill toward the cow pastures and sunset.

When they returned, John and Peter spoke as if their separation had been days instead of half a year. John eased into conversation with Walking Stick, bantering about the new heads of cattle and sheep. Laughing Water and Will gave John a map of the crops planted last spring and shared their anticipation of the harvest's abundance. Each gave John a report fuller than I could have. He listened, eager to hear from each of our tenants. He said, "You all have worked so hard. I'm grateful."

Walking Stick said, "Not as hard as your wife. She planned, we just helped with the labor."

Then, Sunflower took John to meet Marz.

I said, "Quatie brought her. I couldn't turn her away. Georgian Guards burned her mountain cabin and whipped stripes across her back. She slapped a guard for setting fire to her house."

In his mind, he lifted his nose and must have smelled the smoke. Heard, in his head, the cries of the elderly woman cowering before the whip gripped in the soldier's fist. John took her hand and said, "*Sacred mother, I am sorry for your loss. You are safe here.*"

Sunflower cared for Marz like she would have her own mother. Understanding one another was easier now that Sunflower adopted Clarinda's signs. Marz learned them too. The two sat in silence and weaved cloth for all those living at Running Waters.

Tonight, Walking Stick wore the new shirt Sunflower made for him. No one spoke of it, but he and Sunflower had begun a friendship. Sunflower's grief for her husband remained on her face, but she glanced away, hiding it when Walking Stick looked at her. He ran in from his chores, heaping sheep's fleece over his shoulder, so she wouldn't have to carry it. Last month, she rode beside him to check on the new calves. The two rode with their free black hair stretching into the wind. Time would tell whether they'd find one another free enough to attach themselves to one other.

Despite his attentions, from her silence, I feared the cloak of mourning still laid heavy across her shoulders. I couldn't say whether she was ready to find love again, despite it finding her. Walking Stick seemed to sense the same, and remained by her side, unable to ebb his compulsion toward her. If she allowed it, he'd stay.

Even now, Walking Stick sat beside Sunflower, while nearby, Marz's long fingernails never stopped intertwining a basket from vines. Perhaps Marz saw it as her duty to act as a chaperone. But despite such watchful eyes, Sunflower rested her head on Walking Stick's shoulder. Wide-eyed surprise dashed across his face, and he stilled, not daring to move an inch.

Our exhilarated but exhausted children fell asleep in our arms. Will carried a limp Rollin. John toted tall Clarinda. I carried baby Susan. In a short time, we three returned to the fire outside.

When Will's face came into the light, Laughing Water said, "*Just a few years ago, you were that small, Will.*" Will let his father hug him, uncommon for a seventeen-year-old. Then, the two headed to their deserved rest with the father's arm gathering his son by the shoulders.

Across the fire, Honey pulled a humming Peter's hand, forcing him to stand. She rose onto her toes and whispered something in his ear. He shook his head in denial. She stepped behind him and nudged him over to John. Peter looked at her over his shoulder. When he reached John, he stood nearly at attention and cleared his throat.

Peter searched for words and decided on, "Glad you made it home."

John reached for my hand and said, "Thank you, Peter. At least this return was less dramatic than the last."

I let go and slid my hand through my husband's arm, pulling him closer. It wasn't difficult to predict what Peter's following words would be. While Sunflower and Walking Stick had just begun to trust one another,

Yellow Bird's Song

Peter and Honey's conviction was unbreakable.

"This ain't the right time. But Honey say she won't rest 'til I ast you. She right about most things, or believes she is."

Honey swatted Peter's arm, and then, with her impatience, gestured for him to continue.

Peter said, "Thing is, I've changed my mind."

John said, "So, you wish to leave us, then?"

Peter shook his head, surprised. "No! Never known a home like this one here." He looked at Honey, not the house or stables.

John smiled, knowing what Peter meant. John asked, "What's changed then, Peter?"

"Remember dat time we walked through the woods lookin' for them lighter knots? Told you I didn't know what freedom meant. Lovin' Miss Honey has taught me how to live free, not just free on paper. It isn't somethin' you hold in your hand, but somethin' hidden in your chest, lettin' a man take a deep breath. If I ain't bound to Miss Honey, I can't breathe free." Peter finished his request. "I'd like to marry her if'n it's all right with you."

John said, "You might better ask her father rather than me."

Peter looked frustrated. "Asked Major Ridge last week, and he said I best be askin' you when you got back."

John stepped toward Honey, but he addressed Peter. "You don't need my permission, Peter. You need hers."

John took Honey's calloused hands in his. "Do you love him? Can you trust him as your best friend for the rest of your life? You're only sixteen or so. You have seen little of the world."

Honey didn't hesitate. "Let me be sayin' this, Brother John, I've seen all the world I wants to. With Peter, I won't go no further by myself, if'n you say it's all right. Thought no one would want me, but you brought him home, and I'm grateful. Our song is fine."

John said, "Then it seems we are to have a wedding at Running Waters, our first."

The quiet audience listened to the exchange. Walking Stick shook Peter's hand. I took Honey into my arms. I whispered in her ear, "You trust him?"

"Peter know all my truths. Times like they are, many chillern be needin' a mama and papa. Wasn't too long ago when I did. Major Ridge and Mother Susannah and you gave me belongin'. We'll love any of those babies the Lord sees fit for us to find. Sarah, I'm lucky. Peter gives me all his feelin's and sings me the words."

Sunflower hugged Honey before she and Marz left Walking Stick

262

alone, making their slow way to bed. Walking Stick, in similar quiet, followed Sunflower with his eyes when she passed. When their door shut, he offered us his own good nights and walked the distance to his cabin with his head hung low.

Honey and Peter took one another's hands and left our light to stroll the stream. John and I were alone with the fire to warm our faces. The smoke kept the buzzing insects from making welts on my arms. They never would bite him.

Leaning against a log, he stretched his legs and held out his hand, pulling me to sit with my back against his chest. John wrapped his arms around our growing child, lifting the babe's weight from me. When I melted into his chest with relief, he talked into my ear.

"Don't turn around. I don't know if I can say what I must if you're looking at me. But before that, know that I'm so proud of you. You've done better than I could, holding this farm and family together. Running Waters has blossomed under your hands."

I said, "It wasn't only my hands. I kept an account of the household funds. We will profit in the fall if cotton prices hold."

"I trust you, Sarah, but that isn't what I mean. I don't know where to begin." He gathered my hands and trapped both in his larger ones, holding us in a moment's prayer before letting go. Then he pulled a ripped newspaper clipping from his pocket.

"Someone nailed copies to every pine and post down the Federal Road. Georgia's Congressman Newnan reports to the press that our delegation consented to a treaty with the federal government. It isn't true, but Ross believes it without asking. He sees this as confirmation we committed treason. He's using this to blacken my name with my people."[4]

He took a deep breath, one lifting my chest along with his. "President Jackson won't support the Supreme Court's ruling. Georgia refuses to release Worcester and Butler. Chief Ross subjugates removal by delaying, hoping a change in administration will alter Georgia's resolution. But it won't happen. Henry Clay has no chance of beating Jackson in the fall."

Inside me, the baby moved and stretched. John continued, "As much as it breaks my heart to ask you to leave all you've grown. As much as it breaks me to ask our people to leave the graves of their fathers and grandfathers, I must consider removal, Sarah. No. More than that, my intuition tells me it is the only way my people survive."

After hearing such surreal words, I didn't look at him but leaned forward to read the flyer in the firelight. "Have you written to your father about your change of heart?"

"No. I needed to tell you first. I knew you'd either argue against it or

Yellow Bird's Song

rally scripture to support me. Either way, I'd be better prepared to tell him after telling you."

"You give me too much credit. Right now, I have no words. Start over? You're asking us to abandon all we've built and raised? The people and Ross will never concede to removal. Six months ago, you wouldn't have either."

"Nothing more we can do. Nothing left to argue. Time approaches when we must go West. Saying so aloud shifted my disbelief into prophecy."

I raised my voice with little control. "We cannot go now. I am to have another child!"

He continued calmly. "We've signed nothing. No agreement has been made. We have time. I will not put you or our children in harm's way."

I stared forward at the surrounding stream, fields, and trees known by heart. Their fruits and nuts sustained us. Their grasses fed the cattle and sheep. Their lumber kept our family warm and dry. But my husband changed his mind, knew Georgia's violence attacked all the Walking Sticks, Marzs and Sunflowers, Honeys and Peters, Laughing Waters and Wills. I had to listen. What he now considered opposed all he ever fought for.

But uproot our young family from this home I loved so dearly, take us away to some unknown place? We couldn't know whether there was safer than here, whether western land was fertile? Could it sustain our family? Let alone so many Cherokees who'd only known the East as their home.

I said, "Surveyors were here last April. I never heard anything more from them after they left me a copy of their drawing of all one hundred and sixty acres. They did the same to your parents' land. After that, part of me knew our remaining time at Running Waters would be short."

"Hmm," he said, straining the thought. "Perhaps the survey is only an expensive threat. I refuse to allow Georgia to take this land without our consent. Besides, if Jackson wants me to lead a Treaty Party, selling the place where I will do so will not help his cause." He spoke more to himself than to me. "I must think like the lion and the lamb, both predator and prey."

So, President Jackson convinced him? I thought he hated the man.

John said, "Only part of what the Congressman said was true. Ross knows it." I looked at the crumpled page in my hand before John took it, wadded it up, and threw it into the fire. We locked our eyes. Then he looked away. There was more he wanted to say. Did shame keep him silent? Instead of talking, for a moment he just watched the paper burn.

"Ross will attempt to rally my people against me. In their ignorance, it may induce them to assassinate me. Ross teaches them to misunderstand my character instead of viewing me as a friend. He wants them to believe I am a traitor. If they could consider removal, become a happy and civilized people, my blood, if shed, will not be in vain."[5]

My first reaction was to say, "Your friends will never let that happen."

But regardless, if he thought removal a possibility, I couldn't ignore the steep precipice. The thought of losing both John and our home devastated me.

He said, "I must ask you not to speak with Quatie anymore." His words seemed manufactured, produced by a man I didn't know.

I saw a new firmness in his squinted eyes. I said, "Oh, I cannot. Do not ask that of me. She is my sister."

"I know, and I am sorry. Something tells me not to trust either of them."

"You may have lost your faith in him. But I have not lost mine in her."

"Let me tell you why." He shook his head, scolding himself in a whisper. "I never should have kept this from you."

"What? Tell me," I said.

He talked while circling the fire. "The night we met Peter was the same night Vann and I first learned what was happening. But I knew for certain after the war party removed the Georgian guard from Sunflower's house. Foreman, at Ross' request and with his full knowledge, allowed horse theft, whiskey, and slave trading across our land. The guard tortured Sunflower's husband because of two brothers, one a federal Indian Agent for the Creek. They paid off their gambling debts with stolen Cherokee horses. Ross took a cut of the profits, pretending ignorance of the dealings."

I couldn't believe it, wanting to beg him for surety. John never stopped moving long enough to catch him. The more he moved, the more my disbelief grew.

Quatie's unending friendship surfaced in my mind. John's request, asking me to snub such devotion and abandon her, extinguished candles lighting dark corners. Without her, I'd be in the dark.

He took my arms in his hands to stop his pacing. He bent low so his eyes could reach mine. "Ross and his brother Lewis profit from the suffering of others. The men who took you and Honey moved the shipments. Either Quatie knows something and is either not asking questions, which I doubt, or knowingly enjoys the fruits of their labors. During the drought, did you see her family suffer? How many slaves does Ross own now? Near fifty? Think about it."

What he said was true, although I never considered it before. Quatie

Yellow Bird's Song

and Ross thrived while many others, including us, skimped, and saved, hoped for a reprieve from high prices with falling rain. I said, "I overheard them years ago. The day Quatie taught me to fashion candles. One of them mentioned some colonel who wouldn't allow them out of a deal. At the time, their conversation made no sense. Was that what they talked about?"

"Father told me the same. You were so angry with me for going with the war party. In many ways, you were right. Sunflower wasn't the only reason I went." He walked to the kitchen and returned with his coat. He pulled a painted card from its pocket and handed it to me. "I won it from the brother of that colonel. Foreman accepted the money and allowed safe passage for the thieves. Ross doesn't know I know. That revelation needs to come at an opportune moment."

We held onto one another. But shock settled in our paired silence, despite our hearts pumping blood in time. Neither of us had words apt enough, unselfish enough to ease such incredulous thoughts. He was browbeaten. I was devastated. There was no light to escape this cave.

John took the card from my hand. "Say nothing to Quatie about what I did to the men who took Honey and hurt you."

I buried my head in his chest and said, "She knows already or has assumed as much." To think Quatie would betray my confidences pained me as much as the ropes that burned my wrists. He held my scars up to the firelight.

I asked, "What will you do?"

He took another deep breath and pulled me close. "Not what you may think. First, I must convince my father that removal is the only possibility we control."

"Control how?" I asked.

"By negotiating the best deal. If we do not, Georgia will remove the Cherokee from the earth, not only the land. They will suffer as the Creek have suffered. I will not put you, our children, or my people in such danger when I have means to negotiate our survival."

He put his head on top of mine. "If I am elected principal chief, I can stop Ross from any further opportunity to steal from the Cherokee Treasury and negotiate a treaty with Jackson that will serve our people for years."

"Principal chief?" I asked.

He said, "It is my birthright."

Fire's wind blew and shifted the warm June air. I shivered. John felt it too. He caged me in his arms. "I can't do any of this without you. Please do not see Quatie. Keep my confidence. Trust in me, and do not be afraid."

Whatever promises John made, I was afraid and said nothing, leaving

266

my arms by my side. John believed Ross would make him a political lamb for slaughter. Then, in place of Ross, Cherokee would blame John for removal.

Instead, John intended to kick Ross' feet out from underneath him.

Arch came to mind. As Reverend Butrick said, it would be difficult to continue their mission, to convert and educate the Cherokee, without him. With one shepherd gone, the lions came around. John took up the crook.

CHAPTER 27: LION'S ROAR
John Ridge
Major Ridge's Plantation, New Echota, and Red Clay
July and August 1832

S tand, Elias, and I stood while my father interrogated us, seated behind a desk he rarely used. He leaned back in his chair. Two windows framed his stoic head, holding, in portrait, father's sternness against the evening's red sky, both finding immortality in pigment. He made a steeple with his hands in front of his mouth, hiding his scowl. His sagging jowls provided us evidence enough of his disapproval. I'd revealed, in all honesty, a complete account of my meeting with General Jackson and the delegation's interaction with Jackson's man, Cass, the Secretary of War.

Father tried to keep the heat radiating from his face from entering his voice. He spoke slowly and separated each word. *"What. Treaty. Terms. Did. Cass. Present?"*

Elias interrupted, responding before Father finished his question. *"Elisha Chester, the secretary's emissary, sent the government's conditions in writing."*

Father couldn't hold back his eruption any longer. His volume began in the same tones as before, but by the end of his declaration, he shouted. *"Nephew. That is not what I asked!"* He stood and pounded both fists on the empty desktop to punctuate his frustration.

No one spoke for a time while the blue ridges outside absorbed the shock. Mother opened the door, thinking someone, mainly me, might need medical attention. As soon as she entered, Father waved her worry away, and she closed the door quietly behind her with "be careful" written all over her face.

Father spoke with the frustration we all felt. I wished I could stop thinking and just feel like he did when passion overcame reason. I sat in the chair, facing him. Elias handed me Chester's proposal. I read. *"We would receive sufficiently extensive fertile country in the Arkansas territory, where the Old Setters emigrated with Sequoyah. We would conduct our own government there with an agent to look after our affairs in Washington. There is a possibility we could send a delegate to Congress. No whites would be allowed on our land unless authorized by our government. As far as our removal is concerned, we can choose our route and mode of transportation. The United States government would fully support us for a period of a year after our people arrive. We would continue to receive an annuity in proportion to the value of our ceded*

268

land, and all annuities afforded to our people by previous treaties. All improvements here appraised and purchased.[1]

Father turned and stared through the swirled glass panes toward the painted horizon. *"Hmm,"* he muttered. I couldn't tell whether the noise signified interest or disgust. Either way, I knew he thought it was a scheme too good to be true.

Stand said, *"We have no assurances. With so many broken promises, why should we accept this offer now? Look at the Creek's Treaty from '32. Lies, all of it."*

I said, *"The Creek absolved their sovereignty to Alabama. We would not do so. Quite the opposite, really."*[2]

I took advantage of Father's quiet before his earthquake continued. *"In the new land, we would build schools and construct blacksmith forges. The government promises iron and steel for the new construction of churches and council houses. Each adult male would receive a rifle, blankets, axes, plows, hoes, wheels, cards, and looms. Any livestock not transported would receive a fair appraisal and purchased at fair market cost. They would set aside provisions for Cherokee orphans. And I do not know how they could promise this, but the United States offered their protection against warring tribes in the West."*[3]

Father's query did not shake the entire house, just the glass he faced. *"Answer me honestly. Did the delegation agree to their terms?"*

I said, *"The delegation was not at liberty to do either—agree or disagree. We listened and refused to bring a treaty proposition to the people ourselves. That's Ross' responsibility. Cass took advantage, thought our lack of rebuttal enough permission to grant an emissary, Chester, to bring us his and Jackson's proposition."*[4]

Elias said, *"Chester comes next month, the attorney who argued the case against Worcester and Butler."*

Father took his time before speaking again. *"While you've been away, I've ridden through our country. The common man's plight is worse than I feared. Ross continues to do nothing."*

"Father, Jackson knows Ross. I must admit, I've changed my negative opinion of the man. He advised me honestly, knowing how Ross controls our people. No federal troops will arrive to stop the violence, not without Georgians viewing it as an unconstitutional betrayal. Despite what loyalty Jackson feels to the Cherokee, to you, he cannot turn guns on his own people."

Father's tempest erupted. *"Then let Jackson suffer impeachment for denying the ruling of the Supreme Court!"*

Father shouted, so I did the same. *"Crockett suffered political*

Yellow Bird's Song

homicide at General Jackson's hand. Anyone bold enough to bring articles of impeachment against Jackson would fall to the same fate."

Elias resumed his façade of confidence. *"Uncle, no tribe has survived under any state's jurisdiction. Our people will be whipped and crushed under their yoke."*

Stand supported his brother from the distant side of the room. *"I can't imagine the terms will get better than those proposed."*

I said, *"It always gets worse."* Perhaps returning Father's own advice might cool his flames. Or it would turn it to rock.

Father spoke words as if he recited them. At that moment, I understood why my grandfather had given my father his name, The Man Who Stands on Mountaintops. Father said, *"If we resettle in the West, we will govern ourselves. In time, we would meet the whites on more equal footing and petition to become a state. The day arrives, which I've dreaded. I am one of the native sons of the Cherokee, born north in the wild woods. My entire life, I have hunted deer and turkey over these mountains.[5] As a Cherokee warrior, I fought. In business, I offered fair dealings with Georgians who sought to swindle and oppose. Even though the living God gave us this land, I agree, we must remove, but my soul remains behind."*

Elias said, *"Uncle, Chief Ross will never offer cessation as a choice. Chief Ross prays on a false hope that Henry Clay will evict Jackson from office."*

I walked around Father's desk and placed my hand on his shoulder. *"The only way I see to persuade our people is to devise a secondary party, a Treaty Party, and argue publicly against Ross."* Father's support of a treaty offered credibility. He might want the chief's position himself. *"I will stand at your side. You are the greatest speaker of our nation."*

Father listened while Elias and Stand moved beside one another. Elias said, *"The Phoenix is our venue for communication. The silent Cherokee masses do not know the teetering position they are in. How can they judge, decide, and vote for themselves if they continue to hear only what Ross tells them?"*

Father looked up from his hunched shoulders. *"I am too old to be chief. Son, you are not. You three are right; those who sit in darkness vote blindly."*

I looked at my cousins. *"I do not wish to leave the country of my birth, a country I love entirely. My new stand places the people before the power of the executive. I do not want to see our language and customs consumed by the United States, and so diluted that history only records our failures instead of our people's success. If we do not consider a treaty, I fear inevitably, my children's children will no longer speak as we do, will no* longer celebrate the Green Corn, or hold council meetings in the fall. Boys won't face the long night to become men. Women will no longer lead families, recanting stories of our traditions. Only in the West will we be able to preserve our national integrity and sovereignty.[6] Only in the West can we exist, as Justice Marshall said, as a distinct community."

Elias added, "*As long as we continue as a people in a body, with our internal regulations, we can go on improving in civilization and respectability.*"

Father escorted us to the stables with a measured and slower gait. Usually, my limp caused me to follow, but today, I turned around to address him. "*Our timing must be right before we reveal our new perspective to the masses. We need time to learn the true feelings of the voting men.*" And I needed time to build a platform before announcing my run for principal chief, lead negotiator for treaty negotiations with General Jackson and the American Congress.

Not to waste Chester's expense or time, I knew we needed to secure safe ground for an emergency council meeting in July. Since the gathering would host a federal negotiator, Georgia might allow our assemblage, as it supported their interests. In New Echota, council members from the eight districts could convene quickly and hear Chester's proposal. I believed Governor Lumpkin would allow it.

Unsurprisingly, Ross agreed to the meeting with Chester but disagreed about the location. It was beyond me what lengths the man would take to have his way. The only reason not to hold the meeting in New Echota was that I wanted to have it there. So, Ross picked a needless fight to secure his authority. He decided the council would meet in Red Clay, Tennessee, on July 23rd, 1832.

Our ancestors named Red Clay for the iron in the soil, tampered by time, compression, heat, and rain. In a valley between two great hills, groves of white and red oaks sheltered the council house. The pines bordered four springs converging on the grounds. There were no inns near Red Clay, so the entire National Council would sleep rough while Ross and his men made the short ride to Ross' Landing on the Tennessee River, finding the comforts of home.

Many councilmen freed themselves from summer field labor to attend

Chester's hearing on such short notice. After opening remarks, Ross discussed old business instead of allowing Chester to present the government's treaty proposal. Before Chester took to the podium, Chief Ross proposed delaying elections. He said, "Since Georgia's threat remains, all Cherokee government officials should remain as they are, until the people are safe."

Stand exclaimed, "You cannot function as principal chief indefinitely!"

Elias whispered, "That violates our Constitution. The one he wrote." The murmuring from the crowd continued, more in protest than in agreement to bow to Ross' royal decree.

I bit my tongue. Father physically controlled me by pressing his hand into my weak leg. Anything I said now, I would regret. Now wasn't the time for indecorous behavior. But I would have felt great satisfaction punching Ross across his bearded face in front of a United States attorney. Elias left the open-air council house and walked across a wooden bridge over the stream, refusing to look his chief in the eye or listen any further.

My thoughts started in wide circles and then, as they descended, became more pointed. Did Ross assume we planned to unseat him? The only people who knew my plans were Sarah, Father, Elias, and Stand. None of them would say a word. Could this have been a deliberate move on his part to keep control? He must fear that defeat. There was no other explanation for refusing to hold elections.

None of that mattered, though. Since Ross remained our executive, no vote would veto his tyranny. From that moment forward, no further friendship would exist between us. We stood on opposite sides of the Coosa with our backs to one another, shouting at one another in opposite directions.

Ross pulled from his pocket a copy of Congressman Newnan's letter and nailed it, in dramatic fashion, to one of the many oaks near the council fire. Those who hadn't seen it rushed to read, looking over the shoulders of those standing in front of them. Many whispered "bribe," before shuffling to Ross' side of the crowd.

Despite the uproar, Chester offered his proposal. Unsurprisingly, Ross vetoed it, supported by the majority in his circle. Our pro-emigration stance remained the minority. I'd lost this hand but did so in respectful silence. It hurt my pride.

New Echota became a political battleground. Arguments erupted between Cherokee and Cherokee, between Cherokee and the standing militia, between whites and militia, between the Cherokee and the whites. The grid of streets of New Echota marked circles inside circles. No one's back was safe.

As General Jackson assumed, Ross moved against Elias' free press, motivated by his desire for "unity and sentiment and action for the good of all."[7] After Elias printed a fervent editorial presenting Chester's treaty as a practical option, Ross censored him. Refusing to be quiet, Elias resigned as chief editor.

Harriet, Sarah, and I watched from their front porch when Elias, at the print shop collecting his personals, shut the door for the last time and met a smoking Chief Ross as he turned around.

Across the street, Joe Foreman joined Elijah Hicks. After hearing heated words, they crossed the road to stand behind their chief. Neither man ever refrained from a fray, seeking any opportunity to prove their loyalty to the man who increased their wealth in proportion to their service.

Elias raised his voice to refute Ross. "You gave me no choice but to resign! I may be a poor man, but I will have my integrity. I cannot satisfy my own views and the dictates of your Cherokee authority, Ross."[8]

Ross said, "No one asked you to betray your conscience and remain editor."

Elias gritted his teeth when he spoke. "A leader knows that each citizen is entitled to the right to reflect upon the dangers facing his family, to weigh such matters, act wisely, not rashly, and choose a course coming nearest to benefiting the nation."[9]

After Foreman and Hicks arrived, Ross replied with arrogance. "Hicks, you will replace Elias as editor of the *Phoenix*."

Harriet held a handkerchief to her lips. She said, "Elias is heartbroken. He knows that with every loss of culture, moral degradation will follow."

Sarah wrapped her arm around Harriet's waist. Harriet watched her husband, the man in every way a pacifist, hold his ground against Ross.

Sarah said, "It is all slipping away. There is so much here so many, worth saving."

I couldn't watch three against one any longer. I said, "Elias, for one. Stay here."

Sarah followed my eyes, recognizing Ross' threatening stance. She warned, "Be careful."

When I reached the trio, Elias stepped forward. He kept his head high and suppressed his warrior instincts, for Christianity's sake.

He knew I stood behind him and talked to me without shifting his eyes from Ross. "John, I asked you once what the cost of our freedom would

Yellow Bird's Song

be. You said it would be our land. Weak hands of our leaders choose to delay and, without courage, willingly pass it over to the United States."[10]

Foreman snickered and moved his musket from one shoulder to the other. Ross's eyes darted between Elias' and mine.

Hicks spoke with disdain and sarcasm. "No man advocating removal was ever a patriot."[11]

Elias took a deep breath before unleashing his thoughts. "Patriotism is not only a love of country but a love of people. I cannot print peace when there is no peace. I cannot ease the people's minds with any expectation of calm when the vessel is already tossed to and fro and threatens to be shattered to pieces by an approaching tempest. We are in danger, so I must act consistently and raise the alarm, tell our countrymen what is true."[12]

After Elias finished, Harriet called his name from the porch. He looked over his shoulder and answered her by walking home from his print shop for the last time.

After Elias left, Foreman and Hicks walked toward the nearest inn, leaving laughter in their wake. Foreman clapped Hicks on the back.

Only Ross and I remained. He stepped closer so no passersby might overhear.

He said, "You are home to stay. It's best you don't go to Washington again."

"I'm sure you think so."

"Unless you'd like the Georgian Guard to find the corpses you and your father burned in that cave."

Desperate men, losing their hold on power, hold fast with all their might. Some believe one must keep his enemies close, but I refused to heed Ross' threats. I stepped closer to him. "Tell them then, and good luck proving it. I'm surprised you waited to threaten me without your lackeys close by."

"Abandon these plans for this barren mutiny."

"And if I refuse?"

"Let's just say I'll know if you step too far afield. Remain close to your wife and children."

Before I turned to leave, I felt a tug on my pant leg. Rollin crossed the yard and wriggled between Ross and me.

"Papa?" Rollin asked.

I picked him up. *"Remember Chief Ross? You've met him before, but you were little. He's married to Auntie Quatie."*

Rollin extended his hand toward Ross, offering a man's greeting. When Ross didn't return the gesture, I put Rollin's hand on my chest. I didn't want the two to touch, not now, with Ross' threat and my counter

274

still lingering between us.

Ross noticed.

Rollin reached inside my coat pocket, withdrawing my As, carried like a talisman. Rollin took the card and stared at the image.

Rollin spoke in English. "Papa, the mountain cat is jumping on the horse's back."

I said, "I won that card in a game with a Black Crow."

Rollin looked confused. "You play games with crows?"

I spoke to my son, but the words were meant for Ross. "The stallion never suspects an attack from behind."

I set Rollin to his feet with my card still gripped in his hand and moved him behind me.

Ross' guilty face said, "So, there are no secrets between us anymore." His masked words confirmed all he didn't say.

I replied, "If you still don't understand how so much uncertainty predicts our fall, I may not be the man to teach you. Our national existence is suspended on such faith and honor of the United States alone. We are held in the paw of a lion—convenience may induce him to crush us. With a faint struggle, we may cease to be."[13]

Ross offered no retort to my metaphor.

I continued. "Mutability is stamped over every creature that walks the Earth. Your blood is the product of such a union. So is my son's. If my Cherokee blood and that of my children are not destroyed altogether, it will run its course in the veins of fairer complexions who will read that their ancestors—under the stars of adversity and curses of enemies—from outside and within—still became a civilized nation."[14]

A rumble, deep from the fault line between our feet, opened the earth between us.

When Rollin ran back to his mother's arms, I inched toward the metaphorical edge, face to face with my enemy. "Bending doesn't mean the Cherokee must break. Not if turning West keeps us alive, keeps us sovereign. It is the only way the horse throws the mountain lion from his back. But—for now—you are principal chief, and your roar decides our fate."

CHAPTER 28: BETRAYAL
Sarah Ridge
Running Waters
Winter and Spring 1833

Peace was rare with four children. Clarinda wound up the music box and rested her hand on it and lay on the parlor floor. I had to step over her to enter the room. Susan screamed at Rollin from the hallway. Then Honey scolded Rollin for pulling Susan's hair. Both children shouted at one another. Triggered by his siblings, Herman Daggett, our infant son, began the night's entertainment with colicky cries.

The hinges on the front door creaked opened and shut, preceding a blast of frigid air. John was home. From the doorway, I heard him say, "Sounds like home."

He entered the parlor with a copy of the *Phoenix* under his arm, stepping over Clarinda. He took off his coats and tossed them over the sofa back. "Give me the baby."

I passed Herman to his arms. "It doesn't matter who's holding him." The baby arched his back and screamed louder. I massaged the skin on my forehead and temples, trying to rub a pounding headache away. "I can't ease him. The herbs your mother brought keep him content for an hour. But after, he's hurting again."

John cooed at Herman, who burped and somewhat settled. He asked, "What catastrophe is happening in the hall?"

"I don't know. Would you go see?"

John passed Herman back. "Once it's quiet, I have good news to tell you."

He closed the door to the closet under the stairs. "Who keeps leaving this open?"

In a minute's time, passing the archway, John held Rollin by the back of his breeches.

Rollin argued, "I only pulled her hair after she bit me."

Honey followed, carrying a sniffling Susan. As she passed, she said, "Squabblin' and fussin' because it is too cold outside to run out their legs during the daytime."

When they stepped out of my sight, Honey spoke loud enough to be heard over all the crying. "Peter and I don't need no chillern. You twos made 'nough trouble already."

John returned and gathered Clarinda to his lap while I paced in front of the fire with Herman. He signed, "Moonbeam, what did you learn today?"

She gestured. "There's a squirrel under the stairs."

He asked, "Are you letting it out? Is that why the door is open?"

Clarinda nodded her head.

I said, "She said the same yesterday. She clung to my leg when I showed her there was nothing in there but a broom and an ash bucket. I must have closed that door ten times today. Can't pass down the hall when it's open."

He signed to her. "Are you afraid of this squirrel?"

Clarinda signed, "She doesn't belong here."

I whispered, "I'm not laying Herman down to free my hands. Ask her if Will told her about how the *dewa* broke his plow?"

"Hmm. Did Will tell you the squirrel was a witch?" John made up a sign for the witch: a long-crooked nose. Clarinda mimicked him and shook her head, affirming her source of information, confirmed by Honey.

John looked up at Herman and me. "I guess I need to talk to them. I don't have a prayer of persuading the Cherokee not to be superstitious if I can't convince those under my own roof."

"It's time for you to sleep, my Moonbeam," John signed. Then he offered her his arm, bending low so she could put her hand through his elbow. He escorted her up the stairs, leaning over to accommodate her height as if the two were walking into a ballroom.

Herman quieted, finding his thumb. I gently set him in the cradle by the fire and sat, exhausted, on the sofa, pulling John's coat over me like a blanket.

Before I knew it, he nudged me. "You fell asleep."

Barely awake, I said, "You woke me up."

His body blocked the fireplace heat. "Took two stories for Rollin, one for Susan, and another for Clarinda. I'll stay up with Herman tonight and prepare a fifth."

"I wish he'd sleep with stories. You can't nurse him."

"True. Maybe tonight he will sleep until sunrise. I have letters to write. I'll bring him to you when I must."

It took all my strength to open my eyes. He stretched out both hands and helped me stand. Once I was steady, he offered me his arm the same way he had with Clarinda.

"I'd carry you up the stairs if I could. My hip won't allow it."

"Does it hurt tonight?" I asked.

"It's February."

While I changed into my nightdress and socks, John lit the fireplace in our bedroom. I climbed into bed with my eyes already closed.

"Are you too sleepy for a bedtime story?"

I nestled my head on my pillow and curled on my side. "Would it matter? You'd probably tell me one, anyway."

"How well you know me, my good wife. I promise it will be quick. Once upon a time, there were two blackbirds with white stripes around their necks."

I shivered and asked, "Are these real or imagined blackbirds?"

"Such sarcasm, Mrs. Ridge. Where's your husband?" The bed shifted when he turned behind him, pretending others were nearby. "I must tell him of your contrary nature."

"I'm not contrary. I'm exhausted."

He continued, "A man caught the two wild blackbirds and forced them into a cage. No matter how much they squawked and nipped at his fingers, he wouldn't set them free."

I broke my seal under the covers to reach across the bed for his hand and pulled him toward me.

"Hold on. I still have my boots on," John said.

"Never stopped you before. Warm me up. It's freezing in here."

"What would my mother say?" I heard each boot hit the hardwood. He flipped the quilts back, letting what little warmth I'd mustered slip away, and slid into the bed, still dressed in his waistcoat and tie.

He smelled like horse and campfire smoke. When he settled, I asked, "What happened to the blackbirds?"

John kissed my forehead. "This stubborn man had a dinner party. All his guests talked of was how sad the blackbirds looked. Putting them behind bars was a betrayal. Everyone told the stubborn man to release them, even his chief. But the obstinate man refused. He told his important guests that he'd let them go free when the blackbirds stopped nipping at his fingers and remained silent."

I mumbled, "And did he?"

John said, "Did he what? Let them go free? Yes, took a year and four months, but he opened their cage. The two blackbirds, Reverend Sam and Doctor Butler, are on their way home from Milledgeville Penitentiary."[1]

When the robins arrived, river water turned stagnant, covered by a film of yellow pollen. Early one morning, John rode into New Echota with his father to meet Elias, Walker, Vann, Fields, and Starr. They had recently returned from their own visit to the Capitol, a separate delegation from Ross' men. These founding members of the Treaty Party didn't trust Ross to negotiate without their watchful eyes. None had faith in the other.

Heather Miller

When John returned, he said Walker reported how everyone stared at one another's backs, predicting some betrayal. A time must come when John and Ross found a compromise, a unity in the best interests of all. I couldn't wait for the day. When those waters cleared, Quatie and I could be sisters again.

I missed her. We'd not seen one another in months. I wanted to tell her about Herman. See her children. Make sure she was well.

Mother Susannah taught Clarinda that day. She wouldn't return until dinner. Rollin attended Miss Sawyer's school and stayed at the Boudinots'. If I coaxed Susan and Herman for afternoon naps, I could visit her. Only Quatie and I would know.

I put on my bonnet and walked down the hall toward the kitchen to tell Honey I'd be away. The closet door was open again. I looked inside, saw nothing, and closed the door. Marz startled me, standing right behind it. I hadn't heard her footsteps approach.

Her voice was as weathered as her face. "Didn't mean to scare you."

My hand gripped my shawl. "I'm only surprised, Marz." I tied the bow and looked over her shoulder. "Do you know where Honey is? There is an errand I must run. I shouldn't be away for more than a few hours."

Marz said, "She headed toward the barn with lunch for Mister Peter. He's going to Lavender's post."

"Then I'll tell her when he saddles my horse. I'll be home likely before the children wake."

"We'll take care of those babies." She made her slow way to the front room, spinning the wheel, giving me a blessed reprieve from another chore.

I rode beside the yellow river water down the Ross Ridge Road, enjoying the returning warmth. Winter seemed everlasting, but the new buds on the trees reminded me of the child growing inside me. It was early yet. No one knew my secret. I chuckled to myself, thinking about how John would need to invent more stories.

But guilt nagged behind my back. When John returned from Washington, he'd asked me not to see any of the Rosses. I wondered whether Ross asked Quatie to do the same. But surely, they'd allow us an hour to say goodbye.

When I arrived, Quatie wasn't at her churn. The girls weren't hanging laundry in the breeze. Instead, two white men unhitched a wagon full of household belongings, an older father and his adult son. They didn't look the part of politicians, too homespun and unpolished. Curiosity overwhelmed my nudge to turn back, so I spoke to them.

I overheard the younger. "Either she won some of this here bottom

Yellow Bird's Song

land close by, or she's one of them Methody Indian lovers."

Still atop my horse, I held my hand above my eyes to see their faces. I said, "Excuse me, gentlemen." Neither stopped what they were doing to address me with the same courtesy. I continued, "I came to see Mistress Ross."

The older answered. "She's in the slave quarters in the back. This here's our house now."

"What?" I asked, unsure if I heard him correctly. My heart pounded in my chest.

"You heard me. She and her brood got two more days. After that, all of them Indian shells and feathers better be out of my sight."

"But Ross is the chief of the Cherokee Nation! This is his family's house!"

"Ain't no more. Won the house, land, and the slaves in the lottery. I even own those stupid peacocks." He waved me off, throwing a harness over a post. "Hurry on with your business, then."

I found Quatie sitting on a stool outside a one-room cabin, throwing corn to chickens pecking at her feet. Her daughter bounced baby George on her hip. Her sons sat idle with their backs together at her heels.

She coughed. Her face flushed, pinker than its healthy-sunned brown. Her cheeks were flat and muted, less radiant than when I saw her last. When I swung down from the horse, she didn't look up from the hens.

"Quatie, what happened?" I went to her, but she raised her hand and stopped my approach.

She rubbed her nose and sniffed mucus back to speak. "They stormed the door. Told me I had one week to pack our belongings and vacate the house. They won the ground and all its improvements from that swine, Governor Lumpkin, in the land lottery. We must stay until Ross returns."

"They stole your home?" I asked.

"Papers say it belongs to them now. Ross hasn't written us, busy fighting Jackson's Congress or visiting the young, white Elizabeth Milligan."

I took a step closer. "Who's Elizabeth Milligan?"

"Ask your husband. No doubt she's been busy entertaining both sides."

I couldn't forget the name, Elizabeth Milligan. But now, there was little time to riddle Quatie with the million questions it would take to reach the core of her remark. She spoke with emotion, stern and bitter, blaming this disaster on Georgia's politicians who became wealthier by selling land they didn't own. Should I invite her to stay at Running Waters? She wouldn't come. But if she did, how would John react? Stupidly, I looked behind me, as if Ross would ride in any minute. I said, "Ross will come

280

home. He'll know what to do. You won't have to leave."

"It doesn't matter. Ross will probably blame me for allowing them into the house. He'll say I did everything wrong. Besides, you're more likely to know what's happening than he is."

I held my head, confused by her treatment, and frustrated by her statement. I said, "Why would I know?"

She walked toward me, frowning with a fierceness I'd never experienced from her. She said, "Because your husband and Governor Lumpkin are such good friends. Has anyone come to take Running Waters? Stolen all those flowers you grow in your hothouse? Has the guard evicted the Major and Susannah from their orchard plantation on the Oostanaula? I think not. Major Ridge hasn't lost one peach."

No words came to mind that might offer her comfort. What she said was true. Surveyors walked our property last year, but after they left, I heard no more from them. Susannah also mentioned the outsiders, but no one evicted any Ridge.

I knew John had written to his government friends, hoping to keep our land off the lottery. Was Governor Lumpkin who he meant? No matter how he and Ross disagreed on policy, John wouldn't ask the Governor to evict Ross. Would he?

I asked, "How can I help? You don't look well." I reached to touch her forehead. She pulled away. I took a deep breath at her refusal, removed my shawl, and draped it over her shoulders.

She stepped toward me, letting it slide to the ground. "Ross will take us to the Landing, near Red Clay, to our cabin there." Her eyes shifted to the tree line path as Foreman rode in and pulled his reins to stop, watching us. He pulled the long rifle from his saddle strap and rested the barrel on his shoulder.

After seeing him, Quatie said, "Foreman watches over us. I need no sympathy from a traitor's wife."

Quatie's accusation pushed me backward. I picked up my shawl and shook the dirt free. Without another word, I mounted my horse and rode home. I didn't cry until I saw Running Waters, guilty because we were safe.

John's horse was in the stable when Walking Stick put mine in the stall. "He's looking for you."

John stood behind his desk, searching through drawers, strewing papers everywhere. Some scattered underneath his feet. Corners peeked from

Yellow Bird's Song

under his desk. He flipped through letters, confounded by not finding what he sought. In his dismay, he opened another drawer, lifting it above his head, and emptying its contents onto the growing pile.

"Where'd you go?" John said. "I can't find Cass' letter anywhere. I need to show Walker. Have you seen it?" He didn't look up, scanning and shifting letters from one pile into another.

I stood just inside the door, leaning against it. "No, I haven't. Tell me again. Who is Cass?"

John was adamant. "He's the Secretary of War. I must find it."

I watched his frenzy, never having seen him so disorganized or untidy. I asked, "Why is it so important?"

"Hicks wrote how Jackson offered Ross a bribe of $50,000 to treat. No doubt it's a lie. This is another of Ross' ploys, causing the people to distrust the American government. They won't agree to any treaty if they don't think the present administration will keep its word. According to the article, Ross reported that the Commissioner of Indian Affairs would send military forces to expel white settlers.[2] Rumor is Jackson's changed his mind. But it isn't true. Cass' letter proves it."

John grumbled with Cherokee words I didn't know; likely some a lady shouldn't hear. He crossed to a chair at the side of the room and shuffled through another stack, already unfolded. "When I talked with Jackson, I left with a lesson on liberty and little doubt about the man's firm stance on removal."

He walked around the desk and knelt to sort through the papers on the floor. Seeing how the movement pained him, I came to his side and helped. With our heads together, we crawled over handwritten pages. I scanned each salutation, looking for Cass' name.

John tossed papers out of the way. "The letter confirms Ross lied. The military sent by the government protects only Cherokee in Tennessee and the Carolinas. Cass will dispatch no soldiers to Georgia. No one is coming to save us from Lumpkin's lottery or to prosecute thieves forging Cherokee names on deeds. But without that letter, I have no proof to present in council."[3]

When he mentioned the lottery, I stopped helping and sat back on my heels. "Ross' house was sold to whites. Quatie's living in slave quarters."

John stood and said, "I asked you not to speak to her." I felt like my father's daughter, hiding underneath the desk. I couldn't lie to him. "I know you asked me not to, but I had to see her one last time."

He held his hand to help me stand from the floor. I didn't take it. Instead, I looked at the rug in shame. John's tone changed from frustrated to dumbfounded with a single sentence. He spoke above me in a whisper.

"The letter was here last night. No one else has been here. Only you." He withdrew his hand. "Did you take it to Quatie today? When no one knew where you'd gone?" Anger built behind each word. I'd rarely heard him raise his voice in all the years we'd known and loved one another.

Herman cried upstairs.

I put my hand on John's desk and stood by myself. "I haven't been in your study for days. I only come in here to record farm business." So belittled by his accusation, I retaliated in kind. "Tell me the truth. Did you have anything to do with Ross and Quatie losing their house? Did you write to Governor Lumpkin? Keep our homes off the lottery, but leave Quatie and Ross to fend for themselves?"

He walked away from me without answering, studying the view from the window. Silence crackled in the air. But he didn't deny writing to Governor Lumpkin.

I took his silence as confirmation. "How could you?" I asked, striding toward the door. He rushed past me and leaned his weight against it, speaking over my shoulder. "I admit. I wrote Lumpkin, asking that Treaty Party members' homes remain in their care for the time being. Lumpkin has no use for Ross' obstinance. While I said nothing of their house, Lumpkin's actions do send an effective message."

I looked at him as if I'd never seen the man I married before today, haughty, arrogant, manipulative, and uncaring. I tried to pull the door open, but he kept me from leaving.

"Herman can wait," he said. "When I returned from Washington, you said Quatie was like your sister. You agreed to end your friendship. You understood why she couldn't know Treaty Party business."

I turned around, caged on one side by his arm. I said, "No. You asked me to, and I didn't agree." He removed his hand from the wood and gathered both behind his back. Shaking his head, he walked away and leaned with both hands on his desk.

I advanced. "Who is Elizabeth Milligan?"

He looked at me over his shoulder, squinting with confusion. He mumbled, "She's the charming daughter of some of our supporters in Washington. When there, we often dine at their house."

"Why have you never spoken of her? Quatie seems to think something is going on between her and Ross. Or her and you. She offered no more information, and I didn't ask, afraid to hear what she might say. Are you and Ross fighting for Miss Milligan's attention? No doubt the family is wealthy. Who's courting her, you or Ross?"

"Just because I never told you about her doesn't mean I lied. Do you doubt my faithfulness? Ross is twice her age."

Yellow Bird's Song

I said, "Tells me nothing. A guilty man's lie of omission."

"And you believe Quatie's suspicion over the word of your husband? I've not lied to you. Elizabeth is plain and unassuming but dignified. She's an artist and paints portraits, natural copies. She deserves a first-rate husband, not a man like Ross."[4]

"Is that all you can think about? How Ross wouldn't appreciate her? That he's too old for her? Is she the reason you spent seven months in Washington? Left me here to raise our children and run this farm? I know nothing of the world unless you tell me, or I read it in newspapers."

"Most of what they say are lies."

"That isn't the point. I didn't marry you to live alone!"

"You weren't alone, were you? Arch was here!"

"He did come, checked on us, and prayed for you!"

"I didn't marry you to be betrayed! You assured me you wouldn't see Quatie anymore but did so. You talk about lies of omission? They must only teach white children how to do that. Red children never learn. This is the reason we must have every negotiation in writing. So no one can deny what's said."

"Don't be ridiculous. I knew you didn't want me to see her, but don't accuse me of lying because you are mad at Ross."

We locked our eyes, our faces inches apart. I'd only seen him so angry one other time—in the carriage after we married—when Samuel shot at us as we escaped Cornwall's mob. He said, "Have you been feeding Quatie information all this time?"

"How dare you!" I raised my hand to slap him. He grabbed my wrist. "I told her nothing of your business."

"When Ross and I argued on the street, he threatened to tell the guard I killed the men who hurt you. He knew I was going to run against him for chief and suspended elections. He shut down Elias' press so no voting men could hear the Treaty Party's perspective. How could he have known all of that? Father, Elias, or Stand wouldn't tell Ross. Sarah, how could Ross know?"

He looked at his hand on my arm and let go. I didn't turn from him. "Are you accusing me of spying for Quatie?"

His retort was quick. "Should I? What did you tell her? Did you take Cass' letter and give it to her when no one knew where you'd gone?"

Herman's cries became wails upstairs.

"How could I, if I didn't know any such letter existed until fifteen minutes ago?"

His face was confused, and then he turned adamant, believing the story he'd built in his mind. No denial could convince him otherwise. I turned away from his suspicion and made for the door.

His words squeezed my heart. "If I can't trust you, if I can't do treaty business here, I can't stay. My people need me now." His face went from affliction to agony, as if his words were as unbelievable for him to say as they were for me to hear.

"They've never stopped needing you. Not for one moment in our lives. If I can't trust you, I don't want you here. We've proven we can run this farm without you. Go back to Washington for Ross' leftovers at the Milligans'."

Silence.

Honey screamed from the kitchen. We hurried from the study and across the breezeway.

Peter's blood seeped through his hand, dripping to the floor. He stumbled to a chair. Honey grabbed a dishcloth to hold against his wounds.

Gasping for breath, Peter hunched over. "A Ross man at Lavender's store attacked your friend, Mister Fields. Called him a traitor. Why would he do that?" Peter shook his head and continued, "Man said he would die before giving up his land. Fields said it might be sooner rather than later if he didn't agree to a treaty. They argued. Man said Ross would never let that happen. He threatened Fields with the Blood Law. Tipped crates above your friend's head and knocked the man senseless. Fields shook it off and tripped the man. They started wrestlin' right there on the store floor. But, when the man pulled out a knife, I stepped between him and Fields. Nearly cut us both in two."[5]

Honey examined the wound. She said, "I'll sew you up. Yous guts still where they s'pose to be." She replaced her hand with his, keeping the cloth in place. "Hold tight. I'm goin' to get my needle and thread." Honey brushed past John to go to the parlor.

I didn't think before I spoke. "Can't you see what you're doing? What you've done? People are dying."

John dropped the papers in his hands to the floor. He walked backward several steps, glaring at me. With distrust in his scowl, he turned down the hall and opened the front door. When he left, sunlight poured in.

The rest of my week passed with lies.

While Honey and I tended to Peter, John didn't come home that Friday night.

On Saturday, Laughing Water and Will asked whether they could clear another field for cotton. I lied. "John said he hoped you two would do so.

Yellow Bird's Song

Thank you."

I stared out the chapel's windows during services. Harriet led the congregation in hymns. After, Elias said, "Tell my cousin to come see me. We have pressing matters to discuss."

I said, "I'll give him your message as soon as we get home."

On Monday, I washed the children, put their night clothes on, and tucked them in bed. I had not the imagination to invent a story. The truth hidden from them was too fictional to believe.

On Tuesday, Walking Stick brought firewood and asked where John had gone. I said, "On an unexpected journey."

On Wednesday, from his sickbed, Peter asked how John was handling the horses. I told him, "Will and Laughing Water are sure they're fed and cared for. John is at his father's house."

On Thursday, I told Clarinda, "Papa told me how sorry he was to miss your lesson. But, of course, he will bring you back a surprise." He always had before.

On Friday, I took the wagon to pick up Rollin from school. I answered his repeated questions with an apology. "No one knew Papa would have to leave so unexpectedly. I'm sorry he didn't ride with you."

On Saturday, Marz, Sunflower, and I cut flowers. Marz asked whether Quatie would visit soon. I said, "With Chief Ross traveling from Washington, she can't leave home now."

An entire week passed with no word. That night, with a candle in tow, I returned to John's study and made stacks of the disarrayed papers.

When I passed the window, I stopped tidying to listen to every night sound. But the moon's watch remained taciturn, stuck in its phase. With each bend and stretch, I added to the stack, feeling as though someone held me under deep water. I held my breath, kicked toward the surface, but all the while, I knew the distance too great to gasp.

If John came home, what would I say? Apologize, despite having done nothing wrong? Keep the peace? Become my mother, blindly mimicking whatever my husband allowed me to hear? Would he lock all the doors because he didn't trust me? The silence between us would be unbearable. I could never leave home without ensuring his suspicion.

Would he return to Washington and speak of his troubles to the demure Miss Milligan? She'd comfort him while I sat in the parlor sewing regret until my fingers bled.

I'd never taken his letter. I'd never betrayed him by telling anyone his plans. My integrity was worth more than that kind of life. Ironically, he'd taught me the lesson.

From the corner of my eye, candlelight flickered on the brass buckles of John's traveling trunk. It was weather-beaten, far more worn than when he first used it to travel to Cornwall. I lifted its cover. It was empty.

I dragged it out of the room by the handle on its end. Honey heard me and came from her room with a candle. She set her light on the windowsill and said, "What in the world are you doin' with that thing this late?"

"I'm moving John's trunk to the porch. He hasn't returned since we argued. He's going to need it."

"I heard yous two fussin'. Didn't think it was my place to ask."

"Then don't. Just help me." She grabbed the other end, so it wouldn't scratch the floor. We waddled together down the hall and placed it just inside the front door.

Her shock was plain. She refused to pick up the other end again. "Where is he?" She could barely form the words.

"Probably at Major's." I opened the door, dragged it outside, and opened the lid. Honey followed me down the hall when I returned to his study.

She watched, open-mouthed, when I pulled the spines of three heavy law books from the top shelf, stacking them in my arms.

She said, "No, Sarah. Don't do this." When I passed her, she said, "He doesn't know you're having another baby, does he?"

That stopped me. Under my breath, I said, "He'd have to come home for me to tell him." I wondered, "H-how did you know?"

"You whisper to yourself when you're growin' a baby. I seen you do it when we rolled the dough yesterday." She tried to take the books from my arms. "He'll come home."

"No," I said and gripped them tighter.

It took me ten trips before I dropped the last heavy volume inside. What stores of strength I'd saved last winter were empty. The act conquered me. So numb, I couldn't cry. I closed the lid. "Before we married, John told me when a Cherokee wife knew trust between her and her husband was gone, she refused him by stacking his weapons on the porch."

CHAPTER 29: UNSANCTIONED INTEGRITY
John Ridge
Major Ridge's Plantation and Red Clay Council Grounds
Summer and Fall 1833

I thought it would be Father knocking on the apartment door so late in the evening. But it wasn't him. Mother barely gave me time to open the door before she walked in and turned around next to the stone hearth. She crossed her arms and scowled.

I had nothing to say, so I returned to my desk. Time was short. I needed to complete my remarks for council. I had to remember how Cass countered Ross' lies from that stolen letter.

Mother followed with little patience for my delay. She adopted the threatening tone all sons know. *"Skahtlelohskee, put down that quill and listen to me. Let go of whatever you and Sarah disagreed over and go back to being a father and a husband."*

Returning home now was not a possibility. I shook my head. *"Sarah no longer trusts me, Mother. Her actions have made it impossible for me to trust her."*

When I tried to finish writing my sentence, Mother took the quill from my hand and broke it in two. She spat on the floor. *"Does she have reason? Did Sarah say that? Or is that what you want? It is a choice. You are away enough."*

I rubbed my face and passed my hand through my hair. *"We haven't spoken in months. I can't forgive what Sarah did. I can't trust her. Besides, she's put me out."*

Mother said, *"She did nothing of the kind."*

I kicked open my trunk and showed her its contents.

Mother brushed away my dramatics. *"I've done the same to your father many times. Only his tools have changed over the years. When I sat with her today, I respected your wishes and said nothing of your whereabouts. Although, because of Sarah's excuses for your absence, I can't bring my grandchildren here. They'll find you. Sarah told them you were in Washington."*

"I should be." But I wasn't fooling anyone with my bravado. I thought of Sarah and the children. All my work done was on their behalf. I asked Mother, *"Are they well?"*

"Herman is crawling and into everything. Susan is beautiful. She carries a stuffed lamb wherever she goes. It is filthy. Rollin and Clarinda are close. They write together more often than using signs. Honey hovers

over Sarah, and Peter is one step behind them both."

I hesitated before saying, *"Is she well?"*

"Physically, yes, but very tired. I warned her about going to town so often."

I asked, *"Why is she going to town? It's dangerous."*

"She feeds mothers and children. Every kernel she can spare. Walking Stick loads the wagon, and she drives it to the mill. She, Sophie Sawyer, and Harriet Boudinot have passed out sacks of cornmeal for a month."

I held my head in my hands, obstinate. *"She knows where to find me. There is only one place I would go."* I picked up the sharpened end of the quill and dipped it in ink. *"Our personal matters are of little importance. Our people's cause is more pressing. Sarah knows how desperate we are. And she knows what she's done. Feeding people is a sign of her guilt."*

Mother said, *"Leaving the mother of your children! And with her expecting, no less. We raised you to be a better man. More responsible."*

"I didn't know." That news should have broken me, but all I thought about was how she'd betrayed me again by keeping such a secret to herself.

"Skahtlelohskee, stop writing this minute and turn around." I did as she commanded, but I wouldn't look at her face. Finally, Mother said, *"Who are you? What has Sarah done? Tell me."*

I couldn't repeat it. *"Ask Father,"* I said, *"Her colors have turned. She's disloyal. Her priorities have changed."*

"From what you've shown me in these last months, yours have changed. By throwing yourself into saving our people, you've lost what you loved. You barely sleep. Eat nothing. You're weak. All skin and bones. Miserable. How will you lead our people if your heart is so clouded? You'll lose the right words when it matters most because you can't see clearly."

I didn't engage her further. I said, *"I have work to do, Mother."*

She huffed, insulted. And so, I added another woman to the list of people who wouldn't talk to me. She walked to the door. *"Your child arrives in November."*

I returned to my notes but found them too blurry to continue.

When our horses navigated the rolling hills near Chickamauga, close to Tennessee's boundary line, I told Father, *"Don't tell me to keep my voice under control."*

"If you force your tongue, they may kill us before we reach home. Our

opponents know which direction we travel."

"If I remain too quiet, we convince no one. When Jackson surveys the land promised us in the West, if he speaks the truth, it might change the minds of those undecided."

Father said, *"Asking for the survey was wise, despite bypassing Ross' permission. He would never have allowed it, and we need that information. Your letter to Jackson was more successful than you thought. He views you as an ally. Although I believe I'll request a surveying party of my own. Choose land for our family."*

"Ross won't see it that way."

Under the open-air meeting house, the council fire separated two distinct factions. Ross' nationalist numbers were large, crowding around him and extending down the hill where the creek whispered rumors over its rocks. Father stood behind me, guarding the voices of the minority. Ridge, Boudinot, Walker, Fields, Starr, and Vann. Only a few councilmen from the eight districts remained seated on the rudely constructed benches, holding down the neutral middle.

I bit my tongue when Ross gave his state of our nation. Innuendo and insults treated us like a splinter, a slivered annoyance too deep under his skin to ignore.

Father attempted to build a bridge over the fire's divide. *"The sentiments of the majority should prevail, and whatever measure is adopted by the majority for the public good, the duty of the minority should be to yield and unite in support of the measure."*[1]

Ross answered Father's concession by appointing himself head of another delegation.

I could remain quiet no longer. "As president of the National Council, I will draft the terms under which you are to proceed. Then, with wisdom and integrity, we can confide to carry the subject of our difficulties before the legislative branch of the general government, and if possible, draw from it a favorable resolution."[2] Checks and balances.

Before the council's close, Ross laid a new power of attorney on the table, asking both legislative branch members to sign.

Astounded at Ross' audacity, I said, "Doing so will lead the Americans to believe your delegation has all authority to treat."

Ross said, "Jackson will not meet with me otherwise."

I didn't sign. My father wouldn't sign. Stand and Elias refused to sign. Vann, Walker, Fields, and Starr too turned their backs on the Chief.

In retaliation, our band of dissenters enrolled for emigration. I couldn't keep my family bound to this ground and wager their safety against the certainty of Ross' duplicity.

Heather Miller

On the dark ride home, an unexpected addition interrupted our quiet party. We pulled the reins, leading the horses toward the boarding trees and into the shadows. Vann drew and cocked his pistol. But Elias held his hand up. He said, *"Wait. Let the man show his face in the moonlight."*

Father immediately recognized Andrew Ross, brother to our chief. Father said, *"Best not sneak up behind us. Come into the light to speak."*

Then Father leaned over to me and whispered, *"What could he want?"*

The man held his arms free of his sides. "I am unarmed," Andrew shouted in English. "You have every right to distrust me."

He came into the light, a portly man, as short as Ross was, with dark hair combed over and tucked behind his ears. He'd faithfully served on the Cherokee Supreme Court, which gave him the experience to see both sides of any argument. Father said, *"John, tell him how dangerous the roads have become."*

Before I could, Andrew spoke up. "I followed to tell you that your party should send a delegation to watch the delegation in Washington. Major Ridge, if my brother knows you stand directly behind him, he'll be less likely to anger those who may be the Cherokee's salvation. Despite my blood connections, I stand—"

I held my hand to stop Andrew's promise, hoping to understand his motivation further. "Why turn against your family?"

Andrew rode parallel to our party and took a deep breath before answering. "Inevitable question, is it not? My mother. She believed that trust offered a man by his fellows is how one measures his worth. My brothers see the world for what they can gain from it, not what they return to it. They build generational wealth from the suffering of their ancestors. They'd make our canny Scottish father proud."

Satisfied with his answer, Elias reached forward first to shake Andrew's hand. Andrew's promise fostered our solidarity anew.

I said, "Andrew's point is well made. Ross has more authority to treat than we do."

Vann adjusted the reins in his hand and said, "But even a pawn can check the king."

Elias asked, "Could we go to Washington in the name of those who have emigrated? The old settlers? Those who've already been forced to leave?"

With little need for debate, my compatriots volunteered.

With this surprising advice from an unlikely source, we had a new ally.

Ross would feel the pressure of Jackson's frontal assault, while the opposing king, bishops, knights, and Andrew, a lone pawn, attacked from the rear.

I said, "Then it is decided. You go, and I will stay behind and correspond with Lumpkin, in the name of the Treaty Party."

While the emigration delegation spent the summer in Washington, it was the end of September before I addressed the Governor again. I wrote, "It is dreadful to reflect on—the amount of blood which has been shed—by savagery on those who had only exercised their right of opinion. Nevertheless, we must prepare for the work as good generals in times of war. Keep what we have and gain the balance."[3] I signed my name to the missive when another knock came from the apartment door. I huffed at the disturbance, suffering from constant interruptions here more than at home, even with the children running through the halls.

When I opened it, I knew how mentally unprepared I was.

Sarah's back greeted me. She turned around but didn't look at me directly. Instead, she looked at her hands. Her maroon dress was one I'd not seen before. Blousing sleeves tapered at her elbows and tightened down her forearms to her wrists. The bodice's fabric gathered over her shoulders in tiny pleats and crossed at a belted full skirt covering the rise in her womb. A blind man could have seen how her pale skin glowed, and the color in her eyes seemed brighter because of it. Her hair gathered in a crocheted snood at the base of her neck. How could I have forgotten how stunning she was? Rare indeed.

Her presence threw me off balance. So much so that I limped backward, putting weight on my good hip. Air crackled between us. She took a deep breath and, without speaking, extended a letter from her gloved hand. With a glance, I recognized the presidential seal and the hand of the man who'd written it.

She said, "An official messenger delivered it to Running Waters. I brought it as soon as he left. It must be important." She curtsied and said, "I'll leave you to it, then."

What could have happened with the delegation that Jackson felt the need to tell me personally? That he took pains to have a message delivered privately, absent the eyes of the postmaster. The letter burned a hole through my hand. But instead of opening it, I said, "Don't go. I'll read it later," and opened the door further for her to enter. "Come in? Talk to me?"

She looked behind herself, delaying a decision, but nodded, accepting my request. She only took two steps inside the door. When I reached around her to shut it, I smelled her: a mix of milk and soap, sheep's lanolin, and underneath that, the unmistakable hint of rose petals.

In my nervousness, I passed the letter from one hand to another. Finally, I resigned to hold the corner in one hand and grip the other wrist behind my back.

Everything that came to my mind sounded ridiculous.

"Mother told me you've been feeding the people. I cannot offer enough thanks. It is the right thing to do, although dangerous."

She walked toward the window at the corner of the parlor.

"I remember this view," she said. "Best in the fall when the apple limbs light with orange and highlight the maple's scarlet leaves."

Perhaps she didn't know what to say either. Instead of accepting my gratitude, she resorted to talking about fall colors. I didn't want to speak of trees.

If Mother hadn't told me she was with child, seeing her from the back, I wouldn't have known. She carried the child entirely in the front. Her tapered waist didn't reveal her secret.

I asked, "How are you? And the child?"

"Fine."

Not a genuine answer. With her before me, I was anything but fine.

She shook her head in refusal when I gestured for her to sit. "I can't stay long."

I took a step toward her. "The children?"

She retreated. "Rollin can sign his name in script. His handwriting is straight up and down. He rides his pony to New Echota to Sophie's school with Walking Stick or Peter. I won't send him alone."

"Yet you make the journey alone."

She shrugged her shoulders.

"Peter is fully recovered, then?"

"Yes." She turned back toward the window. From her shutter, I knew she'd retrieved the memory of the day I left. She asked, "Are you well?"

"As well as I deserve."

Her response was a nod, followed by lasting silence.

She finally turned around. "It has been months. I cannot lie to the children for much longer. They think you are in Washington. They expect their papa to be home soon and talk of nothing else. It is difficult for me to hear."

"I wish to see them. Very much."

"Come when the new child arrives, nursing two will be all I'll have

Yellow Bird's Song

time to do."

"You remembered what I said. About putting my tools outside." In my imagination, I smelled the stale fireplace from my sick room in Cornwall when we wrote, "Come with me, my white girl fair…" It was where we'd talked of broken marriages, something neither of us ever expected to happen.

"I've not forgotten anything you've said."

That was true, both good and bad. Her honesty forced me to sit in the armchair. Then, my thoughts traveled to our beginnings in this very room. We looked at one another for the first time since she arrived. "You stood there," I pointed, "in that same spot when we argued about Honey, and I found you alone in the strawberry field."

She whispered, shaking her head, "That night, I knew I could never be all you expected."

I countered her self-deprecating thought. "I never expected more of you than who you've always been."

"No wife could live up to your imagination: the good wife created in your perfect mind. To do so, I'd have to be four different versions of myself." She joined her hands in front of her. "It does no good to look behind us." She started toward the door and said, "Mother will tell you when the child is born."

I couldn't let her go, and I couldn't make her stay. I blocked her exit and touched her hand. "Will you allow me to help you when your time comes?"

She pulled her hand away. "No," she said firmly. "Your mother will tell you all you need to know." She made a fist and protected it, wrapped in the other. Then, she said, "Please. Do as I ask."

"Nothing has changed then—" At that moment, I didn't know whether to end the sentence with a question mark or a period.

"Running Waters will not be home for long."

"No, but for now, I'll keep it safe for you and the children."

She spoke just as fast. "What you promise is impossible, and not what you fight for."

Her palpable doubt had me speaking in circles.

She said, "When you came home from Washington and told me you'd changed your mind, that the Cherokee must leave and start over in the West, you gave me no time. You'd had months to consider such a possibility. Planned how it might happen. You told me not to be afraid. You expected me to turn around and swear I'd have no misgivings about leaving what our family built at Running Waters. That I cannot do. And now, alone, I have no choice."

"You've left me no choice but to remain away. Ross cannot know our plans. If he does, the Treaty Party can never remain one step ahead of his next scheme."

She scoffed. "A step ahead. Yes, I see. Not working at home with me there. That is what you meant. Quatie is in Red Clay. John, she isn't here. Regardless, I've never spoken to her about your business, then or now. I never touched the letter you accused me of taking. I do not know who told Ross of your plans to run for chief, but it wasn't me. Besides, the Treaty Party will never stay a step ahead if the people you hope to convince are starving. They can't think about tomorrow or next year when they don't know where their next meal is coming from."

She walked around the room one last time, shoes tapping over the floor. She said, "For years, I sat idly by in this room while you rode hundreds of miles away to protect your people. Not only them, but the Creeks. Yet, you haven't crossed six miles in these last months. Your time to tell me what I can and cannot do has passed."

My shame startled me. I could only retaliate against its assault with a whisper. "You made your desire abundantly clear when you put my books on the porch."

She raised her voice. "No. You made them abundantly clear when you accused me of betraying you."

Sarah walked to the door and turned the knob. She lifted her shoulders and raised her head. She spoke with her back to me. "You told me once the only way to find my voice was to use it." She took a deep breath and pushed open the door. The afternoon sun spilled across the floor. She left it open and stepped outside. "I hope you've heard me because I do not plan on repeating myself."

My heart stopped beating and froze, feet unable to move.

From the Office of the President of the United States -August 1833
    Dear Sir,
    Your chief's delegation met with Secretary Cass. Their first request was that partial land be sold to the government and that your people remain on the residual.[4]
    On my order, Cass refused.
    In another cessation attempt, the delegation offered that those who stayed should revoke their Cherokee citizenship.[5]
    On my order, Cass refused.
    So, Jackson had instructed Cass not to compromise. And Ross'

Yellow Bird's Song

continued attempts to rejuvenate the Treaty of 1819 continued to fail. It might have worked years ago but wouldn't now.

Jackson aimed to remove us entirely, and by doing so, hoped to save the lives and maintain the culture of the Cherokee's noble people. Ironically, Yoholo and I negotiated a similar bargain for the Creeks in '25. But then, as now, such an improbable solution would falter. Hindsight shrunk the list of alternatives.

I returned my attention to Jackson's letter.

It has been my delight this week to see so many old friends. I wish you had joined them. Major Ridge disputes Ross' negotiations on behalf of the entire nation. Your father replied how, under those terms, your people would be "perpetually made drunk by the whites, cheated, oppressed, reduced to beggary, and become miserable outcasts, as the Cherokee body dwindled to nothing."[6] As I told you, these are Ross' schemes, and the results are as I expected.

Others in the emigration delegation know little of negotiation. While I'm not disagreeable to an agreement with a minority, I need to deal with more sophisticated agents. Andrew Ross is hell-bent on signing before returning home. I sent him to negotiate with Eaton, knowing that man's tenacity through and through.[7]

I will say your friend Jack Walker has a future in politics. He, your father, and David Vann agreed not to sign any treaty. Not one solely negotiated by Ross or by his ironic opposition, his brother, Andrew. In all truthfulness, as your father said, neither party has the power to treat on behalf of the entire nation. Ross' stubborn desperation opposes your father's unsanctioned integrity.

My prayer is that both the eagle's strength and its liberty find us in peaceful compromise.

I remain a loyal friend to you and your people.

Gen. A. Jackson

After reading, I took a deep breath, smelling Sarah's lingering presence as clearly as if she had read the epistle over my shoulder. I looked back at the seal on the envelope. It had remained unopened until I slid my finger under the wax. If Sarah had wanted to betray me, this letter would have adequately done so. She didn't take it to Quatie. Instead, she brought it to me straight away, unopened.

I recited Jackson's last sentence again. Was I like Ross, in such "stubborn desperation," so eager to defeat the enemy? While Cass' letter remained missing, should I consider that there was another reason for its disappearance? No evidence existed of Sarah's crime. My anger and suspicion accused her. Could I stare at my reflection in the river and recognize no fault?

Sarah maintained her innocence. Her "unsanctioned integrity," noble and true, had no power to move me. Like her father's dismissals, she accepted my shun. Another abandonment from another man who promised to love her most. She didn't beg for forgiveness. She couldn't find peace, nor could she wage war. So, she waited.

And I delayed too long. I looked away from Jackson's letter. Blame and shame were mine alone.

Oh God, Great Creator, what had I done?

CHAPTER 30: GOLDEN GATE
Rollin Ridge
San Francisco and Sacramento, California
September 1854

Dressed in my best suit, I stood in the dying light beside San Francisco Bay for the second day in a row. Sun-soaked faces of dock workers rowed boats full of pale passengers from the newly arrived steamer, *The Star of the West*. Each small dingy clumped beside ten others, moving through the shallows en masse, heavy with the weight of new Californians or stacked deep with mail bags sent from Atlantic to Pacific.

Many newcomers passed through this "golden gate," as it was called, eager to buy mules, load them heavy with sluice boxes, and head north. I'd read many an eastern paper declaring the locations from the latest gold rush; however, with the sixty days of travel from here to the New England states, too many men arrived, ready to pound through barren mountainsides and pan streams already stripped of their shining ore.

Passengers unloaded, and crews rowed back for another run. I waited on a bench under a tree and, in its shade, studied, for the millionth time, Lizzie's portrait sent last December. Her image returned my stare. Her eyes had exchanged their brightness for tin-type gray. Frozen still, she held no smile.

Mother's last letter said Lizzie planned to travel by coach with a local Fayetteville merchant, a friend of my in-laws, the Wilsons. From Chicago, she'd take a train to New York. After the second leg of her journey, my brave woman boarded a steamer and set sail through Vanderbilt's Nicaraguan route to San Francisco. To get to the other side of the country, one must travel halfway around the globe. Steamer travel remained the safest and fastest means, albeit expensive. How she managed the expense to travel so far, she didn't say. But having experienced the alternative route, the cost was a necessity for her safety.

Lizzie left our daughter with Mother. In her last letter, she told me Wacooli had taken my place and worked in the Missouri fields. Brother Herman had a farm to tend to but said living alone was too sad, so he spent most nights at Mama's. It was probably because he'd rather eat her cooking than burnt cornmeal from his own skillet. Aeneas remained at home because he couldn't decide what he wanted to do. Mama said he should learn medicine and do good. However, if Aeneas chose that road, he'd die a poor man. But, if he practiced law like my brother, Andrew Jackson Ridge, he'd do less good but earn a substantial living. My youngest sister, Flora, studied at the Women's Seminary under Sophie Sawyer. Mother didn't mention Susan's family or my favorite sibling, Clarinda. She and Skili lived in a cabin in the Ozarks, among the forest's medicinal plants. I wanted to inquire about each in my next correspondence. But I waited to write, hoping to deliver good news that Lizzie arrived in San Francisco, no worse for wear.

When I thought of Lizzie's risk, I vacillated from anger at her for endangering herself to giddiness, anticipating holding her again. Lizzie's initiative to come to me during my "illness," reassured me no other man had taken my place. I couldn't stop her, could say nothing if she'd already left. Knowing Lizzie as I did, she deferred my warnings by having Mother tell me of her plans. I could only pray for her safe passage and hope she'd met no single men traveling alone with unrighteous intentions.

Life had offered me few charms since I'd left her behind.[1] Under Joaquín's red canyons and bluffs, Lizzie appeared in my nightmares. Dressed in her shift, she left my side and walked away, never looking back. If a man were to believe his dreams, Lizzie had turned from me, despite my many unconscious calls for her return. I sat by his campfire for weeks, met his beloved Rosita, and listened to the tales of his quest to revive his starving people. I empathized. Had I stayed in Arkansas, I would have become the same duplicitous man, both vigilante and saint, and died in the same manner, trapped by the guns of Ross' henchmen.

It wasn't but a few weeks after I returned to civilization before Captain Love ambushed and killed Joaquín. Afterward, the acid revived the ulcerous pains in my stomach, seeing the noble bandolero's head in a jar paraded across the state as if he were a carnival showpiece. After seeing such horror, I ended my novel with an image of Rosita, Murieta's grieving widow. "Alas, how happy might she have been had man never learned to wrong his fellow man."[2] I couldn't help but imagine Lizzie's heart facing Rosita's grief.

Salty air blew in my face when I looked across the bay to the ship, smoke still barreling from its stacks. The last tiny figures moved down the long plank and boarded dingy boats. Several flouncing dresses blew in the breeze, seated beside men in top hats. The distance remained too great for me to discern any recognizable face. One woman wore silver taffeta, a sheen against the blinding sunlight. Another dressed in homespun indigo blue, the same color as the seas they'd crossed. One tall woman wore mixed shades of brown, like a lucky copper penny found along the road. Once seated, the copper woman raised a parasol above her head when the afternoon's daylight slipped behind the mountainside.

I timed my stroll to the oars' pacing, a consistent plunge and pull by rolled, shirt-sleeved arms. My hand traveled along the smooth wooden rail when the last unloading passengers steadied themselves on the dock rail. Finally, after what must have been an unsteady trip around the continent, they were mere steps from California's dry land.

The woman dressed in plaids of tarnished copper reached for the dock worker's hand and turned her ribboned bonnet upward to step from the boat. All the saliva in my mouth turned dry. Everything I'd planned to say became an arid paste on my tongue. Lizzie's plaid held every shade of soil I'd ever seen, russet brown, thin black stripes against golden seams, all lined with copper patina, the same color of her eyes.

"Excuse me," I said, weaving through idling travelers, moving one man from my way with my hands on his arms. I reached the end of the plank when the ferryman grabbed her gloved hand, and she stepped off the boat. She took a steadying breath, gathered the folds of her skirt, and took the last step.

Would she recognize the man I'd become? Bearded, with hair reaching my shoulders? Thin? But perhaps less mercurial than when we last parted.

As more travelers took charge of their belongings, and porters heaved trunks on their shoulders, the space between us opened. I made my way behind her and cleared my throat. Then, as close to her ear as I dared speak, I said, "Ma'am, are you in need of assistance?"

She didn't turn toward my voice, but stilled and closed her eyes. My voice touched her when my hands hadn't.

Lizzie said, "I am but a stranger in a strange land, too calm to weep, too sad to smile."[3] She recited the first lines of my poem, written as I ached for her near the Sacramento River.

I said,
"The vows of love, its smiles and tears,
Hang o'er this harp of broken strings.
It speaks amidst her blushing fears
The beauteous one before me stands!"[4]

Very aware of the presence of our talkative carriage driver, we headed the last leg of the journey, through the square blocks of Sacramento to the Tremont House on Second Avenue, where I rented a room. Time grew dark.

Our carriage driver's complaints were sufficient to give any aging or careworn man fodder for weeks. He'd recited them all: his popping knees, flat feet, back pain, heart palpitations, a cough that wouldn't end. I wondered whether we'd make it home without him keeling over. I paid him little mind, other than the occasional acknowledgment of his sorrows, thinking of nothing but the fresh smell of her. I counted every second until I could close the door to cold years apart, and in illusive privacy, touch her warmth again.

By now, Lizzie was aware that my illness, the one that drove her to travel so many miles, was more in my mind than in my gut.

She asked, "Did you see a doctor, or are you like most men?"

"Guilty," I said. "My constitution is much stronger now than when I last wrote."

Lizzie looked at the landscape. "I read your book," she said. "Heard your voice from every page. It surprised me to find it on a merchant's shelf in New Orleans with another author's name." She retrieved the copy from her drawstring handbag and handed it to me.

"So many have stolen and published parts of my story, putting their names where mine should be. I expected to make a great deal of money. But after selling seven thousand copies, the publisher put the money in his pockets, and fled, busted up, teetotally smashed, and left me, and a hundred others, to whistle for our money!"[5]

She didn't say much more when she put the copy back in her bag. When she pulled the strings closed, I watched her do so, feeling a similar tightness in my chest.

Lizzie rested her head on my shoulder and looped her hand through my arm. She said, "Then you've earned a fortune they will never have: a clear conscience."

I looked at her over my shoulder and heaved a sigh. "You know me better. My conscience is molasses."

The carriage driver hit a pothole and jostled us apart. Lizzie said, nearly inaudible, "Once, I did. Know you better."

Before I could reassure her, our ailing driver pulled the reins and stopped the rig. Lizzie pulled her arm from mine. I immediately felt its absence, having spent the last hours wrapped like a cord. I watched her face as she took in the humble clapboard house with its lit front room and long front porch, complete with chained swing.

I said, "Let me help the driver with your trunk."

She followed us as we carried it inside, past Mrs. Tremont knitting in the parlor.

Mrs. Tremont, a widow in her sixtieth year, didn't look up from the twists of yarn around her fingers. "Mister Ridge, I hope you've dined elsewhere. I've already cleaned up supper for the night."

"We did." I made hasty introductions, which made the gossipy Mrs.

Yellow Bird's Song

Tremont rise in full attention.

"Your wife?" Mrs. Tremont remarked with a gasp. "But—" She closed her mouth and said, "I had no idea."

"She just arrived."

Kissing Lizzie's cheek, I whispered, "Darlin', you are my secret."

After dropping her trunk in the darkness of my bedroom, I followed the driver back through the still parlor to retake Lizzie's hand and rescue her from Mistress Tremont's polite interrogation.

I pulled Lizzie through the bedroom doorway and, turning around, closed it, and caged her with my forearms. I took her lips with the hurry and passion of a deserted man dying of thirst, crawling toward what he thought was water.

We couldn't see one another, so I listened my way to her skin. I hastily undid the tie of her bonnet and tossed it into the chair beside the door. She tasted like sugared meringue. Her lips responded to me as they always had, a weighty memory triggering my body and mind.

"Why am I your secret?" she asked.

I traced kisses down her neck. With shallow breaths, she pulled the lapels of my coat over my shoulders. I said, "So I can keep you all to myself." I shook it free, letting it fall beside my feet.

Absent vision, she found no trouble unlacing my tie. She threw it behind me, returning her arms to my shoulders and gripping my hair. She took a breath. "Secret keepers—you and your mother both." She unbuttoned my waistcoat, and I shrugged it off.

I pulled my shirt over my head, needing to feel her breasts against my chest. "Last person I want to think about right now." My hands reached and fumbled with the hooks of her dress, distracted by the sound of her suckling my lower lip.

She only let it go long enough to say, "Easy to lose track when keeping so many."

"You see me." I unhooked the last eye. She shuffled her arms, so I could pull the bodice and her chemise over her shoulders and free her arms. Once her bodice wafted to the ground, she gathered my cheek to her breasts. I heard the pound of her heart.

Her chest rose with quickening breaths. She felt her way, gathering my face in her hands to reunite our lips. "No, I haven't, for years. You haven't asked how I afforded to find you."

My hands undid the endless ties of her skirts. One billowed to the ground, followed by another, and another. Then, I knelt before her to untie her shoes.

She followed my movements with her hands on my head. I said, "Then

302

Heather Miller

you have a secret of your own... Raise the other." She kicked one heeled shoe free, and balancing on the other foot, allowed me to pull away the second. "What did it cost you, three hundred?" The other shoe clapped against the floor.

I slid my hands behind her calves, behind her knees, and slid her stockings down. I continued trailing my hands behind the taut muscles of her thighs, across her buttocks until I reached the bones of her hips and let the last undergarment fall down her legs.

She slid her hands from my hair down my jaw to raise my head. "When I left Arkansas, I had four hundred hidden in my handbag. There's five hundred more in the Bank of America in your name. There's enough for me to go back."

How could she ever think...? I lifted her, grabbing her thin waist, raising her to my height. Then, with her taste still on my lips, I said, "Answer enough for you?"

"Show me, then, all you've kept hidden." She traced the lines of my belt and freed the buckle. When she didn't hear it fall, she knelt in front of me and undid the ties of the bowie knife strapped to my thigh. She raised and whimpered in my ear before taking the lobe in her teeth. She said, "It's no secret. I hate that knife."

My pants thudded to the floor.

I stepped free of the pile and used both hands to pull my boots off. "No secret either that what money I sent home didn't come close to that amount." Barefoot, I swept away the pile of clothes and reached for her. "Right now, I don't care how much it cost for you to come to me."

She mumbled, "Ross finally released your father's portion of the treaty money." She shocked me, and I stepped back, hearing her disembodied words. "You and your mother's secrets cost me nearly everything."

I needed to touch her, to find her.

But her back hit the door. "For five years, Rollin, I grieved your loss. In my heart, and in this body, I felt the same agony as if you had died, unable to share my pain with anyone. It wasn't true. Your letters kept coming, confirming you were alive."

I tried to approach her again, hoping to kiss such honesty away. She only allowed me to stand in front of her in the dark, listening to her voice swell.

She said, "I've breathed without you for too long, living a separate life. I won't live any longer without love. God knows I want you, but this love cannot live without trust."

She took my hands, so I could feel her callouses. She confessed, "I've counted our days apart, like so many seeds of wheat chaff."

Yellow Bird's Song

She let me bring the rough edges of her fingers to my lips. "All alone, I've raised our child. Her joy is mine. Her smiles look like yours."

I knelt at her feet and touched my lips to her womb.

"I've cried enough tears, slipping over steep rocks made slippery and smooth by pools I filled myself."

Her words brought tears to my eyes when I raised and kissed hers.

But after, my every attempt at intimacy met with another turn, a withdrawal.

"Yes," she said, her voice rising in anger. "I found the underworld and paid the ferryman enough. You've written letter after letter to me about your pain. You've inflicted it all on yourself. But know, you're not the only one who's suffered trials."

I stumbled backward into the nightstand.

To keep her, if she would stay, I couldn't leave us in the dark any longer. I fumbled with the light. I hunched over the nightstand. It blinded me. Naked, bare to her, I whispered, "I can't show you my secrets because I inherited them. They're here. Inside." I raised my voice. "You want to know what secrets I've kept from you?" I opened the drawer of the nightstand and pulled out an empty whiskey bottle and sat it next to the light. Guilt reached in again and slammed another, half-full, against the wood.

She said nothing. She waited.

I looked toward her over my shoulder. "My secret is that I've failed at everything I've ever tried. I couldn't support my mother and siblings; I was too young and too angry. I hated practicing law; I'm nothing like my father. I didn't finish his intentions; Kell's dead, but Ross is still alive. There wasn't enough money in gold; there has never been enough money. I can write, but my book was stolen. I'm banished Cherokee, Lizzie, separated from my family, from you, from my people. I've authored my own tragedy. So, tell me what you want me to do, but don't say I'm too late to love you. That's the one thing I will never fail to do."

She knelt among the pile of clothes and found her handbag, pulling Joaquín's story from her bag.

She stood, flipping through pages, and walked toward the light and me. She read my words.

"She knew the secret history of his soul, his sufferings, and his struggles with an evil fate, and the long agony which rent up by the roots the original honesty of his high-born nature. More than this, he had told her that he would soon finish his dangerous career, when having completed his revenge, and having accumulated an equivalent for the fortune of which he had been robbed by the Americans, he would retire into a peaceful portion of the state, build him a pleasant home, and live alone for love and her. She believed him, for he spoke truly of his intentions… It mattered not how the world regarded him, to her, he was all that is noble, generous, and beautiful."[6]

Lizzie dropped the book to the floor. She turned my face, so I could see her eyes. "Look at me. Rollin, I'll stay. I can see all of you now."

CHAPTER 31: KNOW NOTHING
Rollin Ridge
Marysville, California, Tennessee, and Georgia
Spring and Summer 1856

To avoid practicing law, I used what renown I'd gained from my novel to accept a position as editor of the *California American*, a revamping of the financially destitute *Tribune*. Despite my new title, my office was no larger than a closet with one window and a sill only wide enough for a small man to lean. Large enough to hold a chair and desk, but small enough that I had to turn sideways to inch my way between it and the wall. All day I'd slashed through blasphemous verbosities from eastern 'slang-whangers' hoping to expand their platforms to the Pacific. Their only proficiency was to talk a donkey's hind leg off.

There was a knock on my closed door. My apprentice, Beatty, didn't wait for me to answer. He squeaked the hinges and let in the tang of ink rolled over type followed by the sounds of twisting iron handles and grunts from the man working the press.

Four-eyed Beatty was one of my typesetters, still a juniper in the news, not yet knee-high to a lamb, skinny as a barber's cat, with his clergyman's collar buttoned to the top and his suspenders pulling his pants too short. The young man was plum stuck between hay and grass. He'd never jump the broom and find a piece of calico shorter than him. But I didn't hire him for his stature. The young man wrote better than a hickory above a persimmon, but talked as though he were translating Latin.

I didn't look up from my work, just extended my hand to accept the submission letters and newspapers from him.

He said, "My quest was delayed momentarily at C Street, at the Pony Express office, while transporting your piece to General Allen."

"Did someone try to bed you down?"

Beatty took off his glasses. "What sir?"

"Air you? Run you through?"

"No sir. General Allen requested that I wait while he absorbed your prose."

"Glad you're still above snakes. And?"

"And what? Oh, Allen. Yes, sir. He replied that your rendition of events was poignant and most proficient."

I looked up, shook my head, rolled my eyes, and put my head in my hands. For someone so adept, Beatty couldn't hit the ground with his hat with three throws.

"You can do better. To write the news, you must find the sweet spot between how people should talk and how they do. Use their voice to get them to understand yours."

Then Beatty, sensing my disappointment, sighed. He took off his glasses to ready himself for battle. After my last attempt to teach him to be a newspaperman, he went home and read Aristotle. Perhaps today, I'd let Beatty win and give the philosopher the night off.

He undid the top button of his shirt and cleared his throat. "Fine. He called you a word-slinger, a sure enough man to ride the river with."

I leaned back in my chair and put my hands behind my head. "The man's a rusher for sure. Thinks he's the biggest toad in a puddle."

"An utter flannel mouth." After such an insult, Beatty covered his mouth with his hand to mask a spurt of escaping laughter.

The paper's owner and proprietor, General James Allen, caused a sensation wherever he walked. He had eastern ties in Pennsylvania and led Marysville's Know Nothings, the secret name for the American Party. They advocated popular sovereignty after the Kansas-Missouri Act negated states' rights. To Congress, none of it mattered if they maintained their corrupt balance of power.

When I took this job, I knew the paper was Allen's voice for his secret society, despite his claims of ignorance. Before I could go to print, Allen insisted on reading every political piece, assuring himself that his paper advocated for the Union against any attempt of Southern Democrats to overthrow it. He opposed political fraud, (as if there is any other kind), and demanded construction of a transcontinental railway.[1] With those guiding principles, and with pay enough to build Lizzie a house, how could I refuse?

I said, "I'd rather ride smiling and pick flies out of my teeth than read anything more about railroad contractors bargaining over the price of steel. It'll only take a week before the deals are nailed to the counter, after the politicians realize how much it'll cost to build a railroad without slave labor."

With a lifetime of blood and sweat shed beside Wacooli and empathy for Spencer Hill, I recognized slavery as an appalling institution. Native nations understood captivity as whites could not. But regardless, I could not vote for politicians who insisted the federals had the right to dictate policy instead of allowing the states their constitutional rights.

Beatty stared out the window watching for gunslingers. "We're living in times of vigilante shecoonery, for sure. Here and in Washington."

"If we believe the *Sacramento Journal*, California's Know Nothing Governor just ordered General William Tecumseh Sherman to lead the

Yellow Bird's Song

militia to enforce the law. From what I've seen, if Sherman mounts his horse from the left, the crack shots throw their legs Indian side and kick dust. They evade him at every turn. You know, I won't let Lizzie come to town without arming myself to the teeth."

Beatty pointed to the townsfolk walking the street and said, "The politicians are hypocrites. They know if they hire the Irish or the Chinese to build track, it'll cost them double. That's why they want to buy steel so cheap. They sit in Washington all down but nine. Doesn't matter. That dog won't hunt. Natives will never allow the whites close enough to build the air line road across the prairie. Not if the tribes keep pulling up the telegraph wires."

I said, "Well, if the Know Nothings don't stop squabbling among themselves, they'll never beat Lincoln and elect Douglas... or get enough senators in Congress to vote to build the transcontinental anyhow. All just a lick and a promise."

Beatty put his hand on my shoulder. "If Allen and his Know Nothings chew gravel, we'll all be rowing up a salt river. Allen won't have a tail feather left to fund the paper, and I'll be out of a job."

I returned to my desk and looked at the pile I still had left to read. Beatty made for the door, hanging his head in assumed defeat.

I stopped his egress. "Beatty, you're my wheel horse. Always have a job with me... Write your story about the Irish and the Chinese. But for God's sake, if your grandma doesn't use the phrase, don't write it for the *American*."

"No offense sir, but you don't know my grandma. She shoots back a doud for breakfast before punchin' dough. She whales away, airin' her lungs. Quite a dabster herself. She'd say no matter how old she gets; she's still aces high. Don't think I learned it all from you, do you?"

With a new mission, pleased with himself and proud of his grandma, he wrapped the end of his glasses behind his ears.

Returning to my desk, I tossed away newspapers and any letters with unrecognizable handwriting. Before the door shut, I laughed, saying, "Don't get cocky, Beatty. Make hay while the sun shines."

When I looked up, he grinned and clicked the latch, perhaps standing a bit taller.

The first letter I opened was from Stand. He said, "The Treaty Party has become the Knights of the Golden Circle." So, I thought, Stand established his own branch of Know Nothings. He said, "Cherokee Nation can't feed its people, let alone overcome our economic disparities without slavery."

But that wasn't his only reason. I knew Stand refused to allow Ross' government to demand anything not voted in by a majority. He wrote, "Either our people enjoy popular sovereignty, or they don't." In Stand's mind, there was no gray middle. What began as Ross' four-year term in '28 continued, with my people suffering under his tyranny for another twenty-eight years.

I sat in my chair, reminded of Uncle Elias, Papa, and Grandpa's wish. If Stand and I could see Cherokee Nation admitted into the Union as a state, then I would be satisfied. Until then, whether I won laurels as a writer in this distant land or whether I toiled in the obscurity of some mountain village over the dull routine of a small practice, I would win my way by slow and painful steps to the purpose in my heart of hearts. And if I failed in all I undertook and lay down to die with this noble purpose unfulfilled, my last prayer would be for its consummation and the consequent happiness of the Cherokee people.[2]

I ran my hand through my hair, hearing Lizzie's voice. She'd say I could do nothing about it today. Better to focus on pressing matters and not to take a drink over problems I couldn't see to solve.

I laid Stand's letter aside and flipped through the other mail. On the bottom of the stack was one from Arkansas. I turned up the wick on the oil lamp and read.

> Brave Brother,
> Mother passed yesterday morning. AJ stopped the clock at ten. Pneumonia. She'd suffered for nearly a month. I tried everything I knew to do. Sassafras to purify her blood, snakeroot for chills, mint to clear her lungs, and elm tree bark for coughing and swelling. No white or Indian medicine can hold a soul to the earth when it yearns to pass beyond. After waiting to join Papa for so long, I must believe they are together again.
>
> When it became too difficult for Mama to speak, she signed. She asked you not to come home. She didn't want you to put yourself in harm's way. She worried Ross' men would lie in wait for you at her funeral. You and Lizzie wouldn't be able to arrive in time, regardless.
>
> I wish you could write her eulogy. Your words would do Mama's sacrifice justice. Susan's husband says he'll speak to what a Christian woman she was. How she suffered her quiet battles alone. We all know, after Papa's death, she bore a dead heart in a living bosom.[2]
>
> Susan decided we should meet you and Lizzie in Memphis, Tennessee in May. I hope her choice gives you and Lizzie time

Yellow Bird's Song

enough to travel. In the meantime, I'll care for your daughter. She grieves Mama as only children can, separating sorrow from playful joy. I wish that part of our innocence remained with us after we grow tall. Alice needs her Mama and her Papa now. Her arms chill without Mama's warmth. Until you and Lizzie come, I'll hold onto her.

Your loving sister,
Clarinda

I knew nothing of grief without revenge, pairing both emotions in my mind. I couldn't think past such loss. Selfish anger struck me first, like molten lava, and I dragged my arm across the desk, sweeping all the newspapers and letters to the floor. I gripped Clarinda's message in my fist and lost my balance. My back hit the corner of the office, and I slid to the floor. Holding my head in my hands, I balled both fists and screamed.

Beatty opened the door.

"Get out," I bawled.

Minutes turned into hours. In disbelief, I drifted aimlessly through such obscurity, with nothing to grab ahold of, to root myself, wandering. Present thoughts jumbled into memories, one intersecting another before the previous finished. Mama had been my constant, a star whose point remained steadfast, enduring, a light never dimmed. She calmed when I raged. When I fought, she steadied. When I hated her, she loved me more. Guilt forced me into the role of a worthless son. I whispered aloud in prayer. "Forgive me, Mama."

I held such animosity to her face, abusing her heart, reminding her of her sin. Mama never stopped reaching, begging me to stay close. Her consistency allowed me space and time to find peace.

The window's daylight turned into evening's amber as I envisioned Mama's face, pictured it in death. For the horror and terror my imagination brought, my anger receded like the tides. I had to trust what Clarinda believed. Mama's soul found what it'd sought each day for twenty whispering years. Papa.

I rolled a fallen pencil toward me with my foot. I uncrumpled Clarinda's letter and scribbled on its empty back.

> Pale lies she now before me,
> Whom late, I scorned with bitter sneers,
> What spell is this comes o'er me,
> That all mine anger disappears?

> My yesterday was clouded

With thinking of her cruel wrong—
But white in death thus shrouded,
I only know I loved her long![3]

Beatty opened the door. He'd fetched Lizzie. And I was not alone.

We boarded a steamship from San Francisco and traveled a month and a day to reach the murky air of New Orleans. From there, the ocean's blue turned muddy brown when we boarded another steamboat, ironically named the *Mayflower*, and made our way north on the Mississippi River toward Memphis.

When we disembarked near the dock, a voice cried out, "Mama." A bouncing five-year-old girl wove through the strangers to reach Lizzie and me. My wife left my side, scooped Alice in her arms, and spun her around in the air, kissing our daughter's cheek.

When I reached them, Lizzie said, "Alice, you were only a baby when your father kissed you last. Will you let him do so now? He's missed you as much as I have while we've been away."

Braids hung over her shoulders, a smooth wave back from her forehead. She had Lizzie's eyes and a more feminine version of my nose. Her lips were thin with a tiny aperture underneath, the only indentation to her oval face. I knew nothing of being a papa, kneeling beside my daughter. She offered me her hand as though meeting a stranger.

"Alice," I said and touched her cheek with the back of my hand.

"Papa." She pointed toward the crowd behind her. "Uncle Anee and Wacooli said they found gold with you. Is that true?" Her tone implied she didn't believe my brothers.

Hearing Alice call me "Papa" was one of my life's most remarkable and saddest experiences, for both the joy and the memories the title brought. How easily time escaped a young man's grasp, caring not for his excuses when he attempted to halt its constant traipse to bind it still.

"It is true," I said. "But you, sweet Alice, are rarer than any gold I ever found." She was petite in her blue dress but deceivingly solid. "You look like a bluebird stopping to rest, taking a breath, perching on my hand." Alice blushed, and I scooped her from the ground and held her close. But, in my mind, I spoke to Mama. "I promise to be Alice's constant. Stand still, so she'll know where to find me."

One by one, my brothers and sisters came into view, walking as a mass rather than individuals. None still wore mourning attire. Susan was dressed

Yellow Bird's Song

in spring yellow and her husband, wearing his minister suit, looked like a magpie. Aeneas' blue suit matched the dress of a brunette on his arm. A weather-beaten hat shadowed Wacooli's face, but I'd know his gait anywhere. My youngest brother, Andrew, wore a lawyer's tie. Herman looked as though he'd only stepped from his cornfields to drive the family's wagon from Fayetteville, in his red homespun shirt, buttoned to the neck, with suspenders covering his shoulders. My youngest sister, sweet Flora, wore a dress covered in her namesake and held Clarinda's hand, whose native dress forced several gawking strangers to step aside. Lumbering behind them was Clarinda's hound.

At our family's reunion, I recognized the dichotomy of joy and grief. I couldn't hold both emotions simultaneously in my hands. I had to let go of one to grip tightly to the other.

Susan said, "You both must be hungry. We have rooms at a hotel here. Let's eat together." She put her arms around me. "There's nothing more Mama would want."

Susan became the Ridge family matriarch, leading the rest of us across the bustle of the street. When one mother passed, it only took moments before another filled her role. With Ridge men causing so much trouble, we needed a matriarch. Susan was ever the responsible one.

Lizzie took Alice from my arms, and they moved with my brothers and sisters while I waited on Clarinda. She only approached me once I stood alone. My oldest sister was somber, living in the visual solemnity of her mind. I looked around her, behind her. Surely, I signed too slowly, but it had been five years since we'd spoken face-to-face. "Where is Skili?" I asked, or at least that is what I hoped I signed. Her husband wasn't there.

She answered. "In the Nightland, Rollin. Two years ago. His heart."

Rather than say how sorry I was, I hugged my sister tight, trapping her hands against my chest so she couldn't talk. When I let her go, she signed, "Whenever I conjure the memory of those who've passed, all I can see are birds."

When we joined the others seated at the restaurant table, I asked Susan, "Why didn't you bury Mama next to Papa in the cemetery at Honey Creek? It is where she belongs." Lizzie grabbed my hand. We'd discussed this on the steamer. She'd begged me not to ask this very question, but I couldn't stop myself.

Andrew said, "Susan worried Cherokee would disturb Mama's body."

Susan responded by lowering her chin, followed by rolling her eyes. From her reaction, I didn't believe this was the first time she'd argued her point. "Not only that. I cannot tend Mama's grave if I must go into Cherokee Nation to do it."

312

Aeneas interjected. "Susan has little need for her Cherokee blood."

"After what they did to Papa and Grandfather, I refuse to breathe their air."

Clarinda interrupted Susan's defiance. She touched my sleeve before she asked, "Brave brother, take me home?"

She didn't need any further gestures to tell me what she meant. After watching her request, the family erupted, all speaking over one another.

Susan said, "Not this ridiculousness again. She knows Rollin won't deny her."

Herman said, "No, sister. Stay with me. Help me work my farm."

Andrew said, "You cannot own land there. How will you live?"

Aeneas said, "What if you are ill? Who will care for you?"

Flora said, "I don't remember the East at all."

When they stopped to breathe, I said, "With Mama's hair, you'll pass as white. No one will say you cannot stay."

Lizzie whispered in my ear. "Take this time with Clarinda. Go. Grieve your mother."

I held Clarinda's gaze but took Alice's little hand. Would I break my promise moments after making it? Leave again the moment she called me Papa? As if Lizzie heard my spirit's vow, she permitted me to make the journey to Ridge land once more. Lizzie leaned against my shoulder. "I'll pack Alice's things back in Fayetteville. When you return, the three of us will go home to California."

Once on the road through the Appalachian Mountains, our horses followed a narrow path through walls of stacked shale and granite. Cherokee spirit orbs followed us on horseback. Clarinda sensed them first, signed the word for ghosts, making two circles with her thumb and forefinger, and stretched the circles like dissipating smoke. On this journey home, we'd reversed removal. She and I traveled backward on The Path Where They'd Cried, passing clusters of our people's gravesites throughout Tennessee. We stopped at each mound or cross and, remembering, offered an apology. Their spectral company departed after each funeral prayer.

Sitting around a campfire near Etowah, the steep mountains kept our firelight close. I threw another log on the fire and scratched a whimpering Digaleni's head. He descended from Clarinda's original hound—the same dog we'd slogged with as children over every pasture and stream at Running Waters.

She signed, "These stony hills remind me of when you and I were lost.

Yellow Bird's Song

Do you remember when Papa found us? We hadn't seen him in months, and suddenly, he was there."

I said, "I was only six, but I remember fragments, images. It was cold. Wind bent over the treetops, bending the pine tops together. As usual, I stayed up after Mama tucked me in, staring out the window. I saw Marz leave her cabin and walk into the woods alone. I remember thinking how she shouldn't be outside alone. She wouldn't be able to see in the dark. She was barely able to see during the day."

Clarinda looked puzzled and gestured with one hand, gripping air surrounding her face. "I remember what she looked like. Skin like stone, nails like claws." Clarinda held the same fist up to the firelight and stacked one atop the other. Then, she signed, "No one believed me, but Marz was a shapeshifter, *dewa* to *tsgili*. She was the squirrel living in the closet under the stairs."

Misty fog surrounded Clarinda's red hair, iridescent beside flames of a similar hue. It wasn't cold tonight, but I pulled my coat across my chest, remembering that November night's biting wind. "If Dick, my appy, lowered his head, I could hop over his neck and wiggle around to face forward."

Clarinda signed, "I watched you mount him from my window. Threw my coat over my gown, snuck to the barn for Equoni, and followed you."

Recalling the story, my perspective changed. I no longer leaned back against a log under the stars, encircled by Tennessee mountains. Instead, from my child's eyes, I stared between Dick's pony ears, captive underneath giant, towering trees. Night owls hooted. Coyote howls chased me. Deer leapt through the brush. "The night was like one of Papa's stories. When I couldn't see Marz, I looked behind me, too scared to turn back, afraid I wouldn't find the path home.

"Marz waited in a clearing. Moonlight made her white hair glow blue. She spoke with a Cherokee man on horseback. He carried a long gun over his shoulder. I tried to be quiet when Marz told the man something about a messenger, a letter from the President. The long-gunned man told Marz how he'd tell War Woman.

"My legs were tired, and I slid from my pony's back. I grabbed his mane to stay seated. In return, he stamped his hoof. Both Marz and the man reacted, suspicious of the sounds behind them. The long-gunned man rode out of sight. Marz approached me in the dark. She scolded me with her gravelly voice.

"I remember only a little after that, like waking up from a dream too fast. Perhaps that's all it was."

Clarinda signed, "No. It wasn't a dream. I caught up to you when Marz

314

grabbed your foot. Equoni and I hid behind bushes where I could see. I watched her hold her arms out to you, and you reached for her. She hugged you and ran her nails through your hair. After that, you fell limp. She threw you over your horse and led your pony further into the woods."

Clarinda continued. "She used her magic to build a stone bridge. It sounded like thunder. Dick's metal shoes clopped over its rocks. I couldn't understand how you could sleep through such noise. Equoni and I kept our distance. After we crossed, lightning struck the bridge, and all the rocks fell away." Clarinda's fists stacked imaginary stones and let her hands fall, imitating how the bridge broke apart.

Clarinda's signs brought me from the memory. I signed a y-shape with my right hand and slapped it against my left. "Impossible," I said, and tilted my head with skepticism.

She signed in reply, "Not for *tsgili*."

The wind changed direction, and Clarinda closed her eyes when smoke blew into her face. She rolled her head, memories taking hold of her conscious mind. She gestured about a cabin made of stone where a fire burned and stood, showing, with her body, how Marz carried me inside. Clarinda explained how she had tied Equoni to a tree and peeked through the stone cabin's window. She showed me how the *tsgili* held me like a baby, sang to me, and ran her long nails through my hair.

Clarinda opened her eyes and signed, "I had to lead Marz away from you."

I said, "I remember hearing your whistle. It sounded like a chickadee, the tiny bird's repeating chirps." I took Clarinda's whistle from around my neck and returned her talisman back to her.

Clarinda held it to her mouth and made the same sound. She signed, "It was all I had that made noise. *Tsgili* set you on the floor by the fire and walked outside, searching for the singing bird. Equoni heard the whistle, and broke her rope, running. I kept blowing, hidden in the brush. Its sound carried on the wind through bare trees. Marz searched in vain, never finding the bird and never finding me.

"Walking Stick and Sunflower rode past first and grabbed Marz. Then, Walking Stick shouted back toward the woods. Papa rode fast with a lit torch, slid off his horse, and followed the sounds. He hugged me for the longest time. I needed him to know you were in the stone house. I kept blowing my whistle, pointing. Soon enough, he reappeared in the doorway with you in his arms."

"If they hadn't found us, what would Marz have done? Your whistle saved my life, then. It protected me when I shot Kell. I should have returned it to you long before now. I remember leaning against Papa,

Yellow Bird's Song

rocked with the gait of his horse. Knew I was safe when I heard his heartbeat in my ear, smelled him."

"He smelled like ink and leather." Clarinda walked to her horse and petted it between its eyes. Then she gathered Mama's hummingbird sewing box from her bag, took the whistle off, and placed it inside. She signed, "That was the same night the great comet streaked the night, collecting all the stars into a single beam."

Her fingers pointed toward the sky as she brushed her thumbs together. I walked toward her, joined her gesture. I gathered her hands in mine, and together, we watched, anticipating the comet's reappearance. She read my lips. I said, "Aeneas was born that night." I held our palms flat together, swaying them horizontally side to side. "Papa and Mama never stopped carrying any of us."

Alone, I knew nothing of mourning. But from those hollows beneath mountains of stone, my sister taught me to remember, to grieve Mama and Papa without rage. Under what stars remained behind, I held my sister and stared into the sky through falling tears, imagining how Heaven, the Nightland, peeked through its nocturnal canopy in weightless light.

For mounting from their depths unseen,
Their spirit pierces upward, far,
A soaring pyramid serene,
And lifts us where the angels are.[4]

CHAPTER 32: HOLLOW
John Ridge
Major Ridge's Plantation and Running Waters,
Red Clay Council Grounds, and the Walker home in Cleveland, Tennessee
Spring and Summer 1834

Walking Stick rode in from Running Waters running cattle between there and here to sell at auction. Once the cows were through the gate, I waved at his approach, eager for news. He rode toward the barn, reined in his horse, and threw his leg over the animal, letting the horse wander under a nearby apple tree and eat its fallen fruit. Walking Stick pulled a piece of fruit and crunched a bite before sauntering into the barn. With a full mouth, he smiled and mumbled, *"You're nearly done."* He wiped his mouth with the back of his hand, then ran his fingertips along the indentions of the nearly finished box. He asked, *"Want me to take it to her when I go back?"*

I blew pine shavings from the carving under my hand. *"Yes. The bottom is just there. Tap on the hinges?"* When he finished crunching, I admitted, *"This is the second one. The proportions of the first weren't true."*

"Perfectionist," he mumbled and tossed the core toward his horse's side-eyed glance. Walking Stick wiped his hands on his pants, picked up a tack, and centered it through the holes in the hinge. His hammer was light, careful not to split the wood.

We worked in companionable silence for minutes. He said, *"She still hasn't named that baby. Calls him Sugar. Horrible name for a boy, although he's a sweet thing. Says you name the children."*

I mumbled, *"She'd have to let me see him to name him."*

"You both are mules. Sunflower told me Sarah believes the trust between you two will never heal if she doesn't prove she's innocent."

I made several last grooves, leaning in with my tool, and blew again, satisfied. I handed him the top piece. *"Is that why she resists? She doesn't need to prove anything."* I handed him the lid. *"I'm the one who has something to prove. She knows I love her."* I watched Walking Stick secure the second hinge with two more tacks with my arms crossed over my chest. *"I've never loved her more, to my detriment and benefit."*

Walking Stick tested his work, opening and shutting the lid on Sarah's sewing box. He left the lid open and handed it back to me. He said, *"Something so beautiful and rare cannot remain empty for long."*

We both leaned on our forearms on the workbench, staring at the box

Yellow Bird's Song

resting between us. I'd spent so much time carving the vines. Unopened buds wound around the panels toward an open trillium on the lid. The hummingbird's bill sipped nectar from its petals. I began carving it the day she brought Jackson's letter. Took me the entire winter to complete.

I said, *"If there's nothing left inside, I'll never trust my intuition again."*

He said, *"Hollow talk. My wife taught me what the word meant."*

Surprised by the quiet man's candor, I said, *"You've rarely spoken of her."*

He looked away. *"She didn't keep her promise. She and her mother put me out so she could live with another man."*

I asked, *"Would you have forgiven her? If she called you home?"*

"If her lies came so easy, whatever she said after would've been just as hollow." His hand slid past me and closed the lid. *"I know what you're asking me. Forgiveness is like those hinges. Open and shut them too often, they break."*

I turned away from his words, dusting my hand across my pant legs. *"I thought Sarah would forgive me after I brought Rollin and Clarinda home, before she gave birth to the child."*

"Strange night when that baby was born. Honey came running, saying Peter needed to fetch Mother Susannah. Sarah was laboring, and Clarinda and Rollin were gone. Already dark before we knew it. I woke Sunflower, and she said Marz wasn't in bed. I hate to think what that witch would've done had we not found Clarinda's horse and heard that whistle. When that comet flew by, I thought the world burned for certain."

I sat on a nearby stool. *"Mine did."*

Walking Stick said, *"You kept your promises that night. Found and protected those children from that crooked woman. Sarah trusted you, needed you. Still does. But hollow words won't show her."*

Walking Stick ambled outside to gather his horse and left me to my thoughts.

When he disappeared into the sunlight, I shouted, *"No sign of Marz?"*

He returned to the barn door with reins in his hand. *"We did as you asked. Sunflower and I took her to Tennessee and left her in a village near Hiawassee. She didn't say a word the entire way."*

I shook his hand and said, *"Had I the opportunity, I would have killed her for touching my children."* I shook his hand and said, *"I owe you."*

"Way I see it, we owe you. Not only for taking me in and giving Sunflower a home, but for keeping your promises to our people. Chief Ross says we'll be all right if we stand our ground. But that's hollow talk too. He wants Cherokee to think you and Major are dishonest. But your

318

actions follow your beliefs."

He mounted his horse. *"I don't want to leave Running Waters. Neither does your family, but if staying means dying? Well. I'm not an important man in the nation, but if I'm asked to sign—"* He looked down, finishing his thought, *"—you'll have my name."*

I said, *"Ross called another council meeting next week. Come. Stand with us."*

Walking Stick shifted his hat, pulling it down further over his eyes. *"Won't talk, but I'll come. Listen from behind."*

I said, *"Behind us may not be the safest place to stand. But it's exactly where I need you."*

I had an idea. *"Don't leave yet. Give me another minute?"* I returned to the barn, grabbed Sarah's gift, and carried it under my arm back into the apartment.

When I passed him, he shouted, *"Where are you going?"*

I whispered to myself. "To the beginning."

The message I put inside wasn't hollow talk, not when I spoke the words by the Housatonic in Connecticut, nor now. All I could hope for was that she believed me now as she had then.

From the packed council house in Red Clay, Foreman lifted his long gun across his chest and stood on a bench behind Chief Ross. Ross raised his palms to quiet the crowd, allowing Foreman, his henchman, to speak.

"Major Ridge had gone around the nation with his chiefs and made speeches telling the people to love their land and, in his earnest, stamped the ground. The ground was yet sunk where he stamped, and now, he talks another way." He gestured toward us and continued, "These men might as well carry a poisoned cup to your mouths and say, 'Drink this, and I will give you so much money!' or, 'Let me give you money to allow me to kill you.'[1] If I had known, I would not have voted for him. Why could these men not be satisfied with property and not try to suck more from the veins of their country?"[1]

The crowd erupted, each man taking to his feet, reaching, and shouting across the aisle at one another.

Father's formidable frame lifted his head above the disquieted others. He kept his stern façade, but his lip quivered. Father said, *"My life is nearly at its end. I am an old man. Foreman has better expectations than he should. By slandering men, he establishes such fame among you. But I have no expectation he will enjoy it long, for we have no government. It is entirely suppressed. Where are your laws? The seats of your judges are overturned. When I look upon you all, I hear you laugh at me. Harsh words are uttered by men who know better. I feel, on your account, oppressed with sorrow. I mourn over your calamity."*[2]

Foreman gripped the stock and barrel. He turned to the men standing behind him and shouted, "Kill them!"[3]

Father boomed over the disarray, attempting to quiet the enraged men. He said, *"What would become of our nation if we were all like Foreman? Could any good grow out of our councils? We should now fall together and twist each other's noses. Our eyes would remain in their sockets, but in general, we would gouge them out."*[4]

I could remain silent no longer and spoke in Father's defense. "Major Ridge has, with distinguished zeal and ability, served his country. He saw it was on the precipice of ruin, ready to tumble down. He told the people of their danger. Did he tell the truth or not? Let every man look to our circumstances and judge for himself. Was a man to be denounced for his opinions? If a man saw a cloud charged with rain, thunder, and storm and urged the people to take care, is that man to be hated or respected?"[5]

Instead of placating them, my words incensed the crowd. Arms gripped and pulled me before Vann stepped in front of me with his hand on his pistol. From my side, Jack Walker said, "I won't stay here another minute and engage with this mob. Mobs do stupid things, John. If you allow men who do not respect you to rage against the truth, you lessen your message by continuing to speak."

Chief Ross slowly walked to the council's clerk. His movement silenced the blind, outraged men. He picked up the quill and wrote a note in the council book. When he looked up, his gaze reached mine. He mouthed the word before raising his voice to repeat it. "Impeachment."

Ross demanded the vote be taken at once. No man hid his thoughts. With each raised hand, "Guilty" echoed. Our Treaty Party remained the minority.

The inevitable happened. Ross silenced us.

Beside me, Vann whispered, *"It's time for a council of our own, at Running Waters."*

Honest Walking Stick galloped into Red Clay between groups of men murmuring amongst themselves, staring over their shoulders, paranoid that someone might overhear. Panting and out of breath, he slid from his horse after finding us packing for home. He hunched over, warning us.

"Assassins waiting in the woods. Shot Jack Walker in the chest."

I came to his side. "Where?"

When his breathing eased, he leaned back. "Near Joe Vann's. Spring Place. He's still alive. His friend carries him home now."

I told Father, *"He lives near Cleveland."*

Father insisted, *"We must ride to him instead of going home. Walking Stick, would you go home and protect my grandchildren. On the way, find the Federal Guard stationed in New Echota. Tell him what you saw."*

Father handed our protector a gourd of water. Walking Stick drank and passed it back. He looked over his shoulder toward the trees. "That woman stirs already murky waters. I heard her on the way here, rallying a group of warriors, ordering them to murder the traitors."

"What woman?" I asked.

Before Walking Stick could answer, Elias interrupted. "Compassed about with so great a cloud of witnesses, let us lay aside every weight, and the sin which doth so easily beset us, and let us run with patience the race that is set before us."[6]

Walking Stick and I would talk later. Saving Jack was the most important thing now.

It was near dawn when we arrived. Walker's wife stood on her porch and washed her hands of her husband's blood in a bucket. Red water sloshed from its uneven side. She recognized us and, shaking, said, "I can't get the bullet out. The shot embedded in a rib, near his heart." She continued stirring up the bloody water, unable to rid her hands of their stain.

Jack moaned inside.

His wife listened, looking through the window, before saying, "He doesn't have long."

Father and I exchanged the same look. There was no naming such anger, betrayal, dismay, or the expectation of grief. Father stayed outside to comfort Walker's wife. I followed Jack's voice to his deathbed.

Blood saturated the top sheet covering him and dripped to the floor. His chest still rose and fell. My friend and ally opened his eyes with a pain-ridden startle.

"John," Walker said, gritting his teeth. "Not going to live long enough to sign my name."

I sat in his wife's chair next to the bed. "Don't worry about that now."

He shifted in bed. Any movement made him gasp. His face was washed in pale green, eyes squinting shut, offering no relief.

"Have little time left for anything else. Just worry about her." He looked through the cabin's walls.

I promised, "I'll make certain she's safe. Who shot you, Jack?"

His breathing was shallow. "Coward finally used that long gun he totes around." He exhaled quickly and sucked in more air. "Foreman and his half-brother Springston. Ambushed us. Hated me since '25 when I caught him."

Jack closed his eyes.

I said, "Caught him?" I stood. "Jack, caught him doing what?"

Jack's eyes found my face above him and gasped several more times. He gripped the sheet in pain and said, "Smuggling whiskey down the Conasauga." Blood spurted from his mouth and dripped down his chin. He said, "Drew my pistol. Confiscated Foreman's barrels." Then he shouted and pointed an imaginary pistol to the ceiling. "'By God, sir, this is my authority.'"[7]

His arm dropped and death's shadow stilled his eyes and covered his face with a graying shroud. Father and Jack's wife stood, framed by the bedroom's open door. I stepped aside and shook my head. Beside their marriage bed, she screamed his name as if volume might bring him home from his last journey to the Nightland.

Days later, when we returned from burying Walker, Ross sent a note to Father's house.

"As to the rumors of threats you say have been made against your life, I have never before heard of them; you say further that reports have also been taken to you of evil designs against yourself and friends by me. With the utmost sincerity and truth, I assure you that whatever may be the character of those reports, they are false."[8]

Father handed me the letter. *"Ross claims he is innocent."*

"What he claims now will be proven false in court. He sent the letter as evidence of that lie. He sent Foreman to intercept Walker. The man barely breathes without asking Ross' permission."

Sad news travels faster than any other. A week later, we received another letter. General Curry wrote from the federal post near New Echota and requested to see us. We didn't delay.

"May I link the words, so my father understands?" I asked.

General Curry nodded and returned to his desk chair, eager to watch Father's response to Jackson's command.

Jackson wrote, "I've just been advised that Walker has been shot and

Ridge and the other chiefs in favor of emigration and you, as an agent of the United States government, are threatened with death. The government of the United States has promised them protection. It will fulfill its obligations to the letter. On the receipt of this, let John Ross know, and his council, that we will hold them answerable for every murder committed on the emigrating party."[9]

Father said, *"People must die to get Jackson's attention. Noted."* His face remained stoic, not allowing General Curry any further indication of his thoughts.

Curry asked, "What did he say?"

I answered, "My father regrets Jack Walker's loss before President Jackson took action."

Curry cleared his throat, took up his quill. "Tell me what Walker confessed." He recorded what I repeated, my friend's final testimony.

Curry said, "I will arrest the guilty. In the meantime, I will order guards to both of your homes and station several soldiers near Boudinot's. These men will escort you there within the hour." He stepped toward a nearby lieutenant. They murmured and saluted one another. All I heard was they should remain for the time being.

Federal Guards would terrify Sarah. Surely, Walking Stick told her what happened to Jack. I needed to go home.

Night fell before our extended party reached Running Waters. When we turned the corner on the path leading to the front door, I saw her. Sarah leaned forward as our horses approached. She swooped low in some instinctual rotation, a swirl of white petticoats, laying the baby in the cradle at her feet, and swirling to rise and embed a musket to her shoulder, aiming it straight for us.

I shouted, "It's me! The guards are with me!"

Before I heeled my horse forward, I asked, "Let me go first. Alone."

Father whispered, *"Stay in the light."*

I nudged my horse forward with my hands held away from my sides. When Sarah could see me, she lowered the barrel, but the stock remained fastened to her arms. I walked up the front steps, not taking the last. We stood eye to eye. The last step was the hardest.

She looked down the road. With panic in her voice, she asked, "Are they arresting you?"

"No," I said. "The soldiers are here to protect us from threats against my life."

She looked confused, trying to process how enemies became allies. After witnessing how Sam had been taken, her assumption was logical.

I put my hands on the gun. The courage she'd gripped so tightly dropped away. Bravery's tears overwhelmed her. Her knees gave way, and I reached for her waist to keep her from falling. Empty hands and weary bones weighed us to the porch floor, so close I felt her lungs exhale desperation. She looked into my eyes and gripped my shirt.

She whimpered a truth she didn't need to say. "I'm hollow…"

I don't know whether I said it or only thought the words, "… without you."

In the next edition of the *Phoenix*, Ross ordered Hicks to print his response to President Jackson. "I pronounce such accusations to be a malicious and slanderous falsehood against our character and was no doubt intended to disturb the peace and tranquility of the nation, and is altogether unworthy of your confidence, no matter by whomsoever reported."[10]

General Curry kept his word, arresting Foreman and his half-brother, Springston, for Jack's murder. Our chief sprang to action collecting funds to provide for Foreman and his brother's legal defense.

In jail, a guard reported overhearing Foreman tell his brother, "Don't worry. We'll be let out by a silver key."[11] It was true; they were. Ross made sure of it.

CHAPTER 33: THE GAMBIT
Sarah Ridge
Running Waters
November 1834

After the guards came to protect us, John remained at home. From that day forward, all the inside doors remained open.

When I passed the study door with a basket full of dirty clothes, he and Rollin sat together in the armchair. John read, "Aeneas sailed to the mouth of the Tiber…" He looked up when he saw me watching them from the doorway.

After his father's distraction, Rollin finished reading the sentence. "From there, he went on a long voy—" John smiled while Rollin struggled to sound out the word. "Voyage," John corrected him, found his place, and continued the story.

I made chicken and dumplings in the kettle while John and Clarinda sat at the kitchen table, bantering question and answer, trading quill back and forth. He laughed at whatever she wrote, filling the silence. Scratching sounds came from the quill. Chair legs creaked underneath them. I looked over my shoulder and caught John doing the same to me while Clarinda took ink from the well.

From the door of my hothouse, the children's laughter stopped my return to the kitchen. John walked the harvested fields with Herman on his shoulders and Susan's hand in his. He lifted Herman by the arms, placing him on the ground. All three of their heads bent low in the grass. John pointed, directing their eyes to a doe and buck, leaping over the thick growth at the edge of the trees.

After supper one night, John rocked Sugar, our infant son, touching his head with its wisps of strawberry hair. John didn't know I was listening. He talked to the cooing babe. "You look so like your mother, Aeneas. He, too, was born of Aphrodite." So, he'd named our son after a warrior who built Rome after the fall of Troy. I wasn't upset, but John's Aeneas would stay my Sugar. The handsome child had a calm temperament and sweet gummy grins, squealing in bursts like a flickering woodpecker.

So, instead of secrets, John hid nothing. Instead of delivering invitations to the Treaty Party's council himself, he sent riders and remained at home. Instead of riding to his father's or Elias' houses, he asked them to come to Running Waters. They made their plans, standing next to the parlor fireplace while I knitted winter socks.

He kept every unspoken promise he made years ago, holding himself

325

to account for the one inside his handmade hummingbird box. Inside it, John had renewed his vow to make so many "crooked places straight."[1]

The Treaty Party's council meeting would fill three days with ceremonies and debates, discussing the business of agreeable terms for the government's purchase. Already on the farm, twenty or more makeshift shelters stood with fires burning. At my request, the men of Running Waters butchered a steer to supply enough meat for so many.

On the first day, Mother Susannah arrived early to grind beans to make bread enough for the masses. Honey formed another loaf in a tin. Sunflower and I fed Susan and Herman their breakfast. After wiping her face, I passed Susan to Susannah so I could remove two crusted loaves from the brick oven, placing them side by side on the biscuit box to cool.

Mother Susannah put her bowl on the table and took Herman from Sunflower's hip. Then, with arms full, she bounced two grandchildren on her lap. She looked up from their faces, and her expression turned more serious. She spoke to Honey who translated for me. "*The soldiers warned us to take the main road here even though it is miles around the wooded path. Quatie and Ross are nearby. I heard him speaking. They steered many to their camp who'd planned to come here.*"

So, Ross closed in on enemy territory. I turned away to hide my face. "What did he say?" I asked, knowing the array of Mother Susannah's expression well enough.

Honey linked Susannah's words. "*Ross spoke English to Quatie, and she repeated his words in the people's tongue. They asked travelers if they loved their land. When they said yes, she encouraged them to sign their name on Ross' petition and go home. Ross doesn't want anyone to hear the wise council of my husband and my son.*"

Honey folded the bread dough, shook her head, and clicked her tongue. "Lonely women do desperate things. If it got that man to talk to her, Quatie would say anything."

I turned around when Clarinda and Rollin entered the kitchen. Clarinda, taller than her brother, grabbed her egg basket while he gathered his milk pails. They headed to the outbuildings to do their chores early, so they could play with other children. They left the door standing wide open. I called after them, but neither returned. Seeing them run side by side made me think.

I said, "When John brought Rollin and Clarinda home, they told me what Marz did. Marz talked to a Cherokee man in the woods. Marz told this stranger about the President's message, the letter I took to John." Thinking backward, I asked Sunflower, "When did Quatie bring Marz to stay with us?"

Sunflower signed around Herman, sitting on her lap. "Two years ago. Spring."

Honey sprinkled flour on her dough. "Quatie showed us the stripes on Marz's back, remember? Sarah, you've got to let that witch and that horrible night go. You couldn't know Rollin and Clarinda ran off after her. You was laboring with baby Sugar." She shook her head. "Could've been worse."

Mother Susannah confirmed. *"Quatie knew your kind heart wouldn't turn the woman away. Makes me never want to let my grandbabies out of my sight."*

Following my reason, Honey's eyes met mine. She pounded her fist into the dough in front of her and threw a towel over the rising bread. "Oh no, Sarah, no. Did Marz steal that missin' letter? Did Quatie bring Marz here to spy on us?"

I shared Honey's suspicion. "The last time I saw Quatie, when I learned Georgia sold her house in the lottery, was the same day the letter disappeared. I told Marz I was leaving."

Sunflower shook her head and signed around Herman's belly. "Find her. Ask her. Only way to know for certain."

Vann entered the kitchen from the back door as I untied the apron around my waist and threw it on the table. He said, "Whoa. Slow down. Came in here to tell you Major's about to call the council to order. John's speaking first."

Honey untied her apron and threw it next to mine. "If I'm guessin' right, you're goin'. I'm comin' too."

Vann said, "Did you hear me?"

We left Mother Susannah and Sunflower with the children and hurried toward the barn, weaving through the Cherokee crowding around the house. When we rode down the road, I looked over my shoulder. Major stepped onto the podium. Behind him, Vann whispered in John's ear. John followed us with his eyes, staring as we passed.

One more time, I had to disobey my husband, evade the guards, to seek audience with a queen.

Ross' crowd was easy to find. Wagons bordered the road. Horses grazed surrounded by pitched tents surrounded by pine trees. Their fires smoked

Yellow Bird's Song

in straight lines, less aromatic when burned under the sun instead of on crisp fall nights.

At the far end of the field, Ross stood on a stump, rallying whooping Cherokee warriors who lifted weapons in anger. I thought about how we'd never find Quatie in this mass of people. But she revealed herself, flapping away the canvas opening to a tent. She stepped forward to stir whatever was inside her pot.

I called her name. She heard me, straightened her back, and rested the ladle handle across the rim.

I approached her from the back. "Mother Susannah told us you were here."

Quatie put her hands on her hips, recognizing my voice before turning around. She spat, "No secret where we are."

I took a step toward her, but Honey stopped me and grabbed my arm. "No secret?" I asked. "You've kept many secrets."

She smirked and sauntered closer. "White women are so slow minded."

I wanted to question her, wanted her confession. But I had no time for her insults. "Why didn't you care for Marz? Why bring her to Running Waters?"

Quatie said, "You made it too easy. You didn't notice how fresh the whip marks were. I didn't even have to lie much to get you to take her in."

I stepped closer to her. "No Georgian soldier burned her home?"

Quatie shook her head. "No, but they've done so to many others."

Appalled, I had a horrific thought. "Did you whip Marz to convince me? Tell me the truth."

"Marz suffered and sacrificed for her people. When your husband changed his colors from red to white, Ross and I needed to know what he planned."

I stuttered and asked her the next logical question. "Did Marz give you John's letter from Cass?" Angry tears filled my eyes, but it wasn't the time to cry.

We all looked toward Ross when his voice bellowed across the field. Underneath his podium, a freed Foreman raised a long gun in his hand. When I looked at Quatie again, she faced me. She pointed toward the man. "Marz took him that letter. And dutifully, he brought it to me. Marz told me your husband planned to run for principal chief."

That is why Ross refused elections. I said, "How could you do such a thing? We were friends, sisters. We stood beside one another, outside of our husbands' courts."

She looked at me as if I were stupid. "Because you have everything I

Heather Miller

ever wanted. Love and children and an ambitious husband who listens to you."

Honey stepped between us, invading Quatie's space with a revelation of her own. "Sarah, when Quatie thought her husband might lose his grip, she took up his gun and fought his enemies herself. Like Nanyihi did." Quatie took a step back as if such truths blistered.

I crossed the dirt ground to the other side of Quatie's cookfire, glaring at her through the smoke. "You told us you revered Nanyihi as a blessed woman, a peacemaker. You're nothing like her. When you sent Marz, you endangered my children. I sacrificed nearly a year with my husband because he thought I stole that letter, gave it to you, and told you everything he ever said to me."

Quatie barricaded me and snarled. "When I heard you sent him away, I hoped you'd leave and take your half-breed children with you. White mother, your children aren't Cherokee. They, and you, are clanless."

After her insult, I couldn't move. I said, "You're lying to your people. Nothing will change. Federal troops are not coming. Georgia will continue to kill the Cherokee if they do not move West. No argument exists that President Jackson will hear. And none of this is John's fault. Place blame where it is due."

Quatie picked up her ladle. She raised it along with her voice. "I blame your people. Yet, here you stand, defending the Ridges against their own. Easy to say with federal troops guarding your porch. I lost my home because of your husband's friendship with the Governor."

I refused to move. She stepped forward, not giving me a moment to deny her accusation. She ranted in my face. "Don't stand on my people's ground and speak of lies. You're a white hypocrite and will never be a chief's wife. I sent Foreman to shoot any passing member of the Treaty Party. Too bad he only found Jack Walker. I will not allow my people to lose what they love, their land. They must see the truth behind these betrayals. Ridges learned greed living like whites." Quatie's tone was rancorous and resolute. She spat her last words when the toes of her boots touched my own. "I told you once, Sarah, there can only be one queen in a hive."

I met her eyes. "You are right," I said. "I'd never behave with such desperation."

Honey's brown eyes stared at me over Quatie's shoulder. She broke the silence. "Only one thing more need sayin', Sarah. Best get to it then."

My eyes darted from Quatie's to Honey's. "What is that?"

Quatie's bloodshot eyes never looked from mine. I returned her gaze. Honey said, "I've watched you carry fear and pain for a long time.

Yellow Bird's Song

Helped tote it right beside you. But we ain't leavin' here with it still strapped to our backs. You know what you need to say."

I didn't know, but if I had, I knew Honey would be right. I denied every human instinct to slap Quatie across her face. I pulled away and walked toward the horses before I realized what Honey meant.

"Quatie," I turned back. "Peter asked Jesus, 'Lord, how oft shall my brother sin against me, and I forgive him? Till seven times?' and Jesus answered, 'I say not unto thee, until seven times: but, until seventy times seven.'"[2]

It took three attempts to mount my horse because my arms wouldn't stop shaking.

When Honey gripped the reins in her hand, she said, "Yep. Them were the words."

Before we reached the barn, I slid off the horse and ran toward John's voice. He shouted over what must have been a hundred heads.

"When the white man arrived and claimed Plymouth, he stole the land belonging to Powhatan, chief of thirty Algonquin tribes. The English had no right, but built their homes, grew their tobacco, taught Indians of their God, and spread diseases no native could overcome. With Indian civilization, education, culture, and religion, whites taught us to turn the other cheek and seek peace. In time, we learned how to be civilized and progressive. We earned white man's respect both here and in Europe."

I could barely hear him from where I stood. He'd never know I returned, that I was listening.

His conviction spread over his words. "But, in our present state, we cannot maintain our culture, our national existence, struggling with the sorrow Fate has placed on our backs."

I watched the wandering feet of the crowd. Men shook their heads; women took the hands of restless children, leading them back to their tents. He lectured the crowd on what they already knew, with language above their heads.

I climbed into the back of an empty wagon where John could see me, taller than the heads of those remaining. At first, he didn't find me, but instead watched the people's faces hovering under him, offering them what consolation he could.

"Cherokee Nation cannot continue in our present circumstances. Our women are raped and whipped. Homes stolen; deeds forged. Soldiers steal your crops, your horses. Warriors put down their bows and arrows and

pick up tin cups full of fire whiskey. Our people lose ground. We must look to the West, where many of our clansmen have emigrated. Will you allow yourselves to be reduced to slavery in this, our Eden? Georgians only think of us with fear and contempt. They will not stop coming, invading, and burning our homes. Are possessions more important than our lives, our children's futures, their children's...?"

I untied the bonnet under my chin and threw it on the wagon's wooden planks beneath my feet. I pulled the cap from my head and shook my red hair free. He saw me, looked up once, then twice at the color falling around my face.

John finished his sentence, distracted. He said, *"... survival?"* He shook his head and repeated the phrase, refocusing himself back to those judging his integrity.

In front of him, I needed him to know I stood behind him, loved him, believed in him, after so much distrust and time apart. I took off my gloves and threw them, inside out, at my feet. I raised my hands to sign, "I laid my blanket over you, and you became mine."

He studied my hands and slowed his speech, both speaking and listening at the same time. He let his written notes fall from his hand and continued. *"Will you throw blankets over your eyes? Deny the violent truth you see for yourselves?"* In our daughter's tongue, he shook his head and returned a sign, throwing his hands to the side. He meant he shouldn't have thrown trust aside.

I signed, "I never lied to you. Quatie sent Marz to spy. She stole Cass' letter. Quatie is the War Woman who ordered Foreman to kill Walker. Quatie is to blame." When I said her name, I raised my hands above my head and made a crown of my fingers.

He returned to his speech, trying to hide the shock rippling off him after such a realization. His words told me he understood.

"Searching for answers has led my family down a dark path, where those once trusted turned their backs to us. But it wasn't me they shunned; they shunned you, our nation's people. Your laws, your treasury, your language, your safety, your humanity. If we are hungry, we are not free. If we are sick, we are not free. If we suffer fear and danger from all sides, we will never be free.

"If we ignore such treachery, we stand in eastern darkness, without the sunlight of transparency. If we keep our eyes closed, we cannot grasp the hand reaching out, pulling us to the West, the direction of day, not night."

I looked around at the wandering eyes of the men and women standing underneath my husband. They planted their feet and stopped moving. Their eyes traced his every movement. Their faces changed from scrutiny

Yellow Bird's Song

to regard. They angled their bodies to face him again. He'd touched their hearts. He noticed the shift, too, and stepped down the stairs.

He asked, with hope in his voice, *"Follow me? I will lead my family beside yours, away from rage and fear, danger, and dying. In the past, we were a commanding people, blessed in ways we couldn't know. If we turn our heads west and chase the sun, we can be so again."*

I took advantage of his pause and answered him. I signed, "Wherever you lead, I will follow, holding your hand."

The people leaned forward, appearing to want John to say more. He silenced, took off his coat and laidit on the porch. He unwound the tie around his neck and let it drop to the ground. He pulled his shirt away from his chest, revealing the tattoo painted on him as a boy. John bent down and grabbed a handful of earth. *"My roots come from this ground."* He covered his heart with the same hand. *"I speak the truth. I've never betrayed you. Help me leave our children a legacy. United, we go West together. When we dig in new ground, fertile soil, the saplings we plant there, under the western sun, will, in a generation's time, give them shade."*

He bowed his head, and the crowd came alive. Some moved toward tables, ready to make their mark. Others circled Major Ridge in handshakes. John limped toward Elias and Vann, and they embraced him, whispering in his ear.

I stayed where I was and watched him make his way through the crowd, shaking hands with some while others clapped him on the back. When he reached me, he looked up and winked. He asked, "Mistress Ridge, have you ever played chess?" He offered me his hand and helped me step down from the wagon.

"No. My father said it was a man's game. Teach me?"

John shook his head and smiled. "Absolutely not. But only because I like to win." He guided me around the corner to stand before him. He didn't let go. "I'd lose for certain. You've already mastered the gambit."

He made the grandest bow, and when he rose, he laid an imaginary crown on my head. His hands slid over my cheeks and held my face. "My queen, to win, she is the one piece the king can never afford to lose." He kissed me.

With his taste still on my lips, I whispered, "Lightning and thunder will crash around us. Cyclones of wind will tear our home apart. Snow will fall so deep the door won't open. Droughts and floods will ruin the harvest. But I will endure whatever each day brings because you stand beside me."

He pulled me close and whispered in my ear, "If I am stronger or smarter than I once was, it is because I know how much I have to lose." John looked around us, over his shoulder. "If I'm granted time and trust to lead these souls to sanctuary..." He rested his forehead against mine. "... it's because your serenity, constancy, and affection provide safety for my soul.[3] If my hourglass yields but little sand remaining, every last grain of hope, I promise—to you."

CHAPTER 34: WITH CLEARER SOUL AND FINE-TUNED EAR
Rollin Ridge
Washington City and Grass Valley, California
May 1866-October 1867

The constant clack of train wheels over the steel track was enough to lull anyone to sleep. When I looked up from rereading Papa's journal, passengers slept with their heads bent back against neighboring bench seats. In such momentary quiet, looking out train windows, I unwound the landscape. Along the plains, taupe fields planted deep with wheat seamed the green forest beyond. Across Kentucky, acres of bluegrass and waxy leaves of green corn touched an azure horizon. In Virginia, the Appalachian valleys blurred gray, as if they still hid widows and orphans wearing mourning cloaks after enduring five years of civil war.

No one was exempt from tragedy. Susan, Andrew, Flora, and I were the only remaining Ridge children. Clarinda's letters stopped in '57. Susan wrote that our brother, Doctor Aeneas Ridge, died in '59, still a young man. Herman fought with Stand's Confederate brigade. Union soldiers took his life at Honey Creek in '64. Still alive, Cousin Stand only recently laid down his saber, serving as a Confederate Brigadier General, the last great man to survive and surrender in the great war.

It was Stand who called me East. He said he needed me to head a Cherokee delegation of second-generation Treaty Party sons: myself, Elias Cornelius Boudinot, Saladin Watie, Richard Fields, and William Penn Adair. Together, we sought to remedy civil unrest still raging in Cherokee Nation. America's war only aggravated my nation's animosity and political division. Stand's letter said President Johnson proposed a new treaty to separate still-warring factions. We had to decide whether to split or unite our Cherokee Nation and settle things once and for all.

Fault lines remained deep between the Ross and Ridge-Watie parties. Anti-Ross advocates chose Stand as the minority's chief in '62 and supported the Confederacy, while Ross earned two hundred and fifty thousand dollars after signing a treaty with the South's Jefferson Davis. But after federal troops arrived, a scared Ross pledged his allegiance and turned his coat to Lincoln's Union blue and fled to Washington. War at home continued after the departure of the Chief with Two Faces. He could do little to feed a starving nation from his comforts in Philadelphia, Delaware, or Washington.

Our delegation would meet Ross in Washington. I would finally sit across the table from the man and use my father's voice. To me, he remained shrewd; the most loathsome reptile that ever fed upon the vapors of a dungeon was a thing of loveliness compared to this fine old patriarch whose head was silvered over by the frost of seventy winters. He cared naught for the government of the United States, nor for the Southern Confederacy, nor for his own people, nor for anything else either in Heaven above or on Earth beneath, whether holy or unholy. But gold. His bloody hands would eagerly stretch forth for some of our money in the United States Treasury by some pretense or other. It remains to be seen whether they would be duped into giving it to him or not.[2]

When our delegation convened, Ross wasn't there, contributing only through notes written from his sickbed at the Medes Hotel. Although, with his absence, I was at liberty to speak freely and tell President Johnson how I feared bloodshed would ensue in Cherokee country if the government delivered us into the hands of the Ross dynasty. The Ridges, Boudinots, and Waties would not raise the flag of war and begin difficulties. "But rest assured, the Ross faction would certainly renew upon us the oppression of old and dig graves for us as they did for our immediate ancestors. Or try to dig them. In that case, we are men enough to resist, and we would—resist—even if it drenched the land in blood."[3]

I left negotiations that day in the company of my cousin Boudi, "Elias Cornelius", and we made our way toward the Metropolitan Hotel, once the site of the Indian Queen. We stopped in front of its marble entryway.

I squinted at the bright dusk, looking up at the sun-glazed windows. I asked Boudi, "What city did our fathers see behind those windows?"

He turned around as if my question required him to look again at the scene just passed. He said, "Certainly not the landscape we see now. The hotel is twice the size it once was."

I said, "That is not what I meant."

"We need your editor's eyes now. Don't turn poet on me," Boudi said, smacking me on the shoulder. He entered the hotel doors while I stayed on the walkway, staring into the street.

From my mind's eye, everything became diminutive, pianissimo. No more were men crossing the street in top hats and canes. Open, horse-drawn barouche carriages replaced fashionable brown coupés. The rhythmic sounds of horseshoes were silenced on the dirt road. Train whistles and steamboat roars faded into oblivion. Tree trunks shrunk and lost their shaded stature. Cobblestones disappeared into beaten dirt under

Yellow Bird's Song

my soles as I watched my feet walk down the avenue toward the Medes Hotel.

With my letter to the *New York Tribune* in the bag at my side, along with Father's journal, Stand's ledgers of Ross' family's financials, Jackson's words, Lumpkin's remarks, General Scott's remembrances, Brigadier General Arbuckle's reports. My leather satchel was heavy with twenty years of confrontation and betrayal: undeniable proof Ross was never the man the Cherokee believed him to be.

I knocked on his hotel door. An unknown woman answered, dressed in a nurse's gray and white. When I asked to see Ross, she curtseyed and granted her kind permission, and gestured for me to enter his suite's front parlor. Had she known our history or announced my presence to him by name, he'd surely denied me entry. But her ignorance became my permission. I followed her across the room, leading me down a brief paneled hall, and opened the door to Ross' bedroom.

She whispered, "He isn't speaking much. Perhaps your visit will help."

With her hand still on the doorknob, she allowed me to pass. She curtsied again and shut the door behind her with petticoat rustles marking her hoop-skirted exit. Finally, I saw the man, and stood beside Ross' sickbed.

He was awake, propped against a mahogany headboard. He wore a red robe with black velvet lapels over a clean night shirt. Someone combed away his silver hair from the wrinkles on his forehead. The skin around his eyes drooped as significantly as his jowls underneath. The creases around his mouth stressed his permanent scowl. Gray whiskers peered along a weather-beaten face down his neck to curling gray chest hair. This old man's existence was sallow, feeble, speckled by protruding moles and dark spots, a residual remnant of his Cherokee mother's blood. My imaginings of him dressed as a devil were not far off the mark.

He examined me as thoroughly as I did him, with no exchange of gesture or word. He didn't appear to recognize my face, as I had expected, not after so many years between last seeing my father. I unbuttoned my coat and sat in the bedside chair while he stared at my face. I took the bag from across my chest, laid it on my lap, and opened its leather flap. From it, I pulled a note from Major Ethan Allen Hitchcock and read it aloud.

"Ross is a man of unbound ambition, a rascal of artful cunning, shrewd, managing, an ambitious man."[3] I set it on the edge of the emerald-green quilt covering him. Ross only threw his hand in the air and grunted with his mouth closed.

I pulled another from the confines of my satchel and opened it to read the shaking script of an aged President Jackson. "What madness and folly to have had anything to do with Ross, when the agent was proceeding well with the removal and on principles of economy that would have saved at least one hundred percent from what the contract with Ross will cost."

I said, "Jackson added a postscript. 'Why is it that the scamp Ross is not banished from the notice of this administration?'"[4]

I set it on top of Hitchcock's note and pulled out a ledger. He watched my hands trace its center ribbon to the marked page. I said, "The deductions from the accounts recorded here vary. From a dollar and a half per citizen for soap, as the people moved slower than expected, to $500,000 added to the cost of removal for your personal salary. I don't believe the federal government paid such an amount. You stole it from the Cherokee's Treasury. You and your brother gained wealth racketeering the government. You took the bread from the hands of Cherokee, sick and dying."[5]

Ross grabbed the ledger and set it on the other side of his bed, out of my reach. I couldn't tell from his defiant silence whether Ross knew who I was. The following recitation from Arbuckle would, no doubt, reveal my identity. By now, I was more determined than ever that he knew my name.

"I have of late received positive information that John Ross was at the Double Spring Council, with many (or most) of the principal men of the late emigrants, on Wednesday before the Ridges and Boudinot were killed. From information derived from the same source, it would appear almost certain that Edward Gunter was in the woods near Boudinot's when he was killed. It has been frequently reported to me that Mr. Lynch, who is now with Mr. Ross, was present when John Ridge was killed, and that the party halted at Ross' house the same day, where they took their breakfast."[6]

Ross shifted on the bed, sliding the ledger and letters to the floor.

From my satchel, I pulled a yellow tattered copy of the *Arkansas Gazette*, an article penned by my Aunt Sollee. I read the last paragraph aloud.

"Experience has too woefully taught me that Mr. Ross and his men do not defend their principles with paper or argument. The knife, the ambush, and the bullet are their means of disposing of their enemies. But if they desire to know who it is that dares expose their principles and atrocities, let them be answered that she is the daughter of him whom a dozen of their young men shot from a loft precipice, the sister of the man who was awakened from his slumbers by twenty-five ghastly wounds, and the cousin of him whom they slaughtered with a tomahawk and Bowie knife, just as he was answering their petition for charity."[7]

Ross' unintelligible grumble turned into a coughing fit. I helped him sit up and patted his back. When he quieted, I covered him again with the

Yellow Bird's Song

quilt. When I returned to my seat, I thought, one more. Let it be Papa's words.

"The Treaty Party and all those who are able to understand and act intelligently meet the commission and treat upon the principles of doing justice to all and preserving their nation in the West. All are notified to attend. A respectable number and much of the intelligence of the nation meet and make a treaty. There are no protests—scarcely opposition. All is peace—the common Indians in their oppressed condition don't care which side succeeds. They are amid starvation, injustice, slavery, and persecution. No opposition is made to the treaty at home but the Ross Council, and that is so implete that to hide their paucity, they sign the protest by their chairman and clerk. Before this, Ross has hired men to run through the nation to collect names and his friends stick them to protests and bring them into the Senate. They are counted. They exceed the whole population taken the last fall by upwards of fifteen thousand souls. No one is responsible for this collection of names and their appendage of protests. Yet they make an impression on senators. They see that it exceeds the truth, but in this tremendous forgery, they believe it showed its preposterousness. Yet enough will remain to embarrass their judgments of what is strictly their duty. If they reject us, where will they put us? How will they save our people from hunger, from degradation, from civil war, or war with the whites? They give us no outlet, no means to escape. Oh, gracious and everlasting God, have compassion upon the poor Cherokee race. Preserve them from despair—preserve them from blood. Oh, lead the hearts of all good men to save them from utter ruin and dispersion. Let not civilization and religion be sown in vain among them."[8]

Ross grabbed at my sleeve, grunting from angry, pale, taut lips. He pulled his cold hand away. After returning Papa's green and gold journal to my bag, I pulled out a copy of the *New York Tribune* and tossed it on his bed. He opened it and held it close to read the title line, "More of the Cherokee Indians". He glared at me, squinting, and hurriedly turned to the last page with sudden realization who I was. I signed the piece with no pseudonym, not with my Cherokee name Yellow Bird, but with the name given to me by my father: John Rollin Ridge.

Every year of my life led to the article in Ross' hands: Miss Sawyer's lessons at the school Mama and Papa built at Running Waters, my time at Grandmother Northrup's in Massachusetts studying at Barrington, Reverend Washbourne's log walls reading the law. From all the scraps of poetry on torn paper to my first article for the *Delta*, the politics of the *California American*, to founding editor of the *Sacramento Bee*, editorials covering native rights and the Civil War, in the *Red Bluff Beacon*,

Marysville Herald, *Hesperian*, and *Trinity Journals*.

I pulled the painted As Nas card from my pocket and handed it to Ross. "My father and grandfather sold the country for the benefit of the nation, but you and yours put the money in your pockets. For the honest and disinterested sale, the Ridges were murdered. For appropriating the money, the Rosses have been sustained, honored, and promoted."[9]

With restrained silence, I collected the ledger and the letters from the floor and left him only my article and Papa's card, still gripped in his shaking hand. I saw myself outside, closing the door behind me. Once beyond the lobby doors, I breathed the cleanest breath, so deep my weightless soul sighed.

The following day of negotiations, Ross' message to President Johnson read, "Yes Sir, I am an old man, and have served my people and the government of the United States a long time, over fifty years. My people have kept me in the harness, not of my seeking, but of their own choice. I have never deceived them, and now I look back, not one act of my public life rises to unbraid me. I have done the best I could, and today, upon this bed of sickness, my heart approves of all I have done. I am still John Ross, the same John Ross of former years."[10]

I thought to myself, "Yes, you've always been the same: a wealthy thief, an honor less traitor, a murderer of the just."

Our delegation healed our nation's wounds and united the Cherokee Nation. Chief John Ross died five days after we signed the treaty, August 1, 1866. He died of old age, or so his doctor said.

In October of the following year, I found myself with a doctor hovering at the foot of my bed, standing between Lizzie and Alice, each holding my opposing hands. They spoke around me, not thinking I could hear.

"Encephalitis," the doctor reported, "a softening of his brain."

With desperation, Lizzie said, "He talks to me, but it's only nonsense. He tosses and mumbles. I can't understand him." She reached across my knees and took Alice's hand. How tight a grip they held over me.

No words came from my mouth, but I understood all she said. My mind answered her. "No, Running Deer. It isn't nonsense to dream of evil men living charmed lives killed by paper bullets. Or of horses stomping the throats of mountain lions. Never wrong to know how injustices done to three men become injustices to the world."[11]

Lizzie asked Alice to show the physician to the door, leaving me and her alone.

Yellow Bird's Song

She rinsed a cloth in a water basin beside the bed, rang its contents free, and placed it on my forehead. I opened my eyes to shocking light, like lightning flashes that leave its witness temporarily blind.

She wiped my forehead and returned to join our hands by my side. She called to me, repeating my name. I knew I couldn't answer her, but hoped she sensed my thoughts. She was my spirit-talker, my Running Deer.

Once Fortune's hand strewed our path with flowers and kindly swept away the thorns. Even in my happiest hours here, words of other days stole along and silently overwhelmed me. Words too deep to be repeated— remembered words. Eternity cannot destroy what would send thrills into my spirit. Forgetfulness is not for us; let us remember.[12]

My needless breaths came in shallow puffs. Dark spots consumed the room. When little air remained, I spent my last saying, "Oh darlin', how I wish I had wings."

With no pain or noise, the weight of the quilts covering my body unleashed their restraints. My shapeless spirit hovered above. My amber light reached out to touch her curls when she wiped tears from her eyes. It is well that woman should, like a weeping angel, sanctify the dark and suffering world with her tears. Let them flow. The blood which stains the fair face of our mother Earth may not be washed out with an ocean of tears.[13]

I tried speaking to her. I said, "Find it. Read it, my love. They were the first and the last words I can give you."

She must have sensed my thought and pulled the filthy and torn parchment from the pocket of my coat draped across a nearby chair. She opened it, touched her hand to her mouth, and said, "Rollin, you finished.

The prairies are broad, and the woodlands are wide,
And proud on his steed, the wild half-breed may ride,
With belt round his waist and knife at his side.
And no white man may claim his beautiful bride.
Oh, never let Sorrow's cloud darken their fate,
The girl of the "pale face", her Indian mate!
But deep in the forest of shadows and flowers,
Let happiness smile, as she wings their sweet hours."[14]

She said, "My love, I make one last promise to you. This world will know your spirit, read your songs." She stopped the clock hanging on the wall, walked to the window, and opened it, with incoming wind blowing hair across her face.

A voice came to me in the breeze. *"Cheesquatalawny, once we chased the dusk. Time to chase the dawn."*

With the overwhelming smell of pleasant earth rising from the ground, my yellow-feathered wings soared. Once again, Papa led me, flying behind his mockingbird's black and gray. If living thought could never die, why should he expire? If there was love within his heart, he must live on. No less than a man's dwelling place above, the mockingbird's notes were far brighter now than ever. And I heard his call, with finer ear and clearer soul, beneath a shade more soft, a sky more blue.[15]

Papa led me higher, away from the Pacific coast, northwest, speeding on endless gales beside Mount Shasta. From a lofted nest above us, broad eagle's wings soared across the night sky. Papa glided underneath, paralleling the eagle's path. I followed, speeding through the star-filled sky. Papa sang, *"Rollin, do you remember?"*

Then we turned east, gliding with wings, soaring faster than tumbleweed blowing across the Nevada desert. Then, we skimmed the surface of the prairies, growing tassels of corn and wheat. Papa sank and dove down next to a running creek, the Neosho. From a nearby branch, two cardinals perched side by side. The red male began its song. It was Peter. The female answered in a voice I knew as well as my mother's, Honey. The four of us flew side by side to Honey Creek, gliding over Peter's Prairie. Papa fluttered and rested his claws on a tombstone engraved with his earthly name. I followed, perching on Grandfather's stone next to his.

The horizon purpled the sky highlighted with rose hues, barely unsealing the sun. It was the hour farmers woke. Testing my strange voice, I asked, *"Where is he?"*

He replied in a tongue my soul understood. *"Your grandfather and grandmother are beyond, in the Nightland. They wait for us. We remain here, never again to leave one another behind. My penance is also yours— to watch above the living. We are nearby, but unable to warn them in a way they understand. My noble son, know I never left your side. What a life you've led. I'm proud of you."* He let go with the breeze and flew southeast.

I followed him toward the morning sun. We glazed over the Mississippi River, yielding to the gray green of morning forests, homeward bound, to the familiar ridges of Cherokee's Blue Mountains.

Papa spoke in my mind. *"Rollin, glide to the oak beneath you. She waits for you."*

I did as he said, tightening the muscles in my wings, holding my golden feathers rigid, close to my breast. I slowed and fluttered, gripping the branch of an oak that held a ramshackle cabin upright.

It was too late. Human bones draped down broken stairs. My heart knew it was Clarinda. I felt abandoned, lost. As I had when I was a child, I sang my sister's name, but she was mute. She could offer no answer.

When the sun peeked over the mountaintop, I heard a woman speak. Her chirps whispered, *"Brave brother."* Above me, a redbird opened her eyes. Her long wings lifted, stretching wider than mine ever could, and circled straight up into the sky. My sister's voice commanded, *"Follow me. The journey is not far."* It was the first time I'd ever heard my sister's voice.

Thin air scorched my tiny lungs. I climbed upward, flying behind her, higher than I thought my wings could carry me, past the morning horizon.

When Clarinda reached the pinnacle between sunlight and space, she tucked her wings close and dove straight down. My eyes closed as we made the searing dive to the Nightland. When the pressure released, we descended, stretching our wings into a field of sunflowers, settling on the branches of the laurel tree.

Clarinda said, *"Papa said we have to fall before we can fly."* She swooped up and joined the owl circling above us, Skili.

I settled and hopped down a branch and perched beside my brothers, Herman, a red bird, and Aeneas, a flickering woodpecker. And then Papa's mockingbird flitted to a higher branch to reveal Mama's red-throated hummingbird form, hovering in front of me.

She said, "My son, there was never any need to ask for my forgiveness."

Did the birds above man only warble warnings of dangerous mountain lions on the prowl? Call their mates nesting far away? Had they only chirped from their need of mere seed and worm? What prophecies did their warnings foretell? What philosophy did their chirps teach when my mind couldn't comprehend such lessons?

Not seeing, I had seen. Not hearing, I had heard.

Grounded on Earth, we come from direct communion with nature in her most sublime and beautiful aspects. We look upon the tall hills that lift into the dome of Heaven above pine-clad summits, filled with weird-like music (as if the thunder whispered), and stoop upon their ridges, breathing in the purer atmosphere which bathes them, a newer life to soul and body. We watch the eagle soar from the cliffs far into the blue ether over our heads or diving into the abyss of air beneath our feet until we could almost have been willing to exchange our immortality for the power of his sun-gazing eye and cloud-cleaving wing.[16]

I joined my family's birdsong, speaking with caws that echoed across endless space. With my senses awakened, all the birds became my soothsayers, shaman seers through yellow glimmer and gaze. As Yellow Bird, I understood such incomprehensible poetry. They sang over their loved ones, flightless beneath.

"*Hold fast,*" they said. "*Steady, nourishing rain falls just beyond the boastful thunder and arrogant lightning.*"

All my earthly life, so many birds flew past—knowing.

To be continued....

SPECIAL THANKS

My special thanks to the guides, hosts, and friends for their many contributions to this narrative. All my gratitude is yours.

Nancy Brown, Ridge Descendant
Paul and Dottie Ridenour, Ridge Descendant
The Rush Family
The Chieftain's Museum staff and Board of Directors, Rome, Georgia
New Echota Historical Site
The Vann House Historical Site, Chatsworth, Georgia
Red Clay Historic Site, Red Clay, Tennessee
Ross House Historic Site in Rossville, Tennessee
Ross Historic Home Site, Tahlequah, Oklahoma
Cherokee Nation Museum, East
Cherokee Nation Museum, West
The Hermitage, President Andrew Jackson's Home
Sarah Ridge Home, Fayetteville, Arkansas
Georgia Historical Society
Dee Dee Lamb and staff of the Fayetteville Arkansas Historical Society
Cornwall Historical Society
DeGolyer Special Collections Library at Southern Methodist University in Dallas, TX
Southern New Hampshire University MFA Faculty and Staff
Claudia Best
Valli Robinson
Norma Gambini
Michelle Mitchell
Penny Lewis
Norma Gambini
Mark Greathouse
Jennifer Miller
Carla Read
Kathy Waldrop
Lauren Forry
Gabino Iglesias
Alex Hammond
Lydia Popiolek
Dee Marley

ABOUT THE AUTHOR

As an English educator, Heather Miller has spent twenty-five years teaching her students the author's craft. Now, she's writing herself, hearing voices from America's past. Miller's foundation began in the theatre through performance storytelling. But by far, her favorite roles have been a fireman's wife, and mom to three: a trumpet player, an RN, and a civil engineer. Alas, there's only one English major living in her house. While teaching, researching, and writing the Ridge Family Saga, Heather earned her MFA in Creative Writing in 2022.

heathermillerauthor.com

NOTES

Prologue
1. Andrew Jackson speech, "To the Cherokee Tribe of Indians East of the Mississippi River."

Chapter 1: Iron and Salt
1. David Farmer and Rennard Strickland, *A Trumpet of Our Own*, pg. 33.
2. John Rollin Ridge poem, "The Still Small Voice".
3. *A Trumpet of Our Own*, pg. 19.
4. Ibid.
5. Ibid.
6. Edward Everett Dale and Gaston Litton, *Cherokee Cavaliers*, pg. 64.
7. John Rollin Ridge poem, "To a Mockingbird Singing in a Tree".
8. John Rollin Ridge poem, "The Still Small Voice".

Chapter 2: The Wild Half-Breed May Ride
1. Chapter title borrowed from John Rollin Ridge poem, "The Stolen White Girl".
2. *Cherokee Cavaliers*, pg. 77.
3. John Rollin Ridge poem, "To Lizzie".
4. Dave Tabler, "The Story of the Wampus Cat."
5. Ibid.
6. Ibid.
7. Ibid.
8. Ibid.
9. Ibid.
10. "Transcription of the Journal of John Ridge, a Member of the Cherokee Delegation."
11. Quote attributed to Thomas Jefferson.
12. John Rollin Ridge poem, "The Still Small Voice".

Chapter 3: Civilized
1. *Othello*, Act 5, scene 2.
2. Cherokee translation of "eclipse".
3. "General Council of the Cherokee Nation." *Cherokee Phoenix*, Volume 1, Issue 34, published October 22, 1828.
4. "The Phoenix de Ave Phoenice"
5. "The Messenger: Samuel Worcester and the Fight for Cherokee Land."
6. Robert J. Conley, *Cherokee Thoughts*, pg. 18.

Chapter 5: Black Drink
1. "Challenge Bowl 2022," pg. 3.
2. "New Echota." *Cherokee Phoenix*, Volume 1, Issue 18, published June 25, 1828
3. Ibid.

4. Ibid.
5. Ibid.
6. Ibid.
7. Ibid.
8. Ibid.
9. Ibid.
10. *History of the Indian Tribes of North America, Volume II. DeGolyer Library.*
11. *Cherokee Phoenix*, Volume 1, Issue 18.
12. Ibid.
13. Ibid.
14. Ibid.
15. Ibid.
16. Ibid.
17. Ibid.
18. Ibid.
19. Ibid.
20. Ibid.
21. Ibid.

Chapter 6: Such Rest to Him who Faints upon the Journey
1. Chapter title borrowed from John Rollin Ridge poem, "The Humboldt Desert".
2. James W. Parins, *John Rollin Ridge*, pg. 63-64.
3. Ibid., pg. 13.
4. Ibid., pg. 64-65.
5. John Rollin Ridge poem, "The Humboldt Desert".

Chapter 8: My Life Upon Her Faith
1. Chapter title quoted from *Othello*, Act 1, scene 3.
2. *The Constitutionalist*.
3. Ibid.
4. *The Bible*, King James Version, Proverbs 31.
5.. Ibid.
6.. Ibid.
7. KJV, Job 28:19.
8. *Othello*, Act 1, scene 3.

Chapter 9: Balm in Gilead
1. Hymn title, "There is a Balm in Gilead." Lyrics by John Newton (1725-1807).
2. Thurman Wilkins, *Cherokee Tragedy*, pg. 186-188.
3. Lyrics to "There is a Balm in Gilead."
4. Ibid.
5. Ibid.
6. Ibid.
7. Ibid.

Chapter 10: It Matters
1. Paraphrased from Dennis Cassinelli's article, "The Tragedy at Susan's Bluff."
   2. *John Rollin Ridge*, pg. 68.

Chapter 11: White Man's Flies
1. Refrain from popular Georgia tune, 1820s. Cited in *Cherokee Tragedy* and Steve Inskeep, *Jacksonland*.
2. Paraphrased from Socrates' articles printed in Cherokee Phoenix, with arguments posed by Kelly Wisecup. "Practicing Sovereignty."
3. Kalsatee's narrative paraphrased from *Jacksonland*, pg. 2-4.
4. *Cherokee Tragedy*, pg. 207-209.
5. Ibid.
6. "How the Honeybee Got Their Stinger, A Cherokee Legend."

Chapter 12: The Garden of the Three Sisters
1. Stanley Rice. *Nanyehi: War and Peace in Cherokee History*,
2. Ibid.
3. "The Story of Nanyehi: A Powerful Indigenous Cherokee Woman."
4. *Nanyehi,*

Chapter 13: Broken Strings

1. John Rollin Ridge's letter to his wife and mother, cited in both *John Rollin Ridge* and in the 2013 issue of *Fayetteville History*.
2. *John Rollin Ridge*, pg. 67.
3. Ibid.
4. Ibid., pg. 70.
5. Modoc Origin Myth, "When Grizzlies Walked Upright."
6. American Experience, "African Americans in the Gold Rush" Spencer Hill story.
7. Ibid.

8. John Rollin Ridge's memory of his father's assassination from the introduction to "The Poems of John Rollin Ridge – A Reproduction of the 1868 Publication plus Fugitive Poems and Notes".
9. Ibid.
10. John Rollin Ridge poem, "Mount Shasta".

Chapter 14: Mercy

1. *Cherokee Tragedy*, pg. 209
2. Cherokee Council Meetins from 1829; Chief Womankiller
3. "In Our Last We Stated..." *Cherokee Phoenix,* Volume 2, Issue 28, published October 21, 1829.
4. Ibid.
5. Ibid.

Chapter 15: Lily of the Valley
1. Edie Smith, "What Is the Meaning of Lily of the Valley?"
2. Ian Newman, "Nightingales in Literature."

Chapter 16: Too Impatient to Wait for God
1. "Cherokee War Dance." *YouTube video*, Lost Worlds Television.

Chapter 18: A Newspaperman's Shoes
1. *Cherokee Tragedy*, pg. 72.
2. John Rollin Ridge, *The Life and Adventures of Joaquín Murieta*, pg. 27.
3. *Cherokee Tragedy*, pg. 72.
4. Ibid.
5. Ibid.
6. *The Life and Adventures of Joaquín Murieta*, pg. 8.
7. Ibid.
8. John Rollin Ridge poem, "The Stolen White Girl".
9. *The Life and Adventures of Joaquín Murieta*, pg. 71.
10. Ibid., pg. 14.
11. Ibid.
12. *Cherokee Tragedy*, pg. 73.

Chapter 19: Worlds Collide
1. Jerimiah Evarts' William Penn Letters in the National Intelligencer, as quoted in William Bruce Wheeler and Lorri Glover's *Discovering the American Past: A Look at the Evidence.*

Chapter 20: Feather, Gobble, Strut, and Spur
1. *Cherokee Tragedy*, pg. 212.
2. Andrew Jackson's message to Congress, "On Indian Removal".
3. Ibid.
4. Jonathan Filler Master's thesis, *Arguing in an Age of Unreason.*
5. George Ellison, "The Turkey's Role in Cherokee Culture."
6. James Mooney, *History, Myth, and Sacred Formulas of the Cherokee.*
7. *Cherokee Tragedy*, pg. 215.
8. James Madison as cited in Jim Powell's "James Madison — Checks and Balances to Limit Government Power".

Chapter 21: Our Liberty, Most Dear
1. Andrew Jackson and John C. Calhoun, contradictory toasts at Jefferson's Memorial Banquet. *Digital History.*
2. *The Men Who Built America: Frontiersmen.* History Channel.
3. "Crockett and the Creek War."
4. Ibid.
5. "Men of Legend: The Battle of the Alamo."
6. *Cherokee Tragedy*, pg. 219-225.
7. Davy Crockett and Farmer Bunce, "Not Yours to Give."
8. Ibid.
9. Ibid.
10. President Andrew Jackson and John C. Calhoun, contradictory toasts at Jefferson's Memorial Banquet. *Digital History.*
11. Ibid.
12. *Cherokee Tragedy*, pg. 220-221.
13. Ibid.
14. David Dobkins, *The Rhetoric of John Ridge,*
15. *The Men Who Built America: Frontiersmen.* History Channel.
16. *Declaration of Independence.*

17. John Ridge's "Cherokee Indians: Memorial of a Delegation of the Cherokee Tribe of Indians, January 9, 1832, Read and Laid upon the Table."
18. *Declaration of Independence.*
19. Ibid.
20. Ibid.

Chapter 22: Cursed
1. Robert J. Conley, *The Witch of Goingsnake*
2. William Setzer's "The Phytochemistry of Cherokee Aromatic Medicinal Plants." *Medicines.*
3. Ibid.
4. *Cherokee Phoenix*, Jan 19, 1833. *Cherokee Phoenix* edition printed two years later, in summation of events beginning in 1831.
5. Ibid.
6. Ibid.

Chapter 24: Riding Blind
1. *The Life and Adventures of Joaquín Murieta*, pg. 24.
2. Ibid., pg. 9.
3. Ibid., pg. 9.
4. Ibid., pg. 27.
5. Ibid., pg. 59.
6. Ibid.
7. Ibid.
8. Ibid.
9. *Jacksonland*, pg. 332.
10. M. Arbuckle, Brevet Brigadier General U.S. to Hon. J.R. Poinsett, Secretary of War. Doc 188 pgs. 27- 28. https://digitalcommons.law.ou.edu/cgi/viewcontent.cgi?article=8100&context=indianserialset
11. Ibid.
12. *John Rollin Ridge*, pgs. 93, 114.

Chapter 25: Bronze Eagles
1. John Ridge's "Cherokee Indians: Memorial of a Delegation of the Cherokee Tribe of Indians."
2. Ibid.
3. Ibid.
4. Elias Boudinot's "Speech to the Whites," 1826, National Humanities Center.
5. *Cherokee Tragedy*, pg. 234.
6. Henry David Thoreau, "Sunday," in "A Week on the Concord and Merrimack Rivers".
7. Elias Boudinot interview with Garrison, quoted in Natalie Joy's "Cherokee Slaveholders and Radical Abolitionists." *Commonplace.*
8. Ibid.
9. Ralph Waldo Emerson, "Self-Reliance" essays.
10. *Cherokee Tragedy*, pg. 235.
11. Theresa Strouth Gaul et al, *To Marry an Indian*. Elias Boudinot quote, pg. 59.
12. *Cherokee Tragedy*, pg. 236.
13. *Cherokee Cavaliers*, pg. 8.

14. John Adams' inscription on fireplace mantle in the White House.
16-. Christopher D. Haveman PhD dissertation, *The Removal of the Creek Indians from the Southeast, 1825-1838*. Auburn University, 2009, pg. 128.
17. Ibid.
18. Ibid.
19. Ibid., pg. 161.
20. *Jacksonland*, pgs. 111-113, 333.
21. *The Removal of the Creek Indians from the Southeast*, pg.161.

Chapter 26: The Shepherd
1. "Memoir of John Arch, a Cherokee Young Man." *Google Books*.
2. KJV, John 1:29.
3. "Transcription of the Journal of John Ridge."
4. *Cherokee Tragedy*, pg. 231.
5. "Transcription of the Journal of John Ridge."

Chapter 27: Lion's Roar
1. "A." *Cherokee Phoenix*, Volume 5, Issue 23, published July 20, 1833.
2. *The Removal of the Creek Indians from the Southeast*, pg. 139.
3. *Cherokee Tragedy*, pg. 239.
4. Ibid.
5. *Cherokee Tragedy*, pg. 294. Originally spoken publicly by Major Ridge in 1835.
6. Ibid.
7. *Cherokee Phoenix*, Volume 4, Issue 52. published August 11, 1832.
8. Theda Perdue's *Cherokee Editor: The Writings of Elias Boudinot*. pg. 163.
9. Ibid.
10. Ibid.
11. John Sedgwick, *Blood Moon*, pg. 202.
12. Ibid., pg. 203.
13. Bethany Henry's dissertation *Cherokee Freedmen: The Struggle for Citizenship*.The University of Arkansas, Fayetteville. pg. 28.
14. Ibid.

Chapter 28: Betrayal
1. Althea Bass, *Cherokee Messenger*, pg. 159.
2. *Cherokee Tragedy*, pg. 253.
3. Ibid., pg. 254.
4. "Transcription of the Journal of John Ridge,"
pg. 98.
5. *Cherokee Tragedy*, pg. 256.

Chapter 29: Unsanctioned Integrity
1. *Cherokee Tragedy*, pg. 245.
2. Ibid., pg. 258.
3. John Ridge's letter, September 22, 1833, from Cassville, Georgia, to Wilson Lumpkin, Governor. *Digital Library of Georgia*.
4. *Cherokee Tragedy*, pg. 261.
5. Ibid.

6. Ovid Andrew McMillion, *Cherokee Indian Removal: The Treaty of New Echota and General Winfield Scott.*
7. Charles C. Royce. *The Cherokee Nation of Indians*, pg. 274.

Chapter 30: Golden Gate
1. *John Rollin Ridge*, pg. 137.
2. *The Life and Adventures of Joaquín Murieta*, pg. 137.
3. John Rollin Ridge poem, "Harp of Broken Strings".
4. Ibid.
5. *A Trumpet of our Own*, pg. 26.
6. *The Life and Adventures of Joaquín Murieta*, pg. 26.

Chapter 31: Know Nothing
1. *John Rollin Ridge*, pg. 117.
2. Angie Debo, "John Rollin Ridge" in *Southwest Review*.
3. John Rollin Ridge poem, "Forgiven Dead".
4. John Rollin Ridge poem, "October Hills".

Chapter 32: Hollow
1. King and Evans, "Death of John Walker, Jr.," in *Journal of Cherokee Studies* Volume 1, Number 1, pg. 52.
2. *Cherokee Tragedy*, pg. 253.
3. Ibid.
4. Paul Ridenour, "Quotes and Stories" "www.paulridenour.com/quotes.htm."
5. Ibid.
6. KJV, Hebrews 12:1.
7. W. Jeff Bishop, "The Walker Murder: The Spark That Lit the Fire."
8. Ibid.
9. "Death of John Walker, Jr.," pg. 13.
10. Ross, John. "Head of Coosa, Cherokee Nation." Received by Andrew Jackson, 15
Sept. 1834.
11. "The Spark That Lit the Fire."

Chapter 33: The Gambit
1. KJV, Isaiah 45:2.
2. KJV, Matthew 18:22.
3. "Transcription of the Journal of John Ridge," pg. 9.

Chapter 34: With Clearer Soul and Fine-Tuned Ear
1. *A Trumpet of Our Own*. pg. 29.
2. *John Rollin Ridge*, pg. 215-216.
3. *Jacksonland*, pg. 332.
4. Ibid.
5. Gerard Reed, *The Ross-Watie Conflict*, pg. 133.
6. M. Arbuckle, Brevet Brigadier General U.S. to Hon. J.R. Poinsett, Secretary of War. Doc 188 pg. 27, 28. https://digitalcommons.law.ou.edu/cgi/viewcontent.cgi?article=8100&context=indianserialset
7. Sarah 'Sollee' Ridge Paschal, "The Cherokees." *Arkansas Gazette*, 21 Dec.

1839.

8. "Transcription of the Journal of John Ridge," pg. 79.

9. John Rollin Ridge. "More of the Cherokee Indians." Published in the *New York Tribune*, 28 May 1866.

10. John Ross, "The Life and Times of Principal Chief John Ross."

11. *The Life and Adventures of Joaquín Murieta*, pg.136.

12. John Rollin Ridge. "To - - -," pg. 1-2.

13. *The Life and Adventures of Joaquín Murieta*, pg. 47.

14.*John Rollin Ridge*, pg. 46-49.

15. John Rollin Ridge poem, "To a Mockingbird Singing in a Tree".

16. A Trumpet of Our Own, pg. 32.

BIBLIOGRAPHY

"A Note on the Language of the Narratives | Articles and Essays | Born in Slavery: Slave Narratives from the Federal Writers' Project, 1936-1938 | Digital Collections Library of Congress." *The Library of Congress*, https://www.loc.gov/collections/slave-narratives-from-the-federal-writers-project-1936-to-1938/articles-and-essays/note-on-the-language-of-the-narratives/ . Accessed 28 Aug. 2022.

Abram, Susan. *"Souls in the Treetops:" Cherokee War, Masculinity, and Community, 1760-1820*. 2009. Auburn University, PhD dissertation. etd.auburn.edu//handle/10415/1828 .

"After John Marshall's Decision: Worcester v. Georgia and the Nullification Crisis on JSTOR." *Snhu.edu*, 2016, https://www.jstor.org.ezproxy.snhu.edu/stable/2205966#metadata_info_tab_conte nts . Accessed 7 Sept. 2022.

"African Americans in the Gold Rush." *PBS.org*, American Experience, 19 Sept. 2017, www.pbs.org/wgbh/americanexperience/features/goldrush-stephen-hill_/. Accessed 3 May 2022.

"Alonzo Delano." *Wikipedia*, 5 Dec. 2021, en.wikipedia.org/wiki/Alonzo Delano Accessed 23 June 2022.

"American Indian Biography: John Rollin Ridge, Cherokee Writer." *Native American Netroots*, 2017, nativeamericannetroots.net/diary/827 . Accessed 17 Feb. 2022.

"The Andrew Ross Home." *Landmarks of DeKalb County, Alabama*, 18 Mar. 2016, www.landmarksdekalbal.org/preserving-dekalb-county-alabama-landmarks/andrew-ross-home/ . Accessed 2 Jan. 2023.

Arbuckle, M. "H.R. Doc. No. 188, 26th Cong., 1st Sess. (1840)." *Letter from the Secretary of War, in Reply to the Resolution of the House of Representatives of the 23d Ultimo, Respecting the Interference of Any Officer or Agent of the Government with the Cherokee Indians in the Formation of a Government for the Regulation of Their Own Internal Affairs*, 14 Apr. 1840, pp. 27–28. *University of Oklahoma College of Law Digital Commons*, H.R. Doc. No. 188, 26th Cong., 1st Sess. (1840). Accessed 16 Sept. 2023.

"As Nas." *BoardGameGeek*, 2014, boardgamegeek.com/boardgame/63501/nas . Accessed 30 Apr. 2022.

"As Nas." *Poker Wiki*, 2022, poker.fandom.com/wiki/As_Nas . Accessed 30 Apr. 2022.

"As-Nas." *Wikipedia*, 25 Feb. 2022, en.wikipedia.org/wiki/As-Nas . Accessed 1 May 2022.

"The Baker Rifle." *Eric Edwards Collected Works*, 7 Nov. 2013, ericwedwards.wordpress.com/2013/11/07/the-baker-rifle/ . Accessed 6 May 2022.

Barbara. "Travel — The White House (Part Two)." *The Enchanted Manor*, 19 Feb. 2015, www.theenchantedmanor.com/tag/the-john-adams-inscription-on-the-mantel-of-the-state-dining-room/ . Accessed 30 Dec. 2022.

Bass, Althea. *Cherokee Messenger*. Norman, University of Oklahoma Press, 1996.

Bishop, W. Jeff. *Running Waters*. Trail of Tears Association, Georgia Chapter, 2008.

———. "Vann's Valley and Head of Coosa: Nexus of Conflict on the Early American Frontier." *Blogspot*, 4 June 2022, cavespringga.blogspot.com/2012/08/vanns-valley-and-head-of-coosa-nexus-of.html . Accessed 4 June 2022.

———. "The Walker Murder: The Spark That Lit the Fire." *Blogspot*, 2022, trailofthetrail.blogspot.com/2010/10/walker-murder-spark-that-lit-fire.html . Accessed 16 June 2022.

"Boudinot, Elias. "An Address to the Whites," 1826." *Social Sci LibreTexts*, July 2020, socialsci.libretexts.org/Courses/Lumen_Learning/Book %3A_United_States_History_I %3A_OpenStax_(Lumen)/22%3A_Jacksonian_Democracy_Reader/22.03%3A_P rimary_Source-_Elias_Boudinot_An_Address_to_the_Whites_1826. Accessed 16 Sept. 2023.

Boudinot, Elias. "First Blood Shed by the Georgians!!" *Georgia Historic Newspapers*, 10 Feb. 1830, , gahistoricnewspapers-files.galileo.usg.edu/lccn/sn83020874/1830-02-10/ed-1/seq-2.pdf . Accessed 3 May 2022.

"Boudinot House Site." *Wsharing*, 2022, wsharing.com/WSphotosNewEchota9.htm . Accessed 20 Mar. 2022.

Boudinot, Elias, and Theda Perdue. *Cherokee Editor: The Writings of Elias Boudinot*. Athens, University of Georgia Press, 1996.

"The Capitol Building, Washington." History, Art & Archives: U.S. House of Representatives. *History House*, 2022, history.house.gov/Collection/Detail/30530 . Accessed 4 Sept. 2022.

"The Capitol from the Virginia Side of the Potomac." History, Art & Archives: U.S. House of Representatives. *History House*, 2013, history.house.gov/Collection/Detail/15032401338 . Accessed 4 Sept. 2022.

Cassinelli, Dennis. "The Tragedy at Susan's Bluff." *Nevada Appeal*, 2022, www.nevadaappeal.com/news/2022/feb/23/dennis-cassinelli-tragedy-susans-bluff/. Accessed 23 Nov. 2022.

"Challenge Bowl 2022." *The Muscogee Nation*, 2022, muscogeenation.com/wp-content/uploads/2021/11/CB-2022-Middle-School2.pdf

"Cherokee Council Meetings from 1829; Chief Womankiller." *National Park Service*, 2021, www.nps.gov/articles/000/chief-womankiller-passage.htm . Accessed 26 Mar. 2022.

Cherokee Images. "The Last Cherokee Midwife ᏍᎯ ᏣᏫᎩ ᎠᏗᏌᏗᏠᏋᎩ." *Cherokee Images*, 11 Aug. 2012, https://cherokeeimages.com/wp/the-last-cherokee-midwife-%E1%8E%A3%E1%8F%82-%E1%8F%A3%E1%8E %B3%E1%8E%A9-%E1%8E%A0%E1%8F%93%E1%8E%A6%E1%8F %98%E1%8F%97%E1%8F%8D%E1%8E%A9/ . Accessed 24 Mar. 2022.

"Cherokee Indians: Memorial of a Delegation of the Cherokee Tribe of Indians, January 9, 1832, Read and Laid upon the Table." *Digital Library of Georgia*, 2022, www.dlg.usg.edu/record/dlg_zlna_pam009?canvas=2&x=207&y=322&w=3410

Accessed 8 July 2022.

"Cherokee Phoenix." *Cherokee Phoenix*, Volume 2, Issue 44, February 17, 1830. *Wcu.edu*, 2022, www.wcu.edu/library/DigitalCollections/CherokeePhoenix/Vol2/no44/cherokee-phoenix-page-2-column-5b-page-3-column-2b.html . Accessed 19 Mar. 2022.

"Cherokee Phoenix." *Cherokee Phoenix*, Volume 4, Issue 52, August 11, 1832. *Wcu.edu*, 2022, www.wcu.edu/library/DigitalCollections/CherokeePhoenix/Vol4/no52/cherokee-phoenix-page-2-column-3a-page-3-column-1a.html . Accessed 8 Sept. 2022.

Cherokee Phoenix, Volume 5, Issue 23, July 20, 1833. *Wcu.edu*, 2022, www.wcu.edu/library/DigitalCollections/CherokeePhoenix/Vol5/no23/a-page-2-column-1a-3a.html . Accessed 3 Nov. 2022.

"Cherokee Words for Eclipse." *Your Grandmother's Cherokee*, 2017, www.yourgrandmotherscherokee.com/blog/cherokee-words-for-eclipse. Accessed 30 Oct. 2022.

Chris. "Men of Legend: The Battle of the Alamo." *Art of Manliness*, 2 Apr. 2009, www.artofmanliness.com/character/knowledge-of-men/men-of-legend-the-battle-of-the-alamo/ #:~:text=I%20would%20rather%20be%20beaten,than%20to%20be%20hypocritically%20immortalized. Accessed 28 June 2023.

Conley, Robert J. *Cherokee Thoughts: Honest and Uncensored*. Norman, University of Oklahoma Press, 2008.

———. *The Witch of Goingsnake and Other Stories*. Norman; London, University of Oklahoma Press, 1991.

"The Constitutionalist. (Augusta, Ga.) 1823-1832, November 27, 1827, Image 3." *Digital Library of Georgia*, 2022, https://gahistoricnewspapers.galileo.usg.edu/lccn/sn84025807/1827-11-27/ed-2/seq-3/ . Accessed 6 Nov. 2022.

"Coosa River, in Turkey Town." *Cherokee Phoenix*, Volume 1, Issue 51, March 4, 1829. *Wcu.edu*, 2022, www.wcu.edu/library/DigitalCollections/CherokeePhoenix/Vol1/no51/coosa-river-in-turkey-town-page-2-column-5a-page-3.html . Accessed 23 Nov. 2022.

"Correspondence on the Subject of the Emigration of Indians, between the 30th November, 1831, and 27th December, 1833, with Abstracts of Expenditures by Disbursing Agents, in the Removal and Subsistence of Indians, &C. &C." *University of Oklahoma College of Law Digital Commons*, 2018, digitalcommons.law.ou.edu/indianserialset/6885/ . Accessed 3 Nov. 2022.

Cox, Donna M. "The Power of a Song in a Strange Land." *The Conversation*, 13 Feb. 2020, theconversation.com/the-power-of-a-song-in-a-strange-land-129969 . Accessed 28 Aug. 2022.

Cremer, David. *Faunal Remains from Fort Mitchell, Russell County, Alabama*. 2004. The Florida State University, master's thesis.

Dale, Edward Everett, and Litton, Gaston. *Cherokee Cavaliers: Forty Years of Cherokee History as told in the Correspondence of the Ridge-Watie-Boudinot Family*. Norman, University of Oklahoma Press, 1969.

Dawson, Patricia. "The Weapon of Dress: Identity and Innovation in Cherokee Clothing, 1794-1838." *SHAREOK*, 2017, https://shareok.org/handle/11244/50932 . Accessed 19 Mar. 2022.

Debo, Angie. "John Rollin Ridge." *Southwest Review*, Volume 17, Number 1, 1932. *JSTOR*, www.jstor.org/stable/43461895 . Accessed 7 Jan. 2023.

"Declaration of Independence: A Transcription." *National Archives*, Nov. 2015, www.archives.gov/founding-docs/declaration-transcript . Accessed 22 Dec. 2022.

Demos, John. *The Heathen School: A Story of Hope and Betrayal in the Age of the Early Republic*. Vintage, 2014.

"Digital History." *Digital History*, 2021, www.digitalhistory.uh.edu/disp_textbook.cfm?smtID=2&psid=3546#:~:text=Jackson%20revealed%20his%20position%20on%20the%20questions%20of . Accessed 22 Dec. 2022.

Dobkins, David. *The Rhetoric of John Ridge: An Analysis of the Conflict of Cherokee Removal.* 1975. The University of Arkansas, master's thesis.

Ealer, John, director. *The Men Who Built America: Frontiersmen*. History Channel, HIST, 18 Mar. 2018.

"Echoes from the Past: The Separate Lives of John Ross." *Stilwell Democrat Journal*, 15 June 2021, www.stilwelldemocrat.com/community/column-echoes-from-the-past-the-separate-lives-of-john-ross/article_80fce828-cd5c-11eb-86d2-bfd1b418b41a.html . Accessed 22 Jan. 2023.

Ehle, John. *Trail of Tears: The Rise and Fall of the Cherokee Nation*. New York, Anchor Books, 1988.

"El Dorado County, California Genealogy Trails: Historical Places." *Genealogy Trails*, 2022, genealogytrails.com/cal/eldorado/history/historical_places.html . Accessed 1 May 2022.

Ellison, George. "The Turkey's Role in Cherokee Culture." *Smoky Mountain News*, 16 Aug. 2006, smokymountainnews.com/archives/item/13183-the-turkey-s-role-in-cherokee-culture . Accessed 26 June 2022.

Emerson, Ralph Waldo. "Essays, First Series (1841): Self-Reliance." *Vcu.edu*, 2022, archive.vcu.edu/english/engweb/transcendentalism/authors/emerson/essays/selfreliance.html. Accessed 30 Dec. 2022.

Endicott, George and Swett, Moses. "Brown's Indian Queen Hotel, Washington City North Side of Pennsylvania Avenue about Midway between the Capitol and the President's House, a Few Doors East of the Centre Market / / Lithog. of Endicott & Swett, No. 111, Nassau Street, N.Y." *The Library of Congress*, 2015, www.loc.gov/resource/pga.06273/ . Accessed 1 July 2022.

"Excerpt of an 1833 Letter from John Ridge to Georgia Governor Wilson Lumpkin, Urging Wilson to Force John Ross into a Treaty." *Digital Public Library of America*, 2017, dp.la/primary-source-sets/cherokee-removal-and-the-trail-of-tears/sources/1505 . Accessed 4 Sept. 2022.

"Experiment in Cherokee Citizenship, 1817-1829 on JSTOR." *Snhu.edu*, 2016, www-jstor-org.ezproxy.snhu.edu/stable/2712531?seq=18#metadata_info_tab_contents . Accessed 4 Sept. 2022.

"The Fascinating History of Brown's Indian Queen Hotel on Pennsylvania Avenue." *Ghosts of DC*, 21 Feb. 2014, ghostsofdc.org/2014/02/21/browns-indian-queen-hotel-pennsylvania-avenue/ . Accessed 1 July 2022.

Farmer, David and Strickland, Rennard. *A Trumpet of Our Own: Yellow Bird's Essays on the North American Indian: Selections from the Writings of the Noted Cherokee Author, John Rollin Ridge*. San Francisco, The Book Club of California, 1981.

"Federal Writers' Project: Slave Narrative Project, Vol. 2, Arkansas, Part 1, Abbott-Byrd." *The Library of Congress*, www.loc.gov/item/mesn021/ November 2022.

Filler, Jonathan. *Arguing in an Age of Unreason: Elias Boudinot, Cherokee Factionalism, and the Treaty of New Echota*. 2010. Bowling Green State University, master's thesis.

Frazier, Charles. *Thirteen Moons*. Anstey, Leicestershire, Thorpe, Random House, 2007.

Gaul, Theresa Strouth, et al. *To Marry an Indian: The Marriage of Harriett Gold and Elias Boudinot in Letters, 1823-1839*. Chapel Hill, North Carolina; London, The University of North Carolina Press, 2005.

"General Council of the Cherokee Nation." *Cherokee Phoenix*, Volume 1, Issue 34, October 22, 1828. *Wcu.edu*, 2022, www.wcu.edu/library/DigitalCollections/CherokeePhoenix/Vol1/no34/general-council-of-the-cherokee-nation-page-1-column-1b-5b-and-page-2-column-1a-2a.html . Accessed 3 Apr. 2022.

Guy, Joe. "The Murder Case That Doomed the Cherokee." *RootsWeb*, 2022, sites.rootsweb.com/~tnmcmin2/jguymurder.htm . Accessed 16 Oct. 2022.

Haveman, Christopher D. *The Removal of the Creek Indians from the Southeast, 1825-1838*. 2009. Auburn University, PhD dissertation.

Hawn, C. Michael. "History of Hymns: 'There Is a Balm in Gilead.'" *Discipleship Ministries: The United Methodist Church*, 2019. www.umcdiscipleship.org/resources/history-of-hymns-there-is-a-balm-in-gilead. Accessed 23 Nov. 2022.

High, MAYFLOWER. "STEAMBOAT: "MAYFLOWER." High Pressure Steamboat "Mayflower" on the Mississippi River. Lithograph, C.1855." *Bridgemanimages.com*, 2022, www.bridgemanimages.com/en-U.S./noartistknown/steamboat-mayflower-high-pressure-steamboat-mayflower-on-the-mississippi-river-lithograph-c-1855/nomedium/asset/3407340 . Accessed 9 Oct. 2022.

History.com Editors. "Andrew Jackson Shuts down Second Bank of the U.S." www.history.com/this-day-in-history/andrew-jackson-shuts-down-second-bank-of-the-u-s. Accessed 7 July 2022.

"History of the Cherokee Indians and their Legends and Folklore." *RootsWeb*, sites.rootsweb.com/~itchertp/history/starr/chapter8.htm . Accessed 2 Oct. 2022.

"History of the Indian Tribes of North America, Volume II [Complete Volume]." *DeGolyer Library, Southern Methodist University*, 2020, digitalcollections.smu.edu/digital/collection/nam/id/426/. Accessed 5 Nov. 2022.

Hogan, William R. "Grand Prairie. By James K. Greer." *The Journal of Southern History*, Volume 2, Number 1, Feb. 1936, pp. 115-117. *JSTOR*, www.jstor.org/stable/2191571. Accessed 2 Oct. 2022.

"How Native American Women Gave Birth." *Sherman Indian Museum*, 2016, www.shermanindianmuseum.org/how-native-american-women-gave-birth.html. Accessed 10 Dec. 2022.

"How the Honeybee Got Their Stinger." *NORTHERN CHEROKEE NATION*, 2023, www.northerncherokeenation.com/how-the-honey-bee-got-their-stinger.html . Accessed 16 Sept. 2023.

"How the Turkey got his Beard: A Cherokee Legend." *First People*, 2022, www.firstpeople.us/FP-Html-Legends/HowTheTurkeyGotHisBeard-

Cherokee.html . Accessed 26 June 2022.

"Slave Narrative of Eliza Whitmire." *Access Genealogy*, Nov. 2012, accessgenealogy.com/georgia/slave-narrative-of-eliza-whitmire.htm . Accessed 28 Aug. 2022.

Hryniewicki, Richard J. "The Creek Treaty of November 15, 1827." *The Georgia Historical Quarterly*, Volume 52, Number 1, 1968, pp. 1–15. *JSTOR*, www.jstor.org/stable/40578764 . Accessed 5 Nov. 2022.

"Image 1 of Cherokee Phoenix, and Indians' Advocate (New Echota [Ga.]), February 10, 1830." *The Library of Congress*, 2015, www.loc.gov/resource/sn83020874/1830-02-10/ed-1/?sp=1&st=pdf . Accessed 19 Mar. 2022.

"Image 1 of John Ross to Andrew Jackson, September 15, 1834." *The Library of Congress*, 2015, www.loc.gov/resource/maj.01087_0182_0186/?st=text . Accessed 16 Oct. 2022.

"In Our Last We Stated That the General Council Was Organized on Monday, and the Message Read on Tues." *Cherokee Phoenix*, Volume 2, Issue 28, October 21, 1829. *Wcu.edu*, 2022, www.wcu.edu/library/DigitalCollections/CherokeePhoenix/Vol2/no28/in-our-last-we-stated-that-the-general-council-was-organized-on-monday-and-the-message-read-on-tues-page-3-column-1b-column-3b.html . Accessed 3 Apr. 2022.

"Indians." *Cherokee Phoenix*, Volume 5, Issue 26, August 10, 1833. *Wcu.edu*, 2022, www.wcu.edu/library/DigitalCollections/CherokeePhoenix/Vol5/no26/indians-page-2-column-1a-page-3-column-4a.html . Accessed 3 Nov. 2022.

Ingalls, Mary. *She Hath Done What She Could: The Story of Sophia Sawyer*. Fayetteville, AK., Washington County Historical Society, pp. 148–149.

Inskeep, Steve. "How Jackson Made a Killing in Real Estate." *POLITICO Magazine*, 4 July 2015, www.politico.com/magazine/story/2015/07/andrew-jackson-made-a-killing-in-real-estate-119727/ . Accessed 2 July 2022.

————. *Jacksonland: President Andrew Jackson, Cherokee Chief John Ross, and a Great American Land Grab*. New York, New York, Penguin Press, 2016.

"Interior of the House of Representatives, Washington." History, Art & Archives: United States House of Representative. *History House*, 2022, history.house.gov/Collection/Detail/42863 . Accessed 4 Sept. 2022.

Jackson, Andrew. "Farewell Address." *University of California, Santa Barbara*, 2022, www.presidency.ucsb.edu/documents/farewell-address-0 . Accessed 17 Sept. 2022.

————. "On Indian Removal." December 6, 1830. Records of the United States Senate, 1789-1990, Record Group 46, National Archives and Records Administration. Message to Congress. www.nps.gov/museum/tmc/manz/handouts/andrew_jackson_annual_message.pdf

————. "To the Cherokee Tribe of Indians East of the Mississippi River." 1835. Macon Weekly Telegraph, Macon, Georgia, USA. Newspaper. *Teach US History*. www.teachushistory.org/indian-removal/resources/cherokee-tribe-indians-jackson .

"Jesse Brown (1788-1847)" *WikiTree*, 6 Nov. 2015, www.wikitree.com/wiki/Brown-42296 . Accessed 7 July 2022.

"John Rollin Ridge." *LocalWiki*, 2022, localwiki.org/yuba-sutter/John_Rollin_Ridge. Accessed 9 Oct. 2022.

"John Rollin Ridge Goes West." *Fayetteville History*, 2009. www.fayettevillehistory.com/primary/2009/06/john-rollin-ridge-goes-west.html . Accessed 24 Nov. 2022.

"John Ross and the Cherokee Resistance Campaign, 1833-1838 on JSTOR." *Snhu.edu*, 2016, www-jstor-org.ezproxy.snhu.edu/stable/2208301? seq=6#metadata_info_tab_contents . Accessed 3 Nov. 2022.

"John Ross and the Cherokees on JSTOR." *Snhu.edu*, 2016, www-jstor-org.ezproxy.snhu.edu/stable/40581546#metadata_info_tab_contents . Accessed 1 Oct. 2022.

Jolly, Tes Randal. "Wild Turkeys Dueling over Breeding Rights." *Mossy Oak*, 2020, www.mossyoak.com/our-obsession/blogs/turkey/wild-turkeys-dueling-over-breeding-rights . Accessed 26 June 2022.

Joy of Fiddling. "Arkansas Traveler"- Katrina Nicolayeff - Camp Summer Sessions." *YouTube*, uploaded by joyoffiddling, 10 Aug. 2015, www.youtube.com/watch?v=PB3tSSlq130. Accessed 6 May 2022.

Joy, Natalie. "Cherokee Slaveholders and Radical Abolitionists." *Commonplace*, 9 Mar. 2010, commonplace.online/article/cherokee-slaveholders-radical-abolitionists/ . Accessed 19 Feb. 2021.

Justice, Daniel Heath. *Our Fire Survives the Storm: A Cherokee Literary History*. Minneapolis, Minnesota, University of Minnesota Press, 2006.

Kelly, Kate. "Traveling West in 1854: The Story of an 11-Year-Old Girl and Her Family." *America Comes Alive*, 6 Mar. 2013, americacomesalive.com/traveling-west-in-1854-the-story-of-an-11-year-old-girl-and-her-family/ . Accessed 28 Sept. 2022.

King and Evans. Journal of Cherokee Studies. United States, Museum of the Cherokee Indian, 1997.

Kosovsky, Bob. "African Americans in Early American Sheet Music." *The New York Public Library*, 2022, www.nypl.org/blog/2011/02/25/african-americans-early-american-sheet-music . Accessed 28 Aug. 2022.

Kyle, Jim. "The Baytown Sun 21 Jul 1985, Page 25." *Newspapers.com*, 21 July 1985, www.newspapers.com/image/7951387/? clipping_id=33305743&fcfToken=eyJhbGciOiJIUzI1NiIsInR5cCI6IkpXVCJ9.ey JmcmVlLXZpZXXctaWQiOjc5NTEzODcsImlhdCI6MTY3Mzk5NjY5MywiZXhw IjoxNjc0MDgzMDkzfQ.F07TM_TDzkt4GvBbfn_r4L6p2lK1BQDdcTt8-K88BG8 . Accessed 17 Jan. 2023.

"Letter from the Secretary of War, in Reply to the Resolution of the House of Representatives of the 23d Ultimo, Respecting the Interference of Any Officer or Agent of the Government with the Cherokee Indians in the Formation of a Government for the Regulation of Their Own Internal Affairs." 14 Apr. 1840, pp. 26–29. *University of Oklahoma College of Law Digital Commons*, digitalcommons.law.ou.edu/cgi/viewcontent.cgi? article=8100&context=indianserialset . Accessed 28 Aug. 2022.

"The Life and Times of Principal Chief John Ross." *Gilcrease Museum*, 2016,https://collections.gilcrease.org/articles/article-life-and-times-principal-chief-john-ross . Accessed 14 Jan. 2023.

Logan, Charles Russell. *The Promised Land: The Cherokees, Arkansas, and Removal, 1794-1839*. Arkansas Historic Preservation Program, 1997.

Loretto, Ed. "Davy Crockett's Advice to Andrew Jackson." *YouTube*, uploaded by TheToe13, 10 May 2007, www.youtube.com/watch?

v=fc94NY9_ZcU. Accessed 4 July 2022.

Lost Worlds TV. "Cherokee War Dance." *YouTube*, uploaded by LostWorldsTV, 8 Nov. 2021, www.youtube.com/watch?v=VjXBYlm4Wp8 . Accessed 6 May 2022.

Love Your Land. "Making Balm of Gilead ~ Love Your Land." *YouTube*, uploaded by 123loveyourland, 3 Mar. 2016, www.youtube.com/watch?v=kNuf78xC-lE. Accessed 19 Feb. 2022.

MacDonald, Craig, MacDonald, Franklin. "Coming Clean — Baths in the Gold Rush." *See California*, 2022, www.seecalifornia.com/history/goldrush-baths.html . Accessed 30 Apr. 2022.

"The Mayapple Is a Hidden Georgia-Native Gem." *Museum of Arts and Sciences*, www.masmacon.org/the-mayapple-is-a-hidden-georgia-native-gem/ .

McDaniel, Herman. "Vann Slaves Remember."
Murray County Mmuseum, 2020, www.murraycountymuseum.com/vann.html. Accessed 28 Aug. 2022.

McMillion, Ovid Andrew. *Cherokee Indian Removal: The Treaty of New Echota and General Winfield Scott*. 2003. East Tennessee State University, master's thesis. dc.etsu.edu/cgi/viewcontent.cgi?article=1935&context=etd

"Memoir of John Arch, a Cherokee Young Man." Fifth Edition. *Google Books*, 2013, books.google.com/books?id=aIleAAAAcAAJ&printsec=frontcover&source=gbs_ge_summary_r&cad=0#v=onepage&q&f=false . Accessed 23 Sept. 2022.

"Memorial of a Delegation from the Cherokee Indians: Presented to Congress January 18, 1831." *WorldCat*, 2022, www.worldcat.org/title/memorial-of-a-delegation-from-the-cherokee-indians-presented-to-congress-January-18-1831/oclc/191239892 . Accessed 8 July 2022.

Miles, Tiya. *Ties That Bind: The Story of an Afro-Cherokee Family in Slavery and Freedom*. Oakland, California, University of California Press, 2015.

Mooney, James. "How the Turkey Got His Beard." *Native History Association*, 2012, www.nativehistoryassociation.org/gvna_beard.php . Accessed 22 Dec. 2022.

Moulton, Gary E. *John Ross, Cherokee Chief*. 1974. Oklahoma State University, PhD dissertation.

"Native American Customs of Childbirth." *Teaching History*, 2018, teachinghistory.org/history-content/ask-a-historian/24097 . Accessed 23 Mar. 2022.

"Native American Symbolism." *Umn.edu*, 2022, www.d.umn.edu/cla/faculty/tbacig/studproj/a1041/eagle/native.html . Accessed 4 Sept. 2022.

"New Echota." *Cherokee Phoenix*, Volume 1, Issue 18, June 25, 1828. *Wcu.edu*, 2022, www.wcu.edu/library/DigitalCollections/CherokeePhoenix/Vol1/no18/new-echota-page-2-column-2b.html . Accessed 30 Oct. 2022.

"New-York Tribune. [volume] May 28, 1866, Page 6, Image 6." *Chronicling America: Historic American Newspapers, The Library of Congress*, 28 May 1866, p. 6, chroniclingamerica.loc.gov/lccn/sn83030214/1866-05-28/ed-1/seq-6/ . Accessed 2 Oct. 2022.

Newman, Ian. "Nightingales in Literature." *ThinkND*, 2 Feb. 2021, https://think.nd.edu/big_questions/nightingales-in-literature/ . Accessed 18 Dec.

2022.

"Not Yours to Give: Davy Crockett on the Role of Government." *Hush Money*, 2022, hushmoney.org/Davy_Crockett_Farmer_Bunce.htm . Accessed 7 July 2022.

Olbrechts, Frans M. "Cherokee Belief and Practice with Regard to Childbirth." *Anthropos*, Volume 26, Number 1/2, 1931, pp. 17–33. *JSTOR*, www.jstor.org/stable/40446137 . Accessed 10 Dec. 2022.

Parins, James W. *Elias Cornelius Boudinot: A Life on the Cherokee Border.* University Of Nebraska Press, 2008.

———. *John Rollin Ridge: His Life and Works*. Lincoln, University of Nebraska Press, 2004.

Payne, Daniel Alexander. "Recollections of Seventy Years." National Humanities Center, 2022, nationalhumanitiescenter.org/tserve/nineteen/nkeyinfo/aarpayneexrpt.htm . Accessed 28 Aug. 2022.

Perdue, Theda. *Cherokee Women: Gender and Cultural Change, 1700-1835.* Lincoln, New England, University of Nebraska Press, 1999.

Perdue, Theda, and Green, Michael D. *The Cherokee Nation and the Trail of Tears*. New York, Penguin Books, 2008.

Pete. "The Messenger: Samuel Worcester and the Fight for Cherokee Land." *Radical Tea Towel*, 2021, www.radicalteatowel.com/radical-history-blog/the-messenger-samuel-worcester-and-the-fight-for-cherokee-land/ . Accessed 30 Oct. 2022.

"The Phoenix de Ave Phoenice." *EWTN Global Catholic Television Network*, 2022, www.ewtn.com/catholicism/library/phoenix-de-ave-phoenice-11464 . Accessed 30 Oct. 2022.

"Pix, Sarah Ridge (1814-1891)." *Texas State Historical Association*, 2021, www.tshaonline.org/handbook/entries/pix-sarah-ridge . Accessed 30 Oct. 2022.

"Plant Lore of the Cherokee." *Blue Waters Mountain Lodge*, 20 Nov. 2010, bluewatersmtnl.com/plant-lore-of-the-cherokee/ . Accessed 24 Sept. 2022.

Poole, Arlen D. Life of Sarah Bird Northrup Ridge. *Flashback*. Vol 57 (Summer 2007): 49–66.

"Popular Sovereignty." *U.S. History*, www.ushistory.org/us/30b.asp .

Powell, Jim. "James Madison — Checks and Balances to Limit Government Power." *Foundation for Economic Education*, Mar. 1996, fee.org/articles/james-madison-checks-and-balances-to-limit-government-power/ . Accessed 29 June 2022.

"Preludes to the Trail of Tears." *National Park Service*, 2021, https://www.nps.gov/articles/000/preludes-trail-of-tears.htm . Accessed 20 Mar. 2022.

"PYRAMID MESA -- Legends." *Archive.org*, 2020,.https://web.archive.org/web/20121023034547/pyramidmesa.com/modoc1.ht m Accessed 16 Sept. 2023.

"Railroads 1850 and 1860; Overland Mail, 1850-1869." *Railroads and the Making of Modern America*, 2017, railroads.unl.edu/documents/view_document.php?id=rail.str.0243 . Accessed 23 Oct. 2022.

Ranck, M.A. "OSU Digital Collections." *Okstate.edu*, 2019, dc.library.okstate.edu/digital/collection/p17279coll4/id/31120 . Accessed 4 July

2022.

Ray, S. *Michigan Journal of Race and Law Michigan Journal of Race and Law*, vol. 12, p. 2007, https://efaidnbmnnnibpcajpcglclefindmkaj/https://repository.law.umich.edu/cgi/viewcontent.cgi?article=1116&context=mjrl#:~:text=In%20this%20Article%2C%20Professor%20Ray Accessed 16 Sept. 2023.

Reed, Gerard. *The Ross-Watie Conflict: Factionalism in the Cherokee Nation, 1839-1865*. 1980. University of Oklahoma, PhD dissertation. www.worldcat.org/title/ross-watie-conflict-factionalism-in-the-cherokee-nation-1839-1865/oclc/7225583 . Accessed 22 June 2022.

"Report of Trial of Stand Watie, Charged with Murder of James Foreman, 1843." *CARLI Digital Collections*, 2019, collections.carli.illinois.edu/digital/collection/nby_eeayer/id/9154/ . Accessed 28 Aug. 2022.

Rice, Stanley. *Nanyehi: War and Peace in Cherokee History*. Southeastern Oklahoma State University. Conference paper.

Ridenour, Paul. "The John Ridge Family." *Paulridenour.com*, 2022, www.paulridenour.com/jridge.htm . Accessed 8 Sept. 2022.

———. "Sarah Bird Northrup Ridge." *Paul Ridenour*, 2022, www.paulridenour.com/comfort.htm. Accessed 28 July 2022.

Ridley, Nicole. "The Story of Nanyehi: A Powerful Indigenous Cherokee Woman." Pearson.

Ridge, John. "Letter, 1833 Sept. 22, Cassville, Georgia, [to] Wilson Lumpkin, Governor of Georgia. John Ridge." *Digital Library of Georgia*, 2023, https://dlg.usg.edu/record/dlg_zlna_krc146?canvas=4&x=1196&y=1487&w=13099 Accessed 2 Jan. 2023.

———. "Success of the "Civilizing" Project among the Cherokee." 1836. *Teach US History*, 2022, www.teachushistory.org/indian-removal/resources/success-civilizing-project-among-cherokee . Accessed 23 Sept. 2022.

———. "Transcription of the Journal of John Ridge, a Member of the Cherokee Delegation." *DeGolyer Library, Southern Methodist University*, digitalcollections.smu.edu/digital/collection/wes/id/3295/rec/2 . Accessed 9 Sept. 2022.

Ridge, John Rollin. "A Letter to Wilson Lumpkin, Governor of Georgia." *In Time and Place*, 2022, www.intimeandplace.org/cherokee/reading/removal/ridgeletter.html . Accessed 28 Aug. 2022.

———. "Humboldt River." *Archive*, 2013, web.archive.org/web/20130906062916/etext.lib.virginia.edu/etcbin/toccer-new2id=RidThep.xml&images=images/modeng&data=/texts/english/modeng/parsed&ag=public&part=4&division=div2 . Accessed 19 Feb. 2022.

———. The Life and Adventures of Joaquín Murieta: The Celebrated California Bandit. London, Penguin Classics, 2018.

———. "More of the Cherokee Indians." *Chronicling America: Historic American Newspapers, The Library of Congress*, 28 May 1866, p. 6, chroniclingamerica.loc.gov/data/batches/dlc_delphi_ver02/data/sn83030214/00206530832/1866052801/0196.pdf Accessed 28 July 2022.

———. "Mount Shasta." *Poets.org*, 2017, poets.org/poem/mount-shasta .

Accessed 3 May 2022."The Poems of John Rollin Ridge -- A Reproduction of the 1868 Publication plus Fugitive Poems and Notes [a Machine-Readable Transcription]." *American Native Press Archives and Sequoyah Research Center*, https://ualrexhibits.org/tribalwriters/artifacts/Poems-of-John-Rollin-Ridge.html . Accessed 3 June 2023.

———. "To - - - -." *DeGolyer Library, Southern Methodist University*, 17 Feb. 1849, https://digitalcollections.smu.edu/digital/collection/wes/id/3290 . Accessed 14 Jan. 2023.

Ridge Paschal, Sarah. "The Cherokees." *Arkansas Gazette*, 21 Dec. 1839. *Arkansas Gazette Weekly from September 11, 1839, to August 10, 1842, Reel G.* Housed in the Little Rock Public Library, Little Rock, Arkansas.

Royce, Charles C. *The Cherokee Nation of Indians. (1887 N 05 / 1883—1884 (Pages 121—378)).* E-book, *Smithsonian Institution — Bureau of Ethnology*, 2014. Accessed 22 Dec. 2022.

Powell, William S. "Ross, John." *NSpedia*, 2022, www.ncpedia.org/biography/ross_john . Accessed 23 Oct. 2022.

"Samuel Worcester." *Savages and Scoundrels*, 2012, savagesandscoundrels.org/people/savages-scoundrels/samuel-worcester/ . Accessed 24 June 2022.

Scholarworks@UARK, and Bethany Henry. *Cherokee Freedmen: The Struggle for Citizenship Cherokee Freedmen: The Struggle for Citizenship*. 2014.

Sedgwick, John. Blood Moon: An American Epic of War and Splendor in the Cherokee Nation. New York, Simon and Schuster, 2019.

Setzer, William N. "The Phytochemistry of Cherokee Aromatic Medicinal Plants." *Medicines*, vol. 5, no. 4, 12 Nov. 2018, pp. 121–121, www.ncbi.nlm.nih.gov/pmc/articles/PMC6313439/ , https://doi.org/10.3390/medicines5040121. Accessed 27 Dec. 2022.

Shakespeare, William. "Othello, the Moore of Venice." *Shakespeare (MIT)*, 2022, shakespeare.mit.edu/othello/full.html . Accessed 28 Aug. 2022.

Shores, Heather. "Chieftains Museum Major Ridge Home." *Chieftains Museum Major Ridge Home*, 2019, chieftainsmuseum.org/ . Accessed 7 July 2022.

Simpson, Dorothy A. *Quatie Ross: First Lady of the Cherokee Nation.* Berwyn Heights, Maryland, Heritage Books, 2017.

Smith, Daniel Blake. *An American Betrayal: Cherokee Patriots and the Trail of Tears.* St. Martin's Griffin, 2013.

Smith, Edie. "What Is the Meaning of Lily of the Valley?" *Garden Guides*, 2017, www.gardenguides.com/13426295-what-is-the-meaning-of-lily-of-the-valley.html . Accessed 18 Dec. 2022.

"Stand Watie." *Angelfire*, 2022, www.angelfire.com/ak2/MannFamilyTree/Stand.html . Accessed 30 Oct. 2022.

"Steamships on the Panama Route — Both Atlantic and Pacific." *The Ships List*, 2022, www.theshipslist.com/ships/descriptions/panamafleet.shtml . Accessed 29 Sept. 2022.

Rennard, Strickland. "Yellow Bird's Song: The Message of America's First Native American Attorney." 1993. https://digitalcommons.law.utulsa.edu/cgi/viewcontent.cgi?article=2291&context=tlr

Tabler, Dave. "The Story of the Wampus Cat." *Appalachian History*, 13 Oct. 2017, www.appalachianhistory.net/2017/10/story-of-wampus-cat.html . Accessed 30 Oct. 2022.

Tanner, Michael, et al. "Fort Mitchell Historic Site." *Clio*, 2020 theclio.com/entry/215 . Accessed 29 June 2022.

"The Cherokee Phoenix: Supreme Expression of Cherokee Nationalism on JSTOR." *Snhu.edu*, 2016, www.jstor.org.ezproxy.snhu.edu/stable/40577233#metadata_info_tab_contents . Accessed 30 Oct. 2022.

"The Conflict Within: The Cherokee Power Structure and Removal on JSTOR." *Snhu.edu*, 2016, www-jstor-org.ezproxy.snhu.edu/stable/40582013/seq=3#metadata_info_tab_contents . Accessed 9 Sept. 2022.

"The Panamá Route to the Pacific Coast, 1848-1869 on JSTOR." *Snhu.edu*, 2013, www-jstor-org.ezproxy.snhu.edu/stable/3633844#metadata_info_tab_contents . Accessed 29 Sept. 2022.

Thoreau, Henry David. "A Week on the Concord and Merrimack Rivers." *Project Gutenberg*, 2022, www.gutenberg.org/cache/epub/4232/pg4232-images.html . Accessed 30 Dec. 2022.

"Through Deaf Eyes. Deaf Life. The First Permanent School | PBS." *Www.pbs.org*, 2007, www.pbs.org/weta/throughdeafeyes/deaflife/first_school.html

Toney, Tabatha. *"UNTIL WE FALL to the GROUND UNITED": CHEROKEE RESILIENCE and INTERFACTIONAL COOPERATION in the EARLY TWENTIETH CENTURY*. 2009. https://shareok.org/bitstream/handle/11244/317770/Toney_okstate_0664D_15737.pdf?sequence=1

Trafzer, Clifford E. *Fighting Invisible Enemies: Health and Medical Transitions among Southern California Indians*. Norman, University of Oklahoma Press, 2019.

"Trails of Tears - David Crockett: The Lion of the West." *Erenow.net*, 2015, https://erenow.net/biographies/david-crockett-the-lion-of-the-west/30.php . Accessed 2 July 2022.

"U`tlun'ta, the Spear-Finger: A Cherokee Legend." *First People*, 2022, www.firstpeople.us/FP-Html-Legends/UtluntaTheSpear-finger-Cherokee.html . Accessed 1 Aug. 2022.

"USA 1830 Coins." *Coinscatalog*, 2016, coinscatalog.net/usa/coins-1830 . Accessed 1 May 2022.

Visit Cherokee Nation. "CHEROKEE WORD of the WEEK: EAGLE." *YouTube*, uploaded by VisitCherokeeNation, 27 July 2016, www.youtube.com/watch?v=8-z_QdgVf5o . Accessed 4 Sept. 2022.

Walker, Jane H. *In the Lion's Paw*. McCrae, Georgia, Longleaf Pine Press. 2008.

Walske, Steven C., and Frajola, Richard C. "Mails of the Westward Expansion, 1803 to 1861, Chapter Eight." *Western Cover Society*, 27 Apr. 2017, www.westerncoversociety.org/literature/books/mails-of-the-westward-expansion-1803-to-1861/mails-of-the-westward-expansion-1803-to-1861-chapter-8/# .YzTsuHbMJdg. Accessed 29 Sept. 2022.

Watson, Stephen. *"If This Great Nation Be Saved?" The Discourse of Civilization in Cherokee Indian Removal*. 2013. Georgia State University, master's thesis. scholarworks.gsu.edu/cgi/viewcontent.cgi?article=1074&context=history_theses , 10.57709/4301370 . Accessed 8 July 2022.

Weiser-Alexander, Kathy. "Chief John Ross of the Cherokee Nation." *Legends of America*, 2021, www.legendsofamerica.com/na-johnross/ . Accessed 23 Oct. 2022.

"Western Expresses | E." *Western Cover Society*, 28 Oct. 2015, www.westerncoversociety.org/early-western-mail-articles/western-expresses-articles/san-francisco-gateway-to-the-gold-fields/western-expresses-e/#.Y0Lss3bMJdg . Accessed 9 Oct. 2022.

"When Government Fears the People, There Is Liberty… (Spurious Quotation)." *Thomas Jefferson's Monticello*, 2022, www.monticello.org/research-education/thomas-jefferson-encyclopedia/when-government-fears-people-there-liberty-spurious-quotation/ . Accessed 30 Oct. 2022.

Wiggins, Melanie Speer. "Sarah "Sallie" Ridge Paschal Pix: Between Two Worlds" *The Journal*, vol. 37, no. 1, Apr. 2013, pp. 44–55. *Ft. Smith Historical Society, Inc.* Accessed 17 Jan. 2023.

"Wild Turkey Behavior." *Nwtf.org*, 2022, www.nwtf.org/hunt/wild-turkey-basics/behavior . Accessed 26 June 2022.

Wilkins, Thurman. *Cherokee Tragedy: The Ridge Family and the Decimation of a People.* Norman, University of Oklahoma Press, 1986.

Wilkinson, David Marion. *Oblivion's Altar: A Novel of Courage.* Thorndike Press, 2014.

Wisecup, Kelly. "Practicing Sovereignty: Colonial Temporalities, Cherokee Justice, and the 'Socrates' Writings of John Ridge." *Native American and Indigenous Studies*, Volume 4, Number 1, 2017, pp. 30–60. *JSTOR*, doi.org/10.5749/natiindistudj.4.1.0030. Accessed 23 Nov. 2022.

Witchdoctaa. "Common Nightingale Singing at Night. The Most Beautiful Bird Song on Earth." *YouTube*, uploaded by witchdoctaa, 8 Apr. 2016, www.youtube.com/watch?v=BWIsYUZP0jM . Accessed 5 Apr. 2022.

Young, Mary. "The Cherokee Nation: Mirror of the Republic." *American Quarterly*, vol. 33, no. 5, 1981, pp. 502–524. *JSTOR*. ezproxy.snhu.edu/login?url=https://www.jstor.org/stable/2712800.

———. "The Exercise of Sovereignty in Cherokee Georgia." *Journal of the Early Republic*, Volume 10, Number 1, 1990, pp. 43–63. *JSTOR*, https://www.jstor.org/stable/3123278?origin=crossref Accessed 6 Nov. 2022.

www.historiumpress.com

Printed in the USA
CPSIA information can be obtained
at www.ICGtesting.com
LVHW040824140324
774242LV00008B/216/J

9 781962 465236